PRAISE FOR GUARDING WHAT REMAINS

"I thoroughly enjoyed this book, not my usual genre but I couldn't put it down. My heart was in my mouth for this poor family whose world is ripped apart by the great depression. The author reels you in from the start and does not let go until the last page. A great variety of believable characters that you can't help but root for them, and you need to keep turning the page every time there is disaster looming and hoping they come through against all odds...superbly written...realistic...an insight into how families fared during this dark time in our history."
– *Gillian Mulligan*

"Loss is life-altering, which Smith deftly demonstrates as readers experience a gamut of emotions from despair to hope as this story progresses through the first half of the Great Depression...While there is no answer to why God permits these experiences, each character grows and changes in different ways, sometimes for better, sometimes for worse...this historical novel is more than a struggle to survive. It is a story of love, redemption, and resilience and readers will readily identify with the experiences the characters face."
– *Historical Novel Society*

"Wow! A fantastic book describing the struggles of a family through unprecedented difficulties. The characters and their different journeys through the exact same circumstances perfectly depicts how God uses good and bad events to get our attention. This is such a powerful story of pain and forgiveness, human frailty and resilience, temptation and grace, hopelessness and steadfast love. I absolutely recommend this book."
– *Cecilia, Goodreads*

"This is one of those books that once you start reading it you can't put it down. I could just imagine myself with the family and having to go through all that they had to go through. Great book and must read!!!"
– *Donna Mackinnon*

"A beautiful and well-researched novel of the Depression. As a lay historian who lives in the Inland Northwest, I was struck by the stark realism of *Guarding What Remains*. Ida Smith has woven an authentic and haunting story of one family of the Depression, whose suffering sobers us even as it reminds us of the hope Jesus brings. I especially loved the ending!"
– *Pam Thorson, Author and Speaker*

"A wonderful book focusing on the Depression years from the end of 1929 into the 1930's in the United States, dealing with the loss of the American Dream and the catastrophic economic effects on families and society. This was an excellent read and, yes, this really happened."
– *Amazing Grace, Amazon*

"Poignant. Heart wrenching. Must read."
– *Ann Webb*

"What a WONDERFUL book! I think it should be a classic! This book kept me up way too late for a couple of nights...a roller coaster ride of emotions...I appreciate Ida's clean writing...such a full, rich story...I am SO thankful that I read this book. It's a literal life changer if one allows it to be...an unforgettable read!"
– *Marge K, Amazon*

"...full of heartwarming scenes of a tightknit family who lean on one another when the world seems set against them...An often powerful tale of steadfastness in the face of adversity."
– *Kirkus Reviews*

"A beautiful story of a 10 year old seeing her family going through many difficulties during a bad period in their lives. Eleanor sees her family nearly come to breaking point and she is brave throughout. A great read. I recommend this book to other readers."
– *Sharmani Jayaram*

"An interesting angle on what so very many, many families went through during the Great Depression."
– *Ray Neu*

GUARDING WHAT REMAINS

A NOVEL

IDA SMITH

GUARDING WHAT REMAINS

BY IDA SMITH

Cover art by 100 Covers

ISBN 978-0997653045 (Trade Paperback)
ISBN 798-0997653052 (ebook)

FICTION / CHRISTIAN / HISTORICAL
FICTION / LITERARY

Printed in the United States of America

To learn more about Jagged Journeys' Stories or sign up to receive free short stories, visit: IdaSmithBooks.com

In honor of Kathleen Anderson.

*You loved us all
and shared love with those who needed it most.
In life and even in death,
you not only survived but thrived.*

Thank you to my wonderful team of beta readers:
Barbara Hamby, Carol Ellis, and Pamela Thorson.
Your input and feedback was invaluable.

A special thanks to my husband, Richard Smith.
I couldn't have done this without your hours of editing, input, encouragement, and support.
You're the best!

ONE

ELEANOR'S HEART QUICKENED AT Teddy's menacing growl.

She dropped next to the tri-colored Australian Shepherd and soothed his bristling fur. She followed his gaze into the pines. "What do you see there, boy?"

He growled again and bared his teeth, eyes focused on the woods.

Eleanor took a few steps toward the trees that edged their home on two sides.

The Australian Shepherd's bark stopped her. His stance told her to return.

She crept back to him. "What is it, Teddy?" She peered into the woods and then glanced behind her at the hitched wagon where her family waited. She tugged at the dog. "Come on, Teddy."

He refused to budge.

She chewed her finger. Something wasn't right.

"Eleanor, we need to leave," called her older sister, Rose, from the back of the hay wagon.

"Just a minute." She turned to the dog. "Teddy!" Eleanor coaxed. "We've got to go."

The dog growled again.

A twig snapped in the woods.

She flinched. Teddy's muscles stiffened; he leaned forward, his growl deeper.

A shiver crawled up Eleanor's spine and radiated into her shoulders. She sensed someone watching her. Eleanor latched onto the dog and peered into the woods. "What is it, boy?"

She froze. There, in the woods, fifty feet away, something moved.

She swallowed.

"It's probably just a badger or coyote," she told the dog, her voice shaking. She remembered talk of cougar tracks at the lumber mill last winter, and she placed a hand on the dog.

"Eleanor, hurry up," William called. "Father wants us in the field."

She tugged at the dog. "Teddy won't come."

William whistled. "Come on, boy."

"Teddy, Teddy," a chorus of childish voices called.

"Leave him," Mother called. "He'll come when he's ready. He probably just wants to chase a squirrel."

Her chest tightened. This was no squirrel. "Come on Teddy, we need to get going."

The dog stood his ground; his focus fixed into the woods.

"Now, Eleanor!" Mother folded her arms.

Eleanor bit her lip. What if it was a cougar? Teddy couldn't defend himself.

He barked, and she flinched.

"Eleanor!" William called.

Eleanor grabbed her worn gloves off the log home's front porch and glanced between the aggravated dog and the woods. If only they could stay. But these were hard economic times, according to Father, who worried about losing the farm. So, they needed to work. Father had explained to her about the stock market crash, but it made little sense.

"Teddy, please."

He ignored her.

"Eleanor, any good fortune you have is running out!" Mother called.

She bit her lip and ran to the wagon, her red braids slapping against her back.

"It's about time," Rose said. "You're wasting the coolest time of the day."

"I know."

Five-year-old Lilly clutched her rag doll and patted the straw next to her. "Sit next to me."

Eleanor settled down and glanced up at Mother. "I'm sorry."

Mitchell and Raymond, the seven-year-old twins, momentarily stopped poking each other with straw to see if Eleanor would get scolded.

"Honestly, Eleanor," Mother's faint Irish accent thickened. "I sometimes wonder if you're not busy chasin' leprechauns."

Fifteen-year-old William glared at her, then flicked the reins.

"There's something in the woods."

"And there's work a-waitin' in the field," Mother reminded her.

The dog remained unmoved, staring into the woods as the hay wagon left the yard.

"Isn't Teddy coming?" Lilly asked.

Eleanor's heart beat in her chest, and she wrapped her arm around her little sister as the wagon jerked and jolted. "He'll catch up." She hoped.

"He always does." Mitchell smiled at her.

Eleanor forced a reassuring smile and watched Teddy until he disappeared behind the trees that lined the drive as they left the yard.

"Maybe he's barking at a bear." Raymond raised his arms in the air, fingers curled like claws, and roared.

Eleanor shivered. Even a badger or coyote could be trouble.

The wagon rattled onto the highway. Eleanor strained to see into the thick tangle of trees and bushes bordering the north and west sides of the property.

She caught her breath. There. What was that? She squinted and saw it again. Something red moved in the woods. Eleanor's heart beat in her chest. Her mouth went dry. Badgers weren't red—neither were coyotes, bears, or cougars.

Eleanor breathed in the strong, sweet, grassy smell of cut hay. She thrust her pitchfork into a clump and lifted. A brown mouse scurried out of its hiding place and burrowed into the hay she had yet to turn. Its movement startled her from her thoughts.

All morning she'd argued with herself about what she saw and if Teddy was in danger. With every lift of the pitchfork, she scanned the tree line, hoping to see the dog.

"Eleanor, what are you doing?" William complained. "Look at this." He kicked at her row of turned hay. "You're missing huge chunks. You've got to turn the wet stuff over so it'll dry."

"Do you think Teddy can fend off a badger?"

He paused. "Teddy can take care of himself. You need to keep your mind on the task at hand." He lifted a pile of the hay from the row she'd already worked and turned it over. "See that? Bend down, feel it."

She huffed and did as he asked. There was moisture on the wilting plants.

"That will turn to mold if it doesn't dry," William reminded.

She nodded, wondering again what the red thing was.

"Now go back to the beginning, and turn over all the hay you missed."

"What about a coyote? Do you think—"

"Probably. Now go."

She took her pitchfork and trudged back to where she'd started. Just because he was the oldest, it didn't mean he could ignore her concerns. Another mouse skittered away. Eleanor wondered if she appeared as a giant to the small creature. She imagined a gigantic bear towering over Teddy. She gulped and tried to push away the idea.

The sun rose higher in the sky and melted the cool air. By late morning, Eleanor was hot and the loaded pitchfork was already heavy in her young hands. She pulled the spare milk can from the shade under the wagon and scooped out a ladle of water. First Lilly, then Raymond, and finally her other siblings and Mother joined her. Father arrived on the tractor and jumped down. Eleanor carried a cup of water and a slice of cornbread to him.

"Do you think Teddy could outrun a bear?"

Father scratched his chin. "Could Teddy outrun a bear? I'm afraid I'd have to hedge my bets on the bear."

Her chest tightened at his reply. "What about a cougar?"

"Oh, my money's definitely on the lion."

Eleanor squirmed at this news and glanced in the house's direction. Hopefully, it wasn't too late.

He looked at her. "What's got you so curious?"

She bit her lip.

"Teddy wouldn't come. He was barking at something in the woods."

"Oh, he was probably just barking at that sow 'coon. She's an ornery thing and loves nothing better than taunting him." Father removed his hat and wiped his shirtsleeve across his forehead. "It's gonna be a scorcher. I imagine, with all that fur of his, Teddy would rather rest in the cool shade."

"Maybe we should go home and check on him, just in case."

"I think you've been reading too many stories." He handed his cup back to her. "Teddy will be fine. Time to get back to work."

"But—" her voice was a whisper, and Father was already climbing onto the tractor.

The rest of the morning, Eleanor worried about the dog. It was not like him to stay away. Had he chased off the intruder? What if he was lying wounded and dying?

Tears welled in her eyes. He could be dead by the time they arrived home. They needed to go back—now! How could she convince Father and Mother that they needed to return? Mother had packed a lunch, and they wouldn't go home until milking time.

She mulled the problem over in her mind as she turned the hay. The *petu-petu-petu* of the tractor's motor gasped in rhythm with her pounding heart as Father cut the hay several hundred yards away. Eleanor waved frantically, but he only waved back.

She returned to working the hay in the middle of the field. Another idea came to her, and she moved with speed. If they finished this section, they could work closer to the tree line after lunch. If she needed to, she could sneak away.

But after lunch, Father sent them to the opposite end of the field. She considered saying she was sick. But Mother would just have her lie under the wagon, and there was no way of sneaking from the wagon to the trees.

She only had one option; though now, it was probably too late. She turned the hay, not bothering to look for Teddy. Instead, she made a game of seeing how long she could wait to stave off the disappointment of not seeing him.

By mid-afternoon, they stopped again for water. Father returned from the far field, and Lilly climbed onto the tractor, her flour sack dress smudged with dirt. She leaned toward Father, pulled his harmonica out of his shirt pocket, and tried playing it. "Keep at it, my little mountain flower," Father encouraged. "You'll get it."

Eleanor took Father more water and mentally rehearsed her speech in her mind. She took one last look for the Australian shepherd in the direction of their log home. She paused. "Father?"

He finished the cup of water. "What is it, Kitten?"

Eleanor pointed to the skyline behind him. "What's that?"

He turned and stared. "No. No! Shannon," his voice was urgent.

Mother approached, followed by the others. "What is—?" She stopped; her face paled.

Eleanor gasped for breath.

TWO

TWO COLUMNS OF SMOKE rose above the tree line. Though light gray at first, the columns grew thick and black.

Eleanor gasped. Her eyes fixed on the sight.

Rose stepped beside Eleanor. "Mother, you don't think..."

Father shoved the cup at Mother. "Everyone in the wagon." He handed Lilly to Eleanor; his forehead wrinkled in worry. "William, get the water can and follow me. Hurry." He shifted the tractor into gear and headed for the truck parked at the field's edge. A vehicle pulled up beside the truck. A man leaned from the door, honking and waving. Soon both he and Father were gone.

Eleanor swallowed. Her hands trembling as she lifted Lilly onto the wagon and climbed up with everyone else. She wished they could ride in the truck, but that meant unhitching the horses and leaving them in the field. There was no time for that.

"Ho, let's go," William called. The horses started their usual slow trek back to the farm. "Faster." He flicked the reins. Their speed increased. Everyone held on; their gaze fixed on the growing plumes of blackening smoke.

Beside her, the twins were wide-eyed—Raymond with excitement and Mitchell with fear. She told herself it was an accident on the highway. Another logging truck had taken a turn too fast or lost its brakes. Last winter, and a truck wrecked and caught fire. Deep down she knew that wasn't right, but she kept hoping.

The horses seemed to trudge along, and Eleanor was sure she could run faster. Even if it was a car accident, that wouldn't explain why Teddy hadn't joined them.

"Why is there smoke?" Lilly asked.

No one answered.

The knot in Eleanor's stomach grew. Hurry, she silently urged the horses. She tried to connect the events of the morning with the possibility that lay ahead. How could a badger or even a cougar start a fire? Was the red thing she'd seen in the woods fire? Were the woods around their home on fire? She bit her lip.

The wagon jostled as William urged the horses on. Smoke scented the air. The horses slowed, shook their heads, and neighed.

Eleanor shared their dread.

Flames danced above the trees. Had Father or William dumped warm ashes from the cookstove some place where they could catch fire?

Her mind returned to the red thing in the woods.

They'd never dump ashes in the woods. Father buried them in the garden and doused them with water.

"Hurry," she whispered, but feared what lay ahead.

The twins, usually roughhousing, sat silent, watching the flames.

"I'm scared," Lilly said.

Eleanor wrapped an arm around her, giving and absorbing comfort. Rose, her face pale, gave Eleanor a pleading look.

Eleanor scrunched her nose at the hot, smoke laden air, tinges of charcoal on her tongue.

At the trees which fenced off the farm from the road, the air chattered with snaps, creaks, and hissing. Eleanor shook. What would they find around the corner?

Several cars lined the road.

A sprig of hope sprouted in Eleanor's heart. Maybe they were putting out the fire.

William coaxed the horses onto the long dirt drive flanked by trees before the animals refused to move further.

Her heart squeezed tight within her chest. She scrambled down and ran to the yard's edge with her mother and siblings. Stepping out from the trees, they stopped. No one spoke. No one moved. Their cheeks flushed from the blaze. Eleanor clamped her hands over her ears as the suffocating air roared with the anger of the devouring flames.

She ran her tongue around her dry mouth and struggled to grasp the scene before her. This was worse than anything she had imagined. Orange and yellow flames danced behind broken windows. The fire chewed through the walls and roof of the once beautiful two-story log home, and climbed into the sky.

Beside her, Rose wailed, hands cupped over her mouth. "No, no. This can't be happening! Why? Why is this happening?"

Eleanor's eyes burned, but she couldn't stop looking.

"Why's the house on fire?" Lilly asked.

Eleanor ran a hand over her little sister's braids. "I...I don't know."

Lilly wrapped her small arms around Eleanor and hid her face in Eleanor's faded blue dress. Mitchell slipped his hand into Eleanor's. Behind them, the horses stamped and whinnied.

"Get away from there," someone yelled.

Eleanor turned to the fiery monster that gobbled the three-story barn with its arched roof. The orange demon had already devoured the doors, revealing the thick blistering red embers that chewed the wood dividing the milking stalls.

She shivered as tears streamed down her cheeks. She turned her attention to their home, the barn, then back to the house. "How? What—?" Her body shook. She closed her eyes, willing the fire to leave, but sensed its presence pressing into her.

William approached Father, who stood unmoving in the drive between the two buildings. Their neighbor, George Glendale, and several other men joined them, buckets limp in their hands. The fire's cruel cackle, muffled voices. George and Father approached Mother and the children. "It was fully engulfed when I got here," George said. "It's so hot we can't get close enough to fight it."

Mother stared into the fire; her tall sturdy frame motionless. Her fair skin was now ashen, and her face was older than just that morning.

Father pulled Mother to him.

"Oh, Charles. What are we going to do?"

"I don't know, Shannon." He touched her cheek. "Let's hope the money will be safe in the milk can."

Mother didn't reply.

A loud crack and a high-pitched screech pierced the air. Eleanor flinched as the roof twisted and fell into the house. A wave of sparks spewed into the yard and garden. A man doused what he could before the fire spread. Others ran to the spring.

"William, get the water from the wagon," Father shouted.

"Gone! It's all gone," Mother said, her voice flat.

Eleanor shivered despite the heat. Her doll! The pretty, green dress Rose had outgrown and given to her. She'd never even worn it. Now she never would. There must be something they could save. But her feet stayed planted on the ground.

The twins and Lilly cried. Mother looked down at them, a deep sadness in her eyes.

"What are we going to do?" Rose asked.

Mother wrapped an arm around her eldest daughter. "I don't know."

More cars stopped. Several men came, two with shovels. Others stood at a distance and watched.

"Mother, why are the house and barn on fire?" Mitchell asked.

Shannon shook her head.

George's wife, a plump woman with a worn apron, touched Mother's arm. "Shannon, I just arrived. What a horrible shock."

Mother only nodded.

"Come, let's find some shade. I've brought some cider."

Shannon allowed her friend to guide her away. She turned and whispered something to the children, her words lost in the fire's screams.

"Rose, Eleanor." The matronly woman looked over her shoulder. "Bring the young'uns."

Rose turned to leave, seeming to ignore Mrs. Glendale's request. Gray tears streamed down her face.

Eleanor gazed at the flakes of ash on her arms and clothes, in Lilly's hair, and filtering down around them. She moved toward the shade, but Lilly clung tighter.

"I'm scared."

"I know." She released Mitchell's hand and picked Lilly up. "Come on, boys."

Raymond stood rigid. "No. I won't." He scooped up a clod of dirt and hurled it at the house.

"Raymond, come. You heard Mrs. Glendale. We should move away from the fire."

"No." He hurled another clod and another. "No one's doing anything."

"Rose, come get Lilly." Eleanor returned to Raymond, who was now throwing anything he could find: rocks, leaves, even sticks. "It's too late."

Rose returned; her gaze focused on nothing.

"Take Lilly and Mitchell. I'll get Raymond."

Rose took them and wandered away.

Eleanor watched her older sister leave. What had happened? Rose was usually the one in control.

Raymond threw a few more handfuls of dirt that rained to the ground in fine powder. "My cowboy hat and guns!" He plopped down, pulled his legs to his chest, and buried his face in his arms. "Our train set," he sobbed.

Eleanor sat down beside him. Gone too were her books and drawings.

A sharp squeal pierced the air, followed by some loud snaps.

"Away from the barn," someone yelled.

She watched the large building, now completely orange, shift and implode. Flames and sparks shot out. A wave of heat hit her face. It was now just a ball of fire. Men rushed to douse water on the sparks that fell on the grass and fence.

Eleanor's hands trembled. A lifetime of memories—the birth of calves, the smell of hay and warm cows, and squirting milk at barn cats pulsed through her mind. She swiped the tears away with her arm. Where the barn once stood was now an empty space. No more quiet afternoons in the loft—daydreaming, sketching, or playing with kittens.

She looked beyond the pile of burning wood at the cows grazing unconcerned beyond. Every morning and evening since she could remember, they had milked the cows in there. Now what? Where would they milk them now?

Raymond rocked back and forth next to her. He mumbled something she couldn't understand. She coughed and stood. "Come on, Raymond." She held her hand out. "We need to join Mother in the shade."

"I don't want to."

Eleanor lifted him, kicking and thrashing. She'd taken only a few steps when a low moan emanated from the house. She turned; a wall twisted and fell inward, followed by another.

Raymond slid from her arms and stood next to her.

Another deluge of warm tears coursed down Eleanor's cheeks and fell onto her ash-stained dress. She pressed her eyes tight. But the harder she resisted, the faster they came. She wanted to run away. Run to her special spot near the spring and be alone—just her and Teddy. To bury her face in Teddy's soft fur.

THREE

"TEDDY!" A FAINT WHISPER escaped Eleanor's lips. Where was he? He should be here; she needed to find him. She took Raymond's hand and led him to Mrs. Glendale and her other siblings. After drinking deeply of the refreshing ginger water, Eleanor slipped into the woods, and behind where the barn had stood. She called for him, but he didn't come.

In the farmyard, a row of men passed buckets and milk cans, wetting the trees and brush bordering the house. A couple more swung axes, cutting trees near the house to stop the fire's spread. She hurried before someone noticed her absence.

Eleanor ran to the root cellar but pulled up short—her heart pounding. The cellar was dug into a low hillside with a thick wood door. This wasn't right! The door stood ajar, as did the inner door. She crept forward. "Teddy—" She stopped. Shattered glass crunched under her feet where ants swarmed over applesauce and pickles. The coolness stung her hot skin; she inhaled the musty, smokeless air, trying to make sense of the empty shelves.

A shiver crawled up her spine. She spun around, expecting to see someone. But she was all alone. Fear gripped her, and she ran from the cellar into the sunshine.

"Teddy?" Determination filled her. She was going to find him. Eleanor climbed to the top of a low hill, scanned the pasture, and called for the dog. A few cows raised their heads, looked at her, then returned to their grazing. A halting breath escaped. "Teddy?"

Eleanor looked down at what had once been their farm. Anger and frustration swelled within her. Had someone left a lantern burning in the barn? Men tossed shovelfuls of dirt on the barn's dwindling flames.

Fire still licked the few charred walls that remained of their home—a black tomb marker of their life. An empty ache squeezed at her chest.

Eleanor hurried through the field, a distance from the house, hoping no one saw her. She entered the small grove of pine trees a safe distance away. It surprised her how the trees muffled the splintering, popping, and cracking of the dying fire. "Teddy. Teddy." A noise to her left caused her to stop and listen. She walked closer to the north side of the house. The noise was louder here. "Teddy."

A rhythmic tap, tap, chink, tap came from near the house. She peered through the woods to see two men chopping trees to stop the woods from catching fire.

"Timber," one yelled and the tree fell parallel to the woods and house.

There was a crash as another wall of the house collapsed and pushed heat and sparks outward.

A weight of helplessness pressed in on her. "Stop! Just stop," she yelled at the fire. She hated this. Hated, hated, hated it. This was her fault. If only she had insisted they see what Teddy was barking at. If only she had said something to William about what she saw in the woods.

She glanced around her. "Teddy. Teddy. Where are you?" The question came out in a whisper. Maybe he was further north. She scanned the area closer to the now burned shell of their home. Wait! What was that?

She skirted pine trees, large thimbleberry, and small huckleberry bushes while the sound of the woodcutters echoed through the trees. Soon she gazed down at a rectangular red metal can with the words, "Shell Motor Spirit" impressed into the side. Something had trampled and broken the surrounding plants, and there were similar sized rectangles and circles smashed into the ground.

Goosebumps spread across her bare arms. She looked about and remembered the feeling that morning that someone was watching her. She took a deep breath. "How did this get here?"

A tuft of white and black fur clung to a low branch. She lifted it off and caressed the soft fur. "Teddy." He'd been here. She swallowed.

"Eleanor."

Her head shot up, and she looked about. At the far end of the woods, where she'd entered, was Raymond. Anger rose within her.

"Eleanor. Wait for me."

"Timber."

She whipped around to see another tree slice through the woods near the garden, breaking off other branches as it fell. "Raymond, what are you doing?"

He stomped through the underbrush towards her. "I've been looking for you."

"You should have stayed with the others."

"I don't want to." A scowl covered his dirty face. "I can't find Teddy."

"Neither can I," her voice a defeated whisper.

"Raymond."

Their heads shot up. Rose followed.

"Great, now you've got us both in trouble."

Raymond glared at her. "You were already in trouble."

"Stop, both of you," Rose called. She reached them, panting. "You...you both are in so much—" She stopped at the sight of the gas can. "Where'd that come from?"

Eleanor shrugged and slipped the tuft of fur into her dress pocket.

"You two need to get back. Mother is in a panic. Eleanor, you should've never run off like that."

"I was just looking—"

"It doesn't matter. Mother—"

"Look." Raymond tugged on Rose's dress and pointed to the charred remains of their house. A tree top had caught fire, and the two men chopped at it.

Rose took Raymond's hand. "We need to get out of here."

Eleanor grabbed the gas can. "I'm taking this to show Father."

"Hurry." Rose headed to the clearing and glanced up at the burning tree.

Raymond reached out his other hand, and Eleanor took it.

To their left, the rhythmic sound of chopping increased.

They reached the yard just as the men yelled, "Timber."

Rose pulled them back into the trees. Eleanor tumbled backward into a large ponderosa pine. Raymond clung to her. The tall, slender pine tree fell fast and crashed into Mother's garden.

She closed her eyes and covered Raymond's as dust and pine needles flew up. The tree bounced and came to rest amongst the corn and beans. Men converged on the tree with water and shovels of dirt, destroying the garden as they put out the flames. Eleanor gasped. How much worse could this day get? A tear dropped to the ground.

Something white caught her attention. She picked it up—a cigarette butt. Where had this come from? Eleanor looked about. She now stood where Teddy had been staring.

"Teddy. Teddy." She turned to the woods behind her. Still no sign of him.

"Teddy," Raymond joined her in calling for the dog; but he didn't come.

They stepped into the open and ran around the burning tree.

Nearby, the flames that devoured the house dwindled and the men, including William, tossed buckets of water on what little remained.

The tap, chop, chop, tap of the axes followed them as they ran around the garden to the front yard.

"Rose. Wait." Eleanor stopped at the chicken coop and scanned the yard. "Where are the chickens?"

Her brother and sister glanced about for the fowl that usually wandered around the yard and garden.

"Nooo," Rose let out a cry. "When will it stop?" She grabbed Raymond's hand. "Come on." She pulled him back to the shade with Mother and the other children.

Hot anger surged within Eleanor; she ran to Father who was talking to the sheriff.

"Was a cookstove left burning?"

Father shook his head.

"Maybe a wire shorted out? Was a light or radio left on?" the sheriff speculated.

Again, Charles shook his head. "Nope. I put our plans to get electricity on hold when the market crashed."

The sheriff nodded and rubbed his chin.

"Father." Eleanor tugged on his sleeve. Her gaze shifted between Father, the sheriff, and the chicken coop.

The broad-shouldered man eyed her. "What do you have there, Missy?"

Eleanor held out the gas can and the cigarette butt. "I found these."

Father's eyebrows furrowed. "Where?"

"In the woods." She turned and pointed. "Teddy was growling and barking at something there."

Father and the sheriff exchanged looks.

The sheriff reached for the items. "Well, Charles, this changes everything."

Father glared at the can. "So, this is how the fire burned so fast." His expression shifted from confusion to indignation. "Why?" He looked about at his destroyed home and livelihood. "Who? All of this—gone. And for what?"

The sheriff looked up from his examination of the items and shook his head. "I am so sorry. These are strange times."

Eleanor fidgeted.

The sheriff raised an eyebrow. "Is there something else you want to tell us?"

She hesitated. "Teddy...he...he's gone—"

Father squeezed her shoulder. "I'm sorry, Kitten." He lifted her chin with his finger. "Is that what you wanted to tell us?"

She pressed her eyes shut and took in a jagged breath. "No. Umm." She shifted her feet. "Well."

"Yes," Father coaxed.

"The chickens...they're...they're gone..."

Charles glanced around the yard and then at the empty chicken coop. He shook his head. "How bad does this hand we've been dealt have to get?"

Tears streamed down her face.

Father wrapped his arms around her.

She sobbed. "Please...please don't...don't be mad at me."

He brushed her tears away. "Why would I be mad at you?"

She struggled to catch her breath. This was her fault. All her fault. "There...there's more."

He and the sheriff waited.

She swallowed. "The...the food in the root cellar...it's...it's gone, too." With these last words, a sense of defeat and emptiness pressed heavily upon her.

FOUR

"WHY ISN'T MOTHER COMING?" Eleanor asked the next morning as she rode with Father back to the farm. In the truck's bed, empty milk cans and buckets clanged together.

"She's staying with Lilly and Mrs. Glendale."

"Is she sick?"

"Sick." Charles scratched at the stubble on his cheek.

"She seems sick," Eleanor reasoned. "She doesn't talk and last night she let Raymond take three helpings at dinner without correcting him."

Father pursed his lips. "Your mother...this is hard for her."

"What do you mean?"

He tapped his fingers on the steering wheel. "She's scared."

Eleanor considered this. "About where we'll live?"

"And how we'll provide for you all."

"Are you scared?"

He sighed. "Not like she is. We live in a land of opportunity. You know how I like to try new things."

She nodded.

"I want to see this as an adventure. An opportunity to try something new—for all of us."

Eleanor worked up the nerve to ask what she'd been wondering. "Rose said we're moving to Spokane."

Charles took a deep breath and grinned at her. "Yes, ma'am. That's part of the adventure."

Eleanor's breath caught and the uneasiness in her stomach from last night returned. She'd hoped Rose was wrong, but now...hearing the words from Father himself... She worked her sweaty hands. "But...what about the farm?"

He reached out a finger and brushed her cheek. "We can't stay here. All the money we had was in that house."

"But...the cows...the...the milking...the...the..." The reality hit her like a bucket of frigid water. Gone. Everything was gone. "But can't we cut down some trees...build a house and barn?"

He cocked his head. A lock of his brown hair fell in front of his blue eyes. "I'm sorry Kitten, there's just no way. George and I have worked it from every angle. With cutting hay, milking cows, delivering milk, mending fences...there's no time to build a barn and even a small, one-room cabin. Definitely not before winter."

Falling! Eleanor imagined the truck's floorboard disappeared from under her. Her sturdy footing gave way. She gasped. The farm was all she'd ever known. How could they leave? Tears streamed down her face and made gray puddles in her lap. "But can't we move the cows somewhere that already has a house and barn? Can't..." The questions crowded her mind. Too many to ask.

"There's no way around it. We've got to sell everything: land, cows, equipment. We need food, clothes, cooking utensils, bedding—so much. Even if we stayed, we'd have to sell most everything just to live. In Spokane, William and I can find jobs."

"No cows?" her voice shook.

He glanced sideways at her. "Sorry Kitten. It's a cow-less adventure."

Eleanor hung her head. She felt foolish. Why hadn't she thought of those things?

Father turned into the drive. "Don't tell the others about this. That's my responsibility."

She nodded. Last night she'd determined to ask Father about Teddy. Now her words were stuck.

He stopped beside the charred ruins of the house. Instead of getting out, he sat in the idling truck and studied the mess. Eleanor stretched to do the same. Steam rose around Mother's scorched Monarch iron range that stood where the kitchen had been. Mother and Father's metal bed frame sat in the living room, like an unwanted houseguest.

Eleanor's heart beat hard against the walls of her chest as she puzzled over the charred beams protruding at odd angles. Here and there, light caught on small pieces of glass or metal, but mostly, everything was black and gray. She turned away.

Charles parked the truck near the pasture fence, and they watched Rose struggle with the horses as she turned the wagon into the drive. The smell of smoke still hung in the air and they refused to move forward. Father got out and assessed the situation. "Tie them up by the apple tree," he told her.

The cows waited in the pasture—anxious. Flies, bees, and yellow jackets swarmed around the curdled milk covering the ground. Last night, after they'd filled the few milk cans they had, they had to leave the extra milk on the ground. Johnny Glendale and William appeared, each with a rifle.

"How did things go last night?" Father asked.

"Ashes are cooling down," William said.

"Spent most of our time scaring away all the critters coming after that there milk," Johnny said.

Rose approached with the twins and smiled at Johnny, who winked at her.

"Coyotes, a fox or two, badgers, you name it," William added.

"Hope you boys didn't shoot any of my cows," Father teased.

"Naw, too dark, shot over them."

Johnny glanced at William. Eleanor was sure there was something her brother wasn't saying.

"All that milk has drawn a pasture's full of bees and flies," William said. "Milking those cows isn't gonna be easy."

Charles unloaded milk cans his buyer had delivered the previous evening. "Well, they need milking and we need the money, so we'll find a way." He handed a rope, wet cloth, and bucket to William. "Start with Martha. Tie her to the fence away from the gate and beyond the milk on the ground." He handed the same to Eleanor and the others.

Eleanor entered the field and skirted the white muddy patches. Bertha, a brown and white Guernsey, followed her. Eleanor tied Bertha to the fence, washed her teats, and sat on a piece of wood Father brought her. As she milked, Bertha bellowed and swished her tail.

Spokane. The city was half a day's drive southwest of them. Excitement and fear fought inside her. How big was it? Was it really as noisy as people said?

Milk squirted into the pail. "No cows," she whispered. A tear slid down her cheek and splashed into the milk.

How odd. She had milked cows every morning and evening since she was five or six.

Bertha shifted her weight, and her belly pressed into Eleanor's forehead. Eleanor didn't back away. She inhaled the cow's scent, absorbed the warmth of Bertha's body against her skin, the softness of her hide. Eleanor let go of Bertha's teats and wrapped her arms around the gentle cow and wept. Bertha lowed and turned her head to watch Eleanor.

Eleanor didn't know how long she'd sat like that, the bucket firm between her feet, her arms around the cow, her face buried into its side when a hand on her shoulder roused her. She looked up to see Father. He lifted her to her feet. She flung her arms around his solid frame. "I don't want to leave."

"There, there," he said, his hand smoothing her un-brushed hair. "None of us do."

"Why did this have to happen?"

"I don't know, Kitten. I really don't know."

She sobbed into her father's cotton shirt until it was wet and she could cry no more.

When she stopped, he lifted her chin with his finger. "Let's get these cows milked and you can ride with me to Eastport."

She nodded and returned to Bertha, determined to convince Father to stay and find Teddy.

"Why does Eleanor get to go?" Raymond asked.

"You two have both come with me," Father said. "Eleanor hasn't come in a long time."

Mitchell looked disappointed, and Raymond slighted.

"Can you bring us some penny cand..." Mitchell stopped and hung his head. "Never mind."

Father uttered something, then climbed into the truck.

Eleanor pushed down the guilt as she and Father drove away from the smoldering ruins of their farm, leaving her siblings to douse the hot spots.

They rode in silence for the first two miles before Eleanor could gather the courage to ask what had been on her mind since yesterday.

"Father."

"Huh?"

"What do you think happened to Teddy? I called and looked for him in the woods." She paused and looked down at her dry, calloused hands. "But I never found him."

Father sighed and tightened his grip around the steering wheel. "I don't know. Your mother said he was barking at something when you left the house yesterday morning."

"He was, and I tried to get him to stop and come." She paused. Should she tell him what she'd seen? She fingered the tuft of his fur in her pocket. "But he wouldn't come."

They arrived at Eastport, with its small general store and gas pump, railroad tracks, loading dock, and several other buildings. Just beyond stood the Port of Entry, where two Canadians checked cars entering and two American border officers searched returning vehicles for alcohol.

Father backed the truck up to a wooden loading dock near the railroad tracks. "You can go look around the store if you like," he said.

"Thanks." Eleanor jumped out of the truck and ran to the wood-plank building whose second-story living quarters looked out over a sagging porch. A bell tinkled as she opened the door. The smells of flour, sugar, and pickles greeted her. She inhaled deeply, and a pain in her stomach reminded her she had eaten little for breakfast.

"Why, Eleanor, is that you?" said a thin woman with graying hair that poked out from a loose bun. The woman stood behind a short counter where only a few years earlier she'd sold hot coffee, soda, and pie when people had money for such luxuries.

"Yes, ma'am."

"Oh my, I was so shocked when I heard about your home. How bad was it?"

Eleanor froze. She looked at all the wonderful things around her—several bolts of material, a few skeins of yarn, fishing lures, nails, tools, canned beans. Though the shelves were sparse compared to several years ago, to her, they were full. "Bad." She hung her head. The enormity of their lack assaulted her. "Very bad."

She looked again at the material and remembered Rose's pretty, hand-me-down, green dress—now, nothing more than ashes. Outside, the train's whistle blew. "I'd better go." She headed for the door.

"Eleanor, wait."

She took a deep breath and turned. "Yes, ma'am?"

"Here." The woman held out a jar of penny candy. "Take one."

Her mouth watered. She stepped toward the store owner and reached out to take a piece, then stopped and dropped her hand to her side. "Thank you, but I shouldn't. It wouldn't be fair to my brothers and sisters, and Father doesn't have any money."

"Pssha," said the woman with a wave of her free hand. "Nonsense. You take a piece for now and I'll put a piece for each of you in a bag. It's the least I can do after all you've been through."

Eleanor looked at the woman, then selected a piece of hard translucent candy. Outside, the train's brakes screeched against the metal rail lines. Eleanor touched the candy to her tongue; her mouth watered. She licked it, then slid the piece in, ran her tongue over it, and moved the candy to touch every inch of her mouth.

The thin woman selected six more pieces, dropped them into a small bag, and handed it to her. "Here you are."

"Thank you."

"These are tough times. Tell your mother I'm praying for your family."

"I will."

She smiled. "You be strong now, you hear?"

"Yes, ma'am."

Eleanor studied the long train towering above her as she walked along the loading dock. The men talked about the fire as they exchanged empty milk cans for full ones.

"Talk is, that two men in Chancy Thompson's old farm truck crossed into Canada late yesterday morning," a railway worker said.

"He finally sold that old thing?" asked the engineer.

"Nope, someone stole it."

The engineer shook his head. "Now that's desperate."

The man turned to Charles. "That's not all. I heard tell they had furniture, tools, ropes, crates of preserves, chickens, and a long-haired dog like the one I've seen with you a few times."

Eleanor's eyes brightened. "Teddy? You've seen Teddy?"

Father glanced at her and she stopped; remembering her manners.

"Were these fellows from around here?" Charles asked.

"Don't reckon so. Earl," he called to one of the border officers. "Earl, come here."

Earl, a hollow-cheeked young man wearing blue suspenders, sauntered over.

"Earl," said the railway worker. "Did you have a couple of men come through here yesterday morning in Chancy Thompson's old truck with some chickens and a dog?" He turned to Charles. "Was your dog black or white? I can't remember."

"He has a black, white, and tan mottled face; white around the collar and chest, with gray and black on his back. Long hair."

"Yeah, I remember seeing a dog like that. Real pretty. The men had him muzzled—said he had a tendency to bite."

"You saw him?" Eleanor leaned forward. "Was he alive? Is he alright?"

Earl shrugged his shoulders. "Looked alive to me."

"What about these men?" Charles asked. "What'd they look like? Have you ever seen them before?"

Earl shook his head. "No, no, I..." he paused and rubbed his chin. "No, wait, come to think of it." He kicked at the weathered wood of the loading dock. "I think I saw one of them last weekend—nosing around town. He was in the diner, asking lots of questions. Later, I caught him checking the back doors. You know, wiggling doorknobs, seeing if any were unlocked. I yelled at him and he ran off."

The railway worker raised his eyebrows. "There you go."

Earl nodded his head. "You know, I thought he seemed familiar."

"Did they have a large milk can with them?" Charles asked.

Earl scratched his head. "I don't rightly know. They had that truck packed awful tight with house wares and such. It's possible."

Charles stared at the border crossing. "Darn thieves." He turned to the railway worker. "Can you tell the sheriff what Earl just told us?"

"Will do."

"Come on, Eleanor. Time we get back."

Eleanor walked to the truck. The candy was almost gone now, but not the excitement that Teddy was alive. She looked up the road that disappeared into Canada. "Can we go look for him?"

Father started the truck. "The man who burned down our house?"

She cocked her head in confusion. "Teddy."

"Eleanor, they're probably miles and miles away by now."

The excitement inside her melted like snow in July. She slumped in the seat and chewed the last of her candy, its sweetness spent. They rode the rest of the way in silence.

FIVE

FOR THE PAST TWO weeks, they had scoured the ash remains of their home and barn, finding very few items of use. Every one of Eleanor's attempts to convince Father to stay failed. She also couldn't persuade him to cross the border and look for Teddy.

"Canada is a big country," Father explained. "I have no idea where to look for him."

Eleanor and the others hung their heads, knowing he was right.

The only joy came in the afternoons. Father took the ash-covered ghost-looking children to the Mojie River. There, they swam, played, and cleaned up before milking the ever-shrinking herd of cows.

Now, Eleanor carried the last pail of milk she'd ever get from Bertha, her favorite cow. Father had given the gentle bovine to the Glendales for all their help.

She wiped away a tear and played through her last idea to convince Father to stay on the farm. But she didn't hold out much hope it would work.

She took the pail to Mrs. Glendale who gave her a bundle of butter wrapped in cheesecloth.

"Have your brother pack this someplace cool."

"Yes, ma'am." She took the butter to the yard where the truck was almost loaded. Stacked at the front of the truck's bed were three new mattresses, along with other things that Father had traded the wagon, horses, and cows for. They packed food and clothing given by neighbors wherever there was space.

Her breath caught at the sight of what little they had. Would her plan even work?

"Eleanor, don't stand there. Help." Rose scowled at her, a hand on her hip.

Eleanor swallowed. "Coming." She handed Rose the butter. "What can I do?"

Mother looked up from a crate she was packing. "Hand me the bowl, William found." She pointed to a nearby stump.

"Yes, ma'am." Eleanor retrieved the beautiful, green serving bowl with hand-painted roses edged in gold.

Mother took it and ran her fingers over the smooth surface. "I'm still astounded this survived."

Eleanor smiled, happy that something had brought Mother joy. She only wished the broken plate she'd found had cheered her mother up. Eleanor couldn't bring herself to toss it. So she hid it in the truck. She watched as Mother wrapped the bowl in several cloth feed sacks and placed it next to a framed picture of her grandparents and the small porcelain figurine they'd found.

Father climbed down from the truck bed. "You all about ready?" He looked at the sun peeking over the eastern trees. "We need to get going."

"Father." Eleanor ran to his side. "Can we please go see the house?"

He rubbed his chin. "Eleanor, that's in the opposite direction."

"I know. But I want to see it—one more time."

"Me too."

"And me," chimed in several of her siblings.

"Please." Eleanor gave him her sweetest smile.

He shook his head and sighed. "Alright. Let's load up."

They said their goodbyes to friends who came to see them off. Eleanor climbed into the back of the truck bed with her siblings, and William latched the wood railing in place. The truck crawled out of the Glendale's farm. Instead of heading south, they turned north one more time. Eleanor and her siblings all stood, taking in the sights. Eleanor's heart surged, trying to absorb it all. She hoped this wouldn't be the last time.

The truck slowed and turned into their drive. Just as they left the road, she noticed something move further up. She squinted, but the truck entered the trees and it was out of sight.

Her heart raced. "Did you see that? Did you?"

"See what?" the twins asked.

"I—I—I'm not sure. There was something in the grass along the highway. It moved...then was gone."

"Probably just a badger or coon," William said.

"No, it was bigger...black and white."

"A skunk?" Lilly guessed.

"Bigger." Her excitement turned to frustration.

The truck stopped and Father got out while Mother stayed in. "Hurry up. Take one last look; we've got a long trip ahead of us."

They all climbed down.

"William, take the empty milk can and fill it with some of that good cool spring water."

"Yes, sir."

"Come on." Father motioned to the others. "I have an idea."

Eleanor slipped a hand into his. "Father, how long did it take you to build the fireplace?"

"Oh Kitten, I didn't build that. My grandfather did way before I was born."

"Do you think it would take a long time to build?"

He looked at the tall stone structure that stood guarding all that remained of their log home. He removed his hat, swiped his bangs away from his eyes, and replaced the hat. "I reckon a week or two, depending if you had to collect the rocks."

Eleanor smiled. "Why couldn't we build a house around the fireplace? It's already here—"

"Kitten, that fire burned hot—I'm sure the mortar's damaged."

"But—"

He shook his head. "We've been through this. We don't have enough money and we need work that pays more than farming."

Her heart sank. She bowed her head and squeezed her eyelids against the tears. She walked behind Father and her siblings.

Charles stopped at the rose bushes Mother loved. He cut off yellow blossoms with his pocket knife and handed one to each child before moving to the pink bush. "Let's give your mother a surprise."

Eleanor dawdled behind her siblings as the younger ones ran to the truck and gave Mother the flowers.

A sad smile spread across Mother's lips. She lifted the roses to her face, inhaled their fragrance, and thanked them.

"Come on, it's time we get on the road," Father said.

Eleanor took one last look around and climbed up into the pickup bed. Her chest shook, and she squeezed back tears. Her brothers and sisters also wore downcast expressions.

Six

FATHER TURNED THE TRUCK around and headed out of the drive. At the highway, he waited for a passing car.

Eleanor looked up the road; again, something dark sat in the tall grass alongside the highway. She wiped her eyes and strained.

Father turned the truck south. She watched as the dark lump stood and barked.

Her heart leaped.

Father shifted the truck, and it picked up speed.

She gasped. "Teddy!" she yelled. "Stop. There's Teddy." She faced the front of the truck while pointing behind her. "Stop. We've got to stop."

Father shifted again.

Her siblings squinted at the dirty critter growing smaller with every tire rotation. "Teddy. Teddy," the younger children called. Rose and William hollered for Father to stop, and William banged his hand against the railing.

The truck's speed increased, and Father shifted again. Teddy was now just a dot in the distance.

Eleanor's heart raced. "Stop. Please, stop," she yelled and stomped her feet to make more noise.

Her brothers and sisters joined her. Father looked at them in the mirror and Rose held out her hand for him to stop. "Teddy," she yelled. "He's back there."

Father shook his head, then slowed the truck.

Eleanor's chest swelled; she jumped around with the others as they all spoke at once.

Father and Mother both hopped out of the truck and ran to the back. "Is someone hurt?" Mother asked.

"No." "No." "It's Teddy." "We've got to go back."

Father's face flushed. "Enough! I know you don't want to leave, but we can't have any more stops."

"But..."

"Enough! You all need to sit down and ride."

Eleanor struggled to breathe, her lips and hands quivering as tears streamed down her face. "Please!" She pointed back to Teddy.

The others stood silent with sad expressions.

"We've been through this. We can't stay."

"I know," her words almost a whisper.

He looked at the others. "You all know we can't stay?"

They nodded.

"Then what is all this about?"

They again all started talking at once.

"Whoa, whoa, one of you."

"Eleanor should tell you," William said.

Father turned to her.

A wave of hope poured over her, and she wiped her eyes. "Teddy, he's alive."

"What?" Father and Mother looked at each other in disbelief.

"Over there." She pointed up the road, as did the younger ones.

Father took off his hat and shaded his eyes. "I don't see him."

Mother squinted. "Where?"

"You can't see him from here, but he's there, along the road, in the grass."

Father looked at her and the others. "Did you all see him?"

They nodded.

He sighed and looked at the sun climbing higher in the sky. "It's late morning and we've got a long trip."

Mother smiled at Eleanor and the others. "I know you all love him, but I'm not sure the city is the best place for him." She returned to the truck.

Father watched her. "You children need to sit down. I'll talk with your mother." He climbed back into the truck and shifted into gear.

Eleanor and her siblings looked at each other in silence and lowered their bodies.

The truck pulled back out onto the narrow highway and headed south.

"Aren't we going back?" Lilly asked.

William shrugged. "Mother's worried about not having enough food."

A tear slithered down Eleanor's cheek. She pulled her knees to her and wrapped her arms around her legs. Across from her, Mitchell and Lilly also wept.

The truck shifted into second and picked up speed.

"I can't believe we're leaving Teddy," Rose said.

Raymond picked at a piece of straw on the truck bed and twisted it. "I thought Mother and Father liked Teddy."

Eleanor's head ached. She slumped with exhaustion. How could they be so close to finding him, only to lose him again? She wept uncontrollably.

The truck slowed and Father downshifted.

The children peered at each other, unsure what to think.

The truck made a left turn onto an old road.

They peeked through the open spaces in the wood railing.

Father backed up and headed north.

"Yay!"

"Father just needed a place to turn around," William exclaimed.

Pulling into their old driveway, Father got out. William lifted the railing off the back and the children started to get out. "Whoa, whoa. Eleanor, William, get out. The rest of you stay."

He held up a hand to their protests. The three of them walked along the side of the road. "Where was he at?"

Eleanor scanned the grass. "I—he..." She turned to William, who looked as worried as she felt. "He was right around here someplace." Her chest tightened again. "He's brown and dirty."

They stepped into the grass and fanned out.

"Here," William called out. He pointed to a flattened area of grass.

Father squatted down and touched the area. "It's still warm." He dabbed at a dark spot and examined his finger. "Blood."

Eleanor's eyes widened.

Father looked about. "Let's look along the tree line."

"Teddy." They spread out, calling his name, then stepped into the woods. "Teddy."

Eleanor looked about; bushes and undergrowth filled in much of the ground below the trees. "Teddy. Where are you?" She stopped and sniffled. "Please Teddy. We're here."

She spun at a soft whine behind her. "Teddy?"

Another whine followed by a whimper and a rustling of leaves. She turned as Teddy limped out from some huckleberry bushes.

Eleanor rushed to him. "Oh Teddy! I've found him." She fell to her knees and wrapped her arms around the filthy dog. "Oh Teddy, I was so worried."

The dog flinched but only looked at Charles and William with sad blue eyes.

"Eleanor, I think he's hurt."

She leaned back.

Teddy whined and tried to wag a muddy, weed-filled tail.

Charles squatted next to the dog. "So, you made it back, ol' Boy." He lifted one of the dog's paws and shook his head. It was worn and caked with dried blood. "I wonder how far he traveled. I bet if he could talk, he'd have quite a story to tell." He turned to William. "Better get that water out. Looks like Teddy needs a drink...and a bath if he's coming with us." He scooped the now malnourished dog into his arms and carried him back to the truck.

Half an hour later, the children loved on the damp dog. They discussed where he might have been as the sum of their earthly possessions
jostled about around them. Eleanor smiled, grateful they'd found him;
while nervous excitement about their new life filled her thoughts with
each farm they passed.

SEVEN

MOTORS, HORNS, AND THE shouts of boys hawking newspapers mixed with strange food smells and exhaust; while buildings taller than any Eleanor had ever imagined loomed over her.

Beside her, Rose pointed to the store windows. "Oh, Eleanor, look at that dress—and that one..."

"Hey, there goes a Durant D-60," William called from the other side of the truck.

The twins rushed to his side. "Where? Where? What's a Durant D-60?"

William pointed out the long car. "I've only seen those in ads."

Lilly squeezed between Eleanor and Rose. "Did you see that tall building with all those windows?"

"Go home sod-busters," yelled a man.

Eleanor pulled her attention from the store window with toy dishes, dolls, and train sets to look at the man.

Another man wearing a new Fedora wagged a hand at them. "This ain't the end of the rainbow," he shouted.

Eleanor's cheeks flushed with embarrassment and shame, though she didn't know why.

Mitchell tugged at her sleeve his; eyebrows bunched in concern. "Who's he talking to?"

"Take your family and leave; we don't need no more Hoovervilles," yelled a man with a fine gold chain spilling from the pocket of his dark jacket.

A Model A crossed in front of them, and the driver yelled something as he passed.

Teddy barked.

Eleanor leaned away from them, as did Lilly and Rose. "I don't like this," Mitchell whispered, while Raymond stuck his tongue out, before Rose scolded him.

"What are they talking about?" William asked.

Traffic started up again, and the truck lurched forward. Eleanor leaned into William. "What'd we do wrong?"

He shook his head. "Who knows?"

Eleanor's insides rocked. 'No more Hoovervilles,' echoed in her ears. Tobacco smoke wafted past. The sun hid behind a tall building with "Gone out of Business" signs taped in the windows. What did the man mean by: ...ain't the end of the rainbow? A car backfired, and she flinched. She wanted to go home.

Eleanor stared absently as Father pulled the truck into a gas station. An attendant sauntered up, wiping greasy hands on a rag. "How much gas do you want?"

"Five gallons."

The man raised his eyebrows. "You got money? 'Cause we don't take barter, and my boss don't need no more workers."

"I do."

The man held out his hand. "That'll be eighty-five cents."

Charles sighed and dug into his pocket. "Do you know of a boarding house we can stay at?"

The man looked over the truck and family. "You got a job?"

"Not yet. My son and I plan to go looking tomorrow."

The attendant glanced up at the truck full of children. "No job, no rent."

Eleanor leaned into William, and he put an arm around her shoulder. What did the man mean? She sensed it wasn't good.

"Well, like I said, we plan to get jobs."

The man pointed toward the river and the railroad tracks. Small spirals of smoke lifted in the air. "You and all the men and boys living down there in that shantytown."

Eleanor's breath caught, and she grabbed her brother's arm.

William looked down at her and forced a smile.

Father looked in the river's direction. "So, you're telling me I'm gonna have to work a little harder to find a job?"

"You're gonna need a miracle." The man lifted the fuel nozzle without inserting it into the truck. "Every day, hundreds of people ride the rails into town looking for work. They think Washington is the end of the rainbow, but there ain't no pot of gold here."

The end of the rainbow. There was that phrase again. Eleanor watched as her father seemed to take this all in. Whatever a shantytown was, it didn't sound good.

"And no one will let us rent from them, even if I have money?"

The man shook his head. "Most boarding houses are full."

Father absorbed this information.

"Listen, mister, I'd only put a gallon, maybe two in your truck. These are desperate times; there are men who will siphon your fuel."

Charles sighed. "Two gallons then."

"That will be thirty-four cents."

Father counted out the money.

The attendant nodded at Father's coin purse. "Hide your money and don't let no one know you have it."

Charles glanced up at the children and nodded.

Fear squeezed Eleanor's arms and chest. She watched Father's enthusiasm for their new adventure drain away like milk out of a bucket after a shotgun blast.

Mother read the street signs, looking for the one listed in the newspaper.

"Shannon, I know this has been hard on you, but this gives us an opportunity to show the children a different way of life and meet new people."

"Oh, fine opportunity. To struggle in poverty like I did as a child."

"Not everyone who lives in cities are poor."

"No. But they come to the city with wealth already in their pockets. They don't find it lying on the ground."

"There are more opportunities for jobs here. This also gives the children opportunities to go to bigger schools and learn a trade."

"And how is William going to learn a trade if he's working?" Her mind flashed back to Chicago and helping her mother clean the homes of wealthy people instead of attending school.

Father looked out the window. "Maybe he'll get a job that will give him an apprenticeship."

"Charles, I've lived in a big city. I know how things work. The people with the money are the people with the jobs. But they won't share it with the likes of us. We are beneath them."

"Shannon, we live in the land of opportunity. Anyone can go out and make something of themselves."

She turned to him. "That's not what the filling station attendant said."

Charles shook his head. "I don't believe it. People just aren't looking."

Shannon massaged her forehead. "You can be so stubborn. If I didn't know any better, I'd think you were Irish."

Charles grinned and slowed the truck. "The address is five-thirty-seven. Do you see it?"

She read the house numbers. "There it is." She pointed to a large, three-story house.

Charles pulled the truck to the curb, and the weight shifted as the children all moved to one side.

"Is that it?" Several of them called.

Charles lifted his hat from the seat and swept the hair off his forehead before putting it on. "Wish me luck, my Irish lass."

Shannon forced a smile; she was tired and ready to be done with travel. "May you meet with open doors and full platters."

He winked at her and headed to the door.

This was the third and last boarding house. She cringed at the thought of where they'd end up if there were no openings. If only she could remember her sister's address. Shannon watched him talk to a matronly woman, his hat in hand, then return down the stairs. Maybe she should have gone to the door with him.

"Do we have a place to stay?" A chorus of youthful voices called.

Before he spoke a word, she knew. Her heart broke. She loved those voices. Children should never have to ask that question. Like the shifting of wind, their luck had changed from good to grim.

"Where are we going?" Eleanor asked.

"On an adventure."

Shannon groaned. Why did men love adventures? Charles' talk of this new adventure excited William, who had sparked a fire in the twins.

Charles entered the truck cab. "I suppose you heard."

"I didn't have to; I saw it on your face."

He squeezed her hand. "This adventure is taking us down a different path."

"You mean our options are dwindling?"

"How you play your hand is all in how you look at it. I'm sure we could pay for lodging at a hotel, but that would take a sizeable chunk of our limited funds. What we hold and what we lay down can mean the difference between winning and defeat."

Shannon understood, grateful that Charles' love of cards had never turned into gambling. She hoped it never would; she knew all-to-well the troubles that could add to their current trials. "So, what's next on this grand adventure of yours?" She dreaded his response.

Charles drummed the steering wheel.

They'd been married long enough for her to know his thoughts. She didn't like them and wished to veer him in a different direction. "We could look for my sister."

He turned to her. "Do you remember her address?"

She pressed her lips together, not wanting to admit the answer.

He brushed a finger across her cheek and turned her chin toward him. "We'll find her, but not today."

She nodded. "Please, tell me we aren't going to that...that...that place..."

He nodded. "I don't know where else to go."

"I suppose." She turned away and stared out the window, but saw nothing.

He shifted into gear and headed back through downtown and across the Monroe Street Bridge. "Can you see the falls?"

"Uh-huh." Normally she loved waterfalls, but not today.

Charles turned off the road and entered a strip of land with small, squat buildings.

Shannon straightened; her muscles tight and jaw set against the collection of shacks. Their indiscriminate scrap construct showcased the disheartened lives of their inhabitants. She sucked air through her teeth. She longed for another woman; someone she could talk with. But how could she share her own hurt and loss with these who already carried so much of their own?

They passed several huts; a mother with seven dirty children stood at the door of one. Shannon's hands shook. The weight of the woman's exhaustion pressed upon her. Her mother's words came to her: Shannon, we are women. Our destiny is knit together with that of our husband, our children, society, and history. She squeezed back an unexpected tear. She must be strong.

Charles stopped the truck by a group of sunken-cheeked men.

Shannon shifted under the emotionless gaze of men with dusty fedoras and hollow eyes. She could do this. For her children, she could do this. She recalled her mother's strength, as she worked to provide for them, even as she died.

"Hello friends, where might we set up camp around here?"

A tall, bony man pointed up the dirt track. "You might find a spot up that way."

From the truck's bed, she heard Teddy growl, then a sharp bark.

"We're not beyond killing dogs."

Shannon startled and turned to see a man standing less than a foot from her door. She leaned away from him and his piercing gaze.

Teddy barked again, and the man held up a knife, examined the blade, then scraped at a scar on his cheek with its point.

"Teddy, shush," William ordered.

"Thank you kindly," Charles said to the men on his side of the truck. He shifted into gear, glanced at Shannon, and nodded at the man.

The corner of the man's lip curled into a smirk.

Shannon took a shallow breath. Her stomach and emotions jostled with the truck over the narrow, bumpy trail.

Shannon flinched at the blare of a train's horn. She turned the ham slices as the train approached, brakes screeching.

Mitchell pointed. "Look, people are jumping off the train."

Shannon looked up to see men, boys, and a few women disembarking. She swallowed and called the girls to help her. "Come on, let's dish up."

Teddy barked, and she turned to see two men approaching. She placed the last slice of meat on her plate. Her heart raced in her chest. To her left, Teddy strained at the rope Charles had tied him to.

"Pardon me, ma'am," asked the older of the two, "but could you spare some food for two weary travelers?"

She straightened and looked at Charles, who nodded and invited the men to join them. She gave the man her plate and Charles gave the other his.

She listened to their stories of life on the rails and cringed at Raymond's excitement and questions. Several times Shannon caught the younger of the two men smiling at Rose, who huddled near her.

Shannon heated food for herself and Charles. How many others would they feed with their limited supply? She eyed the man who'd asked for supper appraising their truck and possessions.

"You have quite a lot of goods," he remarked.

"How long you reckon it's been since we slept on a mattress?" said the younger.

"Near on a year."

The younger one smiled again at Rose.

Rose stood and offered to do dishes.

"Most nights we sleep in a rail car or on the ground by a fire."

Lilly jumped up and wrapped her arm around Charles. "Father, do we get to sleep by the fire?"

"Nope. You and your sisters are sleeping on the truck with your mother and me."

"Oh." Her enthusiasm melted, and Raymond gave her a smile that said, "Ha, ha. We get to sleep by the fire."

Shannon stiffened as the young man carried his plate to the back of the truck where Rose washed dishes. Teddy barked, and she nudged Charles, who nodded and stood.

"Well, fellows, we've enjoyed your company, but my family has had a long day, and we need to get turned in."

The older man glanced at his companion. "Well, I think my friend was looking to take your daughter on a walk."

"I think it's time you two move along."

The man swirled the water in his cup. "That's not being very neighborly."

Shannon's chest tightened. "Our daughter's spoken for."

Teddy barked again, his attention on the young man only inches from Rose.

The man glanced at Teddy and took half a step back.

Shannon's heart pounded in her chest. She glanced from the man, to her children, and finally to Charles. She wanted to take a broom and chase these two rapscallions. The events of the past two weeks weighed heavily on her, and she missed the safety of her home.

The evening's talk and stories now changed to uneasy apprehension. She couldn't stay here.

Eleanor rinsed the soapy water from her face and looked around before lowering her voice. "What did that man say to you?"

"I don't want to talk about it."

"Why not?"

"I just don't." Rose glanced about.

"Are you afraid they're nearby?"

"They give me the creeps. I don't know why Father has to be so friendly all the time."

Eleanor liked that Father was friendly, but she'd never met men like they'd eaten with tonight. "Well, they're gone." She hoped. Her stomach growled. The simple meal of ham and bread with apple butter had only accentuated her hunger. To divert her attention, she had talked Father into playing a few songs on his harmonica. The tunes had both comforted and saddened her.

Lilly thrashed about between Eleanor and Rose on the mattress they shared. "Father," Lilly piped up.

"What is it, my little mountain flower?"

"Why did you tie up Teddy?"

"I don't want him wandering around and getting into things. We've got neighbors now, and we need to not cause any harm or trouble. These folks have had hard times, just like us."

Lilly sat up. "Someone burned down their farm, too?"

"Probably not that. But they've lost their jobs and had to leave their homes because they don't have any money to pay for them."

"Oh." She was silent for a little while, and Eleanor was thinking about what Father had said, when Lilly asked, "What if it rains?"

"Well, I hope it doesn't before I get a shelter built."

Rose now leaned on her elbow; her voice strained. "Why do we have to stay here?"

"Well, in talking to some of the men around here, it looks like it will be more difficult finding and keeping work than I'd first thought."

"Oh."

Eleanor dwelt on this. Back home, Father worked for himself and had plenty of things to do. The milk had always provided for them. She now recalled hushed conversations between her parents about dropping milk prices. Father had said they shouldn't buy extra clothes and machinery so they could pay the property taxes.

"Father?" Rose paused. "Father, is...is our new home going to look like these?"

All was quiet, and Eleanor thought father had fallen asleep. When he spoke, it was slow and drawn out. "Temporarily, until William and I get steady work and can find a place to rent."

No one said anything and Father's words slid over all other thoughts like creek water over rocks.

The sounds of cars, trains, dogs, and distant voices crowded into Eleanor's mind as she replayed the day's events. This was not the adventure she'd imagined.

"I will not look like those women and girls we passed driving in here," Rose whispered.

The image of a frail girl her own age with chopped hair swam in Eleanor's mind. "I won't either," she declared. "So, what are you going to do?"

"I don't know, but I will find a way. And when I can, I'm moving back to Bonners Ferry and marrying Johnny." Rose rolled away, her back to her sister.

Eleanor knew the conversation was over. She was tired but couldn't sleep. Her mind was busy with what-ifs. She couldn't stop thinking of Father's look when the gas station man said jobs were scarce. For a moment, Father had seemed lost and unsure of himself. That scared her the most.

This was her fault and she would do all she could to help—even if it meant sewing. They would not wear flour sacks with holes cut out for their heads and arms like the surrounding children.

As she considered how to sew dresses from flour sacks, Mother's bitter, short syllable whisper pulled her to the present. "How ironic; we can't build a one-room cabin on our own land with our own wood, but we can build a one-room shack on someone else's land with found or stolen scraps."

"Shannon," Father's voice was quiet but firm. "That's enough."

EIGHT

"WE'VE GOT TROUBLE." FATHER set the wood crate with the bread, hard-boiled eggs, and salt-cured ham on the tailgate.

Eleanor's eyebrows bunched at his words. She joined Mother and her two older siblings gathered around him.

"What's wrong?" William asked.

Father lifted a flour sack that contained several loaves of bread. Rodents had chewed holes into it. He pulled the bread out and revealed missing chunks. "Mice."

Eleanor looked at it in horror. "I thought we put the food in the truck's cab to protect it."

"I did. But you know mice, the smallest hole, and they can slink through it."

Mother scowled at the sight; her gray-green eyes were full of fire. "Lie down with dogs and you'll rise with fleas." She turned and walked off toward the river.

They watched her leave.

Eleanor turned to Father. "What do we do?"

"We'll have to make something to protect our food. We need ice anyway; this meat won't last long in the heat."

Rose wrinkled her nose and pointed at the food. "Are we going to eat that?"

"We can't be throwing things away." He handed it to Rose, who held it at arm's length. "Carve out the spots the mice have eaten at and give them to Teddy."

Rose made another face and picked up a medium-sized knife with a newly carved handle, its blade blackened from the fire.

Mother returned as they finished their breakfast of bread, ham, and hard-boiled eggs.

Charles motioned to the tailgate. "There's a plate dished up for you." He stood. "Why don't you sit here?"

She took the plate and sat on the two-foot-tall galvanized milk can. The children watched her as she ate the small breakfast with slow, purposeful bites.

Rose started washing the dishes in the Dutch Oven and Eleanor scooped a handful of the bread and ham pieces Rose had carved and set them down by Teddy.

Shannon stopped eating. "Eleanor, what are you doing?"

"Feeding Teddy."

"Don't give him our food. If he wants to eat, he can find his own food. I don't even know why we brought that worthless creature with us. We don't have enough food for us, let alone a dog who failed to protect our home."

Eleanor and the three younger children stared at their mother. Rose and William looked at the ground. None of them had ever heard their mother talk like this.

Eleanor's eyes filled with tears. "He tried to protect it. He kept barking, but we ignored him."

Father stood and put a hand on his wife's shoulder, then turned to Eleanor. "That's enough," Father said. His voice was soft and his blue eyes understanding.

His rebuke stung, and large tears fell and soaked into her dress. "But..." She looked at Teddy—still thin, tender, and limping. Would they abandon him after he traveled so far to come back to them? It just wasn't fair.

"Don't worry," Father assured their mother, "it's only what the mice nibbled."

Their mother glared at the dog, then handed her plate to Lilly to be washed. "Couple more days and the mice will have all the food eaten."

Eleanor looked at Father, who shook his head.

"William," he said. "Put the meat and eggs in the empty milk can and cover them with cool water. Then put the bread and other perishables on top, out of the water."

William set about his task.

Eleanor looked at the barren ground—not an ounce of shade. "We could dig a cellar like we had at home."

"Yay, let's dig," shouted the twins and Lilly joined in.

"What are you gonna dig with?" Rose asked.

Eleanor and her siblings' enthusiasm curdled. She sighed and helped her family unload the truck. They stacked things around the milk cans trying to create some shade. "There must be a way to keep the mice out."

"We need a trap," Raymond said.

Mother set down the wood crate she was carrying. "You'd need a hundred."

Eleanor swallowed. Everything seemed so overwhelming. There had never been this many problems back home.

She watched Father and William drive away in search of work and building supplies. Around her, the barren ground offered nothing but ramshackle huts. A loneliness like she'd never known weighed upon her.

They sat waiting, waiting, waiting, as the sun rose in the sky, heating the air, burning the dry ground, and scorching their skin.

"Can we go swimming?" asked the twins.

"Do you see how swift that water's moving?" Eleanor replied. "You'd drown."

"Your sister's right. I don't want you playing in that water," Mother said.

Eleanor took in the medley of melancholy huts nearby and the jumble of hesitant children watching them from a distance—some adventure! They sat in silence for so long Eleanor thought she'd explode. "Mother, did you see the beautiful waterfalls we passed over?"

Mother looked up at Eleanor, new wrinkles etched around her mouth. "Uh-huh."

"Weren't they beautiful?"

"I suppose."

"I thought they were gorgeous," Rose added. "So powerful and loud, even amid the sound of cars."

Raymond stopped his restless fidgeting. "And cool and wet. Did you feel the mist, Mother?"

Mother shook her head, and the conversations faded away. The boys wandered aimlessly around their pile of household goods, while Lilly played make-believe with her doll.

Eleanor watched her little sister and thought of her own doll, nothing but ashes now, and regretted that she'd allowed herself to think on it. "Mother, please tell us a story."

"Yes."

"Yes."

"Oh, please," the others joined in.

Mother looked up from her lap at them. "Not today."

There was a quiet but communal groan, and they each went back to doing nothing.

"Mother," Raymond ventured. "Is it lunchtime?"

They each perked up, hopeful.

She took a deep breath and raised her head to the sky. "What does the sun say?" she asked, her voice monotone.

They all looked up, then drooped back to the ground like wilted daisies. It was maybe ten a.m.

Eleanor chewed on her finger—a new habit. Mother had never been like this. Usually she was cheerful—even singing. Idleness had never been allowed; now, none of them knew what to do with it.

A mouse scurried over a food crate and squeezed into a crack. Eleanor jumped up and kicked at the crate; several mice scampered out and Teddy pounced on one, chomping it down like a small biscuit.

"That does it!" Her fists on her hips. "We've got to keep those vermin out of our food."

Mother raised her eyes. "And how do you propose to do that?"

Teddy caught another.

"That dog's caught eighteen mice since we've sat here and they still keep coming," Mother continued.

Eleanor turned and patted Teddy's head. "Good boy." She looked at the crates and the trash strewn around them. "What if we cover up the holes?"

Rose fanned herself. "With what?"

"I don't know. There's all this trash about; maybe we could stuff paper in the cracks...or cover them with cardboard."

"They'd just chew through it." Rose dismissed the idea.

Eleanor thought some more. "Hey, if the metal of the milk cans can keep them out, couldn't tin cans?"

Mother shrugged.

Eleanor turned to her siblings. "Come on; let's go look for tin cans and nails."

The twins and Lilly jumped up, excited for something to do.

"Do I have to?" Rose asked.

"Watch them," Mother said, "and don't go too far."

An hour later, they returned whispering about the small shanties they'd seen. Rose glanced about. "I hope we don't have to live in a shack like those."

The rest nodded.

They dumped about a dozen or more tin cans on the ground and struggled to cut them open. Mitchell took one of the flat strips of metal and held it up to the crack in one of the crates. "Like this?"

Eleanor squatted next to him. "Yes, that's what we need to do."

"We'll need more nails," Mitchell noted.

Rose looked down at their efforts. "You're going to run out."

"It will help." Eleanor sliced her finger and stuck it in her mouth. Rose was right. It wasn't going to be enough. She'd look for more when Father returned. She had to.

The ground vibrated and a low rumble grew closer and louder. Eleanor stood and faced the direction of the noise, then turned to Mother. "Should we hide the food?"

Mother reached for a mattress and motioned for Eleanor and Rose to help. "Hurry. Maybe we can create a wall."

They tried leaning it against the crates, but it only toppled over, knocking several crates with it—mice and food scattering.

"Oh, why can't anything work right?" Mother lamented.

A loud whistle blew, and they watched the train approach. Its brakes screeched against the metal tracks.

Mother sat back down on the milk can. "It's hopeless."

Eleanor nibbled on her finger. Men climbed down from the top of boxcars while others sat inside, legs swinging in the open doors. She counted fifteen men atop loads of logs, metal pipes, bricks, and other items stacked on flatcars. Sometimes there were even women and children peeking out of the open doors.

Eleanor shivered, feeling exposed and vulnerable. She remembered the two men from last night.

"They're waiting for the train to slow so they can get off before the railroad bulls catch them."

Eleanor startled and turned to see a young woman with two small children standing beside them.

"Do you see him, Mama? Do you see him?" asked a boy of four or five.

The woman looked down at him and smoothed his curly blond hair. "No, but he might have been on the other side of the train."

Eleanor and her siblings leaned in, all grateful for someone to break their boredom.

The woman turned to Shannon. "My husband left almost a year ago to find work. Several months ago, they evicted us. In his last letter, he said he was in Spokane." She paused. "I packed what I could carry, and we hopped a train and rode the rails until we got here."

Eleanor and her siblings stared at the woman. The twins wore expressions of awe and excitement.

"You're a brave lady," Mother said. "So many dangers—just getting on and off can cost you a limb, if not your life, and there're pickpockets, brutes, finding food, and like you said, those nasty bulls."

Eleanor turned in surprise to Mother. How did she know all of this?

"Yes, very brave," Mother continued, "especially without a man."

"I had no choice..." She looked down at the ground for a moment, then back at Mother. "I...I thought it was better that we be together..."

"But you haven't found him?"

The woman shook her head.

Eleanor watched as men jumped from the slowing train.

"Does he know you had to leave your home?"

Again, the woman shook her head.

Eleanor's attention was divided between the men disembarking from the train and her mother's knowledge of these things.

Rose and the twins also seemed surprised.

Mother turned to them. "What are you all looking at? How do you think me and your Aunt Fiona and grandfather traveled from Chicago out West?"

Most of the men riding the rails moved toward the shantytown or in the opposite direction of the train. But one man walked straight toward the women and children.

Teddy stood, the hair on his neck lifted.

"Mother..." Eleanor tapped her on the shoulder.

"Eleanor, I'm—" She stopped.

The young woman pulled her children close.

Teddy lunged at the stranger until his taut rope stopped him. He growled.

The man kept coming, adjusting his direction out of the dog's reach.

"I hate this," said the young mother.

"Mommy, do we have to share our food with him?" Lilly asked.

"Shush." Mother stood and faced the man. "That's close enough."

Teddy tried to get closer, but his rope hung up on the mattresses and crates.

Eleanor stepped next to Teddy and motioned to Mitchell to untangle the dog.

Rose pulled Lilly to her while Raymond stood, shoulders straight, fists balled, with a look of resolve on his boyish face.

The man removed his hat and nodded at both of the women. "Ma'am, ma'am. I don't mean to cause any harm." He looked at Eleanor. "I'd appreciate it if you didn't sic your pooch on me. I just have a question, then I'll be on my way."

Eleanor softened at the sadness in his eyes and ran a hand over Teddy's bristled fur.

"If you're asking for food—"

The man held up a hand and stopped Mother. "No, I can't take food from women and children. I'm looking for my son."

The tension among them eased.

"How old is he?" asked the young mother.

"Fourteen." He hung his head, then looked back up at them. "He caught a train out of Saint Louis two months ago, and I've been looking for him ever since. His poor mother is heartbroken."

Eleanor and Rose exchanged looks of shock. She couldn't imagine being all on her own, or what it would be like if William caught a train and disappeared.

"His name's Jack. Jack Paul and he's got brown hair and blue eyes, about yay high." He held his hand up to his shoulder. "He walks with a limp. If you run across him, please tell him we want him home?"

Eleanor swallowed but couldn't stop the shaking in her chest.

Mother sighed—one of the same sad sounds she made a lot these days. "We will."

"Thank you." He turned and started toward the shantytown.

"Sir," the young mother called after him. "Sir, have you seen a man…"

Mitchell stood next to Eleanor, and they watched the woman and her children catch up to the man. "I hope they find who they're looking for."

"Me too." Eleanor nibbled on her nail and hoped they would never be separated.

NINE

CHARLES BOLTED AWAKE AT the loud crack of thunder. Large beads of rain pelted his skin. "Up. Everyone up."

Lightning flashed, illuminating the night as rain now poured on everything not under the one small tarp they had.

"Girls, quick, get all the bedding into the cab." Charles shook his head. "Rain, why not?" he muttered. "Shannon, put anything that shouldn't get wet in there, too. Boys, stack the mattresses on the front of the bed, under the tarp."

There was a rush of movement about the makeshift camp as they tried to see things in the random bursts of light; their bare feet getting dirty as they stepped on dust covered raindrops.

Lightning illuminated the sky, and Eleanor hurried with an armload of bedding, but ran into William when plunged into darkness moments later.

Father lit the lantern he'd purchased. "Shannon, hold this up."

"Boys," he called, "bring over those long boards."

He climbed onto the truck bed and slid the longer of the boards he and William had found between the top two side rails, overlapping the tarp by a foot.

Eleanor watched. "Father, there are gaps between the boards."

"I know. I need you children to collect the cardboard and linoleum."

Eleanor took Lilly by the hand and they, along with Rose, carried the requested items to the truck.

One-by-one, Father laid them atop the crosswise boards. The wind increased and lifted the impromptu roofing materials. Though he tried to hold them down, several fluttered off. "Boys, grab those. Shannon, stand on the tailgate and lift the light so we can all see. Rose and Lilly, get some more boards and hand them to William to hold down the sheeting."

Eleanor peeked between the side railings. "What can I do?"

The wind was now howling, and Charles had to yell to be heard. "Get me the ropes under the truck."

Eleanor handed Father the rope as William placed smaller boards over the pieces of cardboard and old linoleum. Mitchell returned with a section of linoleum and handed it to Father, who laid it over a gap.

"I'm sure glad we've got this," Eleanor shouted.

Charles nodded. "Yes, but I wish I'd splurged on another tarp. I guess it's part of the adventure." He winked at her and worked to untangle a rope. "Eleanor, climb up here and under the boards. I need you to grab the rope I feed down to you, then hand it back to me at the gap I stick my finger through."

He and Eleanor worked to wrap the rope around the roofing materials.

Mitchell ran up panting, his hair, face and clothes wet. "I can't find Raymond."

Charles stopped. "Where'd you last see him?"

Mitchell pointed into the darkness where a large thicket of brush stood. "He went in there looking for a piece of cardboard."

Shannon gasped. "Charles, find him."

"I'm sure he can't be too far; we'll find him as fast as a pair—" Father squeezed Mother's shoulder and let his poker saying slide. He jumped down and grabbed the lantern. "You girls finish up here, then take cover. Eleanor will explain."

"Hurry!" Shannon's voice quavered.

"William, grab Teddy, Mitchell, show me where you last saw him." Images of Raymond falling into the river or stumbling upon a hobo camp and being abducted raced through his mind. He took a deep breath and tried to calm himself. This would have never happened had they stayed on the farm. He tried to push that thought away. He reminded himself that they had to sell the cows and machinery to replace the money that was stolen and provide for their basic needs.

"Raymond!" Charles held up the lantern at the edge of the small thicket and stared into the darkness—nothing. "Did you both go in there?"

Mitchell nodded. "Some things blew in there."

Charles didn't like it. The copse was dense, with very few trails. They stepped in and searched among the trees and bushes while calling for Raymond.

Teddy ran about, nose to the ground, stopping here and there to sniff something or listen. Occasionally, the dog lifted his muzzle and sniffed the air.

"Where was the last place you remember seeing him?" Father asked.

Mitchell shrugged his shoulders. "I don't remember. It was dark, and we were just chasing the stuff." He sniffled and blinked back tears.

"I should have never sent you two after those things."

A streak of lightning lit up the sky. William pointed to his right. "Father, what's that? Over there, on the ground. I saw something."

They made their way, tripping over rocks and exposed roots as branches scratched their arms and legs.

Father swung the lantern in an arc. "Raymond. Can you hear us? Where are you?" He moved in William's direction—hoping, hoping. "What did you see?"

William stopped. "It's nothing. Only a short log."

They continued into the underbrush, the small trees and bushes growing denser, and the ground uneven as it sloped to the river.

"Father," William stopped. "He wouldn't have gone this far, would he?"

"He would if he got turned around."

Mitchell peered into the tangle of trees and bushes. "Too bad we don't have our whistles. Then me and him could call to each other like we did back home."

William grinned at his little brother. "Good idea." He lifted his pinkies to his mouth and whistled several times. They waited, and he tried again—nothing. "I suppose with all this wind it's hard to hear."

Father nodded.

Mitchell sighed. "I forgot. Raymond can't whistle with just his lips. It comes out as a hiss." He looked about. "Do you think he's by the river?"

That same idea gnawed at Charles and gave rise to a greater fear. "It's possible. We probably should look there."

They pressed further in but made their way downward, toward the river, calling and calling.

"Wait a minute." William stopped and held up his hand. "Did you hear that?"

They all paused and listened. The wind wailed, and all around them, trees creaked and moaned as the wind pushed against them. Occasionally a branch or twig snapped, then they heard it, a faint, "Help."

"Raymond," Father and Mitchell called in unison.

Again, they heard the call.

Father cupped a hand to his mouth. "Raymond, stay where you are. We're coming for you."

William shoved branches and vines out of his way as he pressed forward.

"William," Father called. "Where are you going?"

William stopped. "To get Raymond."

"He's over here." Father pointed to their left.

"No, the voice came from up ahead."

They both turned to Mitchell, who shook his head. "I don't know."

They called again but heard nothing.

"Maybe we should split up," William suggested.

Father shook his head. "I don't want to be looking for you as well. Plus, we only have one lantern." He sighed and wished to be dealt a better hand for a change. He assessed the situation. "Alright, we'll split it in the middle. I'll focus on the left, and you focus on the right."

William rubbed his hands against his bare arms. "Yes, Father."

They moved ahead. "Mitchell, keep your eyes open."

Mitchell nodded.

This time, Teddy trudged along behind them, his quiet whines drowned out by the wind. The going was slow as the undergrowth became a thick tangle of bushes. After about forty feet, Teddy nudged first at Mitchell, then Charles and William.

Father stopped. "What is it ol' boy?"

Teddy yapped and moved to their right.

"Come, boys, let's follow him."

They nodded and let Teddy lead the way.

"Fath—"

They all stopped and listened.

"Help."

William pointed in the opposite direction. "Father, that sounds like it's coming from our left."

Charles nodded, then looked at the dog, who had paused ten feet ahead of them, waiting. "Raymond, we're coming." He turned to the dog. "Come on; this wind has the scents all spun around."

They turned and headed further from camp. The dog barked and Father called him to come.

Mitchell glanced back. "Father, William, Teddy's going the other way."

Charles, several paces ahead of Mitchell, paused. "What?"

Mitchell turned and looked back to where Teddy had been, but he was gone. "Teddy."

Charles cupped his hand to his ear. "I can't hear you. Come on."

Mitchell took one last look in the direction that Teddy had gone and followed his father.

"Father, over there." William pointed to something moving roughly twenty feet away between some trees.

"Raymond, Raymond!" They worked their way to the pale-colored object only to discover newsprint caught up in a bush.

Charles fought to keep his fear in check. He gave Mitchell's shoulder a squeeze as a tear slid down the twin's cheek, and Mitchell wiped it away.

William kicked at the newsprint. "We're never going to find him."

"No, don't talk like that." Charles motioned his sons closer to him. He had to be strong for them. "We're going to do what we should have done in the beginning."

"What's that?" they asked.

"Pray."

The boys looked at each other.

Charles removed his hat and William did the same, then they bowed their heads. "Heavenly Father, forgive us for not seeking your guidance sooner. Lord, you know exactly where Raymond is. Please, guide us to him. Amen."

Father shook the water from his hat, placed it back on his head, and looked around. "This is too thick; I don't think he would have gone this way. Let's work our way down to the river. But after searching along the bank and not finding him, they made their way around the thicket and up to the tracks.

Charles worried the whole time if he was making the right decision. The city lights twinkled beyond the Spokane River. Railroad tracks ran east and west—a barrier between the shantytown and the north side of Spokane. What if Raymond had followed one of these tracks away from them?

They walked east, away from the shantytown, trying to see anything in the dark. "Raymond. Raymond!"

Father wiped his brow with his handkerchief. He kept an eye on Mitchell; who looked about but spent more time trying to stay close. It was late. Charles estimated they'd been searching for over an hour; they were all wet, cold, and tired.

Mitchell slumped to the ground, tears pouring down his seven-year-old face. "Raymond and Teddy are both gone."

Father handed William the lantern and picked Mitchell up. "Now, now, let's not cry."

"But I miss them."

"We'll find them."

Mitchell buried his dirty face into Father's chest.

"You're tired and cold, aren't you?"

"Uh-huh."

Father set him down. "Why don't you ride on my back?"

They now called and whistled for the dog.

"When did you last see him?" Father asked.

Mitchell pointed into the patch of trees and brush. "Down there, after we heard Raymond."

"Do you think Teddy found him?" William asked.

"It's possible. Let's backtrack."

They retraced their steps, calling, looking, listening. Halfway back, something light-colored moved in the brush.

"Raymond." Father set Mitchell down, took the lantern, and scurried down the hill. He pushed aside branches and vines. "Raymond." Then he stopped.

"Father, is it him?" William called from the edge of the copse.

Charles turned and shook his head, fighting discouragement.

"What was it?" Mitchell asked, trying to see into the overgrown thicket.

"Just a piece of old cloth."

Mitchell hung his head.

Father put a hand on Mitchell's shoulder.

Mitchell looked up at Father. "Maybe he's with Teddy."

"Let's hope so."

Mitchell rubbed his hands across his wet, bare arms and tried to dry them on his shirt and overalls.

William wrapped an arm around Mitchell's shoulder and pulled his little brother into him. "Don't worry. We'll find him."

The lantern flickered and Father tensed. "Boys, stay close to me and pray we find him quickly."

"Yes, sir."

The rain increased and a streak of lightning flashed far to the north. They made their way to another set of tracks when there was a bark behind them. They all turned. "Teddy?"

He barked again.

There, with wet, muddy, matted fur, stood Teddy, his eyes intense on them—pleading, his body angled.

Hope swelled in Father's chest as he moved toward Teddy. "Where is he, boy? Where's Raymond?"

Teddy whined and turned around, then looked back and barked.

They followed. Teddy ran ahead then waited, sometimes whining, sometimes barking. He led them into the thicket through a narrow path.

Again, the lantern flickered. Charles tensed and whispered a silent prayer. "Raymond. Stay where you are. We're coming."

The lantern sputtered and went out.

TEN

CHARLES STOPPED.

William and Mitchell bumped into him. "Mitchell, grab onto my belt and William, take his other hand." Charles felt Teddy's wet body pressing into his leg. He reached down and grabbed the rope collar he'd made for the dog. "Easy boy."

Like a slow-moving train, they made their way through the thicket, occasionally stopping when one of them lost their grip.

"Father," Raymond called out.

"We're almost there."

Within minutes, they were rejoined and after hugs and assurance that Raymond wasn't hurt, Teddy led them out of the thicket.

Eleanor squatted under the makeshift roof and took the wet clothes that Mother and Rose removed from each of the twins.

The boys' pale chests shivered and only relaxed when dressed in the two extra shirts they had. Mother wrapped them in the quilt, along with Lilly under the tarp by the truck's cab.

Father flung a quilt over the remaining boards and tied it down. "That will have to do. Shannon, you and the girls crawl under the covers with the young 'uns. Warm them up and try to get some sleep. William and I will sleep by the opening."

Eleanor squeezed back the tears. All the pent-up fears and emotions tumbled out. She was helpless. She wept quietly, then stopped. No! She wasn't helpless. She would work harder to watch her younger siblings, so this didn't happen again.

Awake, cold, squished, and with water dripping on her, she longed for their spacious, dry home. Were the people in the shanties dry? Were they cramped? Would the shanty Father and William built be warm and dry? How big would it be?

She shivered. She wanted to curl up next to Rose, but her younger siblings lay with their heads near her feet and their own cold feet poking her in the side.

Why was God allowing all this to happen? A story about God providing for a family in need came to mind. Why hadn't he provided for them? Somewhere amid her cold, confusion, and exhaustion, Eleanor fell asleep.

Eleanor awoke to angry whispers near the truck's cab. She lifted her head and strained to hear.

Mother's hushed words spewed into the early morning air. "This is no place for a family—no place for women and children. While you and William are gone looking for work, any of these men could hurt us and take whatever they want."

Pressure raised in Eleanor's chest.

"I agree Shannon. That's why I leave Teddy here. If it wasn't for him, we'd still be searching for Raymond."

"I know." Shannon's voice cracked. "But why here?"

The farm loomed in Eleanor's mind. Surely, they could have built a new home there.

"Shannon, no one will rent to us if I don't have a job."

"Have you even tried to find Harry and Fiona?"

Eleanor shuddered. No. Not Aunt Fiona.

"We don't even know where they live."

"Well, where does Harry work?"

Father sighed. "I don't remember. I think he works for some place that prints magazines or newspapers or maybe a radio station—something like that. I wouldn't even know where to look."

"Please, try to find them."

Father said nothing.

Eleanor held her breath in hope.

"Charles?"

"Alright. I'll try."

Eleanor's heart sank. What was worse, living in the shantytown or with Aunt Fiona? If they ended up living with her aunt and uncle, she would have to work hard to make her aunt happy.

Several days later, Father and William returned from searching for work with news that they'd learned of a directory and found an address for Uncle Harry and Aunt Fiona.

Excitement and apprehension battled within Eleanor.

The news ignited a flurry of excitement in Mother, who sent the children scurrying to pick up the camp and clean themselves up.

"You sure you don't want to visit with your sister first?" Father asked. "You and I could explain the situation before we all descend on her."

Mother stopped her inspection of Mitchell and Raymond; their faces and necks were red from scrubbing. She looked up at him, puzzled. "Why?"

He shrugged. "Eight hungry, homeless people descending upon them might be...well...frightening."

She licked two fingers and tried to plaster down a stray strand of hair on Raymond's head, then stood. "Charles Cruthers, I declare! We're family!"

Eleanor smiled to see Mother so happy. It was the first time since the day of the fire, though she wished it was for another reason.

"Lilly, come here." Mother straightened the makeshift bows in Lilly's short, braided pigtails, then examined her youngest. "It will have to do." She looked around the camp. "Have we forgotten anything?"

"No," the kids responded.

She looked in the truck's side mirror and tucked a stray strand of red hair into her bun and examined her face, now flush with color. "Then what are we waiting for?"

Rose and the younger children cheered while William and Eleanor exchanged a knowing look.

Eleanor and her siblings leaned against the wood railings of the farm truck. A pang of guilt stabbed her as they left behind the pieced together hovels with their vacant eyed occupants.

"I'm so glad we're leaving here," Rose said.

Eleanor nodded. She didn't want to admit it, but this place scared her. She turned to William. "Are you excited?"

He shrugged, "Yeah. It'll be great."

Eleanor squinted up at him, but he looked away.

It seemed he'd changed since they moved to Spokane. He was more serious and somber. Eleanor didn't like that about him, but if he wanted to be a Gloomy Gus, that was his problem. She turned her attention to the city around her and its many people—more than she ever imagined existed. The buildings were so tall—much taller than their milk barn...

A prick of grief wrapped itself around her, and she shoved it away. This was a happy day—kind of—and she would not ruin it with sad thoughts. Father downshifted, and she clung to the rails as the truck headed up a steep hill.

"Oh, aren't they beautiful?" Rose asked and pointed to several stately homes. "Oh, look at that one with its tall pillars? It looks like the White House."

"Look at that one, and that one, and that one," Lilly called from the other side of the truck.

Eleanor turned, surprised to see a sprawling home, not made of wood or bricks but with smooth walls, like those of the whitewashed cellar. Even though she didn't like Aunt Fiona, she couldn't suppress the excitement of sleeping in a nightgown, between sheets, and behind walls where others couldn't see them. Maybe Mother wouldn't be so sad.

Mary squeezed her arm. "Remember Aunt Fiona's stories of the parties they had, and how they decorated their home for Christmas? And all the food they served?"

Eleanor's stomach rumbled. She could almost taste the sweet, minced meat pie and eggnog. She licked her lips and imaged eating until she was full.

"What do you think we'll have for dinner?" Raymond asked.

"I hope it's not liver," Mitchell said and made a face.

William glanced at them, but said nothing.

A pang of fear clung tightly to Eleanor.

They passed several immense homes with sprawling lawns and long staircases leading from the road to the front porches. "Isn't this exciting?" Rose whispered, her eyes sparkling. "Imagine how rich Uncle Harry and Aunt Fiona must be?" Rose looked down at her faded red dress and worn boots. "I wish I had nicer clothes."

Eleanor sighed. No matter what they had, it wouldn't be as nice as aunt Fiona's.

The truck slowed, then rolled to a stop.

Mother leaned out the window and peered at the large, two-and-a-half story brick home they'd stopped in front of. "Is this it? Come on, Charles, hurry."

Father exited the truck with a sigh and looked up at the children. "You all stay."

"But, Father, why?" Rose protested.

"We want to get out; we want to see," chimed in Mitchell and Raymond.

William glared at his two little brothers. "You heard Father."

There was a communal groan, and all six children leaned against the railing facing the home and watched as Mother and Father walked up the flower-lined concrete path to the large front porch. They waited in silence as Father knocked on the door.

Eleanor nibbled at her nails.

Surprise spread across Aunt Fiona's face when she answered the door. Her surprise shifted to wide-eyed shock when she spotted the truck laden with bedraggled children and household goods.

Mother threw her arms around her sister. "Fiona! Am I glad to see you!"

Eleanor and her siblings stood quietly and listened to Mother tell about the fire. Several times she stopped and gasped for air to starve off the approaching sobs.

"Oh, my! I can't imagine." Fiona looked between Mother and Father and then at the truck full of children. "Come in, all of you," she stopped mid-sentence at the sight of the dog. "Tie him up along the side of the house."

William obeyed as the children scurried up the walk. Eleanor smiled up at her wide-eyed and pale-skinned aunt.

Mother lowered her gaze and put a hand on Lilly's head. "All we have left are the clothes we had on our backs and a few that kind neighbors gave us."

"Oh, my." Aunt Fiona took a deep breath.

Two children about Lilly's age stood near a large stairway, their clothes crisp, clean, and pressed.

"Albert, Suzanne, these are your cousins from Idaho. You probably don't remember the last time we visited them on their farm."

Suzanne wrinkled her nose. "I don't like farms, they smell."

Fiona smiled at her daughter. "Why don't you take—" She turned and looked at Eleanor and Lilly. "Remind me of your names again, girls."

Eleanor obliged.

"Oh, yes. Take Eleanor and Lilly up to your room, and show them your new dollhouse." She turned to her son, "Albert, I want you to take—" This time she looked at the twins.

"Mitchell and Raymond," Father offered and put a hand on each of the boys' shoulders.

"Oh, yes, I don't know how you tell them apart. Albert, take your cousins upstairs and show them your train set."

Mitchell's and Raymond's eyes widened.

"I don't want to. I want to play outside."

"Not now. I don't want you getting dirty before your father comes home."

Albert glared at Aunt Fiona, then stomped up the red patterned rug that ran down the center of the stairs.

Aunt Fiona looked Rose over. "And this must be Rosalyn."

"Rose, ma'am," Eleanor's sister replied.

"Oh, yes. And how you've grown. Why don't you go up and supervise the children?"

Rose opened her mouth to protest, but Father gave her a look that said otherwise. Rose followed the children upstairs, her fingers gently touching the smooth and highly polished banister.

Mother sat on a fuchsia rolled arm sofa. She looked about the stately parlor with its floral wallpaper and dark wood trim. "Fiona, your home is gorgeous!" Shannon smoothed her dusty dress, caught a whiff of her stench, and cringed.

"Why thank you. We were about to update the dining room and entry when the stock market crashed. It has totally affected Harry's work. We've had to cut back on our expenses. It's been such a hardship."

Charles shifted in his seat while William stared at his boots.

Shannon shared their story, while Fiona served them chilled tea. Just speaking the words brought fresh emotions, and Shannon tried to swallow the sobs rising in her chest.

"That is just horrible. It's frightening what some people will do. What are you going to do now?"

"We've had to move to Spokane. Charles and William are looking for work."

"Where are you staying?"

Shannon took a deep breath and looked at Charles.

"We're camping out right now," Father said. "Hoping we can find work so someone will rent to us."

Fiona cringed.

"I'm so glad we found you. It's worse than when we lived in Chicago."

Fiona gasped. "I wouldn't go back to those days for anything."

"Then you understand our plight. It took us a while to find your address. We were hoping we could stay with you until Charles and William find work and we can get a place of our own."

Fiona stared at them. "Oh, my. I...oh. I'll need to speak to Harry about that. Things have been tight...and...well...I want to help...but...I'm not sure we're situated to support...a whole...family."

Shannon swallowed. "It wouldn't be for long."

Fiona looked at her. "You don't understand. Harry tells me there are hundreds and hundreds of men looking for work and very few jobs. It would take more than all the luck of Ireland to find two steady jobs right now."

They sat in silence.

Shannon's breathing increased. "There must be something we can do. We can't keep camping."

"I'll speak with Harry, but we've cut back so much just to provide for the four of us. I don't see how we can support eight people."

"But we'd help—"

Charles patted her hand. "Shannon, let's just enjoy our visit and let your sister and brother-in-law discuss the matter."

Fiona smiled at him. "Thank you, Charles." She turned to Shannon. "In the meantime, let me see if I can find a few outfits for you and then we'll prepare supper."

Upstairs, Eleanor and Lilly spent several hours in their cousin's room. Suzie showed off her dolls with their various dresses and bonnets, her new doll house with its tiny wood furniture, her hair ribbons, and books. Eleanor tired of looking at Suzanne's things and gazed down at the beautiful flower garden below.

Whenever Lilly tried to touch something, Suzanne pulled the item from her hands. "These are mine; I don't want them broke."

Eleanor turned to her six-year-old cousin. "She won't break anything. Why have all these nice toys if you don't play with them? You know, your house could catch on fire and burn all these toys up. Then what would you do?"

Suzie's eyes got big. "I'm telling my mother." She ran out of the room and bumped into Rose. "Mommy, Mommy."

Eleanor panicked. "No. Come back. I..."

Her cries echoed all the way down the hall and stairs.

Rose looked after her. "What happened?"

Eleanor's light complexion paled. "I just—"

"Eleanor, Lilly, come down here right this moment," Father's voice boomed from the foot of the stairs.

In the parlor, Suzie was crying uncontrollably; her pale skin blotched with red spots. When Eleanor entered the room, Suzie pointed at her. "That's the one. She said she is going to burn up my dolls."

Eleanor stared at her little cousin in shock and shook her head. "No, that's not what I said."

"Yes, you did." The child sobbed harder.

Aunt Fiona smoothed Suzanne's brown hair. "There, there, my little one. I'm sure she didn't mean that." She turned her gaze on Eleanor, her eyes small and hard. "Did you?"

Eleanor opened her mouth to protest.

"Eleanor, did you really say that?" Mother asked.

"No. I didn't, I just—"

"Yes, she did."

"Eleanor, what has gotten into you?"

Tears welled in Eleanor's eyes and she fought to suppress them, her lips quivering.

Upstairs, the boys' ruckus quieted, and she glanced up to see each of the younger boys on the staircase watching the interchange.

"I didn't. I promise..."

Everyone stared at her.

"Liar," Suzie exclaimed.

"I'm not." Eleanor struggled to explain, but the words wouldn't come. The weight of her cousin's false accusation combined with the unfairness of all that had happened pressed against her chest. She turned and ran out of the room.

"Eleanor!" Mother called.

"Leave her be," Father said.

The screen door banged behind her, and she scurried around the house and into the garden she'd seen from the window. She squeezed between two plump lilac bushes and huddled near a fence; tears poured forth, each carrying some of the hurt, loss, and disappointment she'd held onto since the day of the fire.

When she quieted, the realization struck her that she was alone for the first time since that horrible day.

On the farm, she could roam the small woods and fields by their home, or sit in the loft with a book or her diary. Her diary! Another ache wrapped its tentacles around her heart and squeezed. Memories of holidays and normal days made special by some unexpected event, like the morning she found a fawn in the tall grass behind the barn, or the first time she milked a cow, the birth of a new litter of kittens. She'd also written descriptions of sunsets, and newborn calves, collecting ice off the pond, and the sounds of toads and owls in the night.

The fire had stolen that from her as well and the memories tucked inside—unless—unless she could rewrite as many as possible. Her heart lifted. She would ask Father for a new diary. It wouldn't need to be fancy...reality slapped her in the face; there would be no diary or any paper for a long time.

Eleanor stared through the leafy bushes up to the pointed roof of her aunt and uncle's home. How long would they stay here? Would she and her sisters have to share a room with Suzie? She hoped not. Behind her, a handful of chickens clucked in the neighbor's coop. She missed gathering eggs and eating them even more. If only they still had chickens.

"Eleanor? Where are you?"

Eleanor debated ignoring Rose.

"Eleanor, come on. Mother wants you to help set the table."

Dinner! She scrambled out from her hiding place at the promise of food—hot meat, mashed potatoes and gravy, breads and jellies, vegetables, pickles, seconds, dessert, and a tall glass of milk to wash it all down.

A short time later, Eleanor sat near the end of the table, squished between Lilly and Suzie and across from the twins and cousin Albert. William sat with the adults and Rose sat at the end, with the responsibility of overseeing the children.

Uncle Harry carved a roast and dealt out thin slices to each of the children.

Rose leaned toward Eleanor and Lilly. "Mother said to take small portions and not ask for seconds."

Eleanor stared at her sister. "Why?"

Her sister only shrugged.

Aunt Fiona turned to her daughter. "Suzanne, darling, hand Mother your plate."

Suzanne did and Aunt Fiona dropped a scoop of potatoes onto it, then handed Rose the bowl. "Rose, please dish up a portion to each of your siblings."

"Yes, ma'am." Rose filled the serving spoon and deposited the contents on Eleanor's plate.

Eleanor licked her lips in anticipation.

"Not that much," Aunt Fiona corrected. "We want to make sure there's enough for everyone."

Eleanor watched, her stomach growling, as her sister removed first a small amount and then more at their aunt's direction.

Raymond and Lilly gobbled their food down while the others ate slower, understanding they weren't getting any more.

"This is a fine meal," Father said.

"Yes." "Oh yes." "Thank you," everyone said.

"Rosalyn, darling," Aunt Fiona said.

"Rose," Eleanor's sister countered.

"Yes, anyway. I've been speaking with your mother and father and we've agreed that it would be an advantage to all involved, for you to stay on with us and help with cooking, cleaning, and the children."

Eleanor's heart stopped. What?

She and Rose stared at their aunt in disbelief, while the boys stopped their chattering and pleas for more food. Only Lilly didn't look up. She instead dropped her hands to her lap and stared at her plate.

"In exchange for your services, we'll provide you with room and board and a small allowance."

Eleanor looked first at her sister, who seemed bewildered by the offer, and then at Mother, whose eyes seemed to coax Rose to accept. Father, like Lilly, looked down at his plate.

Uncle Harry cleared his throat. "Advertising at the radio station has been a struggle in this depressed economy. Companies can't seem to see the many opportunities that await them. With less income, we had to let our regular housekeeper go. But there is simply too much here for Fiona to do alone, and I believe Rose can be of great assistance. Rose can have the spare room on the third floor, and your family will rest in the comfort of knowing she's safe and well cared for."

The food in Eleanor's stomach turned to rocks, and she looked at her parents. "Is Rose staying here?"

Father looked up, his eyes dull and his usual smile gone. "Yes, Eleanor."

"What about us?" Raymond asked.

All the children looked at their father.

Raymond leaned over his plate to see their father better. "Aren't we staying here too?"

Aunt Fiona laughed. "Oh, dear me." She fanned herself with her napkin. "Good gracious, where did you ever get an idea like that?"

"Well—" Looks from Father and Mother stopped Eleanor from finishing. Children are to be seen and not heard, ran through her mind. She looked about at the large, beautiful home with its wide, dark wood trim, windows with beveled glass on the upper portions and lace curtains below, built-in cabinets with leaded glass doors, and the crystal chandelier.

"But you have so much, and we have so little," Raymond pressed.

William shook his head at his little brother, warning him to stop.

Uncle Harry absently straightened his tie. "We've had to make serious sacrifices, and even adding your sister to our household will cost us dearly. But it's a sacrifice we're willing to make."

Aunt Fiona placed her fork perpendicular on her plate, like a clock hand; she looked first at Raymond and then the others. "By your sister staying here, there is one less mouth your mother and father need to worry about feeding and clothing. This will help you all very much, you'll see."

Raymond looked at her and then at his parents. "But where—"

"We'll talk about that later," Father said. "Right now, I want you all to thank Uncle Harry and Aunt Fiona for this fine meal and the enjoyable time we've had visiting today."

The children dutifully thanked their aunt and uncle.

"Now boys," Father continued. "I want you to go up and help clean up Albert's room."

"Yes, sir." Raymond said.

Mitchell only nodded and rose.

"Girls, I want you to help clear the table and wash up the dishes."

"Yes, Father."

"Who's going to help me clean my room?" Suzanne demanded.

"Lilly, you go help your cousin," Father said.

"But they were both in there," Suzanne argued.

Aunt Fiona stood. "When they're done with the dishes, Rosalyn—I mean Rose—will help you."

Eleanor raised an eyebrow at her older sister, who appeared bewildered.

When the dishes were done, Eleanor went with Rose to the truck and they sifted through the box that held their few belongings.

"I can't believe I'm staying," Rose said with excitement in her voice.

Eleanor hung her head. "Me either."

Rose looked at her little sister. "It will be alright. You'll see. This is just temporary. Besides, like Aunt Fiona said, without me, there will be more food for the rest of you."

"One less person eating nothing of nothing doesn't help."

"Come on, Eleanor, this will help us. Besides, I'll be making money."

"And what are you gonna to do with it?"

Rose took a deep breath as she stared up the street. "I'm going to save it up, and when I have enough, I'm going to buy a train ticket and go back to Bonners Ferry and marry Johnny." She pulled out the spare dress and the nightgown. She looked at Eleanor. "You don't mind, do you?" She motioned to the big house. "Aunt Fiona asked if I had a change of clothing. If I'm going to be living and working in such a fine home," she paused, "I'll need to have more than one dress, and I'll need a nightgown."

"You could have told her, 'No.'"

Eleanor stifled a cry. "That only leaves me this dress."

"You have that other one that someone gave you."

"It's too tight." Eleanor looked at the big house. "Maybe Aunt Fiona will give you a few of her dresses."

Rose placed her hand on her chest. "I couldn't ask her."

"Why not?"

William approached the truck with some food and clothes. Eleanor eyed the outfits. "Who are those for?"

"Mother and Lilly," William said. "Come on, Rose, we're about ready to leave."

Rose climbed out of the truck and started toward the house.

Eleanor watched her leave.

Half-way up the walk, she stopped and looked at Eleanor. "Aren't you coming back into the house?"

Eleanor struggled to breathe and shook her head. "I wish you weren't staying. This isn't how it was supposed to be."

Rose ran back to the truck. "I'm going to miss you. But think of the opportunities I'm going to have."

A tear slid down Eleanor's cheek, and she wiped it away with the back of her hand. How could this be temporary if afterward Rose moved back to Bonners Ferry?

Rose threw her arms around Eleanor, who stood stiffly. She wanted to beg Rose to come back with them.

Rose stepped back. "You're just a selfish little girl. You should be happy for me. Aunt Fiona's right. This will help all of us."

"But...this..." Tears streamed down her cheeks. They were all supposed to stay, not go back to the shantytown without Rose. "You..." She turned her back on her sister, the world around her a blur.

Eleanor and Mitchell sat on either side of Teddy, their heads leaning against his neck, fingers entwined in his fur. Lilly sat on the other side of Eleanor, weeping quietly. Raymond faced the other three and voiced his displeasure at the day's events as they rode back to the shanty camp.

Only William seemed unmoved by all that had happened.

Eleanor looked up at her big brother. "Aren't you upset that we have to come back here? And without Rose?"

William turned from the view outside the truck. "Am I sad Rose isn't with us?" He shrugged. "Some, but she was bound to leave sooner or later. That's what children do when they grow up. Am I upset about having to come back here? I'm not happy about it, but it's not unexpected. I would have been more surprised if Aunt Fiona would have allowed us all to stay with them, especially for a long time."

"But they have that big house, and Uncle Harry has a job," Raymond protested.

"And we probably look like a hoard of locusts, coming to eat all their food and tear down their home."

Eleanor's mouth flew open. "We wouldn't do that."

"No, but that's what people think."

Eleanor glared at her brother. "You don't know that."

William leaned in. "No? Have you been out on the streets day after day looking for work? Always being told 'no'? Having doors slammed in your face? Seeing how people glance at you, then look away? Tell you to leave? That you're not wanted around here?" He picked at a loose piece of wood on the rails and flicked it out of the truck.

All four of the children stared at him. His words angered Eleanor. They rode in silence for several minutes.

"Why do people hate us?" Lilly whispered with a quaver in her voice.

"Because people are mean," Mitchell mumbled.

Raymond looked back at the homes and nice neighborhoods as they left the South Hill and entered downtown. "They don't even know us. If they came to our farm, we'd help them."

William nodded. "I know. Father says they're afraid."

"Afraid of what?" Eleanor asked.

"Afraid we'll take what they have. Afraid of becoming like us."

ELEVEN

CRASH!

Rose awoke with a start and glanced about the small room.

A child's wailing snaked up the stairs to her room.

"Rosalyn! I need you downstairs immediately."

Rose sat up and banged her head on the slanted wall. "Owe!" She rubbed the tender spot as the past evening's events drifted into view.

"Rosalyn, do you hear me?"

Butterflies churned in her stomach. "Rose, Aunt Fiona, it's Rose," she muttered. She made her narrow bed and tucked her nightgown under the pillow. A twang of guilt stabbed at her. She'd taken both the nightgown and the spare dress, leaving Eleanor nothing to wear when her only dress needed washing.

She vowed to save her money and buy her younger sister a dress and even a nightshirt.

"Rosalyn," Aunt Fiona called. "Do hurry up. Mr. Morgan needs his eggs, coffee, and toast before he leaves for work in thirty minutes."

"Why can't she remember my name?" She laced up her boots. "I'll be right down."

Rose entered the kitchen to a flurry of activity. Albert chased Suzanne around the table as she squawked at him to leave her alone.

She stared in disbelief. Why were they allowed to run in the house? It was only a matter of time before they hurt someone. And why weren't they helping?

Uncle Harry sat at the head of the table reading the paper, oblivious to the surrounding commotion. The stench of burnt toast wafted from the kitchen. Rose steadied her nerves but flinched as Aunt Fiona banged the cast-iron skillet onto the stove.

"Rosalyn," she called again.

Rose hurried into the kitchen. "Aunt Fiona, my name is Rose, not Rosalyn."

Aunt Fiona gave her a blank look, then handed Rose the spatula. "Fix Mr. Morgan three eggs over easy and don't add too much pepper." She looked at the burnt toast. "You'll need to make him two more slices, medium brown, with butter and strawberry preserves."

"Yes, Auntie."

"Then fix the children each a scrambled egg and toast with strawberry preserves. Don't let Albert dress his own toast; he'll use too much and get it all over his clothes."

Rose nodded.

"After breakfast, have the children clean up, and they can play in their rooms while you do up the dishes."

"And you, ma'am?" Rose wondered what her aunt would do while she did all this work. At home, everyone, including the young children, pitched in.

"Oh, I'll have a piece of toast and coffee after I finish my hair. I have a meeting with my garden club this morning, then lunch at the country club, and a Bridge game this afternoon."

For the second time that morning, Rose stared in disbelief. How did she have time for all of those things while caring for her family and this big house? How could Aunt Fiona go to lunch, knowing her sister sat in a dusty, barren lot with little food and no home?

"Make sure the children get their daily constitutional walk." She pointed out the window. "Two blocks south, two blocks west, three blocks north, two blocks east, and then one block back home. Please make sure you're home before it rains."

Rose nodded, trying to remember all those directions.

"Mr. Morgan will be home from work at six-ten and expects supper served fifteen minutes after he arrives. There are pork chops in the ice-box, potatoes, and applesauce in the pantry." She paused for a minute.

There was a crash in the dining room, and a howl from one of the children followed by arguing.

Rose cringed.

Aunt Fiona seemed unfazed. "Let's have a white cake for dessert. You'll find the ingredients in the pantry."

"Mother!" Suzanne wailed as she entered the kitchen, a goose egg already growing on her forehead. "Albert pushed me into the credenza."

"Oh, my darling Suzanne." Aunt Fiona comforted her daughter. "Ros-alyn, get me a wet cloth."

"Yes, ma'am."

"Fiona, where's my breakfast?"

Fiona bustled past Rose. "I'll get the cloth; you get your uncle's break-fast."

Rose took a deep breath and tried to calm her already rattled nerves. She melted lard on the hot skillet and cracked the first egg. She looked at the gray sky—get the children their daily constitutional walk before it rains. How would her family stay dry?

She sighed. Johnny would have to wait; her family needed her. If today was a glimpse of what her days would be like, she was in for a lot of work.

But it would be worth it. She could only imagine how much money she would make. Maybe she could set a quarter of it aside to go back to Bonners Ferry. With the rest, she could really help her family, and best of all, she didn't have to live in that filthy shantytown.

Eleanor waited for what she hoped would be the perfect moment. Last night had been such a disappointment, and everyone had gone to bed with few words but much tossing, turning, and tears. Next to her, Lilly had fallen asleep crying. When everything was quiet, Eleanor caught faint mutterings from Mother between quiet sniffles.

But Eleanor couldn't sleep. She lay awake reviewing the whole day. Why was her little cousin such a brat? Maybe Eleanor shouldn't have said anything about her cousin's dolls burning up, but she just wanted the little girl to share. Was it her comment that stopped Aunt Fiona and Uncle Harry from letting them stay?

William told her that neither he nor Father expected that Uncle Harry and Aunt Fiona would open their home to them.

Whatever the reason, she was determined to do something helpful for a change. When Father returned from washing up by the river, she approached him.

He smiled at the sight of her. "How's my curious little kitten?"

She took a deep breath and stood straight. "Father...I've been thinking—"

"When aren't you thinking?" he chuckled.

She smiled, knowing it was a compliment. "I know we only have a little money, but...well..." She looked in the direction of the railroad tracks, then down at her shoes. "If we got a goat, we could have milk and butter, and if we bought some chickens, we could have eggs to eat. And if we had enough chickens, we might sell some of the extra eggs."

Father scanned the shantytown growing closer to where they camped. "I don't see enough grass or even weeds here to feed a goat. Though those are some good ideas."

Eleanor slumped.

"Where do you suppose we keep these chickens you want?" he continued.

Eleanor squirmed. "We'd need to build a coop."

"Yes. Yes, we would."

"Can we?"

He sighed. "I don't know. There's a lot to consider, including the money to start this venture. Let me think about it for a while. In the meantime, you see if you can scrounge up some materials to build a coop."

A wide smile spread across her face. "Thank you, thank—"

A loud bang erupted from the truck tailgate, then another. Father and Eleanor hurried over to find Mother banging the iron skillet against the bumper.

"Shannon." He tried to get the skillet out of her hand. "Shannon, what is going on?"

Eleanor's heart raced as she watched from a distance with her siblings.

Lilly coiled her arms around Eleanor. "I'm scared."

Eleanor pulled Lilly close, hiding her own fear.

"We're all going to die. We're going to run out of food and starve to death. It's hopeless."

Charles placed his hand on Mother's back and grasped the skillet handle.

Mother released her grip on the skillet and turned into Father's chest; her body shaking as she sobbed.

Father set the skillet on the truck bed and pulled Mother into him.

"There, there. It's going to be alright. We'll make it through this."

Eleanor's fear increased. What if Mother was right? What if they starved to death?

Lilly ran and threw her arms around her mother's leg.

Both Mother and Father looked down at her with forced smiles.

"How could she not care about us?" Shannon asked. "We'd let them live with us."

"I know," Father comforted. "They're not thinking clearly. This whole stock market crash has everyone scared. People are responding in ways they normally wouldn't."

"But they have a home and food, and we have nothing."

"Oh, we're not completely destitute. We have beds and the truck and some food—including the items your sister gave us. We have each other, and together, we'll overcome this. It may be difficult for a while, but we'll overcome, with or without your sister's help." Father ran his hand over Lilly's messy braids, then pointed to the other children. He motioned with a nod of his head for the children to give them space.

William led the children toward the river. "Come on, leave Mother alone."

"Why?" Lilly bounced beside them.

"She just needs to be alone."

Raymond kicked a rock. "She's upset that Aunt Fiona and Uncle Harry won't let us live with them."

Eleanor picked a flower off a weed. If only they each had a skill or a way to provide food or money, then maybe her aunt and uncle would share their home.

Raymond picked up a rock and threw it as far as he could. "I don't like Uncle Harry and Aunt Fiona. They're mean, and selfish, and stingy."

Lilly tugged on William's sleeve. "Why did Rose have to stay with them?"

William stared at the bushes growing along the river. "They think they can help her."

"But why not us?" Raymond demanded. "What's so special about Rose?"

"She's older and can work around the house."

Raymond picked up another stone. "But you're older than her?"

"I think they want someone to help with housework, cooking, and looking after Albert and Suzanne."

A look of determination came over Raymond. "Someday I'll have a big house like theirs, and I'll let people stay with me. Except them."

Eleanor smiled.

After a while, Father called them back to the truck. "Children, William and I are about to go looking for work and supplies we can use to build a house. We're leaving the truck here." He looked up at the gathering storm clouds. "Eleanor, oversee the younger ones to use the boards and other items. We have to make a shelter in the truck bed like we did before."

"Yes, Father."

"When that's done, I want you to level a place we can build a shanty."

All the children, including William, stared at their father.

Eleanor bit her lip. To build a shanty was admitting defeat. "Is...Is...Is this going to be our new home?" She held her breath.

Father fiddled with his hat. "For a while, until William and I can find steady work, and we can rent a place. Summer will soon be over, and I can't have my family out in the elements."

He picked up a rock the size of a baseball and several thick sticks and a railroad spike. He pounded a stake into the dirt, then measured off five paces, pounded in another stake, and repeated the activity until he had a square and straightened. "That will be our house."

The children stared at the small square.

"That's not even as big as our sitting room back home," Raymond said.

Father looked at it and shook his head. "No, it's not. I'm just hoping I can find enough suitable building materials to make something that big. While we're gone, I want you kids to pull out all the weeds and level it as best as you can. Then, try to find some large, flat rocks we can use as a hearth."

They nodded.

Father looked again at the sky. "But first, shore up the truck, so that you and everything stay dry. Come on, William."

An emptiness settled over Eleanor as she and the others watched them leave.

"Mother." Eleanor started, surprised to see her standing next to them, her back straight and tall, looking after Father and William as they walked toward the more populated part of the shantytown.

"You children heard your father. Get to it." She held her hand out to Lilly. "Come, let's meet our neighbors and get some building ideas."

Eleanor and the twins stared after Mother and Lilly.

"What happened?" Raymond whispered.

"I don't know."

"Mother found her mad," Mitchell said in a quiet voice, then headed to pet Teddy before covering the back of the truck.

TWELVE

"IF YOU'RE LOOK'N FOR work, get going. I don't have any."

William stopped mid-step.

"Are you deaf? Get going. This ain't the end of the rainbow."

William lowered his head and turned back to the street. That was the twenty-seventh "No," that day and the ninth one since Father was hired to fix a truck. William wished he had skills besides milking cows, bucking hay, and cleaning stalls.

He glanced back in the warehouse's direction where Father was. Frustrated, he headed across the river, where he found a long line of men winding around a tall brick building. William approached. "What's going on?"

A gaunt man about his father's age with a dirty hat and wearing an overcoat, despite the warm weather, motioned him over. "Get in line, boy. Get yourself a free meal."

William's eyes widened. "A free meal?" He looked up at the building. Painted high above them in large letters were the words, "Schade Brewing Co."

"A brewery?"

"Not anymore," moaned the man. "Prohibition and all."

"They have turned it into a soup kitchen," said another man.

The line moved forward, and they followed it.

"So, what's your story, boy?" asked the gaunt man.

William stopped in surprise. Every day he rehearsed the events in his mind, but he'd never spoken it out loud. The line moved forward and William shared his tale.

The man, who called himself Tony, shook his head. "As if we all don't have enough bad stuff going on that others got to make it worse."

Inside, William and Tony sat with hundreds of other men at long tables; each with a small bowl, a cup of coffee, and a hard roll in front of them. All talking stopped as men ate; some quickly, as if afraid it would disappear; others ate slowly, savoring each bite of the watery broth mingled with an assortment of vegetables and an occasional piece of meat. William didn't care, it was food. After the first few mouthfuls, he slowed down and enjoyed it.

When he could get no more with his spoon, he tipped the bowl as all the others did and drained the rest into his mouth. All too soon, he and Tony were leaving.

"So, how did you end up here?" William asked.

"Stock market crash, like most everyone else." Tony scratched at the ground with his worn shoe. "I used to have a job, a home, a wife and five young'uns..." He stared across the vacant fields surrounding the brewery turned soup kitchen. "First the food ran low, then the bank evicted us. The children were starving, and I was useless. I..." He looked northeast, where the land rose in the distance. "The Hutton Settlement. It's at the base of those hills. It was the hardest thing I've ever done." He grimaced. "If only I'd saved more. Not owed so much."

William looked in the direction Tony pointed. "I don't understand."

"That's right, you're not from around here."

"No sir," William said.

"It's...it's..." He blinked back tears. "It's an orphanage."

Anger flared in William. He stared at the man. "An orphanage?" How could this man...?

Tony looked away. "I didn't want to. But...we were sleeping under the bridge...they were starving...I couldn't find work..." He bowed his head. "They're safe. They're fed. It's my only consolation."

William's own family's dwindling food supply came to mind.

"My wife," Tony continued, not seeming to care about William's opinion. "She broke up. Couldn't handle all the losses. Quit taking care of herself. Stopped brushing and braiding her hair, wouldn't talk to me, not even look at me." The man swallowed. "She's in a hospital for the insane. Sometimes I visit her...but she doesn't know me. She just sits there—rocks back and forth, mumbles to herself."

Fear gripped William's chest. "I've got to go. I've got to find work." He sprinted toward the nearest group of buildings. "God, I don't know if you exist, but we need food and shelter. Father and I need work. Please, give us work."

A drop of rain splattered on William's arm and then another, and another. He watched as drops splashed in the powdery dirt. He adjusted his hat and ran to a vacant building to wait out the rain under an awning.

"I don't know why we have to make it so small," Raymond complained. He stood and looked around. "There's plenty of room."

Eleanor stopped pulling an especially stubborn weed and rested her fists on her hips for emphasis. "Weren't you listening to Father?"

Raymond shrugged.

"Look at the truck. We barely have enough to cover our belongings with the wood and stuff Father and William have found. Does it look like there's enough there to build a big house?"

"It doesn't even look like enough to build an outhouse," Mitchell interjected.

"So, why did we move here?" Raymond chucked a rock. "There were plenty of trees back home we could have cut down."

Home. The very word caused an ache in Eleanor's chest. "I don't know. I just know we're here, and this is what we have to do."

"It's stupid." Raymond complained.

Mitchell glared at his twin. "Father's doing his best. Now stop talking about it."

By late morning, they had cleared the square area of weeds and rocks and were leveling the ground with a few boards.

Mother and Lilly had returned and worked alongside them. Mother worked hard, but Eleanor could tell she was sad, occasionally sniffling or sighing. Compassion for Mother swelled inside her.

When they finished, Mother straightened and dusted off her hands. "Eleanor, take the Dutch oven to the river and fill it with water so we can wash up. You boys go with her and bring back as large and flat a rock you can each carry."

"Yes, Mother."

They ate a small, simple meal of biscuits and apple butter. By now, they all knew better than to complain. They were just finishing up when the raindrops came and they hurried under the truck's makeshift roof.

Mother lifted Lilly up and climbed in herself. "Might as well lie down and take a nap."

The twins groaned but lay down on their mattress. Lilly curled up next to Mother, and Eleanor wished she could join them, but told herself that she was too old to ask for such a favor. With Rose gone, she now had to take her place; though she often wished to be a child again and coveted the extra affection and attention Lilly received.

She lay on her quilt and listened to the rain plink and plunk against the variety of materials that made up their roof. Would the rain on the roof of their shanty make the same sound? She wished it would stop, so she could look for wood, tin, nails—anything to make a chicken coop with.

As the rain intensified, she longed for a book to read or stationery that she could doodle on, though what would she draw? The Spokane Falls she'd seen the first day they crossed the bridge in search of this place? Or maybe their old home with the barn? Or Bertha, her favorite cow? All before the memory of it faded from her mind.

She peered between the slats that made up their walls. The shantytown—"jungle" as some called it—had grown since they first came.

At first there was a good stone's throw between the other shanties and where they were. But every day more people came and set up shelters—some nothing more than canvas tents, open on three sides, others, tiny buildings about as big as the cellar back home. She wasn't sure if the sketches in her mind of the sad faces of all the homeless people who surrounded them would ever leave her.

Eleanor sighed at the sound and rumble of another approaching freight train. As it neared, the truck bed vibrated, and the precariously placed roofing materials shifted so that water dripped down on them. All four children peered through the slats, watching the train. They cringed as the screech of its brakes and the rumble of the cars filled the air. Through the rain, Eleanor watched men jump off and scatter before the train reached the yard and the railway bulls could catch them.

They all settled back onto their mattresses and into their own thoughts. The boys whispered back and forth, shoving each other. Teddy let out a low growl.

"Enough," Mother ordered. "Even the dog is tired of your fighting."

They stopped, but Teddy continued, his growl growing in intensity and volume.

"Hey, Jack, what do we have here?" called a man probably thirty feet from the truck.

The children lifted their heads to see.

"Hush. Lie still," Mother ordered.

No one moved.

"Some fool's gone off and left his stuff with nothing but a mangy mutt to guard it."

Teddy growled, and Eleanor glimpsed his bared teeth. Teddy was more than a mangy mutt.

"You suppose the keys are in it?"

"If not, I'm sure we can wire it."

Eleanor's heart raced.

"Let's see what's inside first."

Eleanor held her breath. What were they going to do? She wished she was hidden under the quilt.

Lilly whimpered next to Mother.

"What do we do?" Mitchell whispered. Eleanor shrugged.

Mother shushed him.

Teddy barked.

Thud. Something hit the truck's undercarriage.

Eleanor flinched and shivered despite the warm summer day.

Thud.

Teddy's rope scraped against the ground and items stored under the truck as he stepped out from under it, barking in the rain.

Whamp.

Teddy yelped.

Eleanor popped her head up and peered between the slats. Two young men, dressed in tattered trousers, stained shirts, and Brixton caps, approached. One, with a dark mustache, held a rock in his right hand, and the other, who wore suspenders, grabbed another rock. Eleanor bit her lip. She wanted so much to yell out.

Teddy circled a bit, but kept barking.

"How many rocks you figure it'll take to put him down?" asked the one with the mustache.

"Let's find out," said the man closest to the truck, as he hurled another rock.

"No!" Eleanor whispered.

Whamp. Yelp.

Fear and anger arose in her. She wanted to yell to throw rocks back.

Teddy moved sideways but didn't run. Instead, he snapped his teeth and lunged at the men. His body jerked backward when he reached the end of the rope.

The men laughed. "Come on, you mangy mutt. Come and get us." The other one threw his rock.

Eleanor closed her eyes, the tears already streaming out. "Mama, they're going to kill him," she whispered.

"Shush."

Eleanor turned away from the scene outside of the truck to see her mother rise off her mattress. "Lilly, go with Eleanor."

"But Mama—"

"Now." Mother reached her hand under the mattress and pulled something out. "Boys, get to the front of the bed with your sisters."

They turned to see Mother, and their expressions of fear turned to surprise.

"Save Teddy," Mitchell whispered.

"Get," she ordered.

"Yes'um."

Whamp.

A sharp yelp.

More laughter from the men.

Eleanor nibbled on her nails.

Mother hopped down from the truck bed; her back straight. She stepped toward the men; her body so much frailer than the strong farm woman she'd been only a few months earlier.

"Whoa. Would you look at that?"

The other man whistled. "What fool left such a beauty alone in this heap?"

"I'd suggest you leave, and leave now." Her voice was strong and authoritative.

The men chuckled.

"Why don't we crawl into your little shelter there and get a better look at you?" said the one with suspenders.

"They say redheads are feisty," said the other with a wicked grin.

They took a step forward.

"I said leave."

"You really think you can stop us?" asked the man wearing suspenders.

"We've made widows out of women whose husbands were bigger than you."

Eleanor swallowed. She wished Father was here. She and her siblings watched from their hiding place as Mother walked toward the men.

Lilly clung to Eleanor. "I'm scared."

Eleanor squeezed her back.

Mother stopped next to the frenzied Australian Shepherd.

Teddy strained at his rope, still barking at them.

The man with the mustache turned to his friend. "Maybe she needs a man." He straightened and stepped to go around Teddy.

"Stop right now!"

The man grinned. "Come on—" he taunted. But his eyes widened as Mother pulled a large knife from her sleeve. With one swift swipe, as though slitting open a chicken, she sliced through the rope that tethered the enraged dog.

THIRTEEN

WILLIAM KICKED A ROCK across the street. "We'll never leave the shanty-town if it depends on me earning money." After looking unsuccessfully for work all afternoon, he ambled to the business where Father was working.

He'd been so excited to come to the big city, but now he hated it. At fifteen years old, he'd worked hard on the farm, but here that didn't matter, no one would hire him. Forty-three. That's how many "nos" he'd received today. He considered finding a farmer who needed work. But all the fallow fields they passed on their way to Spokane came to mind. Farmers without crops didn't need workers.

He glanced toward one of the city's orphanages. He'd ride the rails before he went to some orphanage. They probably didn't take boys his age, anyway. He swallowed hard and tried to ignore the possibility of starvation for him and his siblings.

"At least Rose has a place and a job," he told himself. "Even if it's with mean Aunt Fiona. But why couldn't she have taken in the others?" He brushed away a tear.

His stomach growled. "Be quiet! You've already had more than the others." He decided he wouldn't eat supper. He'd had a meal the others hadn't. Besides, he'd earned nothing and didn't deserve to eat. He looked up to see Father approaching.

"William, how'd you fare?"

William glanced to the ground, then shook his head. "Nothing."

"Keep trekking. You're bound to find something. It's somewhat like farming. Plants don't grow overnight, and calves take a while until they're milk cows."

William kicked another rock. "Yeah, I suppose. There are so few jobs, and so many men looking." He motioned to the warehouse Father had just left. "I mean, look at your job. You just happened along at the right time, and you've got skills." Wanting to change the subject, he asked, "Did you fix the truck?"

"Not yet. We're getting there. Probably tomorrow."

"Then what?"

"You mean will I have a job?"

William nodded.

"I don't know. They have another truck that might need a little work. When they don't need me, I'll ask them to refer me to others who need mechanical help." Father roughed up William's hat. "Hey, I've got something for you." He pulled an apple from his pocket. "The guys shared their lunches with me and gave me this to share with you."

William looked at it, and his stomach growled again. "I shouldn't. I haven't worked and..."

"And what?"

"I...I ate."

"At the soup kitchen?"

William looked up. "How did you know?"

Charles smiled. "The guys told me about it. I'm glad you found it."

William's sense of guilt lessened.

"How was it?"

"It wasn't Mother's cooking. And there wasn't much of it."

"Well, it's hard to beat your mother's cooking." Charles placed the apple in William's hand. "Eat this. You're a growing boy; if we take it back, it won't satisfy anyone."

William bit into it, savoring the juicy flesh.

"Just don't tell anyone about the soup kitchen. It won't do them any good knowing what they can't have."

William nodded and wiped some of the apple's juice from his chin with the back of his hand. "If we can't find work, why not look for building materials?"

"Great idea!"

The shantytown was abuzz when Charles and William returned carrying a sundry of building supplies, including chicken wire, a pocket full of nails, and a hammer.

"Quite the dog you got there, Cruthers," said a man about Charles' age. Several of the others with him nodded.

Father tensed. "Has he been causing trouble?"

"Depends on who you're asking," said another man.

"What's he done?" Charles sighed.

"Let's just say he's made us all feel a little safer."

William leaned in, the two-by-fours in his arms getting heavy. "What are they talking about?"

"I'm afraid to find out," Charles whispered.

"I'm sure you're bound to get a variety of stories," the first man said. "So, you'd best go ask your missus."

Charles lowered his head in a nod. "Thank you. I'll do that."

Men, women, and children watched Charles and William walk through the shantytown. Older kids told the younger ones that they were the people who owned the dog.

"What has that dog done now?" Charles muttered.

"Father, please tell me we won't get rid of him?"

"I don't know what we're going to do. First, I want to find out what he's done."

When they neared the truck, the children dropped the rocks they'd been carrying and ran to greet them; all chattering and pointing at once. Teddy, off his rope, trotted behind.

"Whoa, whoa, what's all this? Boys, help your brother and me haul this wood to the truck. Lilly, you and Eleanor carry this chicken wire."

"Chicken wire?" Eleanor's face brightened even more.

"You guessed it, my curious little kitten."

She pointed to a small pile of wood and tin cans. "I wasn't able to find much, but I thought we could use the cans for the roof."

Charles grinned. "That's good thinking."

Shannon approached, her hands and face smudged with dirt, and a wry grin on her lips. She kissed Charles. "I'm glad to have you home. Have we got a tale for you?"

"I take it has something to do with Teddy?"

"In part. I have to say, I was mighty grateful to have him today."

They placed the building supplies in a pile, and Eleanor filled cups with water for everyone.

Raymond jumped up and down. "Father, William, guess what happened!"

Father lifted a finger. "Raymond, let your mother tell."

Raymond sighed. "Yes, sir."

"So, what happened here? And why is Teddy off his rope?"

Shannon sat down on a log they used as a bench and called Teddy to her.

Charles raised an eyebrow but said nothing.

"Well, husband, about the time it started raining this afternoon, we had a pair of unwanted visitors." She told him how Teddy had chased the threatening men through the shantytown and then some.

Relief washed over Charles. He watched Shannon; a smile of pleasure lit his face. Her story of the day's events pulled her from her depression and rekindled her former self.

Teddy strolled over, and Charles scratched the dog behind the ear. "You handled that very well, Shannon." He looked down at the tri-colored dog. "And you, my faithful friend, deserve a treat for protecting our family."

"He most certainly does," Shannon agreed. "Eleanor, why don't you wash up and help me make some biscuits and gravy?"

"Yes, Mother."

"Let's make a little extra for Teddy," Shannon added.

Eleanor smiled. "Yes, ma'am!" She turned to her father. "Are we going to make a chicken coop tonight?"

"That we are."

"Boys," Shannon continued. "You go get some more rocks and watch your sister."

They nodded and headed back to the river. William rose to join them. "Mother, you don't need to fix me anything. I'm not hungry," he lied.

"Nonsense, you're a part of this family, and you're eating."

Charles grimaced at William's words and gave him a look that said his mother was right.

After supper, Shannon said she'd wash the dishes, so Eleanor could help with the coop. Under Charles' guidance, William sawed the boards, and Eleanor and the twins took turns hammering nails to hold the chicken wire in.

"The trick," Father said, "Is to get the nail in deep enough that it won't pull out; then pound the head over the wire and into the wood to hold the wire in place."

The late afternoon sun was setting when they finished, and everyone stood back to admire their work.

Charles smiled as Shannon joined them and ran her hand over Eleanor's long braid, praising her for the idea. It was good to have his wife back. He would have never guessed that a threat would help pull Shannon from her grief.

Eleanor could hardly contain her excitement as they stood before the pens at the feed store. Father had given her permission to pick out fifteen chickens. She could almost taste the hard-boiled eggs.

Mitchell pointed to a white chicken with a red comb and wattle and a cape of black feathers and black tail feathers. "How about that one?"

"Or that one?" Raymond asked and pointed to a brown Sussex chicken with white mottling.

Lilly wiggled around. "I like the red ones."

Eleanor looked at Father for guidance. "What's wrong?"

He was glancing between the nearly full-grown poultry and the sign denoting the price. He sighed. "I'd stick with the Sussex. They produce lots and if need be, we can eat them."

She nodded. "But?"

"Well, kitten, they're pretty picked over and I wasn't expecting to pay so much."

Disappointment spread in her chest. "Oh." She bit her lip. "Can we still get some?"

"Of course, but let's just get ten for now."

She nodded, trying to hide her disappointment. Ten meant it would take longer to save up a dozen eggs to sell.

With Father's help and input from her siblings, she selected ten chickens.

The clerk lifted the fowl from their pen and placed them in three crates. "Several of these have already started laying eggs."

Eleanor's smile spread even larger.

"I reckon you'll be having eggs out of all of them within a few weeks. How many bags of chicken feed will you be needing?"

Eleanor looked at the stacks of patterned feed sacks. Her eyes widened, and she bounced on her toes. Cloth bags! An unexpected treat. She and Mother could make herself a second dress and a night-shirt. "Could we get six?"

"Six? How do you expect to keep the vermin out of them?"

"Oh."

"We'll take four," Father told the clerk. "Do you pay a bag refund if we bring the bags back?"

"Sure do," nodded the clerk.

"Oh. But Father, if we keep the bags, we can make clothes." She held her breath.

Father rubbed his chin. He looked at her and the other children. "Don't you have another dress?"

"Not one that fits."

He nodded. "I suppose the boys don't have any other shirts or pants?"

"No pants."

"We'll keep the bags this time," he told the clerk.

The clerked looked at the children milling around and then at Eleanor, who stood straight and smiling next to Father. "Does the pattern on the bags make a difference?"

Father looked down at Eleanor. "Do you want to select the bags?"

"May I?"

"Why does she get to pick?" Lilly asked, her rag doll clung tight in her arm.

"These are her chickens."

Lilly shoved her fists onto her hips. "Well, I want a chicken."

"Eleanor, go with the man and select the bags you want."

Lilly pouted.

Eleanor stared in amazement at the bags of colorful prints. There were beiges with small floral prints of muted colors. Other feedbags had bright yellows, reds, pinks, blues, and greens, some with flowers and others with abstract designs, checks, and plaids. Some even had kittens, bears, bunnies, and horses. She had never seen such a selection in all her life.

A pretty emerald green bag caught her attention, but it would have to wait.

"Hurry up. I've got other customers to help."

"Yes, sir." Eleanor scanned the pile of bags, her mind busy thinking of blouses, dresses, and nightshirts. "I'll take two of the red ones with the white flowers, a beige one with little red roses, and —" She scanned the pile. Lilly ran her fingers over some bags with pink, yellow, and blue bunnies and butterflies. "I'll take that one."

Lilly's face brightened.

That evening, Teddy lay down under the coop, his attention on the men and children who sauntered past, their attention on the chickens.

"Should we tie him up?" William asked.

Eleanor tapped Father's arm. "Everyone's looking at our chickens."

Charles nodded and exchanged glances with Shannon. "I see. I don't think we need to tie up Teddy," Father said. "He's proved he won't run off—unless chasing trouble."

Eleanor let out a big sigh, happy about the chickens, the food they would soon have, and the bonus of fabric. But how much food could eggs provide? She needed to do more. She wished again that Father would let them have a goat.

That evening, she and Mitchell wandered through the camp looking for any scrap materials they could use. "What else can we do?" she asked.

Mitchell kicked at something shiny in the dirt, only to uncover a piece of glass. "Could we plant a garden?"

Eleanor's eyes widened. "Why not?" She slumped. "But where would we get the seeds?"

"They had some at the feed store."

"Do you think Father would give us money for seeds?"

Mitchell shrugged.

FOURTEEN

CHARLES AND WILLIAM WERE back looking for work when they stumbled across a large, two-story barn turned garage some men were tearing down. "Wait here, son. I'm going to see if I can wrangle us up some work."

"Alright." Guarded anticipation crept into William's mind as he watched the men pull boards. Some used crowbars or claw-foot hammers, while others just used their bare hands.

Within moments, Charles returned. "The man who owns this here property is paying $1.25 for a day's wages, but he won't hire boys."

William's shoulders slumped.

"But."

William looked up, the hurt, anger, and frustration etched across his face and in his eyes.

"But he will allow us to haul off any of the supplies we can use, and you can help with that."

"I guess that's something."

"It is. But I've got something else I want you to do first." He reached into his pocket and pulled out the truck key.

"Return to the shantytown, have everyone help you unload it, and drive it back. If we're lucky, we'll have a nice start on supplies for the shanty."

"Will do." It didn't seem like much, but at least it was something.

"And bring that hammer we bought, my axe, the saw, and several tin cans."

When William returned about an hour later, a third of the siding was off and some men were ripping off the roof shingles. He parked the truck up and found Father carrying an armload of siding.

"Good, you're here. That pile of wood over there is ours." He motioned to a small pile. "Pull the nails out and put them in the tin cans; we'll straighten them later. Then load them on the truck."

A tinge of disappointment coursed through William's mind at the small pile compared to other larger stacks. "Is that all you've gotten?"

"No. There are men here who tear a few boards down, then steal boards from other men's piles." He set the boards down. "In fact, I'll help you haul the pile closer to the truck."

Anger rose in William's chest. Everything seemed so unfair. "Why don't we just back the truck up to it?"

Charles shook his head. "Too many nails. We can't afford a flat tire."

William set to work prying nails and was about a quarter of the way through the pile when two men approached him.

"Sonny, what are you doing with our wood?" said a dark-haired man.

William's muscles stiffened. "Nothing, this wood belongs to me and my Pa."

"I think you're wrong." The younger of the men took a few steps closer, so that his body blocked the sun. "This here is our pile."

The older man looked up at the truck. "You think because you've got a nice big truck, that you can just come and take all the wood you want?" The man reached for a board William had already stacked on the truck's bed.

"Hey!" William stood, but the younger man shoved him back down. "Knock it off. That's our truck, and our wood."

"Not anymore, it's not," said the dark-haired man. "In fact." He picked up the board and held it like a bat. "We're gonna teach you to leave our stuff alone."

William's heart raced, and he scrambled to his feet. "Get out of here."

Both men chuckled. "Who you talking to—boy?"

"That's ours. We've worked for it fair and square. Why don't you just get your own wood?"

"Oh, look who's decided he's our boss?" said the older man, squinting at William.

The man closer to William shoved him.

Blood pulsed in William's ears, and he tightened his grip on the hammer. "Leave me alone."

"Or what?"

"Yeah, boy, what'cha gonna do?"

William held up the hammer. "I don't want to hurt you," his voice trembled. "Just go."

"Oh, we're scared." The younger man strutted over to William; his chest thrust out.

William stepped back, tripped over some boards, and fell.

The men laughed.

William, humiliated, seethed with anger and stood, but the younger man shoved him back down.

The man by the truck gathered boards. "Thank you for saving us the trouble of taking the nails out. Now won't you hand my friend here that can of nails?"

William's hands shook. They finally get a chance to get ahead, and now these scoundrels wanted to take it away. He didn't want to give them their hard earned, much needed building supplies. But he was just a kid. He squinted first at one and then the other.

"You heard him," said the younger man. "Give me the nails."

William picked up the can of nails with his left hand and flung them at the dark-haired man's face. He then swung the hammer onto the foot of the man in front of him.

They both let out loud wails, followed by a string of profanities.

William jumped up and shoved the man in front of him backward, then charged after the man unloading their boards.

The noise garnered the attention of several men working on the barn who paused in their work to watch.

The man William had thrown the nails at recovered and turned on William. "You've asked for it now, boy."

William picked up a board and swung it like a bat.

"Hey, what are you doing?" someone yelled.

William turned, just as the other man jump him from behind, and they both fell to the ground.

Soon there were shouts, and men came running.

William struggled under the weight of the older man and gasped for air. He kicked and thrashed about, his arms pinned under him; while the man tried to shove William's head into the dirt.

Men formed a circle around the two and were shouting.

Anger and frustration from the past months fueled William's fight. He arched his shoulders, bent his neck, and worked to keep only his forehead pressed against the ground. He sucked in air and shoved his fists into the ground.

The man on his back leaned near to his ear. "We're gonna teach you a lesson, boy."

Then, like a wild horse, William tucked his chin to his chest and flung his head back while straightening his arms and torso.

The back of William's head struck the man's nose. Blood gushed as the man toppled back; his head thumping on the hard ground.

A sense of power rose inside William.

"Look at that kid go," someone called.

He suppressed a smile and jumped to his feet. In a moment, he was on top of the man; his fist pummeled the man's face and chest.

"Get him, boy, get him," others yelled.

"Those looters have been stealing from each of our stashes, rather than get their own."

The older thief lunged at William to rescue his friend. "Leave him alone, you rotten lad."

"Look who's calling who, rotten?" yelled a spectator. "You thief."

The older thief pulled William off his friend and flung him to the ground. He then rushed at the man who'd just called him a thief. The looter grabbed the spectator by the collar.

But William pounced on his back, his left arm around the man's neck, and his right fist pounding the thief's shoulder and chest. The spectator broke free of the thief and punched the man in the face.

"Break it up, break it up." The property owner shoved through the crowd with Charles and several others at his heels. "What's going on here?"

"William," Charles hollered. "Get off that man."

William let go and slid down the man's back, and wiped dirt and blood from his face. "They were stealing our wood, Fa—"

Father's look told him to be silent.

Humiliation poured over William. He hated being fifteen—not a child, not an adult.

"What's going on here?" the owner asked again.

"This here boy was stealing our wood, then attacked us when we told him to leave it alone," said the older thief.

"I'm not the thief, you—"

Father held up his hand. "Calm down, son."

"But Father?"

"You'll have your turn."

William seethed.

Several men on the sidelines countered the thief's story.

"Quiet all of you, or I'll send you home with no pay. As it is, you're not getting any work done."

The older thief brushed himself off and picked up his friend, then turned to the landowner. "You know these young boys, sir, just roaming the town and getting into trouble."

The boss looked at the beat-up man, then William. "You're telling me this young boy did all this to you?"

"There were several others, but they ran off."

"Liar," William spat.

"Enough," Charles scolded.

"Those fellas have been stealing from all of us," another man shouted.

"Yeah," several others agreed.

The boss turned and looked at William, then Charles. "Is this your boy?"

"He is, sir."

"What do you have to say for yourself, son?"

"This here is wood Father collected. I was just taking out nails and putting it in the back of our truck, when these fellows came and said it was theirs."

"Were there any other lads with you?"

William shook his head. "We just moved here. I don't know anyone."

"You don't have any siblings?"

"Yes, but they're young, and Father didn't want them getting in the way."

The owner looked Charles and William over and the other two fellows. "I've seen you two wandering around, but not doing much. Looks like you're just causing trouble. You'd better get out of here before I call the police."

"But—"

"Now."

William stared in shock. The man believed him. He believed him over two adults.

"What about the building materials they stole?" A man asked.

"Yeah," agreed several others.

The owner raised a graying eyebrow. "Where's this wood they're stealing?"

"Down the street, on the other side of that brick building," someone said.

The boss pulled his pocket watch out of his pocket and sighed. "You've already wasted a quarter-of-an-hour." He looked back at the half-stripped building. "You've got fifteen minutes to go retrieve it. Know that I'll be docking your pay, and will fire anyone caught fighting."

"Thank you, sir," several said. "Our families appreciate it."

Charles and William joined them. On the way, several congratulated William. A warmth spread over him, and he suppressed a smile.

By early afternoon, almost all the planks and floorboards were off and many of the shingles. William stacked the wood on the truck bed, nails and all; he ran back and forth with armloads of shingles, the nails of which poked and scratched his arms. He tried not to mind, grateful for work and materials, and imagined what the shanty might look like.

Collecting shingles, he often glanced up at Father and several other men straddling the rafters, removing boards that spanned the roof. Working in pairs, they lowered the boards on ropes to others on the ground, who stacked them to be divided later among all who wanted them. They were nearly half-way done when the whole structure shifted.

William's heart lurched.

"What was that?" someone yelled. Men on the roof grabbed rafters or sheathing, whatever they could hold on to, while a few swore.

Inside the barn, there was arguing.

Two men worked to remove the corner braces and loose the girts which gave greater support between the posts.

"Hey, fellas, don't remove those yet," Father called to them.

The men who were sawing and hammering at the braces and girts looked up at him. "Mind your own business. We'll do what we want."

William stared into the belly of the barn's skeletal remains. Fear crept up his spine.

"Stop. You're compromising the barn's stability." Charles' firm voice carried.

Others agreed.

"You just do your job, and we'll do ours."

"There's an order to how this needs to be dismantled," Charles argued.

They turned their backs to Charles and the others and continued their activity.

Father slid his hammer's handle under his belt and scanned the lot. "Come on, let's get down," Father shouted to the other men on the roof as the building wobbled again. Some followed, a few didn't.

William watched Father and the man he'd been working with march over to the men sawing away at the braces. Charles clamped his thick, calloused hand around the arm of a man working a saw. "I said to stop."

The man pulled his arm away. "Oh, so now that your son has fought those two looters, you think you're our boss?"

"Have you ever taken down a barn? Or any building?"

"That's none of your business."

"It is when I'm on those rafters, and what you're doing is going to bring this building down with us still up there."

William's eyes widened at this, and he picked up a few more shingles to calm his nerves.

"You don't know that."

"Yes, I do. You take a barn down in reverse of how it's built."

The man spit. "Just a bunch of malarkey."

"Where's the boss man?" asked the man working with Charles.

The man with the saw glared into Father's eyes. "Why don't you just get back up on those rafters? Do your job and let us do ours."

The banging of hammers and the movement of men guiding ropes and pulleys with roofing planks stopped. All eyes and ears were on the confrontation.

Charles took a deep breath. "We have to do this in the right order, or men are going to get hurt. There are lots of things you can do, but removing those braces and girts is not one of them."

"You're not my boss."

Charles looked up at the men peering down from the disappearing roof. "Do you fellows want this barn to collapse while you're up there?"

"No."

"Neither do we," said the ones who'd followed him down.

"Of course not."

He looked at those on the ground. "How 'bout you? Any of you want this barn to fall down on you?"

Men shook their heads.

William smiled and scooped up some more shingles. He hoped one day, when he was grown, men would listen to and respect him the way they did his father.

"That won't happen," argued the man with the saw, and his helper agreed. "This man doesn't know what he's talking about. Look at the size of that piece. It's too small to hold this whole building up."

Charles shook his head. "It's stabilizing the crossbeam to the posts. And as far as the girts are concerned, they are helping hold this entire structure together. Leave them alone."

"What's the holdup?" The owner entered the barn's skeletal remains.

The men grew quiet, and William hurried back to the truck. When he returned, Father and the others were back on the roof, and no one was dismantling the girts.

William made several more trips with shingles, scraps of wood and even a few hinges and large bolts he found. Standing in the back of the truck, William stacked the wood, nail side down, careful not to step on any nails poking up.

He stopped to take a drink and watched the men with the saws return to the barn. "Oh, no!" He looked about for the boss. Then, he caught a movement and turned to see the barn shift.

Shouts rose, and a man fell forward, stopped only by the man next to him who grabbed his belt.

William froze, and his heart pounded.

There were more loud voices, and the men on the roof scurried to ladders. The building swayed with their movement, many jumping from heights of ten or more feet.

"No. No." William wanted to move but couldn't.

Workers spilled from inside while others scooped up boards, shouting and pointing at the barn.

"Father!" William called; his voice hoarse.

Men scattered in all directions as the old behemoth shuddered and leaned to the west. Creaks and screeches filled the air as the posts, beams, headers, purlins, and girts twisted, strained, and rubbed against each other, then crashed down.

Pain seized his chest. "No. No. No." William looked on in horror as a man flew through the air, then landed on the pile of wood, only to disappear in an enormous cloud of dust.

"Father!"

FIFTEEN

WILLIAM GASPED FOR AIR and stared at the scene before him—unable to move.

All was silent. Then, as if on cue, sounds seeped in, and men materialized out of the thick dust that permeated the space around the barn's remains. They coughed and choked. Behind them, screams of anguish and cries for help raised the hair on William's neck.

His teeth chattered, and hands shook. "Father." He had to do something. He had to help. William scrambled down from the truck and ran to the rubble. "Father."

Passing cars stopped, and neighbors ran to the site.

"Father. Father."

Several men grabbed at him as he ran by. "Don't go in there, son," they coughed. "It's not safe."

William ignored them and kept running; the surrounding air was thick with dust.

Two more men stepped out of the dark cloud. "Help." They gasped for air. "Several men are trapped under the beams," one of them called.

A chill ran over William's flesh. "I'll help." He took a big gulp of air and rushed at the dissipating wall of dust.

"Whoa, boy." A man grabbed his shoulders. "You don't need to be in there."

William struggled to free himself. "My father, he's in there."

The man shook his head. "It's not safe. You'll find yourself pinned under a heavy beam."

William inhaled. "I've got to find him." He squeezed back the tears. Men don't cry.

The man didn't let go.

He looked around the man to the jumble of heavy, splintered timber, dust still settling. It resembled a gigantic poorly constructed beaver dam. He grabbed the man's arm. "Please, help me find my pa."

Men screamed from inside the debris, and others ran in to help.

William's face was pale as he stared helplessly at the scene. "They need help. I can help."

The man shook his head. "What's his name?"

"Charles."

"Charles. I think I know him." The man looked across the lot at the crowd of gawkers, and the men rushing over to help. "Is that there your Pa's truck?"

"Yes, sir."

"Do you know how to drive it?"

"I do."

"We may need it to pull the beams off the men. You wait here. I'll see what's needed and let you know."

"Yes, sir."

The wail of sirens grew louder, and soon several police cars and a fire truck appeared.

William inched his way closer to the barn. Others, including police and firefighters, surged around the wreckage.

What would his family do if Father was hurt or...? His chest tightened, and he struggled to breathe. How would they survive? Once again, William wasn't old enough. Why couldn't he be bigger and stronger, like Johnny? How could he ever provide for his family? He sniffled and scanned the scene for Father. He had to find him, even if it meant going in there.

"Father, please," his voice only a breath, "don't be hurt. Don't be—" He couldn't bring himself to whisper it. "Where are you?"

To his left came four men covered in dust, carrying a bleeding, moaning man on a stretcher.

William ran to them. "Father? Father."

The injured man gasped for air.

William's emotions were a mixture of relief and fear. This man wasn't Father, but was he still in there? Injured?

Several more men came out carrying another man. William ran to them and cringed. The injured man's leg stuck out, cocked at an odd angle.

"William!"

He lifted his gaze to one of the dirt covered men carrying the stretcher. William reached for him. "Oh, Father."

"Not now, boy," said a man.

The tears he'd pushed back now fell. He walked alongside them. "Father, I was so worried."

"It's gonna be alright," Charles said. "We need your help."

William smiled.

"Come, take this end." Charles motioned him to the corner of the stretcher he was holding. "Help them carry this man to the truck. Put him on the back."

William nodded. "Where are you going?"

"To help someone else."

"But?" William motioned to a large gash on his father's left arm. "You're bleeding."

Charles glanced down at it. "Huh. Go help them."

William took the end of the stretcher from his father and helped the men carry the injured worker to their truck. "Be careful," he warned. "Some of those boards have nails still in them."

They loaded four men onto the truck, one in terrible condition. Father and William drove them to the hospital.

It was after seven when they returned to the job site. By then, most of the wood and men were gone.

Defeat weighed down on William. "Look, Father." he pointed at where the barn once stood. Several men picked through a small pile of mostly scrap wood—all that remained. "There's nothing left to frame the shanty." His voice shook. Hunger, exhaustion, and disappointment were too much to hold his anger back. "All the sheeting is gone too." He looked up at his father, who surveyed the scene. "You didn't even get paid."

Father put a hand on his shoulder. "I know this is disappointing. But we helped save several men's lives today."

"But it's not fair!"

"It's not fair that they got hurt, either."

William bowed his head in shame. Father was right.

"At least we're alive and well."

William glanced at Father's bandaged arm and nodded in agreement.

"Now, let's see if there's anything we can salvage."

William sighed, "Yes, Father." It seemed all they ever did was scavenge others' garbage. His stomach cramped with hunger, and his muscles ached. All that work, and they wouldn't even be able to start the shelter or buy supplies.

They picked through the pile of remains. Within minutes, William had several slivers, but he tried not to complain. They found a few decent two-by-fours and a splintered four-by-four. Father insisted they collect the rest for firewood.

"Charlie!" one man hollered.

Father raised his head. "You talking to me?"

"Yeah, Mr. Boyer, the boss man said for you to come and see him." The man jutted his thumb down the street. "In that big two-story house over there."

"Come on, William, let's take another load to the truck and go see Mr. Boyer."

The thick chested, square jawed Mr. Boyer welcomed them into his home. It was nicely furnished, not up to the standard of Uncle Harry and Aunt Fiona's, but more like their old house, homey and comfortable.

William's stomach growled at the smell of food.

Mr. Boyer glanced at him and grinned.

William bowed his head in awkward embarrassment.

"Have you—? Of course not. Join us for dinner. We're just sitting down." A woman about ten years younger carried in a heaping bowl of mashed potatoes. "Margaret, this is the man I told you about and his son. Could you set two more place settings?"

She smiled at them. "Of course, Gerald."

"How are the men you took to the hospital?"

"Three of them seem to be alright. They might have a broken bone or two, or sprained ankle, but I think they'll be fine," Father said.

"And the other?" Gerald's voice was grave.

Charles shook his head. "I don't know. He was on the roof when the building came down. William saw him fly through the air. He landed hard on the rubble and got pinned under several large beams. It took quite a few of us to lift them off. I'm afraid he broke his back...among other injuries. He'd scream in pain and then pass out."

"Lord have mercy!" Margaret had returned in time to hear the account and stood pale and grief stricken. "That poor man. Does he have a family?"

"I don't know, ma'am."

"Gerald, we must do something."

"We will, my darling. We will. I'll go around to the hospital tomorrow morning and see what can be done. Nothing to do tonight though, so let's eat." He smiled at William, who was staring at the fried chicken, mashed potatoes and gravy, coleslaw, biscuits and pitcher of milk. "I think this young man is starving."

William reddened and bowed his head.

"Nothing to be ashamed of, young man. You're a growing boy, and you worked hard today. Heck, when I was your age, I would eat a full meal at my parents' table; then wander over to my grandparents or aunt and uncle who lived farther down the lane and eat again. Dish up, son."

William looked at Father for approval.

Charles nodded and smiled. "You worked hard today. You were a big help."

Warmth filled him, and he smiled. Maybe he'd proved to this man that he was worthy of hiring.

Charles and Gerald talked about what brought Charles and his family to Spokane, the economy and politics. Gerald said the old barn had been in bad shape and people were living in it. "About a week ago, someone started a fire. I just couldn't take the risk of people dying."

William listened and ate his fill. He wondered if this man might have other work for them.

When there was a lull in the men's talk, Margaret broke in. "William, save some room for dessert."

"Dessert?"

"Rhubarb cobbler."

A wide grin spread across his lips. "I will Mrs. Boyer, I will."

"You have any siblings, William?"

"Yes, ma'am."

"And where are they at?"

William glanced at Father.

"Go on, son."

William told her about their family, and how they were living in the shantytown, except for Rose.

"I am so sorry to hear that."

They ate dessert, and the men talked some more. As they did, William asked Mrs. Boyer about her garden and flowers.

"You are a farmer," she commented. "Most boys wouldn't even notice."

William grinned. "Back home, I helped in our garden. I enjoyed it. There was something peaceful about it."

"Yes, there is. I only wish I had the time to tend it like it needs."

"If you like, I can come over and help you weed or hoe." He blushed, surprised by his words. "I'm sorry, ma'am. I didn't mean to be so forward."

"Don't be." She dismissed his apology with a wave of her hand. "The truth is, I could use some help."

Charles folded his napkin. "That was a wonderful meal. A real treat. We thank you both, but better get going. We need to get back to our family. They're probably worried."

Margaret rose. "You don't suppose, Mr. Cruthers, that William here could come by and help me with my garden and flowerbeds?"

William's eyes brightened. "May I, Father?"

Father nodded.

"When can I start?"

Mrs. Boyer smiled. "Is tomorrow too soon?"

"No." He turned to Father, who nodded in agreement.

"Oh, before you go," Gerald pushed his chair back. "First, I need to pay you for your work today."

"Thank you, sir."

Mr. Boyer counted out Charles' pay and even gave William a couple quarters.

William's eyes brightened. "Thank you so much."

Charles kneaded the rim of his hat. "Thank you for the opportunity to work and the fine meal." He turned to William. "Come on, son, we need to get going."

"Oh," Gerald looked out a side window. "Did you get your wood?"

Charles and William both stopped. "We got the wood we'd loaded before the barn collapsed," Charles said.

"Well, I had some men set your share of the beams and other wood aside. I'll show you where it's at."

Joy rose inside William, and he grinned at father, trying not to show his excitement. They followed Mr. Boyer to the stack of wood.

Charles stuck his hand out. "Thank you, Mr. Boyer. This will go a long way in helping us provide shelter for our family."

"I'm glad I can help."

As they finished loading the wood onto the truck, Margaret appeared with a basket full of food. "Here, take this back to your family."

"Oh, ma'am. That is so kind of you." Father accepted the basket. "You've all done so much for us already; you don't know what this will mean to my wife and children. We can't thank you enough."

William smiled at Mrs. Boyer; she was one of the most beautiful women he'd ever seen. He hoped someday he'd have a wife as beautiful.

Sixteen

ELEANOR AWOKE TO TEDDY'S low growl. She peered out between the rails of the truck bed into the dark night. Teddy growled again.

"What is it?" Lilly whispered, her small hand gripped Eleanor's arm.

"I don't—" Some lights beyond the train tracks blinked off then on as someone walked by.

"Father," Mitchell whispered. "Someone is out there."

Another growl from Teddy, this time more menacing.

Lilly leaned into Eleanor. "I'm scared."

Teddy barked.

Eleanor stared into the dark. There, close to their supply of wood, was movement...and another...and another. "Someone's by the wood."

Teddy was now barking, and everyone was up.

"Shut that dog up," yelled a neighbor.

Raymond stood at the foot of the boys' mattress. "Hey, get away from our wood."

Father struggled to strike a match and light the lantern. He held it up and its light cast out to the neatly stacked pile of wood that would be their shanty.

Teddy ran back and forth from one end of the stack to the other, barking.

"Who's out there?"

"Oh Charles, be careful," Shannon said, her attention now turned to the commotion outside the truck.

Eleanor could see several men attempting to run in the dark with long boards under their arms. "Father, look, they're taking our wood." She struggled to find her boots and put them on.

Something white flashed past her, and she watched as William chased after the men, Teddy barking beside him and nipping at one. There was a shout and a thud. More barking. Father was on the ground now, running after another man.

Lanterns now shone in several shanties and tents.

Mother climbed down and held the lantern high. Before she could give orders to stay still, Raymond and Mitchell ran past, whooping and hollering after the thieves.

"What's all the racket?" yelled someone in a nearby tent.

Eleanor jumped down from the truck, but before she could take two steps, Mother grabbed her arm.

"And where do you think you're headed off to, little lassie?"

"Mother, we have to stop them." In the lantern's light, Eleanor could see her mother's stern disapproval.

"This is no job for a lass. Your father and brothers will get them."

"But they're stealing our house."

"No."

She climbed back onto the truck bed and looked out into the darkness. "Get 'em Father, get 'em William."

Beside her, Lilly repeated, "Get 'em, get 'em. Go Raymond. Go Mitchell. Go Papa. Go Will'am. Get 'em."

Eleanor lifted Lilly up so she could see, though there were only shadowy figures in the dark.

"Eleanor," Mother called. "Get into the truck and turn on the headlights."

Within moments Eleanor had the headlights on, revealing a lanky man with a board under each arm. The twins rushed at him. Eleanor fidgeted, wanting so badly to join in the chase.

"These are mine," yelled the man over his shoulder. "You all have lots."

"Give us our wood," Raymond ordered and lunged for a board.

The man tried to swing the boards around to hit Raymond but they were too heavy; he lost his balance and stumbled.

The boys each grabbed a board and wrestled them away.

The man fell to the ground, cursing. "It's not fair you should have all that wood, you filthy farmers. The rest of us have needs too."

"Get out of here," Raymond said. "My father and brother worked hard for this."

The man scrambled to his feet and charged Raymond. "You don't talk to your elders that way, boy." The man raised a hand to strike Raymond.

Raymond swung the board at the man's knees, and he howled in pain. "You're nothing but a thief. Get out of here." Raymond shoved his board toward Mitchell and lunged at the man, who held out his hands to grab Raymond.

Eleanor leaned out of the truck. "Raymond, no—"

Teddy bounded into the light, barking; the dog clamped onto the seat of the man's pants. "Ouch, get away from me, you mangy mutt."

His pants ripped, and Eleanor giggled. The man pulled free and fled, chased by Teddy and Raymond.

Minutes later, Raymond and Teddy returned and Raymond took his plank from Mitchell, who was trying to drag both long boards.

Eleanor watched several neighbors take one last look and return to their own shelters.

Father and William returned, each carrying wood. "They're gone now," William said. "Good job Teddy."

Teddy sniffed around the woodpile and herded Mitchell and Raymond back to the truck.

"I chased a man too," Raymond boasted.

"Yes, you did." Father ruffled Mitchell's hair. "And you helped too. Thank you both."

Shannon stood near the woodpile and held the lantern high as Father and the boys re-stacked the wood. "Oh Charles, what are we going to do?"

Father massaged his stiff neck. "I'm afraid we're going to have to start on the shanty tomorrow. Remove the temptation. In the meantime, you sleep with the girls in the truck bed. I'll take our mattress and Mitchell and sleep by one side of the supplies; William and Raymond can sleep by the other. I'd bet a pair of twos those fellows won't be back tonight, but I'm not taking any chances. We worked too hard for this and fall is coming."

At the mention of autumn, Eleanor pushed aside her idea of a garden. It was too late to grow much else than lettuce and radishes. Would everything be as difficult as the past two months had been?

Rose placed Uncle Harry's eggs and toast on the table only moments after he sat down and already had the toast for the children on the stove.

"You're a very efficient worker," her uncle said. "That is a commendable attribute."

"Thank you." She bit her lip and pushed forward with the speech she'd rehearsed for the past few days. "I was wondering if I might ask a question."

"You know that this is my time to read the paper?"

"Yes, sir. But I was wondering when I might get paid?"

"That is under your aunt's discretion. I suggest you take that up with her and not interrupt my reading time anymore."

"Yes, Uncle."

Rose turned and marched into the kitchen and snatched the toast off just before it burned. She hoped the spoiled brats wouldn't complain. She'd scrape the charcoaled flakes off and hide them under a more generous amount of butter and preserves—not that either of them deserved the extras.

The problem was, she'd already asked Aunt Fiona about her pay and was told that Uncle Harry took care of it. She knew that Uncle Harry's mornings weren't to be disturbed, but there was no other time she could ask him. Otherwise, Aunt Fiona was around, or kept her so busy from morning until bedtime, that she couldn't slip away and ask.

Now, he was telling her she had to ask Aunt Fiona. Would she ever get paid? She poured the whisked eggs into the hot fry pan and stirred.

Suzanne and Albert ran down the stairs and into the kitchen, arguing.

"Rosalyn." Suzanne tugged on her sleeve. "Tell Albert that if there are only three cookies, I get two, because I'm a lady, and I'm older."

Albert slapped at Rose's dress. "Rose, tell her I would get the extra cookie because I'm a growing boy, and I'm younger."

Rose squinted at her uncle, who sat reading his paper and drinking coffee, oblivious to his children and their tiresome selfishness. Her father would never allow such behavior. She couldn't understand how two men could be so different.

Rose squatted down and looked her little cousins in the eyes. "Children who argue over cookies don't get any. Now go sit down, and I don't want to hear another word out of you."

Albert's eyes widened, and he stared at Rose.

Suzanne stared, then opened her mouth to protest.

"Go. Now."

"I'm telling Mother."

"Your mother doesn't have time for your nonsense. Now go sit down and be quiet."

Tears welled up in Suzie's eyes. Rose ignored the fake tears and turned back to the stove.

By the time Aunt Fiona arrived for breakfast, Uncle Harry had left for work, and the children were already back in their rooms playing. Rose set a porcelain egg cup with a soft-boiled egg and a plate with a golden-brown slice of toast topped with strawberry preserves beside a slice of bacon, and a cup of hot coffee before her.

"Rosalyn, several ladies from the garden club are coming over tomorrow for lunch. I want you to make three dozen tea sandwiches and some fresh squeezed lemonade, and clove cookies."

Rose bided her time, not wanting the subject of her pay to be swept under the concerns of her aunt's luncheon. "Are the recipes in the cookbook?"

Aunt Fiona looked at her oddly. "Are you telling me you've never made tea sandwiches?"

Rose opened her mouth.

"Of course, you haven't." Aunt Fiona straightened her napkin. "Why would you need to? Living on a farm in the middle of nowhere." She sighed. "I'll explain." She stared at Rose. "Why are you just standing there?"

"I...I spoke with Mr. Morgan today about my pay—"

"You did what?" She dropped her spoon. "While he was reading his paper?"

"Yes, ma'am."

"You foolish girl. I will never hear the end of this."

"But it's been two months since I started working for you, and I haven't gotten paid. My family needs the money."

"What do you think the food is that you eat? The nice bed? The roof over your head?"

Rose stared at her in shock.

"Not to mention you're living in a nice, respectable home with a respectable family and not in that squalid hobo jungle. And didn't I give you one of my dresses the other day?"

"Yes." Rose swallowed, and she stared at her aunt in disbelief. This was not how Aunt Fiona and Uncle Harry presented the arrangement to her or her family. She pushed back the tears that came at her aunt's implication—her family was respectable. Far above her aunt and uncle.

Aunt Fiona ate a bite of toast and took several sips of coffee. She looked at Rose and sighed. "I suppose. I feel I'm being robbed blind, but what can I do?" She went and retrieved a petite red handbag with small beads and sequins sewn into the shape of flowers. She pulled out four quarters and placed them on the table. "There. Don't be foolish and spend it all in one place."

Rose looked at the money and didn't know if she should take it or fling it back at her aunt. At this rate, she could never help her family and buy a train ticket back to Bonners Ferry and Johnny.

"What are you waiting for?" Aunt Fiona waved her hand at the money. "You've got things to do."

Rose scooped up the coins—gritting her teeth to keep the curses at bay.

Shannon watched as William sprinted down the dirt path to his job with the Boyers. "All the times he's looked for work," she said to Charles, "and he gets it when we need him here."

Father shrugged. "That's the way of it. Looks like I may need your help."

Shannon looked at the small square scratched in the hard ground that outlined where their new home would be and bit her lip. "I suppose." She retied her scarf around her head, hoping to protect her fair, porcelain skin from the sun. "Where are my gloves?"

Charles smiled at her. "Under the truck seat."

That morning she measured the depth of the holes Raymond dug for the posts, pulled nails from boards, and kept Lilly on task with whatever minor jobs they could find for her. She tried to keep her own mind focused on the job at hand and pushed aside the memories of the peaceful farm.

By mid-morning Charles and Mitchell had sawed the posts to the sizes they needed, and she helped hold them steady as the twins poured and compacted dirt into the holes around them. She had to admit; it felt good to be doing something—even though she didn't like where she was doing it.

By lunch, a six-foot post stood like a limbless tree at each corner. Two more stood midway between the corners of the east and west walls. Three taller posts ran north to south down the center for the roofline. It was so small, but larger than most of the surrounding shanties.

She surveyed their soon-to-be home and the stack of building materials. "Do we have enough?" she asked Charles, as the children cleaned up the lunch dishes.

He surveyed the pile. "I doubt it. We may have to pare down."

She walked inside the perimeter, and Charles pointed out how they would arrange things. "You've really thought this through."

He nodded. "Unless you have a better idea."

She looked at the area to be the all-purpose kitchen, eating, and living area. "There's not a lot of area to prepare meals."

"No, there's not."

"But I don't imagine we'll be eating any large meals, anyway."

His countenance changed.

Shannon sucked in the hot, dry air, fighting against the grief that clawed at her. She looked through the walls to the shanty jungle around them. "I guess it's bigger than most of these."

Charles nodded. "There's one family that must have five children and their hut is barely more than a quarter of ours." He measured it off. "It must be maybe ten feet by seven feet."

Shannon walked the small area Charles had pointed out. "How do they all sleep in such a small space?"

"They must be on top of each other. I imagine the poor father wakes up each morning with someone's toes up his nose."

A chuckle escaped her lips, and she clamped her hand over them. "Charles! You little imp." For a moment, there was a flash of playful fire in her eyes.

He grinned. "And you love me."

She glanced between the start of their shanty and the stack of wood. She estimated how big a shanty on their own land would have been. Shannon considered the parallels between the men who destroyed their farm and last night's thieves. Anger and resentment grew within her, and she struggled to gain control.

"Looks like you're finally getting some walls," called a neighbor woman.

Shannon forced a smile. "Yes." She put her gloves on and dusted the dirt off them. "Let's get that wood on here before it walks away."

"Look Father, there's William." Eleanor pointed to the path that wound through the shantytown.

Shannon looked up and smiled, grateful for him to be back. She didn't like him out in the big city alone.

It was mid-afternoon, and they had the cross boards connecting the corner and center posts nailed three feet from the ground.

Charles stood. "Just in time."

William quickened his pace.

Raymond and Lilly pointed to a paper sack he carried. "What's in there?"

William smiled. "That Mrs. Boyer is a nice lady. She had me thin her lettuce, carrots, radishes, and beets and let me bring them home." His smile grew bigger. "She also made some cookies for us."

"Can we—"

William held up his hand. "After dinner. I'm taking these to—" He stopped when he saw Mother and held out the bag. "I'll swap you the hammer for this food."

She smiled and thrust out the hammer.

Fresh vegetables brightened Shannon's mood that had sunk with every nail into their new home on someone else's land. This would be better than living in the back of the truck, she told herself, and tried to appear chipper for the children.

With William's help, the work went faster, and by sunset, they had the top and bottom cross boards nailed to the poles.

"Tomorrow we'll run the beams across the top and hopefully put up the rafters," Charles announced.

"Why don't we just make a flat roof, like those?" Raymond asked and pointed to several shanties.

"Because it snows," William said.

"When do we get to add the walls?" Eleanor asked.

"After we get it all framed in," Charles said.

Mitchell looked from the fifteen-by-fifteen frame to the pile of wood. "Are we going to have enough wood?"

Charles removed his hat, pushed the loose locks of hair back in place. "I don't think so."

Even in the fading light, Mitchell's anxiety was obvious and paralleled Shannon's.

Charles gave Mitchell's shoulder a squeeze. "We'll find more materials."

"What if we don't?"

"Then we'll live in the half that's finished."

They all looked at the portion between the two tall posts and the corners. It was roughly fifteen by seven feet, not much larger than the truck bed.

"Cheer up," Charles admonished. "Let's not worry until it snows."

Snow. Shannon shivered at the word. How could he be so optimistic? It had taken so long and a leprechaun's luck to get what they had. Her mother's Irish saying came to mind: May misfortune follow you the rest of your life, and never catch up. Shannon was sure that not only had misfortune caught up, but it had moved in to stay.

When they nailed the last board on a few days later, they all stared in silence at their half-built shelter. It had three-quarters of a roof, two full walls, and two that only spanned half the distance, leaving the whole southeast corner open. Charles had built the chicken coop into the southwest corner for easy access and to prevent anyone from attempting to steal chickens or eggs without them knowing.

Shannon sighed at the cracks between the thin boards. They were nothing like the thick logs she was used to.

"Boys, stop climbing through the windows."

Mitchell paused midway through. She wondered at Charles' decision to add them. Sure, they would bring sun and light, but where did he plan to get the glass?

"Papa." Lilly tugged on his shirt. "What do we do now?"

Charles examined the partially finished shelter. "We move in and go back to looking for work and wood."

"But it's missing walls, Papa."

"It's got more walls and roof than the truck."

But like the truck, people could walk by and look right in. Shannon felt more exposed. She understood Charles was trying to make up for losing their large home—but was this better or worse than the smaller, enclosed shanties around them? What if they didn't find the materials they needed? She took a deep breath. She had to trust Charles. He'd always provided for them and he would now.

Charles gave instructions for moving in, but she lost his words in the forest of her thoughts. "Rose should be here," she whispered to herself. Fiona's indifference to their plight stabbed at her again. Not only had her sister not offered any more help, but she made no effort to bring Rose to see them.

Eleanor touched her arm. "Mother, I think Father wants the cooking supplies by the chicken coop."

Shannon looked at the skillet in her hand and the mattress she was about to set it on. "Where is my mind?" She followed Eleanor to the area where Charles was nailing crates to the wall. He'd already added boards inside as shelves. "Look at this." She pointed to the makeshift cupboards. "Your father is so clever."

Eleanor smiled.

Shannon took a deep breath; she was going to be positive. Maybe she could find a job cooking or cleaning like her mother had. She and Fiona had often gone with their mother to her jobs. She couldn't imagine taking all four children with her and feared leaving them alone. Still, there must be a way.

SEVENTEEN

ELEANOR EMPTIED THE LAST sack of chicken feed and looked about. It had been a week since they'd run out of building supplies and moved into the partially finished shanty. Father and William had been out every day looking for work and building materials. Occasionally, they brought something home or found an odd job, but usually it wasn't much. She'd overheard her parents talking about the money running low.

She looked at the bright red feed sack with white flowers and her too-tight, worn-out dress. She knew she looked and smelled awful, but what else could she do? Her other dress was even smaller. She wanted so badly to make a new dress rather than return the sacks to buy more feed.

Father and William were about to go looking for work. She walked to where Father stood by the truck. "What can I do for you, Kitten?"

Eleanor lifted the empty feed sack. "This was the last bag."

His smile grew grim, and he nodded. "I suppose."

"Can you get me another bag?" she paused. "With the same pattern?"

He reached out and took it. "I can sure try. You don't have any aces in there, do you?" A glint of mischief in his eyes.

"No." She kicked at the dry ground.

"I take it there's something else you want?"

She took a deep breath and pressed forward with her request. "I know we don't have much money." She gave him a look of innocence. "But...could I please have a needle, and thread...and pins and—" She swallowed. "And sheers to cut the fabric with?"

He squatted down until he was eye to eye with her. "Eleanor, I have so appreciated your helpful attitude, and how much you've helped your mother with your siblings. I know this hasn't been an easy time. I'll see what I can do." He looked over at the chicken coop. "You don't suppose you have any extra eggs I could sell?"

A wide grin spread across her face. She leaned near him, cupped her hand around her mouth, and whispered into his ear. "I've been setting a few aside."

He took what she had. "Eleanor," he said in a quiet voice. "You're a very resourceful young lady."

She smiled, but was apprehensive about what he might say next. "Maybe you could find a way to get the needle and thread you need?"

She pressed down the anxiety rising in her and nodded that she would.

After Charles and William left, Lilly and the twins disappeared into the shantytown to explore and play with other children. Mother's concern over them staying close by had faded.

Eleanor looked at the empty feed bags with their colorful patterns and thought of the things she could sew. She really didn't enjoy sewing, but it was something she could do to help. She held up the beige bag with little red roses. This would make her a nice nightgown. A twinge of guilt nagged at her. She had planned to make two items for herself out of the fabric, and a dress for Lilly, but nothing for anyone else. She hung her head. The fact was, everyone had extra clothes except her. But if she was honest, the dresses Aunt Fiona had given Mother were too big and thin for winter.

Next time she bought feed sacks, she would use the fabric to make the others some clothes.

With the other children gone, Mother returned to bed, as was her new habit. The sunshine beckoned Eleanor, so with bucket in hand, she walked out the open wall. It was odd to be in a house that people could look into. Teddy tagged along beside her, jumping and prancing.

All morning she'd been contemplating how to earn money so she could buy a needle and thread. If only she was older and could leave the jungle to earn money. She knew no one in the shantytown had money.

Then, an idea came. She could barter. But with what? She'd given Father all her extra eggs.

What could she barter with that the women of the shantytown might want?

She passed several hovels and smiled at an exhausted woman standing in the doorway, her three little children playing in the dirt at her feet. Eleanor passed several other shanties and tents before an idea occurred to her and she returned to the woman.

"Ma'am?"

The lady looked up at her.

"Do you sew?"

She nodded.

Eleanor smiled down at the children. "Would you like a little quiet?"

The woman cocked her head. "What are you suggesting?"

"Well, I know how hard this has been on my mother, and sometimes she needs to be alone. If you like, I could watch your children for you, play games with them or take them on a walk, and you could lie down and rest, or sit by the river—whichever you prefer."

"And what do you want in return?"

"A needle and some thread."

"Your mother didn't think to pack sewing supplies?"

"No ma'am. Our home burned down."

A flash of compassion sparked in the woman's eyes. She looked at the children and then at the river. "What's your name?"

"Eleanor."

"Well, Eleanor, I thank you for the offer, but not today."

She turned and tried several other huts, to no avail. She offered to fetch water—more "nos." Eleanor now understood how Father and William felt. She wandered through the shanty jungle with its haphazard dwellings, occasionally glimpsing Raymond and Lilly with a group of children, mostly boys.

One lady gave her a wad of thread after Eleanor brought her three buckets of water, but usually the women just shook their heads or even scowled at her. Eleanor was about to retrieve some water and go home when an old woman beckoned her.

"Child."

"Yes, ma'am."

"Did I hear you're offering to fetch water?" She motioned at the bucket Eleanor carried.

Eleanor nodded.

"What do you need in return?"

"A needle and thread, ma'am."

The woman looked her up and down. "Your dress is getting a bit tight on you."

"Yes, it is ma'am. I have some feed sacks, but no needle or thread."

She nodded. "Well, if you'd be willing to fill my two buckets inside and water my garden—" she pointed to a small patch of ground with Swiss chard, potatoes, carrots, and beets. "I'd be happy to supply you with a needle and thread."

Eleanor's countenance brightened. "Oh, yes ma'am. I'll be right back."

After watering the garden, the woman handed her a needle and half a spool of white thread.

Joy sprung up inside Eleanor. She pinned the needle inside her pocket and, after turning the thread over in her fingers several times, placed it alongside the wad she already had. "Oh, thank you. Thank you so much. You've made me very happy."

"Well, a girl needs a proper dress that fits her."

A huge smile spread across Eleanor's face.

"I hope you'll come by and show it to me."

"I will. What is your name?"

The old woman now smiled. "Sadie Johnson."

"Thank you, Mrs. Johnson, I will."

Eleanor hummed a song as she skipped to the river. She filled the bucket and set it down, not yet wanting to return to the shanty. She gazed out at the water and up and down the opposite bank and then the bank on this side. Eleanor squinted. Was that one of her brothers wading alone at the river's edge?

Teddy barked and ran ahead of Eleanor, who followed. Her heart raced as she drew near. "Mitchell. What are you doing?"

He looked up and scurried out of the water. "Nothing."

Teddy jumped and yapped.

"Where are Raymond and Lilly?"

Mitchell petted Teddy. "Playing with some kids."

"Back by the shanties?"

He nodded.

"Why aren't you?"

"I don't want to."

She sat on a large rock and motioned him over. "How come?"

"I don't like some of those boys. They're mean and they like to fight." He paused and looked at Eleanor. "Promise you won't tell?"

She nodded.

"They're always daring each other to do things—like throwing rocks at some of the older men or stealing things."

"They shouldn't do that!"

"That's why I don't want to be around them."

"What does Raymond do?"

"He's the one who comes up with lots of the dares."

Mitchell's words only slightly surprised Eleanor. Raymond had always been the one people followed, even when they were at school back in Bonners Ferry.

"So, what are you going to—"

A scream back at the shanties filled the air.

The hair on Teddy's back bristled, and a low growl rumbled in his throat.

Another scream and Teddy dashed off toward their shack.

Mitchell's eyes widened. "That sounds like Mother."

A third scream raised the hair on Eleanor's neck. She grabbed the bucket. "Come on."

They arrived at the shanty to find Mother screaming and throwing things at a man Teddy had pinned against an inside wall. Teddy's large front paws pressed against the man's chest; his bared teeth were only inches from the man's face.

"Help me. Get this dang-bum beast off me."

"Get out of here," Mother screamed.

"Get this varmint off me and I will."

Mitchell stepped closer to the man. "What are you doing in our home?"

"I thought it was abandoned." He motioned with his head to the two missing walls. "...and people were scavenging it."

"I don't believe you," Mitchell replied.

Eleanor dropped the bucket and grabbed a long sharp stick she used to poke the dead rats Teddy often caught. She turned the stick on him. "You should ask around before you just enter a house."

Mother pointed at the man with the knife she kept near her. "Check his pockets. He was stealing things."

The man stiffened. "Do you always assume the worst about someone?"

Mitchell stood before the man. "When we find them snooping around our home, yes."

"Make sure you check his shirt pockets," Mother advised.

"Get away from me, boy. I'll hurt you."

Teddy's growl intensified, and Eleanor poked the man with the stick. "You leave my brother alone."

"Alright, alright. Inside my shirt pocket."

Mitchell reached inside the pocket and pulled out some tea bags.

"There, you happy. Now let me go."

Mitchell appraised the man. "You're hiding more."

"Leave me alone, boy."

Teddy growled and snapped.

"He's got something inside his shirt." Mother pointed.

"Get it out," Eleanor said and pressed the stick into the man's flesh, her grip firm.

Mitchell reached inside the man's open shirt and removed a can of beans, a few slices of ham Mother had wrapped in a cheesecloth, and several pancakes.

"Hey, that was already mine."

"No," Mitchell held up the pancakes. "These were left over from our breakfast and the ham from last night's supper." He searched the man's other over-sized pockets and found a fork, and Eleanor's feed bags.

"My cloth." She grabbed them from Mitchell and poked the stick deeper into the man's chest.

"Ouch."

"Those are mine—to make clothes out of." She wanted to slap him. She'd come very close to losing her new dress and nightgown. Fortunately, Mother had screamed, and they'd arrived before he escaped.

Mitchell glared at the man. "Abandoned homes always have fresh food and feed sacks. Maybe we should tie you up and let Father deal with you when he gets back."

The knife shook in Mother's hand. "Send him away before I use this on him."

The man glanced between Mother and Teddy, trembling.

Mitchell glared at the man and stepped back.

Eleanor backed up; her stick still trained on the man. "Come here Teddy."

Teddy looked at her, but didn't move.

"Good boy, let him go now."

Teddy's front paws dropped to the floor, and he barked. The man shoved his hat further on his head and inched out of the shanty; his attention never leaving Teddy. Teddy and Mitchell following a short distance as the man scurried off.

Eleanor watched from the shanty's opening; she must find some place secure to hide her feed sacks. But was anyplace ever really safe?

EIGHTEEN

ELEANOR WATCHED HER YOUNGER siblings wander off to play and explore. She turned her attention to the lunch dishes and the dress for Lilly she was sewing. Jealousy rose inside her. "Mother?"

"Yes." Shannon was already sinking back into the bed.

"Can I leave the dishes and go play?"

Shannon looked up, her eyes tired, jaw slack. "You're too old to play."

Her words hit Eleanor like a punch to the gut. Too old? She was only ten. Before the fire, even fifteen-year-old William played.

"Stay with me," Mother continued. "I don't want to be alone."

Eleanor took one last glance at her siblings disappearing into the shantytown that now surrounded their still unfinished shack. It wasn't fair. Mother rarely talked to her. She just slept or cried—occasionally mumbling to herself. If she got up, it was only to walk down to the river alone and stare at the water and the buildings on the opposite riverbank. Eleanor washed the dishes and put them away, banging the blue metal plates onto the shelf.

"Eleanor, please, I have a headache."

"Sorry Mother." But she didn't feel sorry. It wasn't fair. Yes, she had a new dress, which she'd sewn herself, but she'd lost her doll, books, and sketch paper in the fire. Now she didn't even get to have any fun unless Father played his harmonica in the evening and would make up games for them to play. Even then, Mother would sometimes insist she sit out.

She picked up the blue material with bunnies and butterflies printed on it and stitched the sleeve onto the shoulder. She hoped they would finish the shanty before winter, and they would have more than these feed sack clothes to keep them warm.

"Don't you miss her?"

Eleanor started at Mother's words. She looked up from her sewing and pricked her finger. "Ouch." She shook her finger. "What did you say?"

"Don't you miss her?"

"Rose?"

Mother nodded, her eyes red and puffy.

Eleanor set her sewing on the rough, makeshift table Father and William had made. She moved to sit next to Mother on the bed. "I miss her a lot. I didn't know she wouldn't be living with us."

Mother started crying again. "Nothing is as it was...it's all gone—" She gasped for air. "Now Rose too. Fiona has so much; why did she have to take Rose?"

Eleanor stroked her mother's arm; her own words gone like so much else in their lives.

"She doesn't even visit. Why should she? Fiona has everything and we have..." The tears returned.

Eleanor reached down and hugged her mother. "I'm sure she still loves us. But how would she get here?"

"Fiona or Harry could bring her."

Eleanor couldn't imagine her aunt or uncle coming near the shanty-town.

"When I die..."

Eleanor startled at her mother's words.

Shannon bit her lip. "Will...will you visit my grave? And put flowers on it?"

Eleanor recoiled. Confusion and fear gripped Eleanor's chest. She tentatively touched her mother's forehead; it was warm but so was the day. "No." She shook her head. "Please Mother, don't die. We need you."

"If I die, then there's one less person to feed. Besides, you can take care of everything."

Eleanor struggled to breathe. What? She needed Mother's help. She didn't want to be Mother. "I...I don't..." words wouldn't come. She wanted to scream. A heaviness pressed upon her. No. Please no. I'm only ten; she wanted to say.

But Mother had turned over with her back to Eleanor and was weeping and mumbling something to herself, blind to Eleanor's own tears.

She spent the afternoon sewing outside in the shade, unwilling to stay in the dark shanty any longer. More than once, she caught herself watching the activity in the camp; her sewing limp in her hands. Teddy yipped, and she looked up to see Father and William with their arms full. Her heart swelled at the sight, and she hurried over to help with the load.

Father leaned two single-pane windows against the shanty while William set down a wooden crate containing a bag of nails, matches, and groceries.

"Milk!" Eleanor pulled out one of the two-quart bottles.

Eleanor tried to remember when they'd last had milk—once a daily staple—now a rare treat.

"Eleanor," Charles looked about. "Where's your mother?"

Eleanor lowered her head. "She's in bed."

"How come?"

"She says she doesn't feel well...but—" Eleanor stopped.

"But?"

She glanced into the shanty; not sure she should say more.

Father motioned her and William to the truck. "What's wrong?"

Guilt pressed in on Eleanor, like she was betraying Mother.

Father bent down and looked her in the eye. "It's alright, you're not in trouble."

She shifted her weight. "I know. I'm...I'm scared."

"Why?"

William stood silent, watching.

"Mother says she doesn't feel well, but it's the sadness. Mother's sad about the house and farm, about Rose. She thinks we don't need her."

Charles pondered this for a moment. "This has been hard on her." He turned to William. "We need to take the truck tomorrow and pick up those other items. Might as well drop in on your aunt and arrange a time to visit Rose."

Eleanor's countenance brightened. "Are we going to see Rose?"

Father put a finger to his lips. "Don't say anything until it's planned."

She nodded. "Wait, did you say you have more things?"

"We do." Father grinned at William. "I met a man tearing down a house that's badly burned and he gave us those windows. Tomorrow I'm going to go over and help him and he's promised me a sink, a small cookstove, a few doors, and some more wood. Maybe even a few pieces of furniture."

Eleanor jumped up and down. "Yay. Will we be able to finish the shanty?"

Father smiled. "Possibly."

"That ain't all." William's grin exploded. "Looks like I'll be making dough for a little while."

Eleanor paused, unsure what he meant.

"He got a job," Father leaned in and whispered.

She threw her arms around him. "I knew you could. Doing what?"

"Cleaning up at a swell new movie theater they're building. I'm hoping the boss man will let me paint and install chairs. It's real darb inside. My boss might also let us have the odds and ends."

"I'm going to offer to haul off what they don't need," Father said.

Eleanor was awash with joy. "That's wonderful."

After Father left to talk with Mother, William leaned in. "Before I got the job at the theater, I did some work for Mrs. Boyer and you know how she's always giving us stuff?"

Eleanor nodded, salivating at the memory of the fresh produce and baked goods the kind woman would send home with William.

"Well, Mother had me give her some of your eggs as a thank you."

"That's where they went. I thought maybe someone stole them."

"No. But Mrs. Boyer insisted she purchase them. She said she knows what it's like to be poor." William reached into his pocket and passed several coins to Eleanor.

"Thank you. I'll save it for feed or thread."

"Good idea, less for Mother and Father to worry about."

Eleanor looked down at the coins, then back at William. "Poor? Is that what we are? Poor."

He nodded. "What did you think we were?"

"I don't know. I knew we didn't have a lot, but...I guess I thought we were just...in between times. Like, getting by until you and Father found a job, and we got a house to live in."

The idea seemed strange. "Poor," she whispered to herself. Stupid—that's what she was. Stupid. She'd been so intent on helping her family that she missed the obvious.

"William, Eleanor, where's Father?" Raymond called in his loud voice.

Eleanor and William stopped their conversation.

Raymond ran ahead of Mitchell and Lilly, all three with sticks in their hands. "Look what we've got."

Eleanor stared in surprise. "How did you—? William, do you see that?" She pointed.

Father exited the shanty.

"Looky, looky," Lilly jumped up and down, dropping her treasure in the dirt.

"Be careful," Mitchell admonished.

Raymond held up his prize. "Look what we caught."

"Well, I'll be!" Father adjusted his hat and squatted down to get a better look. "Why didn't I think of that? Fish."

The children swarmed around him as he fussed over their catch, and they told him how they'd found some old fishing line and hooks and made some poles.

"Well, aren't you the smart ones? Let's get these cleaned and take them in to your mother."

"Give them to Eleanor," Mother said from the shanty opening. "She'll cook them."

They all stared after Shannon as she disappeared into the shadows in the back of the hut.

Eleanor sighed. "Give me the fish."

"No," Father said. "Children, part of fishing is taking care of them." He gave William a knowing look. "Your brother will show you how to clean your catch."

Eleanor and Father watched them head back down to the river. "Eleanor, can you put the food away? I need to have a talk with your mother."

Tension rose in her chest—a mixture of nerves and hope. "Can I go play when I'm done?" she asked, knowing she was disobeying Mother's earlier orders.

"Yes, and don't worry about fixing dinner."

NINETEEN

"Hurry," Eleanor called. She smiled at the almost finished shanty and climbed onto the back of the truck. Her siblings, all bathed and in clean clothes, joined her. She couldn't wait to see Rose. The truck rocked with everyone's excitement.

They parked in front of her aunt's home. Aunt Fiona and the cousins were waiting on the front porch for them.

"Where's Rose?" Mother asked.

"Where is she?" chirped the others.

"Oh, she's in the house preparing the evening meal. She's quite excited to see you." Aunt Fiona looked Eleanor and the younger children up and down. "Why don't you children play outside?"

"We want to see Rose," came a chorus of voices.

Shannon straightened her back. "Please, Fiona, we haven't seen Rose in almost two months. That's the longest we've ever been apart."

Charles stood behind her, his hand gently on her shoulder for support; his eyes met his sister-in-law's with a look that said not to push the subject.

Fiona sighed. "Of course. Come in."

"But Mother?" Suzanne said.

"Never mind, Darling. Come along."

Suzanne glared at Eleanor and Lilly.

Irritation at her little cousin arose in Eleanor's chest.

Aunt Fiona flitted about nervously as the entire family piled into the kitchen, all seven talking at once.

Rose stopped stirring a pot of gravy and threw her arms around Mother, who held her tight. "I've missed you so much. Mother, why are you crying?"

Shannon dabbed at her eyes. "Oh, look at you. You're a beautiful young lady."

"Rosalyn," Fiona's voice was loud above the surrounding noise. "The gravy is going to burn."

Eleanor stepped up to the stove. "I can stir it."

"Eleen, I don't think that's such a good—"

Charles put a hand on his sister-in-law's arm. "Eleanor is fine. She helps with the cooking all the time."

Raymond tugged at his aunt's sleeve. "Why do you call Rose, Rosalyn?"

Fiona stared at Raymond, then pushed past him toward the door. "Let's all sit on the front porch out of Rosalyn—Rose's way."

At supper, Eleanor savored the variety and flavors. Aunt Fiona was more prepared for their visit this time and had more food and larger portions. "Rose, this is delicious."

"Very good," Father added.

"Your cooking just gets better and better," Mother added.

Everyone agreed.

Rose's cheeks turned pink. "Thank you." She appraised her sister. "Eleanor, is that a new dress?"

Eleanor smiled. "Do you like it? I sewed most of it myself."

"I do."

"I also helped Mother make hers," Eleanor continued. "The fabric is from the feedbags for my chickens."

"You are quite industrious."

Eleanor tried to suppress a smile.

Suzanne wrinkled her nose. "Why do your dresses match?"

"I liked the fabric so much I thought Mother would look good in it," Eleanor lied, feeling stupid.

Lilly's eyes brightened, and she held up her doll. "Eleanor made me and my doll matching dresses."

Rose smiled at Eleanor. "Your sewing has really come along."

"Thank you." Eleanor fingered a crease in what should have been a smooth hem.

Fiona poured herself more coffee and offered some to Shannon. "So, tell me, sister, where are you living now?"

Shannon's smile wilted. "Down by the river. Charles and William are building us a place."

"Where at by the river?"

Shannon pressed her lips together and avoided eye contact with her sister. "Near the rail yard."

"Isn't that where the Hooverville is?"

"I believe so," Harry said, and eyed Charles.

The table grew quiet. "Did you bake the rolls also?" Eleanor asked, trying to change the subject.

Rose nodded.

"Don't tell me you're building close to that hovel?" Her aunt continued. "I've heard such horrid things about that place. The city really should do something—it's an eyesore and a disgrace to our community!"

Eleanor and her siblings stared at their plates.

Uncle Harry cast a disparaging look on Father and the rest of the family. "One shouldn't have more progeny than one can sufficiently provide for."

Shannon's green eyes flashed momentarily at her brother-in-law, then moistened.

Charles squeezed her hand. "Planning only goes so far. No one can predict the future. Besides—" he looked around the table at his family. "Our progeny is a blessing. Every one of them."

Fiona's posture straightened more than usual, and a look of pride shone on her face. "I imagine it's good for you that we've taken Rosalyn in to work for us."

"Rose," Shannon corrected. "Her name is Rose."

"We're glad for this opportunity to spread her wings, learn new skills, and have new experiences—while earning an income," Father added.

At the word, 'income,' Eleanor noticed her aunt and uncle appeared to squirm a bit.

"But Rose, why don't you come and see us?" Lilly asked.

Mitchell looked intently at his sister. "Why don't you come and visit on your day off?" He paused and in a quieter voice, he said, "Do you not like us anymore?"

Rose smiled across the table at her little brother. "I think about you all the time, and I want to come and visit..." She looked at her aunt and uncle, but they avoided her gaze. "I don't know how to get down to the—to your house, and Aunt Fiona doesn't feel I should walk about alone."

"She's right," Father put in.

"But Uncle Harry could drive you," Lilly put in.

Eleanor watched her sister and sensed there was more.

Aunt Fiona jumped in. "I'm afraid we've kept her quite busy on her days off, haven't we, Rosalyn?"

Rose nodded, and Eleanor was certain her sister was hiding something.

"In fact, why don't you tell your family about your visit to the Manito Park Zoo with your cousins?"

"Yes, ma'am. Well, a few weeks ago, at Aunt Fiona's suggestion, I took Albert and Suzanne to the zoo. I never saw so many kinds of animals in one place before," Rose said. "There were lots of bears—including black, brown, grizzly, and even a polar bear—it had beautiful white fur. There were buffaloes, beavers, coyotes, cougars, a bobcat, and monkeys."

"Monkeys?" Lilly bounced in her chair, and the twins' eyes widened with excitement.

"But what I really liked was the ostrich they call Queen Marie and the emu."

"You forgot the raccoons and ducks," Suzanne said.

"And the deer and elk," Albert added.

"Yes, well, we're used to seeing those back home."

"What about the goat?" Albert asked. "Do you have goats in Idaho that chew tobacco?"

At this, the boys all giggled.

Rose blushed.

Fiona looked at her sister. "Shannon, you just have to take the children to see the zoo. It's very cultural and will expand their education and knowledge of the world."

Raymond, Mitchell, and Lilly's eyes brightened at the idea. "Can we, Father? Can we, Mother?"

The light in Shannon's pale green eyes faded more, and all her energy seemed to drain away.

"We'll discuss this later," Father said.

Eleanor remembered what William had said about them being poor and pondered how she could earn money for such a treat.

Fiona clapped her hands. "Listen up, the meal isn't finished. Rosalyn, why don't you serve us dessert?"

Rose left and returned with a white frosted cake.

"Oh."

"Wow."

Sounds of approval lifted from those around the table.

Rose smiled. She looked at Mother, whose sadness changed to a look of pride.

"Rose, did you make this?"

She nodded.

"You have done a splendid job on this entire meal." And, as if her sadness was gone, Mother added, "And this cake...it's like a bouquet. So beautiful, and I'm sure it's as delicious to the mouth as it is to the eyes."

"You mean it?"

"Yes, Darling. I'm very proud of you."

Eleanor smiled at Rose, happy her sister was getting some praise, suspecting it was a rarity. Seeing Rose reminded her of how much she missed their time together.

Raymond finished his last bite of cake. "That was great. Maybe someday, when Suzanne is older, she can come and work for us."

The room quieted and Aunt Fiona paled while Uncle Harry choked on his coffee.

Eleanor glanced at William, and they suppressed a laugh.

Suzanne looked around the table. "What? Me? I...I..."

"Suzanne, why don't you take Lilly up to your room to play?" Aunt Fiona suggested. "And you boys can go outside. Shall we adults retire to the sitting room? Rose, why don't you and your sister clean up the table and dishes?" She pushed her chair from the table and stood, not waiting for an answer.

Eleanor closed the kitchen door. "Whew! I'm finally alone with you. Is it always like this?"

Rose looked at her. "Like what?"

"You doing all the work?"

Rose set down the stack of dessert plates, and her smile faded. "Every day. Why don't I come to visit you?" she asked. "Because I never get a day off."

"What about the day you went to the zoo?"

"I walked there with the—" she glanced about to make sure no one was nearby. "—the little demons while Aunt Fiona was having a luncheon that I'd prepared. She wanted me to serve, but they were being horrible that day, so she had me get them out of her hair, and they begged to go to the zoo, so she, of course, gave in."

"Don't Suzanne and Albert have chores to do?"

Rose shook her head. "No, I do everything for almost everyone. All those little brats do is dress, eat, breathe, fight and whine. The only thing I don't do is the laundry. Aunt Fiona has a laundress come in once a week."

Eleanor raised her eyebrows. "No wonder they're such brats." She was quiet for a moment.

"What is it?"

Eleanor sighed. "Raymond, Mitchell, and Lilly don't do much either. It's not like it used to be on the farm."

Rose lit the stove to heat the wash water and turned to her sister. "You're just saying that."

"No. Especially Lilly. Mother rarely makes her do anything. The boys bring water and search for firewood and helped when we built the shanty, but other than that, they do very little. William goes with Father looking for work, but I do most of the cleaning and some of the cooking. Mother's sad most of the time, and after Father and William leave for work, she often goes back to bed. She helped me make the patterns for the dresses, but I sewed them."

"I wish we were back on the farm."

"Me too." Eleanor slipped a piece of cake into her mouth. "So, what does Aunt Fiona do all day?"

"She goes to meetings and lunches or plays Bridge."

"What's Bridge?"

"A card game she plays with other ladies; they take turns having it at each other's homes. When it's here, I have to make sure the house is really clean and fix a pleasant lunch with tea sandwiches."

Eleanor cocked her head.

"Don't even ask."

Eleanor pretended to pour imaginary tea into an invisible cup. "How would you like your sandwich, ma'am?" She asked in a mocking voice. "Oh, I'll have mine in my tea, please."

Rose chuckled and poured the hot water into the sink and added dirty cups and glasses. "Oh, before I forget." She pulled two quarters from her pocket and handed them to Eleanor. "Here, this is to help you all out."

Eleanor looked at the two quarters. She made that much a month just selling eggs, and this was all her sister had for them?

"I wish I could give you more, but they only pay me a dollar."

"A dollar a week?"

Rose teared up and shook her head. "No...a dollar a month."

Eleanor stared at her sister. "That's not fair. You work so hard."

Rose wiped her eyes with the back of her hand. "They say most of my pay goes for the food I eat, the small room I sleep in, and this." She held out the faded, too big dress she wore. "Aunt Fiona gave it to me from her closet."

Eleanor wrapped her arms around her sister and hugged her. "I'm sorry. I miss you so much and so does Mother—everyone does."

"I miss you too."

They stood hugging by the sink for several minutes. "We'd better hurry up, or Aunt Fiona will be in here wondering why I'm not out watching the demons."

Eleanor snickered. She lifted her sister's hand and placed the quarters in her palm. "You work hard, you deserve these."

Rose shook her head and pressed them back into her sister's hand. "No, I have plenty to eat and a safe, dry home. You take them."

"I'll take one, you take the other."

"Alright."

Raymond slipped back into the house, past his sisters washing dishes, and up the servants' stairs to Albert's room. He marched straight to his cousin's shelf and opened the cloth bag of marbles. He selected seven multi-colored marbles, stuffed them in his pants pocket, and closed the bag.

He then walked across the room and opened a cupboard. He reached behind several sweaters and pulled out a cast iron mechanical monkey bank; and within seconds had it opened and removed several coins. Raymond placed the bank back in its hiding place and shut the door.

He examined a toy train piece, replaced it, then stuffed a small metal car in his sock.

"Cousin?" Albert's voice called from the hall. "Cousin?"

Raymond hid in the closet, closing the door just as Albert entered. "Cousin?"

Raymond ran the cable of a thick sweater between his fingers. It was too bad his cousin was younger and smaller than he was.

"Cousin?" Albert stood just outside the closet door.

Raymond moved further into the corner, kicking a toy firetruck whose bell tinkled.

"Cousin?" Albert opened the closet door and peered in.

Raymond held his breath, hidden behind a long wool coat, probably belonging to Uncle Harry.

Albert shut the door. "Cousin?" His voice was now in the hall near Suzanne's room.

Raymond smiled and slipped out of the closet, down the back stairs and outside.

Before long, it was time to leave, and they were hugging Rose goodbye.

Mother was the last to hug her. She pulled away and looked Rose in the eyes. "Please, promise me you'll come and visit? Please?"

Rose glanced at her aunt.

Mother turned to Fiona and Harry. "Please, promise me you'll make sure she comes?"

Eleanor held her breath, knowing what Rose had said about no days off.

"We'll try." Fiona said. "You best head home; it's late, and you look exhausted."

"Yes, thank you again for supper."

Eleanor took her mother's arm and guided her down the walk to the truck. Her mother, who had always been so strong, felt frail. "Thank you, Honey. Please, sit in the front with your father and me."

"Yes, Mother."

Eleanor had never sat in the cab with Father and Mother.

On that hot summer evening, Mother grasped Eleanor's hand with her cool, shaking one. Eleanor pulled her mother's quivering body next to her and together they wept.

TWENTY

RAYMOND STOOD OVER THE washbasin. "Why do we have to go to school? William doesn't have to."

"Because you are children, and that's what children do." Father surveyed the finally completed walls of the shanty, then at the collection of rocks he'd laid out on the worn wood floor he and William had salvaged from an old feed store. "William, I think we should use bricks for the hearth. It'll create a level base for the cookstove."

"What about the rocks?"

"We'll put them behind the stove to keep the shanty from catching fire."

"But Father." Raymond dried his face and tried to straighten his thick, wavy brown hair. "If I stay home, I can help you and catch fish."

"And get into trouble. No. You're going to school and that's the end of it."

Eleanor hummed next to him as she finished braiding her long red hair and tied the end with a strip of cloth.

"Why are you so happy?" Raymond glared at her.

"I get to go to school and read books and talk with other girls." She smiled in anticipation.

"How dull!"

Eleanor rolled her eyes. "Hurry up; we're going to be late."

Shannon watched the children from the table.

"Lilly, stand still." Eleanor struggled, braiding her little sister's hair.

Mother arranged the stack of dirty dishes before her. "Eleanor, leave your sister be. She's just going to stay here with me."

"I want to go to school," Lilly protested.

"Not this year," Shannon announced. "You're too young."

Charles looked at his wife. "Shannon, she needs to be at school."

"But Charles, she's so young."

"She's as old as the others were when they started school. There's nothing productive here for her to do."

Eleanor finished Lilly's braid and wrapped a strip of the bunny fabric around the end, grateful Father agreed Lilly and Raymond should be at school.

"Well, if it's productivity you're concerned about, then Eleanor should stay. I need Eleanor's help here. She needs to be gaining practical experience, not a bunch of head knowledge she'll never use."

Eleanor froze at Mother's words. "No, Father, please! Don't make me stay."

"Eleanor, you're needed here," Mother insisted.

"Everything I do, you can do."

Charles rose from his place on the floor. "Eleanor, that is enough!"

"I'm sorry." Hot tears filled her eyes. She had thought of nothing else since Father had mentioned school three days ago. "But it's not fair."

"Eleanor."

She bowed her head. It wasn't fair. Why did she have to do everything? Why couldn't she still be a child?

Charles went to Shannon and put his arms around her. "This is not a good place for the children to be. They need to be away from here, learning."

Shannon pushed him away; her body trembling. "Sure. Leave. All of you. Leave me here alone in this human rubbish pile."

Eleanor faltered under her mother's angry gaze, drilling into her. "What do you care about me?"

"Shannon—" Father reached for her, but she slapped him away.

"You're all selfish—all of you." Her mother's breaths came in gasps. "Leave me. All of you—everyone always does." She turned and fled the shanty.

Father looked after her, then back at the children. "Finish getting ready. William, you know where the school is. I need you to walk them there."

"Yes, Father." William looked at his siblings as Father left the shanty. "Come on, you're going to be late, and it's a way to walk."

As they walked, Eleanor took in the road signs and businesses to find their way back after school. All the while, her mother's words chanting in her head. Arguing with herself. Was she being selfish? No, she wasn't. If anyone was, she decided, it was Mother.

But what did she mean by everyone always leaving her? They hadn't left her, so who—?

Eleanor waved to a new classmate, then walked to where her siblings waited by the flagpole. "How was your first day?"

Lilly slipped her little hand inside Eleanor's as they all walked home. "I met some new friends."

"Good." Eleanor hoped they were nicer children than the ones Lilly played with near the shack. Some of those children were good. But Lilly and Raymond gravitated toward a rougher bunch. Children who threw rocks at birds and animals, fought with each other, picked on other children, and sometimes used bad words.

"We played tag and horsey; I was a black stallion and Marybelle was a chestnut mare," Lilly said.

As they walked, Lilly and Raymond chatted about the friends they had made, while Mitchell read as he walked.

Raymond skipped a stone across the street. "I met a boy named Joey Brown; his father owns a shoe shop, and a boy named Frank O'Connor, whose father works for Washington Water Power." He picked up another small rock. "We played marbles, and tomorrow we're going to play jacks." He turned to Mitchell, whose nose was still in a book. "Why didn't you play marbles with us?"

Mitchell looked up from his book. "What?"

"Why didn't you play marbles with us?"

Mitchell shrugged. "I'm not any good. Besides, I only have five."

"I can show you how to play."

"Maybe." Mitchell returned to his book.

"I'll even spot you a few of my own marbles."

"I guess."

Eleanor looked down at her little sister. "Do you like your teacher?"

"She's nice when she lets us go outside and play," Lilly said. "But she wants me to know my letters and numbers and write them out."

"Well, you know your letters."

"A, B, G, D, Q, L, I, L, L, Y, X, Z," Lilly said and nodded her head once in a show of "see-there," confidence. "But Miss Dodge says that's not all of them."

"You are missing some. We'll work on them at home."

"She says I have to write them, too."

Mitchell looked up from his book. "Do we have any paper?"

Eleanor shook her head. "Only old newsprint."

Worry sketched itself on Mitchell's face. "We're supposed to write a story about what we would do if we were the boy or girl in this story." He held up the book he was reading. Raymond chucked another stone down the road. "Ha! No paper, no homework."

Eleanor cringed at Raymond's words. She let go of Lilly's hand and reached inside her pocket where she'd sewed another secret pocket to hide her egg money. She fingered the coins. "Come, we're going to the store."

"Are we getting candy?" Lilly asked.

"Popcorn or Post Toasties?" Raymond added.

"No, we're getting paper and pencils."

Lilly and Raymond hung their heads, but Mitchell's eyes brightened.

"I want candy," Lilly said.

Eleanor ignored her.

They turned in to Tom King's Grocery. The smell of fresh meat, cloves, and onions overloaded their senses. All around them were canisters of coffee, tea, and tobacco, jars of pickles, cloth bags of flour, salt, and oats, and cans of fruit, vegetables, and meat.

They stood and stared at the abundance of it all and inhaled the smells that taunted their empty bellies. Eleanor longed for the days when they had a full pantry.

Lilly reached out to touch a red apple when a man's sharp voice yelled, "Hey, can't you children read?" A clerk in his fifties with a white apron pointed to a sign on the door.

Only two children allowed in the store at a time.

Eleanor nudged her siblings. "You wait outside. I'll buy what we need."

They each looked about in disappointment at all the wonderful food and filed out.

Eleanor counted her money again and selected two scribbler pads, an eraser, and two pencils. That would be enough if they shared and were careful not to waste any. She handed the man a quarter and asked, "Do you buy eggs?"

"Twelve cents a dozen."

"Thank you." A sense of pride swelled inside her; she could help provide for their needs.

Outside, the twins were arguing.

Raymond leaned into Mitchell. "It's your own fault."

Eleanor separated them up. "What's his fault?"

"He's hungry."

"We all are."

"But he didn't eat all of his lunch."

Eleanor looked at Mitchell. "Why not?"

Mitchell's gaze moved from the ground to Eleanor's green eyes. "I made a friend, and he didn't have one. So, I shared mine."

Eleanor smiled. "That was nice of you. Come on."

Mitchell opened his book and continued reading.

"How can you do that?" Raymond asked.

Mitchell turned a page. "Do what?"

"Read and walk."

He shrugged. "I don't know."

"Well, I had my biscuits and half of Joey Brown's peanut butter sandwich."

"A peanut butter sandwich?" Lilly's eyes widened, and she licked her lips. "Why'd he give you half his sandwich?"

"I won it."

Lilly was all engaged. "How?"

"With these." He lifted a small bag of marbles he'd tied to his belt loop. Mitchell looked up from his book. "Where'd you get those, anyway?"

"I found some and won others."

Mitchell squinted at his brother.

"What?"

"Did I say anything?"

Raymond grabbed his brother's arm. "You don't believe me?"

Mitchell struggled to free himself, but Raymond only held on tighter.

"Listen to me," Raymond spat. "I hate being poor. When I'm grown up, I'm going to live in a big house with lots of food and nice things. I'm going to have a job like Uncle Harry's that pays lots of money."

"What does Uncle Harry do?" Lilly asked.

"He's the boss of a radio station or something," Eleanor added.

"Yeah, that's what I'm gonna do," Raymond said.

Mitchell pulled free. "Fine."

Raymond knocked Mitchell's book to the ground. "You're gonna be poor and hungry."

Mitchell chased after the book and dusted it off. "I am not."

Raymond was face-to-face with his twin. "Yeah, you will. You don't get rich reading and giving your food away."

"You don't get rich fighting and stealing, either."

"Oh, yeah?" Raymond shoved him.

"Yeah!" Mitchell shoved him back.

Eleanor spun around. "Raymond. Mitchell. Stop it now."

Raymond lowered his head and plowed into Mitchell, knocking him down and pinning him to the ground. "Why can't you be normal? Like the rest of us. You embarrass me. The boys keep asking me. 'What's wrong with him?' 'Why does he eat lunch with that stupid Lenny?'"

Mitchell scrambled to his feet. "He's my friend."

"He's a mama's boy."

Mitchell charged after Raymond. "You don't know that."

Raymond held out his hands and stopped his brother. "Ask him where his dad is."

"His dad went looking for work."

"Yeah, and he never came back."

Mitchell struggled to grab Raymond's shirt. "It's not his fault."

"Maybe his father just doesn't want to be around him."

Eleanor's good day was falling apart. "That's enough." She pulled them apart. "You two stop it." She grabbed each of her brothers by the arm. "Raymond, apologize to Mitchell."

"Me?"

"Yes, you. You started this."

"He's accusing me of stealing."

"Well, you did," Mitchell said.

"He should apologize to me. He's embarrassing me in front of my friends."

"He's your brother; he's more important than friends. If these friends of yours don't like Mitchell, then they aren't very good friends."

Raymond yanked free of Eleanor's grip. "They're better friends than he is a brother. At least they're fun." He stomped off toward home.

Mitchell hung his head.

Eleanor glared after Raymond; she was not happy with how he was changing. She tried hugging Mitchell, but he pulled away.

"Why is he like that?"

"I don't know. I think he's got a little of Aunt Fiona in him."

Mitchell suppressed a grin.

Twenty-one

"I don't understand why this man can't pay you?" Mother asked as Father and Eleanor climbed into the truck while the twins joined William in the back.

"I told you; no one has any money. At least the children can take the apples for lunch."

She shrugged and took an angry Lilly by the hand.

They drove through town and were soon in the country. Eleanor rested her arms and chin on the open window and gazed at the passing scenery. It was good to leave the city with its stale, smoky, rancid air and see the open spaces of fields and farms. "I wish Mother could have come; these beautiful fields would cheer her up."

"Or make her miss the farm more."

Eleanor nodded. "Do you miss living in the country?"

"Of course, I do; I think we all do."

"Even William? He seemed excited about coming to Spokane."

"Well, Spokane hasn't been what we expected. Back home, we didn't see the effects of the crash. We didn't know how many people were homeless and out of work. I think William was hoping for the excitement of big city life, but that's not what we're experiencing."

Eleanor sighed at Father's last words; she turned and took in the sight of orchards and fields, many with crops languishing on the stalks. "Will we ever go back to our farm?"

"I don't know. We'd have to buy back our land, rebuild a home and barn, and buy the cows." He paused. "It doesn't seem likely."

Eleanor sighed, and hot tears streamed sideways from the force of the warm air speeding by. She hated living in town and missed the cows, especially Bertha. She wiped away the tears and summoned her courage. "Father."

He glanced over at her.

She took a deep breath. "Father, will...will we..." She swallowed hard, and forced herself to ask the question she'd considered for weeks. "Will we live in the shanty forever?"

He stared at the road. "I don't think so. It's time we get dealt a good hand. We've been trying hard. They say God helps those who help themselves, but I'm not seeing it."

"There's an awful lot of people who are hungry and homeless. Do you think God even sees us and all we're doing?"

Father looked at the blue sky. "I don't know. I thought so, but maybe not."

Eleanor pondered this; she'd never heard Father waver in his convictions, and it frightened her.

Father turned down a dirt drive at a mailbox with the name Schmidt on it, and soon a barking dog and a farmer in his fifties met them. He shook Father's hand and leading them all to the edge of a large orchard; he gave them each a cloth bag that slung over their shoulder.

Eleanor climbed ladders and sometimes even the trees; she put apples in her bag then transferred them to round wooden baskets, being careful not to bruise any. Despite the hard work, Eleanor loved being on the farm—although a tinge of sadness crept in at the lowing of a cow.

Several times Eleanor caught her skirt or sleeve on a twig or branch, creating a small rip. She was glad she'd worn her old dress.

The loud clanging of a bell announced lunchtime, and Mr. Schmidt climbed down from his ladder and encouraged the others to follow. "Time to wash up. The Missus has prepared a good spread of vittles."

Raymond and Mitchell jumped to the ground. "Yay!"

The farmer smiled. "That's what I like. Eager young-uns. You boys." He turned to Eleanor. "And you, young lady, have worked hard. Let's go see what the Missus has cooked up."

They arrived at the white, two-story farmhouse to find a large table set under a tree by the back porch. There was corn on the cob, biscuits and jelly, green beans, pork roast, mashed potatoes, and gravy.

The children inhaled the wonderful smells, their eyes wide with anticipation. Eleanor was grateful Father allowed them to come.

Mr. Schmidt prayed over the meal, thanking the good Lord for His bounty and asking Him to bless the Cruthers family for all their help.

Mrs. Schmidt handed the bowl of mashed potatoes to Father. "Mr. Cruthers, we so appreciate your helping my husband get his truck working Tuesday and coming out and helping us bring in our crop."

Father took some potatoes and passed them on. "Well, ma'am, we appreciate the opportunity to provide our family with some fruit."

"I was hoping you'd bring your wife with you. A woman gets mighty lonesome out here."

Charles nodded. "I apologize. We have a younger child and didn't want her getting in the way. We figured it would be best to keep her at...at home. But I'm sure my wife would have enjoyed the company of another woman."

"Well, you'll have to bring her out to visit sometime."

"Yes, ma'am."

Mr. Schmidt handed Charles the platter of meat. "You mentioned you used to farm."

As Father began telling Mr. Schmidt their story, Mrs. Schmidt looked over at Eleanor. "Are you the oldest girl?"

"No, ma'am. I have an older sister, Rose. She lives with our aunt and uncle and works for them."

"So, I imagine you help your mother out a lot."

"Yes. I help cook and clean, and watch over the younger children. I care for our chickens and help Mother make clothes from the feed bags. But it takes a while to collect enough feed bags to make outfits for all of us."

"That it does." The woman examined Eleanor's tight dress. "That it does." She looked around the table at the Cruthers family. "Are there seven of you at home?"

"Yes, ma'am."

"That's a lot of mouths to feed and bodies to clothe."

Eleanor blushed, remembering Uncle Harry's comment about planning to provide for their family. "It is." She almost asked if Mrs. Schmidt had other work but stopped before embarrassing everyone.

The closer it drew to winter, the more Eleanor worried. What would they eat, and how would they stay warm?

That evening, stiff and sore from her work, Eleanor watched Mr. Schmidt load four crates of apples into the back of the truck. She couldn't remember the last time they had fruit. She wished those delicious apples would last forever. It seemed so little compared to the size of the truck.

Her last visit with Rose came to mind. Her sister worked so hard and made very little money—but she had a warm home, clothes, and three meals a day. Things they didn't have.

Her conversation with Father came to mind. Maybe God didn't see that they were starving. Maybe he didn't care.

Discouragement settled in. She had been sure being in the country would make her happy. Instead, it made her miss home. She gathered her courage and stood tall. "Mr. Schmidt?"

The kind farmer smiled at her. "Yes, young lady."

"Thank you so much for having us out here."

"Well, thank you for all your help."

"Sir, do you know of any other farmers that might need help?" She ignored Father's look of disapproval.

Mr. Schmidt rubbed his chin. "Lots of farmers need help, but most don't have money to pay. Many aren't even bringing in their crops."

Eleanor's eyes widened, as did William's. That explained the fields with dried and withering wheat, lentils and barley still on the stock. "But why aren't they harvesting their crops?"

"The price we would get for them is less than it would cost us to harvest them."

William's muscles flexed, and indignation flashed in his blue eyes. "So, while people starve, food rots in the fields?"

Mr. Schmidt nodded. "I'm afraid so. It hardly makes sense. Some of these farmers have already had their farms foreclosed on. The rest of us are trying to do what we can to hold on."

Panic squeezed Eleanor's chest. "Do you mean there aren't any farmers around here that can hire us?"

Father gave her a stern look. "Eleanor, that's enough."

Mr. Schmidt held up his hand. "It's alright, Charles. She's a hard worker and trying to help." He turned to Eleanor. "Old man Evans is one of the few farmers I know around here who doesn't depend on the banks to buy seed and equipment, but he has a hired man who chases off anyone who stops by the gate he built across his drive."

Eleanor slumped. What was her family supposed to do?

Charles thrust his hand out to Mr. Schmidt. "Well friend, we appreciate the opportunity to pick apples and to make a new friend."

"The pleasure is all mine." He reached into his shirt pocket and pulled out a small wad of bills. "This isn't much and I'm sorry I can't pay you more, but consider it a thank you for all your help."

Eleanor watched Father put the money into his pocket.

"I understand," Father said. "These are hard times, and I don't want to see a fellow farmer lose his livelihood and go through what my family is. I appreciate the money you can spare and the opportunity to provide my family with some food. We have all enjoyed getting out of town. I only wish I'd brought Shannon."

Eleanor walked to the truck. Her only consolation was hoping she could talk Mother into baking an apple pie.

"Best of luck to you," Mr. Schmidt said.

"And you too, my friend."

As they climbed into the truck, Mrs. Schmidt came out with a crate of food. "Here, I've packed up some potatoes, fresh picked green beans, butter, and preserves, sugar, and the rest of the roast."

Eleanor stared in surprise.

Charles paused, overcome with emotion. "Thank you, thank you so much. We really appreciate all your kindness."

"And we too." She touched Eleanor's arm. "Wait here, young lady." She returned shortly with a plump flour sack. "This here is for you." She handed Eleanor the sack.

Eleanor peered inside, and her eyes widened at the sight of a green woolen dress with a white collar. She smiled at Mrs. Schmidt. "Oh, ma'am. Thank you. Thank you so much."

The woman smiled. "Winter will come soon, and a dress made from feed sacks won't keep you very warm."

Joy swelled in Eleanor's chest. "Thank you."

"My pleasure. And that dress there." She nodded at the too tight dress Eleanor wore. "There is still some suitable material there you can use to make a quilt."

Eleanor smiled. "I will. I will." She waved at Mrs. Schmidt, wondering how warm a quilt made of worn-out clothes would be. She fingered the thick green wool of the dress; it would definitely be warmer than anything else she had. But the conversation about quilts aroused a fresh worry that brought the chill of winter with it.

TWENTY-TWO

THE FRONT DOOR OPENED, and William's prepared speech to ask for work fell from his mind at the sight of the teenage girl before him. He grew hot, and his mouth was dry.

"Hel...hello." He glanced down at the porch floor between them. "I...I was wondering if you need any work done? I'm...I'm a hard worker and can rake leaves, clean gardens and flowerbeds, chop firewood, wash windows..." his words came out faster and faster. His grip on his hat tightened and loosened; sweat beaded on his forehead.

The girl watched him with deep brown eyes; a mischievous smile spread across her lips. "What's your name?"

"William. William Cruthers, ma'am."

She giggled. "Well, William Cruthers, I'm not the lady of the house."

"I..." William bowed his head, embarrassed. "I apologize."

"My name's Clara." She held out her hand, palm side down, wrist bent. He looked at it, unsure how to shake it.

"Gentlemen, kiss the top of a lady's hand."

He wiped the dirt and growing sweat off his hand and gently took hers. His lips just touched her soft skin; his heart pounded so loudly; he was sure she could hear it.

"I'm pleased to see you're a gentleman. We can't have thugs working for us. I just won't stand for it. Wait here while I go see what tasks Gloria needs accomplished." She paused and looked him in the eye. "You don't mind waiting?"

"Yes, ma'am. I mean, no, no; I don't mind."

She smiled, and her brunette bobbed hair lifted in a slight swirl as she left.

William swallowed hard and took a deep breath. Her beauty and confidence overwhelmed him. He looked about the white, two-story Victorian with its rounded pillars and wrap-around porch. A four-foot chair hung by chains from the porch ceiling. An image of him and Clara sitting in it flashed into his mind, and his cheeks grew warm.

The screen door opened, and a woman about his mother's age with a white and pink floral apron appeared. Clara stepped around the woman. "This is the young man I spoke of."

"Yes, Clara. I can see."

William stood straight and forced himself to focus on her mother, who introduced herself as Mrs. Turner. She gave him directions to rake the Ponderosa pine needles out of the yard and flowerbeds and place them in a pile near the burn barrel.

"You can put some in the barrel, just don't let it get too full and smother the fire."

"Yes, ma'am."

"Clara will show you where the rake and shovel are."

William bowed his head. "Thank you."

He worked hard all afternoon; hoping Mrs. Turner would hire him another day so he could see Clara again. He sometimes sensed he was being watched. He would turn and see the girl's face disappear behind an upstairs curtain. Twice, Clara brought out some milk and cookies.

"Did you bake these?" he asked, holding up an orange-colored pump-kin cookie.

"I did. Do you like them?"

"Yes, very much."

"What do you like to do?"

William took his time chewing the cookie. It had been so long since he'd been able to do what he wanted; he didn't know how to respond. "Fishing, tinkering with motors, building things."

"Do you like movies?"

"Yeah."

"Have you been to the new Fox Theater?"

William smiled. "I got to help paint the inside and get it ready to open."

"Did you see George O'Brien, Anita Page, and Little Mitzi Green when they were here for the grand opening?"

William shook his head. "No. I wasn't able to be there."

"I got a glimpse of Anita Page before some tall guy in front of me lifted his daughter on his shoulders. She is so beautiful."

William could only nod at the slender girl with a milky complexion and strong cheekbones standing in front of him. He couldn't imagine anyone being more beautiful than her.

When William had finished, Mrs. Turner counted out his pay. "Thank you very much. You've helped Mr. Turner out of a task he abhors."

William nodded, unsure what she meant by abhors. Clara smiled at him from the parlor room window. Anxiety crept inside him. What if he never saw her again? He had to see her. Mrs. Turner was looking at him; he had to do or say something. "Do you have any other work I can help you with?" His voice cracked, and his cheeks warmed. "I can wash windows, weed..." His mind went blank. "Chop wood."

Mrs. Turner glanced behind her and Clara moved away from the window. "I'll check with my husband. I'm not sure if he has someone lined up to do yard work, but I'll ask him."

The words took a moment to sink in. "Oh." He pushed down the panic rising inside him. "I...I hope you're happy with the work I've done today."

Mrs. Turner surveyed the yard. "You've done a fine job."

William smiled. "If you don't mind, I'll be back by in a few days."

Mrs. Turner smiled. "We'll see if we can find anything."

William forced himself to wait until he was in front of the next house before he looked back and spotted Clara looking at him from an upstairs window. What if she didn't hire him back?

"Ma...Ma...Mo-th-er, it...it's cold out there." Lilly ran into the shanty and to the small cook stove; her fingers and face were red from cold. She stood within inches of it and rubbed her hands up and down her arms; the sleeves of her dress were not thick enough to keep out the cold.

Shannon looked up. "Maybe you should stay inside. It is late October."

"Uh, ah. It's boring in here." Warming up for a few minutes, she ran back out.

Shannon sighed. "What are we going to do? We can't go through winter with these thin clothes." She patted Eleanor's arm. "I am so thankful Mrs. Schmidt gave you this warm dress."

"Me too." She touched her mother's hands—they were ice cold. Shannon wore the dress Eleanor had helped make for her. "Mother, you should make yourself another blouse to help keep you warm."

Shannon nodded. "We need sweaters and coats."

Eleanor agreed. The clothes she had helped Mother sew were not enough to keep them warm. "I wish we had some yarn. Father or William could whittle us some needles and you could knit sweaters and I could knit some scarves, hats, and gloves."

Mother patted Eleanor's arm, and a sad smile spread across her lips.

Eleanor wanted to throw her arms around her mother and hug her. She wanted to tell her she loved her and hear her mother say, "I love you." Deep down, she knew her mother loved her, but since the fire, it seemed Mother no longer could express anything but sorrow.

Eleanor sighed, and they sewed together in silence for a while. "How much bigger does this need to be?"

"Let's see." Shannon stood and stretched out two corners of the quilt and Eleanor did the same. They looked at their handiwork; the squares had no color pattern; it was strictly functional. "Let's lay it on my bed. That will give us an idea."

The quilt top covered most of the bed, but with little left to go over the edges. They both sighed in disappointment.

"I'd say six more rows on the sides and four on the bottom." Mother fingered the remaining squares. I'm afraid we only have enough for maybe one or two more rows."

Eleanor fingered the thin quilt top. "How is this going to keep us warm?"

Mother sighed. "We need more material for the backing and something thick to fill the quilts."

"Like what?"

"Batting would be best, but even old blankets would work."

"What about grass or gunny sacks?"

Mother looked down at the piecemeal quilt with its small squares—some made with two or more smaller triangles. "We may have to."

They returned to their sewing, Eleanor sewing squares together and Mother sewing those two blocks with two more to make the long strips.

Shouts and voices called from outside. The door flew open, and Lilly ran back in. "Mother, Eleanor, guess what?"

"Shut the door; you're letting in the cold."

"Guess who's here?"

There was a knock on the door-jam, and a young lady carrying a couple of ten-pound flour sacks stepped in.

"Rose!" Mother and Eleanor jumped to their feet.

"Oh Rose." Eleanor's discouragement slipped away.

"Oh, Darling. Come in."

Rose set the bags on the table, then hugged her mother and sister before looking around. "Oh, I brought some friends." She motioned to someone outside, and two girls and a young man entered, followed by the twins.

Rose and her friends looked around at the small but clean shanty.

Shannon's excitement cooled, and her gaze lowered.

Rose straightened and grabbed her mother's hand. "Mother, Eleanor, these are my friends, Marguerite and Shirley, and this is Liam, Marguerite's brother."

Eleanor liked them at once, especially Liam with his sandy blond hair, wide grin and dimples.

Shannon took a breath and managed a smile. "It's nice to meet you. Thank you so much for coming with Rose to see us." She turned to her daughter. "I've missed you so much."

"I miss you too, Mother."

Sensing her mother's desire to be the good host, Eleanor moved toward the cookstove. "Would you like some tea?" She filled the kettle with water, then added more sticks and scrap wood to the fire.

"Please, have a seat." Shannon motioned to the other bench and the two mismatched chairs Charles had found and brought home.

Rose and her friends sat.

"It looks like you're making a quilt," Marguerite said.

Shannon glanced at the quilt top, now in a pile on the table. "Yes, it's really nothing. We're trying to make something warm from the scraps we have."

"Oh." Rose jumped up. "I almost forgot." She reached for the packages she'd brought; her face shining with excitement. "I was baking bread and molasses cookies, so I made some for you." She pulled them from the first bag, along with a few more cloth sacks from the bottom. "I figured you and Eleanor could use these."

Eleanor's eyes widened, and she fingered the fabrics. The sizes varied, but the colorful patterns were beautiful. She estimated they could finish the quilt top they were working on and maybe start another. "These are so beautiful."

Rose flipped through them. "Aren't they? Aunt Fiona picks out the prettiest sacks, then does nothing with them."

Shannon shook her head. "Thank you."

"What's in the other sack?" Lilly asked.

Rose untied the string. "A lady Aunt Fiona knows brought over some yams, but Aunt Fiona doesn't like them. I remembered the delicious yams you would make on holidays, so I brought them along with some butter." She smiled.

Mother chuckled. "Fiona never did like yams."

Mitchell and Raymond's eyes grew big at the sight of the food.

Tears filled Shannon's eyes. "Thank you. Thank you so much." She hugged Rose.

"What's this?" Eleanor held up a dozen or more clumps of yarn.

Rose picked up a tangle of yarn. "I'd forgotten I put those in there. The demon—kids were playing with this and made a mess. I was going to untangle it, but I never had time."

Shannon picked up the wads of navy yarn and looked at Eleanor. "Can you believe it?"

Eleanor grinned. "We were just talking about yarn."

Mother looked at the twins. "And I know two boys who can work to untangle this."

"Oh, no. Not us," Raymond protested.

"Yes." She handed a clump to each of the boys. "Don't break it and you know how to roll them into balls. If there's enough, you'll each get a pair of gloves."

Eleanor poured tea, and Rose shared how she'd met Marguerite and Shirley after walking the cousins to school. They both worked cleaning people's homes and shared a room at a boarding house.

Eleanor glanced at Liam. He was gazing at Rose, and she couldn't help but smile.

"Why don't you live with your families?" Mother asked.

Marguerite and Liam exchanged looks before Marguerite bowed her head.

Rose put her arm around her friend. "It's alright Marguerite. It's not your fault."

Marguerite didn't look up.

Liam cleared his throat. "I'm sorry, Mrs. Cruthers; life has been hard for us, and it's hard not to believe we are unworthy."

Shannon cocked her head.

"About a month after the stock market crashed, Marguerite and I came home from school to find our parents had moved."

Eleanor almost spewed out a mouthful of tea. How could a parent do that?

Shannon stared into her tea but said nothing.

"There was a note," Liam continued. "It said that father had lost his job, and they were going to San Francisco to look for work. They would send for us when they had money."

An ache of fear burned in Eleanor's chest. Mother and Father would never do that—would they?

"But that was October 1929," Mitchell said.

"Two years ago," Liam added.

Eleanor and the twins stared at them.

"Where do you live?" Mitchell asked.

"I live in a chicken coop behind my employer's house. It's small; so fairly easy to keep warm." He looked around at the scraps of wood, cardboard, tar paper, linoleum, and newspapers tacked to the inside of the walls. "I've done some of the same things you have to insulate my house."

Shannon sighed, looking around their small shanty with thin walls. "And what about you, Shirley?"

"My parents have ten children. After the crash, we had to move into a smaller house and sell lots of our furniture. I quit school and started working. Liam and Marguerite stayed with us for a while. She and I shared a bed with three of my sisters."

Eleanor was grateful she only had to share her bed with Lilly.

"We found several jobs cleaning houses," Shirley continued, "and decided to rent a room from a lady Marguerite cleaned for. I know it was hard on my parents, but it leaves more room and food for my family."

Shannon nodded while Eleanor realized she wasn't the only one missing her sister.

Rose looked around. "Where are Father and William?"

"They're working, or looking for work," Lilly said.

Rose nodded. "It seems everyone is."

Too soon, Rose and her friends had to leave. "Tell Father and William I love them and am sorry I couldn't stay." She grabbed Eleanor's hand. "Walk us to the road?"

Eleanor squeezed her mother's shoulder and stepped into the cool of the late fall day. She rubbed her hands over her arms, grateful for the warmer dress.

Rose wrapped her arm around her sister. "Eleanor, I'm worried. Are you going to be warm enough this winter?"

Eleanor didn't answer. How could she? It was only October and—.

"Eleanor?"

"I'm scared." She squeezed back the tears. "We're always hungry, and now we're cold too. We need warm clothes, and coats, quilts, and yarn."

Rose nodded. "I'll see what I can do, but Aunt Fiona hasn't paid me, and she keeps complaining that Uncle Harry isn't making enough money."

TWENTY-THREE

ELEANOR WATCHED HER SIBLINGS mingle with the other students and scurry to their classrooms before exiting the school.

"Miss Cruthers, oh Eleanor Cruthers, where are you going?"

Eleanor paused. She hadn't bargained on Mrs. Jones, the school secretary, seeing her. She stopped, her heart beating, and turned to face the woman.

"Miss Cruthers, where are you going? Your class is that way." The woman pointed back to the building.

"I know, Mrs. Jones, but—" Think Eleanor, think. "But Mother...Mother isn't feeling well and needs me to—I mean, needs me there."

"What's wrong with her?"

"Huh? Oh. She's awful tired and weak and cold. I can't leave her alone."

Mrs. Jones nodded. "I see. I hope she gets well soon so you can return to school."

Eleanor nodded. "She should be better tomorrow."

The older lady raised an eyebrow.

Eleanor knew she'd gone too far. "I mean, I hope she's better tomorrow."

Mrs. Jones gave her a look that made Eleanor nervous, but Eleanor didn't stay to answer more questions.

Eleanor had walked several blocks before the pounding in her chest calmed, and she was sure Mrs. Jones wasn't following her. She looked about, noting the street signs and buildings. She had never been this way before, but was determined to find what she was looking for.

She started with several shops, asking the clerks if they had any work she could do. "I can sweep, wash windows, stock shelves..." The men she spoke to often shooed her away or gave her looks that made her skin prickle.

Eleanor entered a clothing shop where a young lady stood and greeted her. "Hello, ma'am," Eleanor started. "Do you have any work I could do? I can clean and organize, put things on shelves—" her gaze fell on the clothing. "I can also sew, if you have mending or alterations."

The young lady with shoulder length hair smiled. "Shouldn't you be in school?"

Eleanor shifted. "Well, I'm taking a break to help my family earn some money."

"Oh, you are, are you?"

"Yes, and I'm a good worker."

"I'm sure you are." She leaned an elbow on the counter and rested her chin on her hand. "How is your search for work going?"

Eleanor took a few steps closer. "Not well."

The woman nodded. "Where all have you looked?"

"Up and down both sides of this block and the one before it."

"Are you alone?"

"Yes ma'am."

"Has anyone hurt you?"

"No."

"Well, that's good. But you need to be careful. There are men who, if they see you alone, might hurt you; if you know what I mean."

Eleanor nodded, clueless, but the memory of the strange feeling returned. "Then it's probably a good idea that I work for someone like you."

The woman smiled. "I like you; you've got spunk."

Eleanor smiled. Spunk. Whatever it was, she liked the sound of it.

"The problem is, I don't have a lot of money to pay you."

Eleanor looked around the shop. Besides dresses and coats, scarves and nylons, there was also material, thread, buttons, and other notions, including yarn. "Do you make all these clothes here?"

"Oh no, we get most of them from factories in New York, Chicago, and California."

"Oh."

"Sometimes we make a special item for a customer or do alterations."

Eleanor's countenance brightened. "Who does that?"

"Usually my mother."

"Oh." Eleanor looked at the skeins of yarn. They were so beautiful. There were reds and blues, greens and pinks. She stopped at several skeins of mustard colored yarn; Mother would look so good in a sweater that color.

"Do you knit?"

Eleanor nodded. "I can't make sweaters, but I can knit scarves, shawls, hats and mittens."

The woman walked away from the counter and pulled out a skein of emerald yarn and held it out to her. "This would look wonderful with your hair and eyes and match your dress."

She looked at it and wanted it more than she ever wanted anything. She touched it. "It's beautiful."

"You like it?"

Eleanor nodded.

"How about this? I've got a storeroom that needs cleaning, and I can't watch the store and clean. If you clean it out, I'll give you..." She paused. "A skein of this yarn."

Eleanor's eyes widened. "Really?"

The young woman smiled. "Yes. And if you do a real good job, I might give you one of those too." She pointed to the mustard yarn.

Eleanor's hand shot out. "It's a deal."

The woman smiled and shook it.

For the next two days, Eleanor worked cleaning out old catalogs, display props, and odds and ends. Among the items were some outdated swags and swatches of fabric, which she set aside. She was just finishing up when the young woman checked in on her.

"Oh, my, Eleanor, it's hard to believe this is the same room. It will be good to use this space again." She picked up the small stack of fabric. "Did you forget to toss these?"

"Well, I was wondering if I could keep those?"

"Sure. Come, I'll even wrap them up for you, along with your yarn."

Eleanor tried to calculate how big a quilt the fabric would make. She arrived at the flagpole just as school let out. Lilly and the twins gathered around her, full of questions about the package in her arms.

"What's in it?"

"Where'd you get it?"

"I'll tell you when we get home."

At home, Eleanor made a big production of unwrapping it, being careful not to tear the brown paper or break the string. She gasped. The lady at the store had packed the fabric swatches, but rather than packing two skeins of yarn, she'd added a third, blue skein.

"What is it?" everyone asked.

"Oh," Eleanor picked up the extra yarn." I'd forgotten about this. She suppressed a smile and showed them the fabric. She handed Mother the skein of mustard yarn. "Is there enough for a sweater?" she asked.

Mother smiled. "No. But I'm sure I can knit you all some hats or mittens."

"But, that's for you, Mother."

"Thank you, but you children need it more than I do."

Eleanor's heart sank. "But we're in the warm schoolhouse, and you're in the cold shanty."

Mother nodded.

"If we add the yarn from Rose to the blue..."

Mother smiled. "We'll see what we can do. Maybe your father can buy another skein or two. But where did you get all of this?"

"From my teacher. She had me clean out a closet and let me keep some things."

"Including the yarn?" Mother asked. "It looks brand new."

"Well..."

Mother looked at her.

"Someone gave them to her, and she doesn't knit, so she asked if I'd like them...for helping her clean out the closet." Eleanor squirmed under Mother's scrutiny and changed the subject. "How big a quilt do you think we can make with the fabric?"

Mother sighed over her suspicions and started laying the fabric out on her bed. "Well, if we just use the sizes we have here, and don't cut them into smaller pieces—" She rearranged a few pieces. "We probably have enough for about half a quilt top. I still don't know what we're going to use for backing and batting."

Eleanor's excitement fell. "Oh." It was the same story—never enough.

Mother lifted Eleanor's chin. "It's a start."

Later that evening, Mitchell sidled up next to Eleanor. "You're lying," he whispered.

"What?" Eleanor's heart beat hard in her chest and her icy hands grew sweaty.

"The fabric and yarn. Your teacher didn't give them to you. You're lying. You haven't even been at school."

"Shush. We need it. Father and William are busy providing food and stuff for the shanty."

"You shouldn't lie."

"Do you want to be cold this winter or warm?"

"Warm."

"Then keep your mouth shut."

"I'm coming with you."

She stared at him. "No."

"Then I'm telling. It's not safe."

The words of the kind lady at the clothing store came to mind.

"But if you come, Raymond will know."

"He doesn't pay any attention to me."

Eleanor wasn't so sure. But in the end, she agreed, and for the next two days they knocked on doors and stopped by stores, asking for work but were turned away every time.

Mitchell flopped down on a curb. "We should be back in school."

"I'm not giving up."

"What else can we do?"

Eleanor watched the cars and trucks drive by.

"Pee-ewe." Mitchell plugged his nose.

"That's it!"

"What?" His face still scrunched up from the smell.

"Garbage. That was a garbage truck. Sometimes people throw out usable stuff."

"You want to make quilts out of stuff people have thrown away?"

"That lady was going to throw away that fabric I brought home."

"I don't know."

"Mitchell, you said you wanted to help—"

"Alright."

They spent the rest of the afternoon wandering through alleys, looking in dumpsters and piles of junk. Finding nothing but a few old crates and a chisel with a chipped end and a broken handle.

On Friday, they explored an unfamiliar area with still no luck at jobs or finding tossed items of use. The clock at the train station chimed.

"Is it only nine o'clock?" Mitchell asked.

"It feels like noon." Eleanor's discouragement grew with each block.

"Hey, you smell that?" Mitchell's eyes widened, and a smile spread across his face.

She inhaled. "Bread. Oh, that smells so good."

They walked faster; the smell growing stronger. Soon, there it was. A large brick building with the words BAKERY printed above the door. A delivery truck pulled away, and they watched it go.

"I could eat a whole loaf of bread," Mitchell announced.

"Me too."

In the front was a counter with several men helping housewives with their purchases. Eleanor and Mitchell waited their turn in line.

A middle-aged man glared down at them. "What'll it be?"

Eleanor swallowed. The bread in the case looked so good. "Do...do you have any jobs?"

"Get out of here. We don't hire children. Next."

They slunk out, both almost in tears. The delicious smells only made the pain in their bellies worse.

"He didn't have to be so mean," Mitchell said.

Eleanor's hurt turned to anger. "You're right. He didn't." She looked about then and motioned for him to follow her around the corner of the bakery. "I bet they have a dumpster." She grinned.

Mitchell's eyes widened. "Yeah."

She crept along the narrow space between the bakery and another building, her finger to her lips. They peeked around the corner. A man dressed in white with a funny white hat dumped a handful of flour sacks into a large bin. Someone said something, and they darted back to their hiding place.

"How are we going to get into that?" Mitchell asked, a look of fear creeping across his face.

"Let me think." She peeked around and watched the men.

"Hey, Tony, I need your help over here."

She watched as the man who had dumped the items left to another part of the lot. "Come on." She motioned to Mitchell. "I'll lift you up and you can grab stuff."

They scrambled onto the loading dock, over to the large bin, and glanced in. The smell wasn't inviting.

"Ewe," Mitchell whispered. "I don't see any bread."

Eleanor stared at the mishmash of egg shells, empty tins of yeast and shortening, along with bags that once held salt and flour. "No. There's no bread. But look at all the bags." She glanced at the men. Still busy. "Come here." She interlaced her fingers and held the step out to Mitchell. "Get in and toss those bags out."

He, too, looked at the men and sighed. Within moments he was tossing out large muslin bags, which Eleanor quickly stuffed inside the first few he'd tossed.

"Some of these have egg and stuff on them."

"I don't care. Toss them anyway."

"Hey, girl. What are you doing?"

Eleanor looked up to see the man called Tony looking at her. "Come on, Mitchell, we gotta go." She gathered up as many bags as she could.

Inside the dumpster, Mitchell struggled. "Eleanor, I'm stuck. I can't get out."

The man was walking her way. "Get out of here, you scamp."

Eleanor's heart was beating. She dropped the bags and reached down. "Mitchell, grab my hands."

He tried but was too short.

She looked at the man. He was closer, and the other one was coming too. "Hurry."

"I can't reach it."

"Over there." She pointed to the side. "The garbage is higher there. Can you grab the side?"

Mitchell struggled to make his way there.

"Jump."

He did and clung to the side.

She reached down and grabbed his wrists. The man was now only forty feet away. She pulled him, and he scrambled onto the loading dock. "Quick, grab those bags."

"Stop. You're trespassing," yelled the man, now twenty feet away.

They each scooped up a pile and ran to the edge and jumped.

Several men from inside the building ran onto the loading dock.

"Catch them," ordered the man.

Eleanor and Mitchell ran as fast as they could, dropping a few of the bags. They ran between the two buildings; the sound of men's footsteps pounding behind them. At the street, they turned and ran south, then dived between two other buildings.

The men had given up their chase, and the two leaned against a brick wall, panting.

"That was scary," Mitchell said.

"But look at all the bags we got?" Eleanor was holding up a bag. "24 1/2 lbs. Pataha Flour Mills Bleached Fancy Patent XXX Flour 'A Flour for Particular People' Houser & Son Pomeroy, Washington." She folded it and stuffed it into another bag. "Where is Pomeroy, Washington?"

Mitchell peered into one of his sacks. "I don't know, but this one has some flour still in it."

They headed home with their loot.

"I think we have enough here to back all three quilts."

Mitchell was quiet, then he asked, "How are we going to explain these to Mother?" his voice was full of worry. "I think we should tell her the truth."

Guilt tugged at Eleanor. He was right, but she feared the trouble she would get into.

TWENTY-FOUR

WILLIAM AND FATHER TRUDGED across the Monroe Street bridge; the wind bit at their exposed faces; the wool coats Shannon and Eleanor had sewn from blankets provided minimal protection from the cold. They made their way through town and trudged up the South Hill where they daily looked for work among the large homes of businessmen, lawyers, doctors, and those who were faring better during the Depression.

The rose bushes were trimmed back and gardens cleaned out; so they held little hope of bringing home unwanted squash or green tomatoes. Most of the work they found now involved shoveling sidewalks and driveways, chopping wood, and filling coal chutes.

They parted ways, each going to the neighborhood where they'd found semi-steady work. William spent the morning chopping wood for Clara's neighbor, Mrs. Jacobson, who always invited him in to warm himself by the fire and served him soup, bread, and tea with a cookie or three.

"I noticed that young Miss Turner watching you from her room," Mrs. Jacobson mentioned as they ate lunch.

William blushed.

"She is quite the plucky gal."

"She's a bearcat—a swell bearcat."

Mrs. Jacobson smiled. "I think you two are good for each other."

He looked up at her grandfather clock. "I'd better get going. Mrs. Turner needs my help this afternoon."

Mrs. Jacobson pulled several coins from her purse. "Thank you for all your help and for taking time to converse with an old lady."

"You're not an old lady, and I enjoy our conversations. You've lived a very interesting life."

She squeezed his hand.

Across the street, Mrs. Turner had several evergreens leaning up against the front porch. She had him trim the lower boughs off two large trees and carry them into the home. This was the first time Mrs. Turner allowed William inside, and he was careful not to track in snow or break anything.

Mrs. Turner guided him to set up a tree in the parlor and another in the large dining room.

"Can William help us string the Christmas lights?" Clara asked. "You know how much Father hates it."

Mrs. Turner looked at the task. "That he does. Do you mind, William?"

"No. I don't mind at all."

Clara smiled.

He retrieved boxes and boxes of lights and other decorations from the Turners' attic. Clara opened box after box while her mother disappeared into the kitchen.

Clara handed him a string of colored lights, which he wound around the top of the tree, then passed back to her.

"Is this alright?"

"Ab-so-lute-ly," she smiled back at him and batted her dark eyelashes.

He grinned.

"You know, Will," her voice was low. "I could stare at those dimples of yours all day long."

He blushed, and she giggled.

Together they draped first the lights and then foiled garland around the trees, then hung the blown glass ornaments.

William stepped back and looked at the tree. "That is one swell looking tree."

"Doesn't it sparkle like ice?"

"Ab-so-lute-ly!" His face flushed as the desire to wrap his arm around her surfaced, and he busied himself with an ornament.

"Have you decorated your tree?" Clara asked, her eyes twinkling brighter than the lights.

William paused, knowing there wouldn't be a tree this year; not wanting to lie, but reluctant to explain the reason. He'd never told Clara where he lived, for fear of how she'd respond. "No, we haven't put one up yet."

"What do you want for Christmas?"

The room seemed to grow hotter with every question. He shrugged. "The usual."

Clara put a hand on her hip. "Oh, aren't you elusive?"

"You know, guy stuff, tools—" What would he have wanted if they weren't poor? He hoped she wasn't planning to give him a gift. He avoided the question as he always did by asking her what she wanted.

"Oh, you know, the usual." A coy smile spread across her painted lips.

"Let me guess, jewelry and furs?" He wished he could buy her a beautiful fur muff or necklace like he'd seen displayed in store windows. He thought about the few coins he'd held back from his odd jobs. Did he have enough to buy Clara a gift?

She handed him another ornament, and he noticed, really noticed, her store-bought dress and thick stockings. She had so much, and his family was cold and hungry. How could he justify a necklace?

She smiled at him, and her deep brown eyes twinkled. How he'd love to see those eyes dance with joy at a gift he'd given her. Why was he toying with her? She was way out of his league.

Eleanor pulled the emerald green stocking cap she'd knitted over her ears and rolled over in the top bunk to watch Father start the fire in the small cookstove, though it did little to heat the shanty. His frame had grown thin, as had everyone's, and his usually round cheeks were hollow.

Ice covered the windows, and there was frost on the inside of the walls. How she missed the warmth of their log home. Why hadn't Father built the shanty out of logs? But then, where would he get them?

Her stomach ached with hunger, as it did all the time. She used to dream of the fat, fluffy pancakes, bacon, and canned fruit with cottage cheese Mother made on the farm. But now, those thoughts only made her grouchy, so she tried to think of the good things they had—like the bed and Lilly's small but warm body pressed against hers.

She snuggled under the two quilts, thankful for the army blankets Father and William had purchased. She had helped Mother sew them inside the quilts, creating soft, warm coverings they wrapped up in during the day.

From the left-over pieces of Father's and William's coats, she and Mother had patched together a coat the twins took turns wearing.

Unfortunately, they'd run out of money to buy more wool blankets, so Mother and the other children rarely went outside except for water or firewood.

Only Lilly was moderately warm. She'd received her cousin's old coat, boots, and several dresses.

Though they were collecting more feed sacks, their fingers were too numb to sew anything, so they hung them over the windows or stopped up cracks in the walls.

It had become so cold Mother forbade them to go to school. Instead, Mother and Eleanor would quiz the twins and Lilly on their schoolwork. Then, they would all climb in bed and Eleanor would read to them from under the covers until the letters and words blurred on the page. They spent most of their days in bed to conserve candle wax and firewood.

At night, the wind howled. When would all this end, so they could live in a normal home with plenty of food, heat, and candles? Now that they lived in town, would they someday have a home with electricity? That seemed like too much of a luxury to wish for.

Eleanor often went to sleep imagining a spacious home like the ones on the South Hill near Rose. In her imagination, she sat reading and sipping hot cocoa in front of a huge fireplace with a toasty fire burning.

Eleanor loved this dream. She dozed, the smell of smoke and the snap, snap, pop of the fire more real than usual. Outside, children called to one another as they played in the snow.

Beside her, Lilly's voice cut through the fantasy. "I smell smoke."

"I do too," Mitchell said.

Eleanor forced her eyes open, and fear seized her.

Lilly now sat up in their top bunk, letting precious heat out, and pointed toward the east wall. "What's that orange light?"

TWENTY-FIVE

"FIRE!" FATHER JUMPED OUT of bed and grabbed his boots. "Someone's shanty's on fire."

Eleanor jolted up at Father's words, her heart huge in her chest.

"Oh, Lord, not again," Mother exclaimed. "Children, get up. Get dressed."

Eleanor scrambled down from her bunk above the boys and helped Lilly down.

"William. Come. Get your coat and grab the buckets."

At the door, Teddy was barking.

"Charles, how close is it?" Mother pulled her dress on over her nightgown. "Hurry children."

The smell of smoke was thick in the air, and from outside came shouts for water and the sound of children crying.

Eleanor's hands trembled as she buttoned her dress, then helped dress Lilly.

"I'm scared," Lilly's words were almost a whisper.

"It will be fine." But Eleanor wondered at that. Would it? It may just be a neighbor's shanty, but it could spread to others. To all of them. They must try to save all they could. It was winter. They couldn't lose their home again. They would die in the cold. Would Aunt Fiona take them in if it was winter?

Father and William left, each with a bucket. The twins stared out the window by the stove. "The shanty behind us is on fire," Raymond announced.

Mother wrapped a quilt around herself. "How close are they?" She hurried to the window. "I don't like it. I don't like it at all." She turned and looked about the shanty, its one room illumined from the fire outside and a candle Eleanor had lit.

"Should we pack stuff up?" Eleanor asked.

"Yes." She turned to the window. "Boys. Put on all the clothes you can, and pile everything else in your bedding. Then fold it up."

Eleanor was already stacking food and supplies on the table.

"Where are we going?" Mitchell asked.

"Hopefully nowhere. But if that fire spreads, we're fleeing. When you're done, do the same with your sisters' bed and mine. Lilly, come help me and your sister pack the food and dishes."

"Yes, Mother."

They piled dishes inside the Dutch Oven skillet and packed cups, bowls, silverware and food inside flour bags.

The noise outside quieted some, and Mitchell ran to look out the window. "The fire's almost out."

They gathered around the window and stared at the dim silhouettes of men standing around what now looked like a wide and dwindling campfire.

Shannon slumped to a chair, weeping.

"Mama," Lilly took Shannon's hand. "What's wrong?"

Shannon looked up. All four children stood around her. "I was so scared." She started crying again. "I...I..." She pulled the children into her, and they each hugged her. Eleanor soaked up the unexpected affection.

Father and William entered and looked about at the disarray, and their family gathered together. "Well, we got it put out. Several men are working to finish it."

"Was anyone hurt?"

"By the grace of God, no."

Shannon closed her eyes and sighed. "Where are they staying?"

"Marcus said he's done with this cold weather. They're catching the midnight train to San Francisco."

"Were they able to save anything?"

"The clothes on their backs."

Shannon stood and started rummaging through the crates. She pulled out a flour sack and added some apples and biscuits. "Eleanor, get me four hard-boiled eggs."

"Yes, Mother."

Shannon added some matches, newspapers, and a couple of potatoes. She handed the bag to Charles. "Give them this. I hope it helps."

Charles took it and kissed her forehead. "You're still the angel I met in my mother's kitchen nineteen years ago."

Eleanor smiled to see a glimpse of the woman her mother used to be.

TWENTY-SIX

CHRISTMAS 1931

"HURRY, GET UP," SHANNON'S voice was loud and shrill in the dark, early morning hour.

Eleanor jolted up in bed, her heart racing.

"Quick, grab the plates, get the silver. Now. We must get out, now," Shannon's voice rose. "Oh, Charles, the milk can, yesterday's pay. We must grab it. The walls, they are burning. Why? I know I put out the cook flame. Children, hurry. Get your clothes. Oh, Charles. Our beautiful home!"

"Shannon." Charles gently shook his wife. "Shannon, wake up. It's just a dream. Just a bad, bad dream."

Eleanor lay on the top bunk listening to her parents in the dark. She knew from past exchanges what would come next.

"No. No. Charles, the—" Shannon mumbled something through sobs. "There, there."

Eleanor watched him soothe Mother. His large hands caressed her long, red ringlets.

"It's just a bad dream."

"No, it's not. Look around you," her mother sobbed. "It's real. The fire was real."

"Yes, it was. But we are all safe."

"Safe but starving."

"Every day we eat. Maybe not a lot, but every day we eat."

"When will it end, Charles? How long will we be hungry and cold? When will our bellies be full every day? When will we live in an actual home? Why has God forsaken us?"

There was silence. Eleanor lay there, considering Mother's questions—always the same questions. Ever since the neighbors' shanty burned down, Mother awoke one or more times a night with nightmares. Every time, Father worked to comfort her and answer her questions as best he could. Yet as the days turned into weeks, Father's responses came slower and slower. This, more than Mother's nightmares, frightened her.

Today was Christmas. Father had tried to hide it from them, knowing there would be no treats. But Eleanor had secreted away some flour, sugar and a few other ingredients with plans to bake a simple coffee cake. She hoped it would be special and make up for the reduced egg supply.

Just last week, someone had tried to steal some chickens before Father could let Teddy out to chase them away. Because of the poor light and extreme cold, the chickens didn't lay many eggs. Eleanor knew frightened chickens would lay less.

She looked around the dismal shanty and wished for something more to cheer her family up. Should she cook a chicken for dinner? A hen that had stopped laying eggs? If she stewed it and made noodles, then everyone might not be as hungry.

After the breakfast dishes were washed, Father announced he and William had a surprise. Father had everyone close their eyes and William placed a small piece of paper in each person's outstretched hand.

Eleanor smiled at the small gift. "Thank you." She slipped the piece of penny candy into her mouth and savored its sweetness. This was more than she'd expected. "Father, maybe you could play a song or two on your harmonica?"

"Yes, Father, please," chimed in her siblings.

"I suppose I could do that, but you all need to sing along."

Eleanor smiled. It was good to have Father and William home with them.

The harmonica vibrated a few notes and joined by voices outside the shanty singing, "We wish you a Merry Christmas, we wish you a Merry Christmas..."

Father put down his instrument. "Shannon, go see who it is."

Mother stood and tightened the blanket around her before opening the door.

"Merry Christmas!" shouted Rose, Marguerite, Liam, and Shirley.

"Oh, Rose!" Shannon embraced her.

Rose and her friends hurried in, wearing second-hand wool coats, and home-made hats, scarves, and mittens. Liam carried in a heavy wooden crate, while Marguerite and Shirley each had a colorful bag of flour and rice. Rose clung to two lumpy, red calico patterned bags.

The children jumped with glee; even Eleanor forgot her age and joined in the excitement. Only William refrained from a joyous response.

Shannon smiled at the surprise of seeing Rose. "Oh, sit down. All of you."

Rose threw her arms around her mother. "Hugs first."

"You just missed breakfast," Father said. "And I'm afraid this hungry crew ate all the delicious coffee cake Eleanor made."

Warmth spread throughout Eleanor at Father's compliment.

Rose smiled at her sister. "Look who's becoming the little housekeeper."

After some tea and small talk, Rose and her friends shared the gifts they'd brought. Besides the flour and rice, there was a bag of plump Idaho potatoes, carrots, salt, sugar, spam, butter, and several cans of beans.

The family stared at the food. There would be a Christmas meal after all.

"I know it's not a lot—" Rose began.

Mother hugged her and ran a hand across her daughter's cheek. "Oh, Rose."

Father put an arm around her. "It's such a generous gift, especially when you're saving up to return to Johnny."

Rose bit her lip and looked at her feet. "Actually, I don't know if I'm going back to Bonners Ferry." She paused, and Marguerite reached up and squeezed Rose's hand. Rose stifled a sob. "I don't know if I'm going to marry Johnny."

They all looked at her in surprise. "Why not?"

A seed of excitement grew inside Eleanor, and she sneaked a look at Liam.

Rose swallowed hard. "Johnny..." She blinked away tears and took a deep breath. "Johnny hasn't written me in a while." A tear slipped down her cheek, though she attempted a brave face.

William folded his arms. "Hooey! It means nothing. Fellows don't like writing."

Rose shook her head. "He hasn't written in months."

They all stood in silence, surprised by this new information. Eleanor ached for Rose. Since they had been little girls, Rose had loved Johnny. She had always assumed that Rose and Johnny would marry.

Mother's shoulders slumped, and she pulled Rose to her. They hugged for several moments before Rose straightened.

"Well, I didn't come to have you all get sad. And I didn't come to just bring food. Though there is one more treat." She opened one of the lumpy bags and pulled out a tin of sugar cookies cut in the shapes of stars, bells, trees, and even reindeer with colored sugar sprinkled over them.

Her younger siblings leaned in. "Oh, ah."

"Can we have one?" Lilly asked.

"Of course, you can."

They passed the bright red and green tin around, and everyone savored the sweet treat.

Then, one-by-one, Rose pulled out small brightly wrapped bundles, read the name on the tag and handed them out. "Go ahead, open them," she said, once everyone had theirs.

Raymond and Lilly quickly ripped open the paper; while the rest carefully untied their packages. Inside, each family member had received a pair of woolen mittens.

"Marguerite helped me knit those. She'd knit a pair for my family, then a pair for Shirley's family."

Eleanor's were from the same emerald green yarn she'd used for her hat. Already her fingers were warmer; she knew she'd be wearing them inside the shanty.

Everyone thanked Rose and hugged her.

"I'm sorry I have nothing for you," Eleanor whispered in her sister's ear.

"That's fine. I know you would if you could. Getting to see you all was enough for me—" She paused and looked at her family with their gaunt frames wrapped in quilts. Her gaze shifted to the ice caked window panes and frost on the inside walls of the shanty. "I know you're here, helping care for them when I can't." Her eyes welled with tears. "Thank you. Keep at it. I love you."

Eleanor returned her hug. "I love you, too."

Rose looked at her friends, and they all stood.

"Must you leave already?" Mother asked, as the sparkle in her eyes dimmed.

"Yes. We still need to drop off food and mittens for Shirley's family; then I need to get back and fix dinner for Aunt Fiona and Uncle Harry."

Everyone said their goodbyes. Mother hugged Rose last. As Rose pulled away from the embrace, she removed the too-big blue wool coat that Aunt Fiona had given her and wrapped it around Mother's shoulders. "Here, Mother. Merry Christmas."

"No, Rose. You need—"

Rose put a finger to her mother's lips. "No Mother, you need it." And she was gone.

Mother ran her hands over the blue wool coat. "I shouldn't have accepted this. What will Rose wear to keep warm?"

"She'll be fine, Shannon."

"You think?"

"I know," Father said.

She snuggled into the coat's warmth. "For the first time in a long time, I feel like a lady and not a vagabond," she said to no one in particular. She turned to Eleanor. "And look, these mittens match the hat you knit me."

Eleanor smiled and picked up the ten-pound bag of rice. "I'd better get these provisions put away."

Mother picked up the bag of flour. "Let me help you."

William stood. "I'm gett'n some wood."

"Can I come?" Raymond asked.

"No."

"How come?"

"'Cause I said. Now beat it." William slammed the door behind him, and the shanty rattled.

Everyone was silent for a moment.

Eleanor considered how he'd responded when Rose and her friends arrived with the gifts. Something was definitely bothering him. He hadn't been his normal self lately.

"What's wrong with Willy?" Lilly asked.

Father looked at the closed door. "Your brother just needs some time alone." He picked up an old newspaper he'd found and read some articles out loud. After about a half hour, there was a scratching at the door.

"There's Willy," Lilly said, and opened the door. "Ew. Teddy, yuck!"

Eleanor turned to see Teddy stride into the shanty and lay a dead rabbit by the stove.

They all stared in surprise.

"Even Teddy's brought a Christmas gift," Eleanor remarked.

Mother patted him on the head. "Good dog. You keep the rats away and now you've brought us some Christmas meat." She turned to the others. "Looks like we'll be having rabbit stew for dinner."

Father patted Teddy on the head and took the offering. "Come along boys, let's skin this."

"Can I try tanning the hide?" Mitchell asked.

"Sure."

Eleanor wondered how William would respond to Teddy's contribution.

William pulled his wool coat around himself and looked at the mittens Rose had given him. His hands warmed for the first time since working inside Clara's house. "It's not fair," he mumbled to himself. "Father and I work hard, and all we can give them is penny candy, while Rose lives in that nice warm house and comes with food and mittens and even gives Mother a coat."

He thought about the money he'd set aside to buy Clara a gift. In the end, it wasn't enough, and he'd given it to Father for food.

He wandered to the river and threw a small rock into the cold water. How could there be any rocks left? He'd thrown so many in already.

A train rumbled by, and he glanced up to see men closing boxcar doors. What if he left? Rode the rails to California? He took a step toward the train and then another. Would he find work there or just be one of many other hungry men? The train picked up speed.

He stopped and watched it pull away.

A blast of icy wind sent a shiver through him, and he headed to the ever-shrinking thicket Raymond had gotten lost in those early weeks in Spokane. Several other men also collected firewood.

He chopped at anything he hoped would burn.

"Finding any?"

He looked up to see Father.

"Not much left," William grumbled.

"I imagine not."

William tossed a branch to the ground.

"You're feeling outdone, aren't you?"

"It's not fair." He voiced his earlier feelings and looked down at his navy-blue mittens.

"Yes, it seems that way. But who provided the roof we have over our head, the chicken feed, heck-the chickens? Who provided the food we've been eating and the blankets Eleanor and your mother used in the quilts and make our coats out of?"

"It just seems like so little."

"I know. But every bit helps. These are hard times. We need to persevere. We're all doing our part, some in small ways every day, some in bigger ways occasionally."

"I guess."

"Come on, let's bring this wood back and rekindle the stove. Teddy's contributed a rabbit to our Christmas dinner, and your mother and sister are making stew."

William snapped a twig in two. "So, Teddy brought a rabbit?" A faint smile tugged at his lips. "Yea, I guess you're right. It's hard to see the efforts of all we do, but we're all alive."

Father nodded.

TWENTY-SEVEN

JANUARY 1932

ELEANOR AWOKE TO THE mid-January wind howling, forcing cold, and bits of sharp ice and snow through even the smallest cracks in the shanty walls.

She pulled the quilt tight against her shivering body. She hadn't bothered to remove her dress the night before, hoping the thicker material would keep her warm. Her toe wiggled at the hole in her stocking. She pulled her hat down as far as it would go, and inside her mittens, she rubbed her fingers against her palms, attempting to warm them.

She was sure it was her mother's frantic, nightmare induced cries that drew her up from her sleep. She looked to the window, but the ice glazed panes denied the morning light entrance.

There was no reason to get up. They'd eaten almost all the rest of their food from the night before in a meal of rice soup flavored with the meager gelatin from the empty spam can and weak tea. She was so tired and dreaded checking the chicken coop. The chickens, too, were cold, hungry and not laying eggs. They'd already butchered all but two, and Eleanor was sure she could eat a whole chicken all by herself. Soon, the chickens would be gone. Then what would they eat?

She dozed off, but awoke again to harsh whispers.

"I can't watch this, Charles. I can't watch them starve. You must do something."

"Shannon, I'm trying. There's no work! I've even tried selling the truck, but no one has money."

"Then do what the Hills did," Mother whispered.

Eleanor stopped shivering and turned her head to see her parents' bed. She strained to hear their hushed conversation. Had Mother said to do what the Hills did? She leaned over the bed and looked down at her brothers. The twins, like Lilly, were sleeping, but William looked up at her with hurt in his eyes.

Her chest tightened.

Do what the Hills did. The Hills lived in the shanty two doors down. They had three children and no food. Last week, while Mrs. Hill sobbed and tried following her husband through thick snow in thin shoes and with a cloth wrapped around her thin dress, Mr. Hill took the children to the children's home.

Eleanor tried to swallow, but her mouth was dry. She was so weak and cold and hungry, yet she couldn't imagine an orphanage could be any better.

"I can't bear to watch this," whispered her mother. "We're all going to die—here in our beds—we'll starve to death, and someone will find our frozen bodies in the spring."

Tears streamed down Eleanor's face, but turned cold and stung her dry, windblown skin.

Charles sat up. "Shannon, please, please, don't lose hope. We'll get some food and make it through this. We need to stay together. What has happened to the strong woman I married?"

"Gone."

"Where?"

"You know."

"No, I don't."

"Burned up in the fire—and anything left withered away with the hunger, wind, and cold."

"Shannon, please," Father's voice cracked with desperation and hurt. "Please, Shannon. I need you to hold on."

Fear crept throughout Eleanor's limbs and the voice inside whispered, "You're dying."

"I need you—"

"I can't," Shannon whispered.

Eleanor strained to hear her mother's words. Though they were painful, Eleanor was drawn to them like a hungry mouse to poisoned crumbs.

Shannon grabbed Charles' shirt. "I'm dying. Can't you see that? I want to know they are safe and warm and fed. Don't let me die knowing they will follow me."

"Shannon." He reached down and pulled her to him. "Shannon, no. Please. Please, don't give up. You can do this. We can do this."

She strained against him. "If you love me, you'll do what I ask."

He set her down gently, and she turned away.

Charles rose, and Eleanor closed her eyes and feigned sleep.

He pulled his trousers and shirt on over his long-johns, buttoned up his coat, and left the shanty without starting the stove.

As soon as he left, William and Eleanor wrapped themselves in whatever they could find and followed Father as he picked his way over slick, snow-covered rocks, headed to the river.

"Do you think he's going to the orphanage?" Eleanor whispered.

William cut between a few shanties, followed by Eleanor. "I don't know, but we can't let him see us."

They darted between clap-trap Hodge-Podge buildings, staying a hundred or more feet behind him. When they ran out of shanties to hide behind, they scurried to hide behind spindly bushes or large rocks. Father stopped, and they peered from behind a garbage pile.

"How can she do this? How can she give up?" His husky voice rang out in the frosty morning air, then mingled with the river's chatter.

Eleanor strained to hear him.

"Can't she see I'm trying?" he cried to the sky.

"Can you hear him?" Eleanor whispered.

William shook his head. "Barely, let's move closer."

"Where?"

William scanned the river bank before them. "Over there, to the side of him. You hide behind that rock and I'll hide behind the bush."

Eleanor nodded, and they crept closer, hoping he wouldn't see them.

"She could have helped," Charles continued. "Can't she see I need her? The children need her? How can I give them away? What am I supposed to do without her? Without them?"

Eleanor peeked around the rock.

Father lifted his face to the sky. "God, what am I supposed to do?" he yelled. "Can't you see how hard I'm working?"

He hung his head. "Was this all a mistake? Should we have stayed in Idaho? Should I have rebuilt the farm? How could I? I had no money. They stole it. Remember?" Great sobs racked his body.

The tears Eleanor had held back for so long came.

"Why?" he screamed. "Why did they have to steal it? Why did they have to burn it? Everything? Why? Why didn't you stop them?"

He stooped, picked up a rock, and hurled it. The rock flew nearly a hundred feet before falling near the opposite bank with a splash.

He glared up at the sky. "Do you really help those who help themselves? Do you? I don't know how we can try any harder. Do you even see all we're doing? Do you see my family starving? Freezing in that house made of scraps?" He turned back and glared at the shanty jungle before carrying on.

Eleanor and William ducked just in time.

"They say you love us," he continued. "Is this your idea of love? Is it? Making me watch my family die? Making me abandon my children to an orphanage? What kind of love is that? What am I supposed to do? Tell me!" he screamed at the sky. "I'm out of options."

An emptiness like she'd never known consumed her. She exchanged glances with William.

Father continued to walk along the river, but Eleanor and her brother trudged home. Quiet. Her father's words, "...abandon my children to an orphanage," played in her head.

The next several days were quieter and more somber than usual. They ate what little scraps of food they had, with Shannon and Charles refusing to eat anything. Charles and William looked for work and visited the soup kitchen, bringing the dry biscuits back for the children.

William called Eleanor outside late one evening. "Every day, Father tries selling the truck."

"No one wanted it, did they?"

"No." William shook his head.

Mother slept or lay in bed weeping. When she was awake, she would glare at Charles and ask him in strained whispers why he hadn't done as she asked. "Do you care that little for them?" she asked.

Father bit his lip and squeezed back the tears. "Give us one more day."

"Their deaths are on your head," she spat and rolled over in bed.

These conversations swirled about in Eleanor's mind, getting jumbled in her exhausted state. She tried sewing together some bags, but her fingers were numb and her eyes couldn't focus.

The next day brought no work. No money. No food. Charles and William stayed out later than usual, looking for work.

Eleanor and William scavenged for sticks. "Did you tell Father we know about the orphanage?"

William shook his head.

"Has Father said anything?" Eleanor asked, her words almost too heavy to speak.

"He tries to act as though nothing is different. He'll start talking, then stop, never finishing."

Eleanor wanted to cry, but it was too much work, so she stared at the barren ground.

The following morning, Charles got up early and started the fire. William climbed out of bed to join him.

"Go back to bed," Father ordered.

Eleanor watched her brother, so thin his clothes hung on him. William looked at their father, then crawled back under the quilts.

"There's no point in both of us getting cold. You stay here and mind the fire."

William nodded.

After a cup of weak coffee, Father donned his coat and left.

William hurried out of bed and put on his boots and coat.

"Where are you going?" Eleanor whispered.

"To see where he's going."

Eleanor's stomach ached when the door closed. She looked about their shanty. She looked at her mother and siblings. Trying to remember it all. She wondered if she would see her brothers and sisters at the orphanage? Would they be split up? Would they even take an eleven-year-old? How would they be treated?

Dread, mingled with sadness, weighed heavily on her. Would her parents come and visit them, or would they leave and go to California? She wanted so badly to tell Rose. Why hadn't she thought to run to Rose? Maybe she could help. Maybe Aunt Fiona would take them in rather than let them go to the orphanage. Would the orphanage take William? Or was he too old?

Her mind swirled with questions. She cried quietly into her pillow. She had tried so hard. Sewed quilts and clothes, raised chickens for eggs. Despite it all, it wasn't enough. She had failed.

After a while the door creaked open, and William came in, somber, and she could see he too had been crying—outside, in the early morning—where no one would see him.

"Where'd he go?"

William looked up at her on the bunk and pointed north. The direction of the children's home.

Eleanor tried to swallow the fear rising in her.

TWENTY-EIGHT

CHARLES TRUDGED NORTHEAST IN a zigzag pattern. He must go to the children's home. He'd put it off too long. No work. No food. No heat to speak of. Charles wasn't even sure how he would feed himself and Shannon.

They would be better off at the children's home with its thick brick walls and honest-to-goodness meals. He swallowed at the reminder of his failure. He would talk with the director. Make arrangements. The truck had no gas, and the children couldn't make the seven-mile walk. He wasn't sure he could. Surely, they could pick the kids up? He squeezed back the tears.

Despite what he told himself, he wandered in a daze and looked into the windows and doors of every building he passed. Just one sign—that's all he needed. A sign that someone was looking for workers. But many businesses were boarded up, and those that weren't hadn't opened yet.

Maybe, maybe if he wandered southeast, into a different neighborhood, he'd find work. He turned away from the children's home several miles away and made his way south, across a bridge, through downtown, and up South Perry. The town was so quiet this frosty January morning.

He stopped at a gas station but was turned away. The area was more residential. Smoke rose from chimneys and stove pipes of homes. Occasionally, he caught the scent of bacon in the air. His stomach ached.

A man dusted snow off his car.

Charles approached him. "Do you have any work? Please, my family is—"

"No." The man turned his back to Charles.

Charles turned and wandered on. He stopped at a small diner, two grocers, and another business that hadn't opened yet. Charles was cold and hungry and more discouraged than he'd ever been. He wandered down an alley and came upon a small store with the door ajar.

He knocked. "Hello, is anyone there?"

No answer.

"Hello?" He pushed it open and entered a butcher shop. Meat sat in chilled cases and behind them stood a walk-in freezer. He called.

Nothing. He opened the freezer. A side of beef hung along with a couple of pigs. His stomach growled; he licked his lips.

He looked out the open door. No one.

Charles stepped back into the butcher shop and looked around. Roasts, steaks, hamburger, stew meat, pork chops, bacon, and whole chickens sat waiting to be cooked and eaten.

His mouth watered. He took a step closer, then another. Maybe this was providence pointing the way. God might have seen how hard they tried to find work and was rewarding them. Maybe...

Charles shook his head. Thou shalt not steal. He could never eat that meat. And if he did, he'd retch it up. He'd never read the whole Bible, but he knew God didn't provide through stealing.

He walked out; locking the door behind him.

He'd walked only a few feet when a rough hand squeezed his shoulder and turned him around.

"Hey fella, what do you think you're doing?"

Charles stared at the burly man with muscular hands and a clean-shaven face. "I'm...I'm looking for work."

"Yeah, I saw you. Wandering around in my shop. Thought you could take some meat, did you?"

"No. I didn't take any."

"We'll see about that." The man grabbed the lapels of Charles' coat and ripped it open. The mismatched buttons popped off. Charles shivered as the man stared at his thin frame and patted him down. "What'd you do with it? Hide it so you could come back later?"

Charles shivered in the cold. "Nooo...I...I took nothing. I wanted to. But I couldn't. It's wrong. It's not who I am." He looked past the man to the shop. "I...I even locked the...the door." His teeth chattered in the cold.

The man glared at him, then with one hand on Charles' collar, he yanked him back to the butcher shop and tried the door. "Huh." He dug out a key and pulled Charles in. He examined the meat case and then the freezer.

"I didn't take a thing."

The butcher looked Charles up and down. "I don't know what's worse, a thief or a fool. Get out of here."

Charles pulled his coat around himself and left; stooping to pick up the buttons on his way.

"What's worse," he asked himself, "a thief or a fool?" He wandered past bungalows and simple two-story homes as he pondered the question. He didn't like either and had never thought of himself in those terms. Near the end of the block, the sound of singing rang out. Before him was a small, white church.

He rubbed his icy hands together and entered, if for no other reason than to find warmth. He slipped into the back pew near a coal stove and picked up a hymnal. His stiff fingers fumbled with the pages as people near him turned and glanced at him. An usher leaned in and whispered a page number. Charles nodded.

On the stage, a medium built man with stooped shoulders and white hair led a small choir in dark choir robes singing "Jesus, Savior Pilot Me." On the right side of the stage, a young blond girl about Eleanor's age played the piano, and on the left of the stage, a tall wiry man with broad shoulders and a dark suit with a white, clerical collar stood singing.

Charles mumbled along, trying to understand why these people were meeting today. Was it a holiday? Today was Friday, wasn't it?

"Now turn to responsive reading number thirty-seven, Enduring Life," said the cleric.

Charles turned to the back of the hymnal and found the reading. The pastor read the first line and all around him, people responded with the next line.

Was it Sunday? Charles looked down at his hands. They shook, more from hunger than cold. His trousers were baggier than just last week when he'd punched another hole in his belt to cinch it tighter. Maybe Shannon was right. Maybe she was dying, maybe they were all dying—slowly starving.

His breath caught in his throat and he choked back tears. He didn't want to make a scene. What day was it? When had he last eaten? There was the small meal he and William ate at the soup kitchen; both of them only eating the soup, each taking their small piece of bread home to be shared with the other five.

He was sure today was Saturday—but no, here were these people, dressed in their Sunday best, sitting in church, now singing another song.

"There is no shadow of turning with thee..."

He was dying. That was all there was to it. He had lost track of the days and was no longer thinking clearly. Shannon was right. He and his family were dying. Everything around him slowed.

"Thy compassions they fail not..."

What? What had they just sung? He flipped to the song; the page numbers listed on the side wall. "Thy compassions they fail not..."? He disagreed. What was compassionate about losing his home and livelihood? What was compassionate about his family starving and freezing to death?

"Morning by morning, new mercies I see. All I have needed thy hand hath provided..."

He shook his head. He'd tried to look on the bright side of things and work hard when given the opportunity. Hadn't he and William looked unceasing for employment?

Growing up, his father had taught him that God helps those who help themselves. Hadn't he done that? But what had it gotten him? Living in a freezing cold shanty, watching his family starve.

The singing stopped, and everyone sat down. Charles followed their lead.

"Good morning, friends." The pastor looked out over the congregation. His eyes met Charles', and he smiled. "Welcome. This is the day the Lord has made. Let us rejoice and be glad."

Heat radiated from the stove and for the first time in months, Charles felt warm. But with the warmth came a foul odor.

The people in front of him shifted, and someone glanced back at him.

"Please turn in your Bibles to first Peter chapter one. Calvin Olmsted is going to read for us."

A young boy of ten or eleven came to the podium.

There was a rustling of pages, and Charles bowed his head in shame. It had been over six months since the fire, and he'd never missed the family Bible. In it, he had listed his and Shannon's wedding date, and the birth date of each of his children. So much hope and excitement—but for what?

"Last week we talked about God's promise of a new birth into a lively hope," said the pastor. "This hope comes through the resurrection of Jesus from the dead. But let me ask: Is our hope just for this life?" He paused and looked out over the congregation. "No!" He pounded the pulpit in excitement.

"Through Jesus' death and resurrection, we have an inheritance waiting for us in heaven. And not an inheritance like any we can receive here on earth. No. This inheritance can never be defiled, corrupted, or fade away. It is permanent."

"Amen!" shouted a woman.

"Yes, Amen, sister Collins."

Charles tried to listen to the pastor, but the smell of his unwashed body and clothes distracted him. How long had it been since he or any of his family members had bathed or washed their clothes? Back on the farm, they bathed regularly, and Shannon would have never allowed the laundry to go even a few days without washing.

"That inheritance is kept in heaven for each of us who has believed in the sacrifice of Jesus' life on the cross, which he gave freely, to pay the price for our sins." The tall pastor, about ten years older than Charles, leaned in, his blue eyes bright with excitement, and looked again at Charles.

Charles shifted in his pew, sensing the man spoke to him and only him.

"We all rejoice in this salvation, though now, for a season, temptations, trials, and tribulations weigh us down."

There was a murmuring and shifting among the congregation as people agreed.

The reverend gripped both sides of the podium and leaned further toward his congregants. "Do not give up!"

Several in the pews nodded.

"Remember what is vital. Remember what lasts. These trials test our faith. Will it stand, or will it fall?"

Charles pondered the man's question. He'd never considered himself a very religious man. And if he was honest, what little faith he had was slipping through his fingers like the ash of his home and farm.

"Do you not know how precious your faith is? We value gold and place it as the standard. But I tell you that your faith is worth more than gold." His voice rose to a new level of enthusiasm.

"A goldsmith refines gold in a fire to remove the impurities. Similarly, the impurities of our faith are being removed through trials. But gold perishes and becomes nothing. Not so our faith; when refined by the troubles of this life, our faith will bring praise, honor, and glory when Jesus Christ is revealed." He paused and allowed his words to sink in.

"Amen, preach it brother," sister Collins shouted.

Several others nodded or murmured their agreement.

Charles sat stunned at the man's words. He, Charles Cruthers, could receive honor from God for his faith? Was that true? He had never put much stock in his faith.

Charles' stomach rumbled at the smell of ham, potatoes, beans.

He forced his mind back to the message and the song that said God does not turn from them, but shows mercy and compassion. Charles considered God untrue to those words. But could it be that he, Charles Cruthers, was the unfaithful one?

A familiar tune played on the piano.

The pastor spread his arms before him. "The altar is open for all who wish to pray and seek forgiveness for sins."

Everyone stood and sang, "Tell Me the Old, Old Story."

Charles stood too, intending to slip out before the service ended, but the pastor's words held him captive. He made his way to the front, hat in hand. The reverend smiled at him.

He knelt, and the hurt and grief of the past months gushed out like a beaver's dam blasted open with dynamite. Why did Shannon no longer walk by his side? Why did she leave him alone to contend for their family's survival? Loneliness and anger swelled along with grief, exhaustion, and failure. It all spilled forth.

"Oh, God! What have I done?" His words were a hoarse cry mingled with sobs he'd held inside since the fire. "I've tried so hard without you. I never sought you, but just pushed ahead." He paused and took a deep breath. His sobs were louder now; his chest heaved while voices sang around him.

"Oh, God, it was my pride. I leaned on me and not you. How could I have been such a fool?" He wiped his tears on his coat sleeve. His body shook.

A large, slender hand pressed gently on his back, and he sensed someone kneeling beside him, but he cared little about what people thought of him. He had to make things right. He had to lay this heavy weight down. His pride had stopped him from turning to God for help. Could he forgive himself? Could his family ever forgive him?

"Oh, God, I've been such a fool. God, I don't deserve it, but please, please, can you at all forgive me? Please, look after and care for my family," he paused. "Please, provide for them where I have failed." He continued to weep even as the choir director dismissed the congregants, and around him respectful whispers and shuffling feet faded.

"God has forgiven you, my friend."

Charles pressed his lips together and looked at the preacher kneeling beside him. "I...I..." More sobs.

The man reached a long arm around Charles' shoulders and comforted him. "Grief is the pressure valve of the soul. You must release the hurt and pain or it will destroy you. Woe to the man who refuses to grieve. Grieve my brother. Grieve, wail, and mourn, for God blesses those who grieve and shall provide comfort."

For the first time in months, maybe even years, Charles didn't feel alone. The man introduced himself as Reverend Jake Hamilton. By pieces and in broken sentences intermingled with tears, moans, and sobs, Charles shared how he had tried to provide for his family without asking for God's help.

"You are not alone, my brother. Many of us, especially of our sex, have bought the lie that God helps those who help themselves."

Charles picked at the hole where a button once was.

"God does not encourage laziness, but He expects us to humble ourselves and seek after Him."

Charles stared at his dry, cracked hands. Why had he been so late in learning this?

"The same holds true for salvation," Hamilton said. "Many feel they must work to earn it, but nothing could be farther from the truth."

"You mean my goodness doesn't get me to heaven?"

"There is no way we can ever do enough to save ourselves from our sins."

Concern loomed up in Charles. "Then what are we to do?"

"Lean fully on the grace of God and His gift."

"Gift?"

"Yes. His gift of salvation. Think of your sin as an enormous debt that you can never repay."

Charles listened.

"No matter how hard you work, you could never, in a million years, earn enough money to pay off your debt." Reverend Hamilton looked at Charles, who nodded.

"God knew we were incapable of ever paying the debt our sin produced, so He provided a way out. He sent His son, Jesus Christ, to pay the debt for us. Jesus took the punishment our sins deserve—a punishment that is so severe, it requires death."

Charles rubbed his stubble. "You mean he allowed himself to be killed to pay my debt?"

"He did."

"But why? What did I ever do to deserve that?"

"Nothing. It has nothing to do with anything you or I or anyone else has ever done or could ever do. It is who God is."

"I don't understand."

"God is love, and it is because of His great love for us that He saves us."

"So, God saves everyone?" Charles asked.

Hamilton shook his head. "No. Only those who accept His gift of salvation."

"How do I do that?"

"Romans 10:9 says, 'That if thou shalt confess with thy mouth the Lord Jesus, and shalt believe in thine heart that God hath raised him from the dead, thou shalt be saved.'"

Charles pondered this, then turned to the pastor. "Can you help me?"

A wide smile spread across Jake Hamilton's lips. "I'd love to."

When they finished praying, Jake invited Charles downstairs to join their pot luck.

A mixture of emotions, including exhaustion, tugged at Charles as he and Reverend Hamilton entered the church basement to join the others for lunch. The sight of so much food still available, even though everyone else was already eating, cheered him up.

A lovely woman at least a foot shorter than Reverend Hamilton approached them, along with the young girl who'd played the piano.

Jake extended his hand to the woman. "Mr. Cruthers, I'd like you to meet my wife, Olivia, and my daughter, Eva."

Charles shook their hands and thanked them for inviting him to join them. "I must admit, I feel guilty for partaking of this wonderful food while my family—" He paused and looked to the ground.

Jake pressed his hand into Charles' back. "No need to feel bad. We have plenty and will pack some up for you to take home."

Charles kneaded the rim of his hat. "Oh, I didn't mean to—"

"No, I insist. We have plenty and consider it a privilege to share."

"Thank you. You don't know how much this means to us."

Jake and Olivia both smiled.

Charles turned to Eva. "That was some mighty fine piano playing this morning."

"Thank you."

"I have a daughter about your age."

"Does she play any instruments?"

"She used to play the piano back home. But not anymore."

Jake and Olivia made sure Charles had two large plates of food. He measured his intake, not wanting to be sick. After the meal and much conversation, people gathered their dishes and children and headed home. As Olivia helped several women clean up the kitchen, Jake inquired about Charles, his work skills, and family.

Charles talked about his children and Shannon before her sadness set in, but skirted the issue that brought them to Spokane.

Jake stood. "How about I give you a ride home?"

Charles looked toward the door, remembering again why he had left the shack. "I would like that, but I have an errand I need to attend to."

"On a Sunday?"

Charles sighed and the familiar grief he'd been battling came back. "I suppose Sunday is not the best day for it." He could already see the look in Shannon's eyes. Had she lost all respect for him?

The church fellowship hall was empty and tables and dishes washed. Olivia approached. "Jake, Eva and I are going back to the parsonage. There are several crates of food in the kitchen."

Jake nodded.

Olivia held out her hand to Charles. "It was nice meeting you. I hope we'll see you again." She smiled. "Please bring your family. I'd love to meet them and I know Eva would love to meet your daughter."

Charles only nodded; he had trusted God too late. By next Sunday, his family would no longer be together.

TWENTY-NINE

Late Tuesday afternoon, Jake returned to the Cruthers' shanty, this time with blankets, socks, sweaters, and even coats for the twins and Eleanor. He also had firewood and more food—mostly staples this time.

Charles looked at Jake's gifts. "I can't accept all this."

"The people in our congregation care deeply for the plight many find themselves in these days. I actually come down here every Wednesday. I just rarely get this far in before I've given away the supplies I've brought."

Charles nodded. "Can we go outside and talk?"

Outside, both men pulled their coats tighter around themselves to ward off the bitter wind.

"What can you tell me about the Hutton home and the Spokane Children's Home?"

Sadness settled on Jake's countenance. "Is that what you're considering?"

"Yes," Charles' whisper lasted only a moment before the wind carried it away; his eyes were already watery.

"You don't really want to give your kids away."

Charles bit his lip. "Of course not. But they're starving to death and with those thin walls—" He thrust his thumb at the shanty. "It won't be long until we all die from pneumonia or starvation." Charles looked down at his dry, cracked hands. "I've always provided well for my family. We used to have a large home and dairy farm. We worked it together..." He stopped, unable to continue.

Jake let Charles compose himself.

"We lost it all."

"In the crash?"

Charles shook his head. "No, in a fire..."

As he listened to Charles relate the events of that day, Jake's blue eyes clouded with grief.

Teddy, thin and bedraggled, came around the shanty, a rat in his mouth. Charles pointed at him. "Somehow, Teddy got away and made his way home." The image of Teddy, not much worse than now, flashed through his mind. "We almost missed him. Made one last stop at the homestead before heading here. The kids saw him along the roadside."

Teddy ate his catch.

"Shannon had already sunk into her sadness and resented another mouth to feed. Maybe we should have given him away, but how could we? We'd already lost so much. He's also been a great protector."

The minister shook his head. "I'm so sorry, my brother. I'm always astonished at how selfish and cruel people can be to one another."

The sun was setting, splashing deep pink in the sky, and the wind had calmed.

"I know this may seem like a cruel question, but have you forgiven those men who did this to you?"

Charles stiffened at Jake's question. "How can I? All I feel is this growing hatred toward them as I see my family suffer. Taking the money would have been bad enough. But to burn down our home? To destroy our livelihood? How could they?"

"I don't know why they had to destroy your home and barn. My guess is jealousy, wanting to cover their tracks, or just plain cruelty. But holding on to your anger and hate will only eat you up. I've seen it too many times, especially since the market crash." He gestured at the surrounding shanties that had crowded around them.

Charles clenched his fist and squinted at what was now his family's home. "They don't deserve to be forgiven."

"None of us do. But not forgiving them does nothing to hurt them. It gives them more power." He let his words sink in.

"More power." Charles nodded. The past six months had aged him. "I never hated anyone. I never even felt anger the way I have since all this happened. At first, I thought we could overcome this, treat it as an adventure; teach my kids how to handle adversity, work hard." He shook his head. "Back home in the mountains of Idaho, I had no idea that things were this bad." He looked again at his shanty and the empty chicken coop.

"I don't want to take my children..." Charles lowered his head. "I'm trying to trust God. I really am. The food and supplies help. But we've been down this road before. William and I find work for a few days, and we buy food, or someone—like our daughter—gives us food, and we eat for a few days or maybe even a couple of weeks. But eventually it runs out, and we're left eating one, maybe two meager meals a day."

Charles could no longer hold back the tears. "We're dying, Jake. We're all slowly dying." He paused. "Shannon begged me over a week ago to take the children so they wouldn't die. But I couldn't. I don't know if it was my pride or unwillingness to let go of them." He turned his face away from several people walking past. "But now we're thinner, closer to death—" He swallowed. "And now I've also lost Shannon's respect." His voice cracked, and he covered his face with his hands.

Jake put his long, slender hand on Charles' shoulder. "Oh, my brother."

A hawk flew overhead.

"I want to trust God; I really am trying. But how is this any different from previous times? What if the orphanage is God's way of providing for my family?"

"Well, I believe God led you to the church and us for a reason," Jake said. "You've repented of your sin and corrected your thinking. You now have food and extra clothes and blankets. And I won't stop there. I'll continue to help you, as will our congregation."

Charles stared at the ground.

A train rattled past.

Jake pointed at the chicken coop. "I see you had chickens."

Charles forced a smile. "That was Eleanor's idea. We had eggs for quite a while. But now it's too cold and dark for them to lay eggs, and people kept trying to steal them. We were so hungry we ate them."

Jake listened patiently.

"What we really need is work. Without work, we're never going to stay fed. It's just a patch on the hole in our bellies."

Jake nodded.

"Work can also provide decent lodging," Charles continued.

Jake rubbed his chin. "I'm sure the orphanage is an option for some. But like I said, God brought you to us for a reason. There's plenty of food for the next week, and I'll bring you more. I can also get some lumber to help thicken those walls. But most importantly, I know lots of people. Let me see what I can do to find you and your boy work."

Charles sighed. "That would all be great, especially the work. I warn you, we've searched high and low."

Jake nodded. "I don't doubt it. Sometimes it's not what you know, but who you know."

Charles cast him a sideways glance. "You sound like my wife."

Eleanor tried on the new-to-her coat that Reverend Hamilton had given her. It was a little small, but immediately blocked out the cold better than the quilt she usually wrapped herself in.

She and William slipped out the door and hid around the side of the shanty, listening to Father and Reverend Hamilton talk.

She teared at Father's words that they were all dying. Mother had said the same thing nearly a week ago. She wanted so much to believe it wasn't true.

When the pastor left, Eleanor and William headed to the river to talk. "Do you think Father will still take us to the orphanage?" Eleanor asked.

"Maybe not right away, but eventually."

"But the pastor said he'll provide us with food—"

"Right now, but like Father said, it never lasts."

"But he said he'd help you and Father get jobs."

William shrugged. "I'll believe it when we're working."

Eleanor was quiet.

"I'm not going to any orphanage," William blurted.

Eleanor stared at her brother. "We're not going to an orphanage. You heard Father and the Reverend."

"Not now. But if we run out of food again..."

Eleanor swallowed. She hoped that wouldn't happen. That maybe, this time, things would be different. "If you don't go to the orphanage..." her voice was weak and her words halting. "What will you do?"

"Run away. Catch a train and ride the rails."

Eleanor stared at him. "What—? Ride the rails! Where?"

"California."

"Why?"

"It's warm and I hear there are fields and fields of farms. I can go from farm-to-farm working."

"But—?" She struggled to breathe. "I don't want to lose you."

The anger in his eyes softened, and he straightened her coat collar. "It hasn't happened yet. Who knows—maybe this preacher fellow will come through." He smiled at her. "You like your new coat?"

She smiled and snuggled into it. "It's warm."

He nodded. "So is this sweater."

Shannon ran her hand over the sweater they had given her and sighed at the feel of her clean skin next to the freshly washed dress. She'd forgotten how good it felt to be clean. As soon as she could, she'd wash the sheets and nightclothes. Her skin crawled at the thought of lying between them until then.

She took a deep breath. The Reverend Hamilton had brought boards on Wednesday and Thursday and helped Charles and William nail it to the inside of the shack. He'd even brought sheets of cardboard which they nailed to the rafters, creating a ceiling. Overnight, the shack grew warm. It wasn't hot, but the water didn't freeze and they all felt comfortable to move about.

Shannon had embroidered a simple design on a couple of tea towels she'd made from flour sacks. It seemed like ages since she'd embellished anything with needlepoint, and she'd forgotten how much she enjoyed it.

She turned her attention back to her appearance. Her fingers trembled as she braided her hair. Today was the big day. They were all going to church and to lunch at the home of Reverend Hamilton and his wife and daughter.

Shannon looked at her reflection in the small mirror. She hadn't been out of the shantytown since her last visit with Rose in the fall. Excitement swelled in her, but would the church women judge her for living in the shantytown? She fingered the cable knitting on the sweater. What if the woman who'd donated this sweater was there? Would she look down on her?

A sweat broke out on her upper lip.

Shannon sat in the back pew with Lilly and Raymond on one side of her and Mitchell and Eleanor on the other. She absorbed the heat from the coal stove and wanted to purr like a cat.

A couple of women approached and welcomed her. They exchanged pleasantries, but Shannon became more self-conscious with every word until they expressed their pleasure at meeting her and wandered off.

An older lady marched forward, thrust her hand out to Shannon and introduced herself as Mrs. Lidgerwood. "My husband was the late Harry Lidgerwood," she announced.

Shannon smiled. "I'm sorry to hear about your loss."

The silver-haired lady cocked her head. "Why thank you, but he passed on thirteen years ago."

Shannon's cheeks warmed.

"Are you new to the area?"

Shannon nodded.

"Well, your mother raised you with good manners. Where are you from?"

"Chicago, but most recently, Bonners Ferry."

The woman smiled.

"Have you been to the gorgeous Uptown Theater?"

Shannon's muscles tightened. "No…Is it new?"

"I believe it opened in 1925. We didn't make it there until the following summer."

Shannon relaxed. "I left in 1911."

"Well, next time you're there, you really must see it. It is a work of art!"

Shannon nodded, sure that wouldn't happen anytime soon.

Mrs. Lidgerwood turned to Eleanor.

"You look like an adventurous young lady," commented the small woman; her feisty eyes twinkling.

Eleanor smiled.

"I imagine you have all sorts of schemes up your sleeve."

Eleanor giggled.

"The Reverend tells me you raise chickens and sell the eggs."

"I do, but they're not laying right now."

"It is pretty cold for them. Well, you let me know when they do. I love fresh eggs." The old lady smiled; her soft skin creased around her cheeks. She patted Eleanor on the arm and shuffled off.

Mitchell leaned in. "We don't have any chickens."

"We will," Eleanor replied.

Shannon smiled at her daughter's optimism.

Jake approached with his wife and introduced Olivia to Shannon. Olivia grasped Mother's hand with both of hers, a large smile on her broad face. "I'm so pleased to meet you. Charles and Jake have both told me so much about you. I look forward to our time together this afternoon."

Shannon nodded. "Yes," was all she could say.

At the end of the service, Pastor Hamilton asked that Father stand. He noted that because of the evil deeds of others, Charles and his family had lost their farm in Idaho and needed work. "Charles and his son are both hard workers, and Charles has building and mechanical skills. If anyone has need of such work or even chores around the house, please speak to Mr. Cruthers after the service."

Several people approached them and offered condolences for their struggles. An elderly lady asked William if he would come and do some work for her, and a man asked if Father was good with car engines. A thrill of hope rose in Shannon's chest.

THIRTY

AT THE HAMILTON'S HOME, Eleanor joined her younger siblings and Eva in the parlor. She thrilled at playing her favorite board game, Uncle Wiggily, while Father, Jake, and William talked, and Mother helped Mrs. Hamilton prepare soup and sandwiches.

"Mitchell, come on," Raymond called. "It's your turn."

Eleanor turned around to find Mitchell gazing intently at a piece of framed art. "What are you looking at?"

"It's a sketch of a fox." He turned to Eva. "Who made this?"

Eva jumped up and stood next to him. "My mum drew that." Her lips spread into a wide smile, and her blue eyes sparkled.

"That's great."

Now all the children gathered around the sketch. Eva then showed them more of her mother's art, from sketches of animals to flowers and even Eva when she was little. "Mum also does needlework. Does your mom do needlework?"

Eleanor smiled at the memory of the beautiful embroidery settee pillows, wall hangings, and even dish towels. "She used to."

In the kitchen, Olivia let out a deep-throated laugh. Eleanor turned to see her mother setting the table, head down.

"Oh Shannon," Olivia's voice rang out. "I just must remember that." She laughed some more.

Eleanor's chest tightened. What had Mother said that caused Eva's mother to laugh? Did Mother mean to say something funny? Mother was usually very serious, and now she looked embarrassed. Eleanor glanced at Father, who also looked concerned.

Eleanor turned to Eva. "Why is your mother laughing?"

Eva shrugged her shoulders. "Mom's always laughing. Come on, let's get back to our game." Eva looked at Eleanor's siblings. "How fun it must be to have sisters and brothers to play with."

Eleanor had never thought of it that way. "How come you don't have any brothers or sisters?"

"Mother said she couldn't have any other children." Eva glanced into the kitchen at her mother, then lowered her voice. "She used to get pregnant then lose the baby."

Eleanor furrowed her eyebrows. "Lose the baby?"

Eva leaned in closer and whispered, "You know, have a miscarriage."

"Oh." Though Eleanor didn't know. "What's it like being an only child?"

"Lonely. There's no one to play with or talk to."

Eleanor hadn't considered that. Besides Eva, she had only known two other children who were only children. She had never understood why their parents didn't have more children.

"Lunch is ready," Mrs. Hamilton announced from the parlor entrance. "Children, go wash up."

Eleanor brushed her fingers over the smooth white porcelain plate and lifted her sandwich. She'd forgotten about such luxuries. Mrs. Hamilton asked Mother about her favorite recipes and interests, while Father and William talked with Reverend Hamilton. Occasionally, the reverend would turn and tease the twins and Lilly.

Eleanor answered Eva's questions about school and learned they were in the same grade, but attended different schools.

"We haven't been to school since the weather turned cold." Eleanor's stomach clenched at the familiar fear she'd pushed away all winter. "What are you studying?"

"We've just started long division and studying the Industrial Revolution."

Eleanor winced. What was long division?

"When do you think you'll be able to return to school?"

"I don't know. Maybe now that we each have coats, we can go back."

Eleanor chewed on her thumbnail. Long division, the Industrial Revolution. Would she ever catch up? Or would she fail fifth grade?

"Oh, I wish we could attend the same school. Wouldn't that be lovely? We could play hopscotch or jump rope together during recess. It would be so fun," Eva said.

Eleanor smiled; she'd never had a friend she'd spent time with outside of school. Eva could be such a friend.

Next to her, Mother and Mrs. Hamilton discussed gardening and baking.

She wanted to ask Mother about school, but before she could, Mrs. Hamilton praised Mother on the embroidery towels Mother had given her and asked if she sewed.

Before Eleanor knew it, Mrs. Hamilton was asking Mother to help her with some mending jobs she had while the children were at school.

Eleanor smiled at the mention of school.

"They did what?" Mitchell's voice raised above the others.

Eleanor turned to see her younger siblings all staring with shocked expressions at Reverend Hamilton and Father.

"I'm afraid it's true," Reverend Hamilton said.

"But why?" Mitchell wanted to know.

"They're just animals," Raymond said.

Mitchell was clearly upset. "But buffalo and a polar bear?"

"What are you talking about?" Eleanor asked.

"The Manito Park Zoo," Father said.

"Is that the zoo Rose took Suzanne and Albert to?"

"Yes." Father nodded.

"What about it?"

"But why?" Mitchell repeated.

"With these tough economic times," Reverend Hamilton started. "The parks department couldn't afford to care for the animals. They tried to find homes for them, but every city is struggling and so are their zoos."

"So, what did they do?" Eleanor asked, still confused.

"They killed a polar bear and three buffalo," Mitchell lamented, his voice shaking.

"And two grizzlies," Raymond added.

"But a polar bear and buffalo." Mitchell's blue-gray eyes were wide with sadness. "They live far away. I may never get to see one and they killed them."

"It is a terrible loss," Reverend Hamilton agreed. "They were all beautiful creatures."

"What did they do with the meat?" William asked.

"I don't know."

"They should have given it to all the hungry people."

"I agree, William," Reverend Hamilton said. "At least something good could have come from this horrible loss."

"It was awful," Mrs. Hamilton added. "We heard the gunshots and the howls of the animals."

Eleanor glanced at Mitchell, who was fighting tears and tried to make sense of the story.

"It's one thing to kill an animal for food, but—" Father stopped mid-sentence. "Lilly, are you alright?"

Lilly shook her head. "I don't feel well."

Mrs. Hamilton looked across the table at Lilly. "That child is as white as cream."

Mother scooted her seat back. "Lilly, come here."

Lilly obeyed, and Shannon pressed a hand to her youngest child's forehead. "Charles, she's burning up."

"Nooo. I'm cold." Lilly rubbed her skeletal arms.

"Eva, go get that blanket off the foot of the spare bed."

"Yes, Mother."

"Charles, we need to get her home."

Father nodded.

"We have a spare bedroom," Mrs. Hamilton offered. "You can care for her in there."

Eleanor held her breath, unsure how Mother would respond.

Mother cradled Lilly. "Thank you." She looked between Father and Lilly.

"I want to go home," Lilly murmured.

"I think with the paneled walls and lower ceiling, the shanty will be warm enough. Thank you so much for the lovely meal and conversation."

"My pleasure. I'll be praying for you." Mrs. Hamilton squeezed Mother's hand.

Reverend Hamilton stood. "I'll drive you home."

Eleanor carried dishes into the kitchen, sad the delightful afternoon was over so soon. She looked at her frail little sister, who seemed to melt in Father's arms and hoped it wasn't serious.

THIRTY-ONE

"I CAN'T BREATHE," RAYMOND complained.

Eleanor wrung a cold rag and placed it on his forehead. The cool water sent chills through her fingers and to the rest of her body. "Try sitting up."

"I'm too tired."

Eleanor found a short board and a school book to prop up his nearly flat pillow.

"I'm thirsty," Mitchell croaked, beads of sweat on his forehead as his body shivered.

Father and Lilly coughed.

Eleanor was thankful for Mother's help. The crisis had shaken off Mother's sadness.

William arose early, split some of the wood Reverend Hamilton brought, and went looking for work. He shoveled snow for some of the older parishioners, but he insisted on staying outside in order to not make them sick.

Many of them left bags with sandwiches, cookies, and fruit on their doorsteps, along with his pay. He would share these meals with Mother and Eleanor.

Reverend Hamilton came daily, bringing food and medicine. Several times, Olivia joined him with a large pot of chicken noodle soup and homemade bread.

Eleanor always appreciated their visits. She could tell Mrs. Hamilton was trying to help and befriend Mother. But Mother guarded her friendship and never chatted with Mrs. Hamilton like she had with Mrs. Glendale.

"Don't you like Mrs. Hamilton?" Eleanor asked after one of their visits.

Mother turned her attention away from Eleanor and fiddled with some medicine. "I don't have time for friendship right now."

Eleanor's hands went to her waist. "Mother, you've got nothing but time right now."

Mother faced Eleanor, her eyebrows raised with a look that said: Missy, you've overstepped your boundaries. "It appears to me that we are both too busy for friends."

"Mother, that wasn't what I meant. Not while everyone is sick, but when they get better."

"If they get better."

Eleanor swallowed at the fear Mother's words brought. She would not believe it. They would get better; she would do all she could to make sure they did.

"Besides," Mother continued. "That Mrs. Hamilton seems pretty uppity."

"Uppity? Like Aunt Fiona?"

"No." Mother glared at her. "And don't talk about your aunt that way. I think you forget your place. You are a child, not an adult."

Eleanor stepped back; tears stung her eyes. "A child?" Her voice was inaudible; her lips trembled. Is that all she was to mother after all she'd done? She stirred the chicken noodle soup on the small stove.

Lilly whimpered.

Mother wiped the sweat from Lilly's brow. "Spoon me up some of that soup."

Eleanor reached for a bowl, then stopped. "No. Ask Aunt Fiona to help you if she's so wonderful. I'm just a child." She grabbed her coat.

"Eleanor."

She glared at her mother. "No." And stepped outside.

Rose reread the letter from Johnny Glendale, though she knew the words by heart:

Dear Rose,

I know I haven't written for a while. A lot has changed here since you left. The Sumners had their farm foreclosed on and so did the Dewitts. Talk is that the Morgans will be next. Father says he doesn't owe much, so we are fine for now.

There is a new family at school, and they have a daughter in your old class. Her name is Stella—

A knock at the door startled Rose, and she stuffed the letter back into her apron pocket and wiped her eyes with the back of her hand. "Coming."

She composed herself and opened the door. "William!" She threw her arms around him. "Am I happy to see you. Can you come in?"

"Is anyone home?"

"No, just me." She looked behind him. "Where are Father and the others?"

"That's why I came."

They sat in the kitchen and drank tea with milk in it; a treat for William, and he told her about the family being sick. He shared about Mother wanting Father to take them to the orphanage, and how Father ended up at the church instead. "They've all been so helpful," he added. "They've provided food, clothing, wood for the shanty, firewood, and even jobs."

"I'm glad they could help where I can't."

"It's interesting; Father has changed."

"How?"

"It's hard to explain. He's—calmer. It's like he's accepted that this is our new life. He said he used to believe that God helped those who help themselves. Now he believes we need to trust God to provide."

Rose stopped her teacup midway to her mouth. "Does that mean we don't need to work?"

"That's what I asked him. He said no. It's our attitude. Something about trusting God to provide rather than thinking it's all up to us and being prideful for any success we have."

She shrugged. "I guess."

"It's kind of complicated. He spends a lot of time talking with Reverend Hamilton." He paused. "Are you alright?"

Rose straightened. "Yes."

"Are you sure?"

She looked away. "I'll be fine."

He examined her. "You've been crying," his voice rose. "Are they hurting you?"

She shook her head; tears welled in her eyes.

"What is it?"

Rose stirred her tea.

"Johnny?" his voice was tentative.

She nodded, not looking at him.

"What?"

She pulled the letter from her pocket and thrust it at him.

He read it, then looked up at her; tears now streaked down her cheeks. "I'm sorry."

"How could he do that? Just go and fall in love with the first new girl at school?"

"I don't know." He wondered if this new girl was a looker.

"Maybe I should come home and help," Rose said, changing the subject.

William shook his head. "No, you'll probably just get sick, and then who would take care of you?"

Rose nodded. "You're right. Or Aunt Fiona and the little demons would get sick, and I'd have to care for them." She made a face showing how horrible that would be. "But I want to do something." She stood and perused the kitchen cabinets and refrigerator. She pulled out a blue and yellow printed bag and placed several potatoes, apples, onions, and some oranges in it.

"You probably shouldn't give me the oranges; I can't imagine Aunt Fiona wanting to give those away."

"She buys them for the brats to eat at school, but they don't. They usually trade them for something else or leave them in the school bags to rot."

William looked about at the abundance. "To be unhappy with all this..."

"And yet want more," Rose added. She found another bag with a matching print and poured dried beans in the bottom, then put some salt, flour, tea, and sugar in smaller bags and tied the ends with string. She placed two cans of peaches on top of the dry goods and handed the bags to her brother. "You'd probably better go. Aunt Fiona will be home soon."

"Should you really be giving me all of this?"

"She's always bragging about helping people in need. I'm just helping her."

William smirked then sobered. "Hey, I'm sorry about Johnny."

Rose hung her head. "I guess I've known for a while." She straightened. "If he can find a new girl in Bonners Ferry, I'm sure I can find a big six around here. One with some dough!" She smiled mischievously.

William grinned at her use of the slang for a strong man. She was getting out.

They hugged, and William left, thinking of his sister with a big strong rich guy.

SPRING 1932

Spring rains brought mud mixed with sewage, clinging to the floors and walls of the Hodge-Podge shacks and spreading disease. Those already barely surviving now struggled with influenza, pneumonia, scarlet fever, mumps, measles, whooping cough, polio, and tuberculosis.

Though the Cruthers family battled pneumonia, they all recovered after several weeks and weren't among those visited by the undertaker's daily trips into the shantytown.

"Where do they expect us to live?" Charles asked Jake as he fixed a leaking pipe in the church kitchen. "The newspapers blame the disease on the filthy conditions of the 'Hoovervilles,' but they don't help us."

Jake shook his head. "I don't know why people fear the downtrodden."

"We live in fear for our lives and what little we have."

"Why is that?"

"The shantytowns are seen as 'disease infested eyesores.' New comers tell us stories of being chased from their shelters by angry men brandishing torches and setting their shanties on fire."

Jake grimaced. "My guess is they hope people will catch the rails and leave—find somewhere else to put down roots. People are fearful."

"So that gives them the right to take away what little we have? As if we don't have enough trouble in our lives?"

"Oh, I agree." Jake handed him a wrench. "But people don't live rational lives."

"I'll say. We take turns patrolling the perimeter day and night to protect our families and shelters." Charles yawned.

"I take it you were on duty last night?"

Charles nodded. "I carry a stick and metal lid to bang together to announce danger. It's hard. There are so many places people could sneak in and catch us unawares."

Jake nodded in agreement.

"If only I could find a permanent job and move my family out of there." Jake was silent.

Charles leaned out from his spot under the sink. "You're awful quiet."

"Well..."

"What?"

"Well..." Jake paused again. "I'm leery of getting your hopes up..."

"But?" Charles' chest lifted in anticipation.

"Well, I've heard rumors of a job opening with one of the hospitals. If it's true, I think you would be well qualified."

"A hospital?"

"Yes."

"I don't have any medical training unless helping cows birth or mending their cut legs or wounds from coyotes counts."

Jake laughed. "I think that qualifies you for a position as a surgeon."

"Farmer surgeon," Charles chuckled. "That ought to scare any patient away. We farmers aren't known to have the most conventional methods."

"It's good to hear you joke."

Charles sat up and leaned against a cupboard. "I'm working on putting into practice your words about forgiveness and trusting God."

"And?"

"And I'm finding things to be thankful for. Seeing how God is providing for us, even though it's not always how I would do it or exactly what I want. We haven't missed a meal since I stepped through the doors of this church."

"I told you God would provide." Jake smiled.

"He has. But he's also taking away my anger at those men. Yeah, I still fight it, but I keep praying about it. I can't imagine living knowing that I destroyed someone's home and livelihood. I'm trusting that God will punish them in His own time and way."

"That's good. God is much better at dealing out discipline and punishment than we are. He knows the heart of man and can punish fairly."

They were silent for a few moments before Jake continued, "Eva has been asking if Eleanor could come over some afternoon. As an only child, she gets lonely and hasn't found many girls at school with common interests. She really likes Eleanor, and Olivia and I would be grateful for an opportunity for them to become friends."

Charles smiled. "That would be good. Eleanor works so hard to help; if I didn't know better, I'd suspect she feels responsible."

"Maybe she does."

"That's ridiculous!"

"Is it? Children often take responsibility for things out of their control."

Charles pondered Jake's words. "I wonder if you're right? She was the one trying to coax Teddy from the house the day of the fire." He massaged his chin. "And all that morning she was worried about him—" He shook his head. "No wonder she's put her childhood aside and works so hard to care for us."

He took in a jagged breath. "My little girl." He wiped tears away with the back of his hand. "All this time, she blames herself."

Jake nodded, following Charles' reasoning. "It's very possible."

"And now she's stuck between our current condition and Shannon's depression." He looked at the pastor. "I'll talk to her tonight."

"That's a good start."

Charles nodded. "Tell Eva I'll bring Eleanor over tomorrow afternoon." His mind returned to the job Jake had mentioned. If that happened, she could go back to being a kid. He smiled at the idea.

THIRTY-TWO

Olivia and Shannon sat at the table mending clothes to earn money while Eleanor and Eva read to Lilly and quizzed the twins on spelling and math before playing Old Maid.

"So, tell me, are there others in the congregation as bad off as us?" Shannon asked, her question laced with a tinge of resentment.

Olivia considered the question for a moment. "There is a family who lost their home to the bank and had to move in with family in Ritzville. And then there's Mrs. Dexter, a widow, who lost her job and savings when the stock market crashed. She rents out a few rooms to some bachelors and cooks for them, but she still struggles. And then there's Mrs. Springer. She found a job doing laundry at a hotel. It doesn't pay much, so she cleans a few businesses in the evenings. She's not getting fat, but she's surviving."

Shannon took this all in, then looked down at the mending she was finishing up. "You don't have much to sew today."

"No, we're going for a drive; there's something I want you to see."

"Oh, I don't know. I probably should get the children home."

"They'll be fine. Won't you Eleanor? Eva?"

They both nodded.

"We're fine, Mother," Eleanor assured her. "Go."

"Listen, Missy. I'll determine whether things will be fine." She looked at the children all watching her. "I don't feel safe with you all alone."

"If they have any problems, Mrs. Blackhouse is across the street, or they can call Jake at the church or the operator for help," Olivia offered.

Shannon considered her options.

"Jake can take them home when he's finished at the church."

Eleanor looked between Mrs. Hamilton and Mother. "We'll be good, we promise."

The others agreed.

Shannon glared at Eleanor. She didn't appreciate her siding with Mrs. Hamilton.

"You rarely get to go do anything fun. Go."

"Yes, Mother." Lilly added, and Mitchell nodded in agreement.

Shannon looked from one sweet face to the next and shook her head. She put on her coat and turned to the children. "You children don't be breaking your shin on a stool that's not in your way, you hear?"

"Yes, um," they giggled at one of her favorite Irish sayings.

She sighed. She hadn't said that since before the fire.

In the car, Olivia drove through downtown, pointing out the architecture of several beautiful buildings. "I grew up in Chicago with lots of grand buildings, so I can't help but admire some of the beautiful ones I see here."

Shannon turned to her. "Chicago? You're from Chicago?" there was a thread of hope in her voice.

"Yes, have you been there?"

Shannon smiled. "I was born and grew up in Chicago."

"What neighborhood?" Olivia drove westward into a neighborhood Shannon had never been.

"In Hyde Park in Chicago's south side; it was a strongly Irish neighborhood."

"I can't believe it. I grew up on the South Shore; we used to go to O'Leary's Fish House in Hyde Park on Saturday nights."

"O'Leary's! I had forgotten all about O'Leary's," Shannon said with a laugh. "It was one of my father's favorite restaurants. It's been ages since I've had fish and chips like those."

"I agree. So, when did you leave Chicago?"

Shannon's mood returned to somber, and she looked down at her hands. "In 1911, after my mother died. Father got the itch to try something new. He'd read about the vast woods out west, and that they were looking for loggers and decided that's what he wanted to do."

"Is that how you ended up in Bonners Ferry?"

"No, we moved to Sandpoint, and I met and married Charles and we moved to Bonners Ferry."

"Why didn't your father work in logging around the Great Lakes?"

Shannon pondered this. "I believe when Mother died, his heart broke. He wanted away from Chicago and all the memories of her."

"Some people are that way." Olivia wound her way through a neighborhood with a mixture of beautiful stately houses and simpler, one and two-story homes.

"When did you leave?"

"Fourteen years ago, before I was pregnant with Eva." Olivia sighed. "I'd had several miscarriages, and the doctors said I would never have children. I doubt I would have moved if we did." She pulled along the curb. "We're here."

Shannon pulled her thoughts away from this, another sad, shared experience. She stepped from the car and inhaled the fresh air. "Oh, this clean, cool, spring air reminds me of home."

Olivia's wide smile spread across her round face and accentuated her dimples. "And that is just the beginning. Come." She motioned Shannon to join her on a path that led to a modest two-story home. "I want you to meet my friend, Virginia."

Shannon admired the spring flowers that lined the walk. "You said there was something you wanted me to see, not someone."

"Yes, well, this someone has something she wants to show you."

Shannon stiffened but couldn't resist the fresh air and the escape from the shantytown. "Oh, look at the beautiful grape hyacinths oh—" She pointed to a flowerbed. "And those white and yellow daffodils!"

An older woman with straight white hair opened the door and welcomed them in. "I'm so glad you could make it. There's sandwiches and coffee, but—" She pointed to the graying sky. "I'm afraid it might rain, so let's first enjoy the garden."

Virginia picked a flower here and another there as she chatted about the pink and red tulips and the bright yellow forsythia bush. She pointed out the different rose bushes and what color they were. "Shannon, what is your favorite flower?"

Shannon took in the beautiful garden, still in its young stages. "As beautiful as these all are, I love roses with their many layered petals and beautiful scent."

"What is your favorite color?" Virginia asked.

Shannon smiled. "Yellow, yellow roses."

"I will keep that in mind."

Inside, Olivia sat back and allowed Virginia to share her experiences of raising children on a farm in nearby Cheney. "I loved the country," Virginia said. "But when my husband died in a farming accident, I had to move my four children to town and start a new life."

Shannon nodded in understanding.

"We have something for you," Olivia said and motioned to Virginia, who handed Shannon a small package wrapped in brown paper with several grape hyacinths tucked under the twine.

Shannon's heart softened. "I—I don't understand. Why?"

"Just open it, my dear," Virginia said. "We'll explain."

Shannon tugged at the twine and folded back the paper to find a handmade diary inside with a fountain pen. "Oh, my. It's beautiful." Her fingers caressed the cardboard cover, which had a piece of watercolor paper laced to it on the edges with pink and purple flowers. She looked at Olivia. "Did you?"

Olivia nodded.

"After I left the farm," Virginia continued, "I replayed my memories daily; afraid I would forget them. A friend suggested I write those memories down, sketch some if I needed to. That way, I would always have them."

Shannon fingered the book, then held it to her chest. "Thank you. I will."

"I know you ladies must go, but I've so enjoyed our visit."

Shannon hugged her. "Thank you, I've so enjoyed meeting you."

"Please know, you are always welcome." With that, she handed Shannon a blue vase with the flowers they'd picked.

"Oh, I couldn't. You've given me so much."

"No," Virginia smiled. "Your visit has given me more than you know."

They were quiet on the drive home, the sky already darkening. Shannon sighed at the sight of the shanty. "Thank you, Olivia. This was a wonderful day." She twirled the twine between her fingers. "I'm sorry. Even though I haven't been a very good friend, you have always been very kind to me. For so long, I didn't see that there was ever going to be a way out of this." She motioned to the surrounding huts. "When we lost everything and had to move here, I gave up hope. But I see that I...we don't have to be stuck here. Thank you."

She exited the car and watched Olivia drive away. A thin woman wearing a threadbare coat shuffled by. Even with the woman's head down, Shannon saw the black eye, and she steeled herself against the sadness.

It was late March, and signs of spring were everywhere. Eleanor and her younger siblings had been attending school for a couple of months. As they walked back to the shanty, Eleanor pondered her meeting with Lilly's teacher. How could they get Lilly caught up and interested in school? It was the fourth meeting with Miss Dodge in two weeks. Meetings Mother should have attended but were left to her.

"See the new marbles I won." Raymond held out his hand as they walked home. "I also got an apple, half a sandwich, and two cookies."

"Good for you." Eleanor looked at Mitchell. "How about you? What have you been doing at recess?"

Mitchell shrugged, and Raymond finished for him. "He just mopes around. His little pal Lenny, doesn't come to school."

Eleanor turned to Mitchell. "How come?"

"He has polio and can't walk." Mitchell kicked a stone in the road.

"He's a dumbbell," Raymond taunted. "That's really why he's gone."

"Is not." Mitchell pushed him, and Raymond pushed back.

She pulled them apart. "Enough you two." Eleanor turned to Mitchell. "So why don't you play marbles with the other boys?"

Mitchell shrugged. "Don't feel like it."

"'Cause he's a chicken."

"Dry up."

"Knock it off, both of you." Eleanor massaged her forehead. They were all so far behind in school, and Mitchell was the only one she could trust to do his work. Raymond, like Lilly, excelled on the playground, but battled with both his teacher and Eleanor over schoolwork. Why did she have to manage this?

Lilly skipped alongside Eleanor, unconcerned about her teacher's rebuke. "When we get home, I'm going to play with Molly and Antonio."

"Lilly, it's not our home, and no, you won't play with them. You're going to sit down and work on writing your letters and numbers. You should know this by now."

"No, I'm not. I'm going out to play."

"Not until your letters are done."

"Who cares about letters? I want to play. You sound just like Miss Dodge."

"That's because Eleanor's smart like your teacher," Mitchell said.

Raymond chucked a pebble down the road. "Oh, leave her alone, both of you. Why do you make such a big deal out of everything?"

Eleanor stopped and, with fists on her hips, glared at Raymond, then Lilly. "Because it's important."

"Because it's important," Raymond mimicked and Lilly giggled. "You think everything is important. 'Wash your face, wash the dishes, sweep the floor, don't track mud in, wash your socks.' Who cares if our face is clean? Who cares if our dishes are clean? We're just going to put more food on them and make them dirty. What difference does it make if our socks are clean or not? It's just a bunch of stupid work."

Eleanor's pale complexion turned as red as her hair, and her eyes almost bulged. "It's important because...never mind. You're too stupid to understand. Sometimes you have to do things because you're told."

"Sometimes you have to do things because you're told," Raymond repeated.

"I'm going to go tell Mother."

"Go ahead, she doesn't care. She's probably sleeping and will be mad at you for waking her."

Eleanor stomped off, afraid Raymond was right. She walked past the small garden patch she'd planted; she needed to thin the radishes and carrots.

Inside the shanty, Mother sat by a window sewing. Eleanor set her books on the table and approached her. An enormous pile of their own mending sat on one side, and a few repaired items sat on the chair beside her.

"Mother, can we talk?"

Shannon raised her head and rubbed her eyes. "This light is pathetic for sewing in." She sighed. "What is it?"

"Mother, I need your help."

She sighed again. "I hope it's not much. I'm tired."

Eleanor fought off the temptation to bark back that she was tired, too. Tired of cooking and cleaning. Tired of caring for her younger siblings, helping them with their school work, and trying to provide food. "I need your help with Lilly and Raymond. They won't help me out around the house, and they don't want to do their schoolwork. Miss Dodge said Lilly needs to work harder, or she'll have to do this year over. Miss Dodge also said that Lilly is getting in trouble at school."

Mother glanced around the shanty. "I told your father she wasn't ready for school and should stay home with me," she mumbled, and set the shirt she was sewing down. "But no, he insisted it was better for her. Now look where that's gotten her. You just need to stop picking on her."

Mother's words stabbed. "I'm not picking on her. I'm trying to help—"

"Eleanor, Lilly's not even six years old yet. Poor thing, she never even got to experience the farm. She's had her entire childhood taken away from her."

Eleanor stood. "And I haven't? Other girls my age get to play hopscotch, and jump rope, have tea parties and play with dolls or board games. But not me. No. I have to cook and clean and be mother to your children, while you lay about sad all the time."

Shannon stared at Eleanor.

Eleanor's fists clenched. "That fire didn't burn just your home; it burned our home too."

Mother crossed her arms.

Eleanor leaned in and pointed her finger at her mother. "You act like you're the only one who lost everything. Well, you weren't. We all did. You're not the only one who lost their home and clothes and special things. So did we. We all had to move away from the place we loved." She brushed away a stray tear.

"Do you think I want to be here? No. I don't. I want to be back on the farm milking Martha and Bertha. But that isn't the way of it. Instead, we're here. And I'm trying to help Father and William provide for all of us. The least you could do is help."

The slap of Shannon's hand across Eleanor's face stopped her outburst. She touched her stinging cheek.

Silence.

She turned at a sound behind her—the younger children watched from the doorway.

Her face flushed. She pointed to Lilly and the twins. "They're your children. You take care of them. I tried to help, but all it's done is make you lazy." Eleanor pushed past them and left the shanty.

"Where are you going?" Mitchell called.

"Away from here."

THIRTY-THREE

"WHO'S READY TO MOVE?" Father bellowed.

Eleanor's eyes shot open, and she sat up in bed. "It's here!"

Three months had passed since her and Mother's fight and so much had changed. Father had explained to Mother Eleanor's guilt and convinced Mother that in spite of her grief, her family needed her. Mother admitted that it wasn't Eleanor's responsibility to care for the younger children. They both apologized and worked together caring for the family, with Mother carrying the heavier share.

Yesterday, they had packed their meager belongings except for what they would need in the morning.

The job as head of maintenance at the hospital had become available, as Reverend Hamilton predicted it would. And through a series of events Father said were answers to his prayers, they had hired Father for a temporary position. He'd so impressed the retiring head of maintenance that he had recommended Father for the job as supervisor.

The position, though it paid little, came with a modest home complete with indoor plumbing, electricity, and a coal furnace.

After a quick breakfast, the family loaded Eleanor's new chickens and other belongings on the truck while Teddy danced around yipping, his mouth open, in what looked like an excited smile.

Eleanor stopped outside the front door. Inside the fenced off area for the chickens was her little garden with green carrot tops sticking several inches out of the ground, radish, lettuce, beets, and a few corn stalks. "Father, what about my garden?"

He stopped and put his arm around her shoulder. "You have worked very hard to help provide for us, Eleanor, and I couldn't be prouder of you. But I'm afraid if we try digging this up, it will die."

"I thought you'd say that." She bit her lip, trying not to cry on this happy day.

"We're going to a better place, a home with a fenced-in yard and a garden spot. If Mr. Hugo, the previous occupant, hasn't already planted a garden, then I'll buy you some seeds, and you can plant another one."

She nodded, avoiding eye contact.

Father looked at the neighbors who watched their activity. "These folks are still struggling. How about we leave it to them?"

"But what if they don't water it?"

"That's the chance we have to take. But I'm sure someone will see the value in it and care for it."

Eleanor took a deep breath and looked at the young Asian family across the narrow dirt path, watching them. "You're right, Father. I'll tell Mrs. Lee."

"That's my girl."

When they'd loaded the last item, Father and William tied everything down as best they could, and the children climbed aboard.

"Watch that stuff, will you, William? I don't want it shifting and squishing any of you or pushing someone out of the truck."

"Yes, Father."

Their shantytown neighbors stood by as Father pulled the old farm truck away from their shanty. Eleanor watched as they passed small and even tiny shanties. This had been their neighborhood for almost a year. She looked back at their shanty, wanting to see, one more time, the second home she'd ever known.

They weren't a hundred feet from it when shouts rose as people fought over who got to live in it, while others were already removing boards.

Eleanor turned away, saddened that all their work and striving was so easily destroyed.

"It's sort of sad, isn't it?"

Eleanor turned to see Mitchell standing beside her. "Yes, it is." She sighed. "It's like we're losing another home."

"I meant it's sad that there's still so many people in need. They're desperate, just like we were."

She pondered his words for a moment. "Yes, that too."

"Do you think we'll have to leave our new home?"

"I hope not."

They drove across the Monroe Street Bridge and Eleanor smiled. She loved the water, all frothy and white, as it tumbled down the falls and west toward the ocean, or so William had told her.

As they maneuvered through the busy streets, several people yelled at them to go back to where they came from.

"Ignore them," William said. "This is our home now."

This is our home. Eleanor let the idea take root. These streets were hers now. She watched people stroll along sidewalks in front of businesses and stores. Someday, she told herself, she would enter those shops and purchase a new, store-bought dress and maybe even a fancy hat like some ladies wore.

The engine growled as Father shifted into low gear, and the truck ascended the steep South Hill. Eleanor and the boys clung to the side rails as a few pieces of furniture shifted to the back of the truck.

"Are we going to live next to Aunt Fiona and Rose?" Mitchell asked.

Raymond pushed a crate toward the front of the truck bed. "I hope not."

"Don't worry," William assured them. "Our house is within walking distance, but not that close."

"What's it like?" Eleanor asked.

"Yes, what's it like?" chimed the others.

"I've only seen the outside, but it's nice. It's smaller than our home in Idaho, but it's nice."

Eleanor watched as they passed a variety of homes. "Does it have a front porch?"

William pursed his lips and pretended to think. "Hum, does it have a front porch? I don't remember."

She slugged him. "Quit teasing."

"I'm jesting."

She rolled her eyes at another one of his hip words.

They neared the hospital, and Father turned one block up from the large brick building. He drove a few blocks before he pulled in front of a white craftsman with a covered porch. A wooden swing hung from the porch ceiling next to a large front window.

Eleanor's eyes grew wide, and excitement swelled in her chest. "Is that it? Are we here?"

Father jumped out of the truck; a smile spread across his broad face. "Well, children, this is your new home."

Mother wore an expression of pleasure accented with moist eyes.

Father wrapped an arm around her. "What do you think, Shannon?"

"It's not the log home..." she turned to him; a smile gracing her lips. "But it's nice."

"And there's no outhouse to scrub, and no well you need to haul water from. It's all indoor plumbing."

"So, you've said. I think I could get used to that."

"I hope so."

The front door opened, and a man in a suit and tie came out.

Father took her arm. "Come on children, I want you to meet Mr. Lunders, my boss."

Eleanor smiled at several neighbors standing or sitting on their front porches watching; a few others looked from their windows.

Mother also noticed and tried to smooth her worn dress.

A man crossed the street and approached Father's boss, ignoring Charles and his family. "Mr. Lunders, when Roy said he was retiring and moving to the Oregon coast, he never mentioned that you were selling the house." He now sneered at Charles and the family.

"Mr. Potter, this is Charles Cruthers, his lovely wife, Shannon, and his family."

Mother blushed at Mr. Lunders' compliment.

Teddy barked at the man, who squinted. "That dog better not be dangerous."

"Only to thieves," Father responded with a smile. "He's well behaved, but very protective."

Mr. Potter looked at the dog and then back to Mr. Lunders. "He'd better not be barking all the time."

Mr. Lunders ignored the man. "Mr. Cruthers is our new head of maintenance at the hospital." Mr. Lunders removed his fedora and his bald head shone in the morning sunshine, and his eyes twinkled with pride. "He's taken Roy's position."

Mr. Potter shook Father's hand out of duty. "It's good to know you haven't sold it." He looked at the farm truck with its mess of mattresses, mismatched chairs, wooden crates, and children dressed in play clothes pressing around him, eager to see their new home. "If someone didn't know better, they'd think you're a bunch of those homeless tramps that are invading our city," he said, as much to Mr. Lunders as Father.

Eleanor's pulse quickened.

"Mr. Cruthers and his family are new to our fair city. They've recently moved here from north of Bonners Ferry, where Mr. Cruthers owned and managed a large dairy farm." Mr. Lunders' bright eyes and serious smile exuded pride. "We at the hospital are quite happy to have Mr. Cruthers and his fine family here to join us in caring for the needs of our community for many years to come." He glanced at Eleanor and winked. "Now." He turned to the children and then Mother. "Who wants to see their new home?"

Eleanor smiled straight at Mr. Potter and marched into the house.

"I hope that Mr. Potter won't be a problem," Mother mused as they climbed the steps.

"Don't worry about small-minded men like him," assured Father's boss. "This is a wonderful neighborhood; we've never had a problem."

His words soothed Eleanor's nerves, which rattled behind her confident facade. But once inside their new home, Eleanor's nerves stopped their rattling altogether. She walked through the front door into a spacious dining area with wood floors. To the left was the kitchen and, on the right, the living room.

Eleanor had just entered the living room with its wool carpet, long drapes, and brick fireplace when a cry from mother sent her running into the kitchen. She slid to a stop, confused.

Mother stood in the center, looking about. "Oh my, Charles, would you look at this? After how we've been cooking for the past year..."

Eleanor let out a sigh of relief. "Mother, you scared me."

Shannon turned to her. "Can you believe this? It's—What's that?" She moved to the wall and two buttons. She pushed the white one, and a glass fixture on the ceiling lit up. Mother turned to her. "Did you see that?"

Charles grinned at Shannon's excitement.

She pushed the dark button below, and the light switched off. "Imagine, no cooking by oil lamp."

"Father, Mother." Lilly and the twins ran from the back of the house to where the others stood. Lilly's blue eyes sparkled with excitement. "There are lights that turn on."

"I take it electricity is new for you?" Mr. Lunders said.

Father nodded. "There was electricity at the border and train depot a few miles away, but I hadn't had the time to wire our home and barn to connect up to it."

Mr. Lunders gave Father the keys and said his goodbyes.

Eleanor ran her foot over the smooth, red-marbled linoleum floor. Mother opened cupboard doors and drawers. "Real cupboards." She shook her head. She opened the refrigerator. "Look Charles, it's cold, and it even has a light."

The children rushed to see.

William turned on the faucet, and Mother stared. "Running water!" She smiled; her eyes growing moist.

Father wrapped his arms around her, and she buried her face in his chest. "I know it's not like our log home," he said. "But it has some conveniences our other home didn't have."

"Why is Mother crying?" Lilly whispered.

Eleanor shrugged her shoulders and followed her brothers outside.

Neighbors watched with curiosity and Mr. Potter with disdain as her family unloaded their few belongings from the truck.

"Look at that car," Raymond shouted as a green and black convertible Cadillac V-16 Roadster slowed.

William turned and shouted. "Mr. Turner."

The man stopped and Eleanor watched with unease as his eyes perused them and their ratty makeshift furniture. His look changed from concern to contempt.

"William, are you helping someone move?"

William set the chair down and approached the vehicle. "Yes, sir, Mr. Turner. "I'm helping my family move into our new home. They hired my father as the new maintenance supervisor at the hospital."

Apprehension spread throughout Eleanor's limbs as the light complected skin on Mr. Turner's slender face drew tight, and he clenched his jaw. "I see. I'm glad I happened by this morning."

"Nice car," Raymond said as he and Mitchell approached the vehicle.

Eleanor cringed seeing the look of horror on the man's face. "Boys, come back here."

Mr. Turner's lip curled in contempt as the boys stepped away.

Eleanor smoothed her too-tight faded dress and wished she was wearing her other one.

"Yes, very fortuitous," said the man. He adjusted his Fedora and drove off.

"Who was that?" Raymond asked.

"Mr. Turner."

Raymond looked after the Cadillac Roadster. "Is he rich?"

"He's got dough. He wouldn't have that breezer and a nice, two-story house if he didn't."

"Do you work for him?" Mitchell asked, concern in his voice.

"Yes, but you should see his daughter." William whistled.

The twins looked at him as though he'd sprouted another head.

Mitchell looked down the road where Mr. Turner's car had disappeared. "I'm not sure I like him."

William turned to his little brother. "Dry up."

Eleanor glared at her brother. "William!"

A hurt look crossed Mitchell's face. "I'm just saying I don't like the way he looked at us."

"Who cares how he looks at us? It's Clara I'm interested in."

"Clara?" Eleanor grinned. "Who's Clara?"

William handed her a box of kitchen stuff, ignoring her.

"Clara," Raymond mocked and made a face of disgust at Mitchell.

Mitchell nodded and scrunched his face in agreement. "I don't know. I think he's sneaky."

William set another chair on the road. "Just take this stuff in the house and mind your beeswax."

Eleanor followed the boys back to the house.

"Mind your beeswax," Raymond repeated, and they both laughed. "Why would we want beeswax?"

Mitchell shrugged. "I still don't like the guy."

"So what?" Raymond said. "I like his car, I mean his breezer. Maybe I'll have one like that someday."

Eleanor fidgeted behind them; her load growing heavy. "Would you two hurry and quit your jabbering?"

Inside, Mother placed the beautiful green and gold edged serving bowl with hand-painted roses on the middle shelf of the built-in china cabinet. "I still can't believe this survived." She stood back to admire it. "To think it fell through the floorboards and was just sitting on the ground. I'm so glad William found it."

Eleanor looked at the bowl with a mixture of pleasure and sadness. Moments earlier, she had stashed the only remaining piece of Mother's good china on the top shelf of her and Lilly's closet. When she'd found the broken plate, Mother had dismissed it, telling her to toss what Eleanor felt was a special find. She couldn't understand why Mother didn't want it, and the rejection of that day coursed through her veins anew.

"Eleanor, I want you to collect all the linens and clothing; we need to wash them before putting them back on the beds."

"Can I go out and play?" Lilly asked.

"Not yet," Eleanor said. "You need to help."

"I wasn't asking you."

"Sure, hun."

Lilly stuck her tongue out at Eleanor and hurried out the door.

"Mother!"

But Shannon headed into the living room; the smoke-stained figurine of a red-haired woman with a yellow dress in her hand. She placed it on the fireplace mantle. "Your father bought me this on our honeymoon."

"Mother, Lilly should help us."

"Eleanor, she's little; let her play."

Eleanor sighed in exasperation. She hoped all the progress they'd made over the past few months wouldn't unravel and leave her doing everything.

"Take the bedding downstairs."

"But won't it be easier to wash them outside, closer to the clothesline?"

Mother shook her head. "Your father and brother found an electric washing machine in the basement."

Eleanor's eyes widened. "Oh, wow!"

"We'll see if it really knows how to clean clothes," Mother added.

Eleanor stuffed a dirty, smelly sheet into the Thor electric washing machine's tub and added some Naptha laundry soap before Father showed her which knobs to push.

Father stepped back as water poured into the tub from a hose attached to a nearby sink. "Would you look at that? I still can't get over it."

William wandered around the machine, looking at the chains and gears and cranking the wringer. "There are all kinds of timesaving devices in this house."

"The time saving machine I'm most interested in right now is a hot bath." Father grinned. "I imagine we'll all be needing one before we go to bed in clean sheets."

Eleanor's eyes lit up. "Father, can you play the harmonica tonight so we can dance and celebrate our new home?"

A wide grin spread across his lips. "Kitten, I think that's a great idea."

William stood. "Maybe we could have some popcorn and—"

Crash!

Teddy's barking filled their ears.

Father stepped toward a basement window. "What in tar-nations?"

Eleanor raced up the stairs behind Mother, William, and her father, who took the stairs two at a time.

Upstairs, her siblings ran in from the backyard with Teddy barking and pushing his way through.

They all stared in shock at the hole in the bathroom window, cracks spidering out. Everyone talked at once.

"Whoa, whoa." Father lifted his hands in the air to get quiet.

"What happened here?"

"He did it." Raymond pointed at Mitchell.

"I did not, you threw it."

"But you're the one who didn't catch it," Raymond said.

"You threw it too high."

"You're supposed to jump. Everyone knows that."

"Enough!" Father held up his hands. "Everyone, back away and watch where you're stepping."

Eleanor sighed.

Teddy wiggled around them making his arrarrarr sound; his head down and tail wagging.

"What were you boys throwing?"

Mitchell pointed at the dog. "We found a baseball."

Father squatted and held out his hand. "Come here, boy."

Teddy wiggled with the find in his mouth, then released it in Father's hand.

Father looked it over. "Let's not be throwing balls toward the house and until you have mitts, throw underhand."

"But Father—" Raymond whined.

Father held up a finger. "Underhand, or you don't get the ball back."

Raymond folded his arms and glared at Mitchell.

Mother massaged her forehead. "What are we going to do now?"

Father pulled her to him. "I'll run down to the hardware store and get some glass."

"How much will that cost?"

"Not much. I'm working now, remember?"

She nodded.

He turned to the children. "Why don't you head back outside? Eleanor, please help your mother clean this up."

She nodded, suddenly tired.

"William, come with me. We need to find something to measure that window with."

"Yes, Father."

Eleanor picked shards of glass from the windowsill. She couldn't believe they'd already broken something in their new home. So far, things hadn't gone as she expected.

"Ouch!" She yanked her hand up and watched the blood pool on her finger.

Mother stood and held out her hand. "Come here. Let's get that washed up and wrapped."

She put her hand under the water, tears flowing.

"Eleanor, it can't hurt that much."

She shook her head. "It's not that. It's...it's everything." She sniffled. "The window, Mr. Potter, the people tearing our shanty apart...why is everything against us?"

Shannon pulled her close. "Not everything is against us; it just appears that way sometimes."

Eleanor looked into her mother's gray-green eyes and forced herself to ask the question, suffocating her. "Is...is that how you feel—when you don't want to get out of bed?"

Mother brushed a tear from Eleanor's cheek. "Yes. I suppose it is—and so much more."

Eleanor listened.

"This is not the first time I've had my world ripped away from me. Life was hard before my mother died; afterward, it was impossible."

"How?"

"Her small income from cleaning houses was gone; we were starving. One evening, Father had us pack our few belongings, and we hurried to the rail yard where we climbed aboard a boxcar and traveled to Sandpoint. We stayed at a boarding house with a very gracious lady who took care of Fiona and me when Father was in the woods felling trees."

"Were you scared and lonely?"

She nodded. "When I married your father, and we joined his grand-parents on the dairy farm; I thought I'd never have to leave. I felt safe there."

Eleanor squeezed her mother's hand, and Shannon smiled.

Mother stared at the hole in the window and swallowed. "Apparently, bad luck will find you anywhere."

Eleanor looked at the window. "Maybe bad luck can hurt us, but only we can allow it to break us."

THIRTY-FOUR

ELEANOR STILL COULDN'T BELIEVE that Mother was letting her go to the schoolyard with Eva—alone—no siblings. They skipped down the sidewalk, chatting in excitement.

"After the schoolyard," Eva said. "Let's go to Finnegan's Market. He has a soda fountain, a candy bin, and magazines."

Eleanor fingered the coins in her secret pocket, hoping she had enough.

Eva skipped along beside her. "I'm so excited for you. Isn't it wonderful how God has answered our prayers? Not only did he give your father a job but also that nice house, and so close to us we can see each other all the time." Her face, of light complexion, shone with excitement.

Eleanor paused. "Are you sure it was God? Maybe it was just your father and all the people he knows."

Eva cocked her head. "Eleanor, God rarely drops things like jobs from the sky. He works through people to answer our prayers."

Eleanor pondered this.

"Do you believe in God?"

"I think so. I mean, I believe he's out there. But I don't understand him, and why he lets bad things happen."

Eva stooped down and picked a daisy from a crack in the sidewalk and spun the flower between her fingers. "I don't always understand everything either—I don't think anyone does. Father says God is too big for us to completely understand. He also says that bad things happen because people disobey God, and when we do, we hurt ourselves and others."

"But why would God allow us to do that?"

"Father says God doesn't want to force us to love and obey him. He lets us choose."

Eleanor pondered this.

"I believe God helped your father get that job. My father didn't meet Mr. Lunders from the hospital until this spring."

Eleanor looked at Eva. "Oh."

"Violet and Pauline are nice." Eva paused, her legs dangling as she sat atop the seesaw. "Mother says not to gossip."

"But?"

Eva scrunched her face in thought. "Well, just watch out for Helen White."

Eleanor pushed against the ground with her feet and rose as Eva descended. "How come?"

"She's not very nice. Her two friends, Georgina and Camile, are fine by themselves, but don't tell them any secrets or personal stuff."

"Let me guess, they'll tell Helen?"

Eva nodded. "She can take the nicest thing and twist it into something awful to embarrass you and make sure everyone knows." She grimaced. "There I go gossiping. It's so hard. I just don't want you to get hurt by her."

Eleanor nodded. They raced around the playground and had a contest to see who could swing the highest. As much as she tried to enjoy herself, guilt tugged at her. She should be at home helping—but wasn't this what she'd been wanting?

She pushed the merry-go-round harder and jumped on. The girls lay on their backs and stared up at the fluffy white cumulus clouds, laughing as they grew dizzy.

At Finnegan's Market, Eleanor inhaled the smell of fresh produce. She took her time perusing the aisles and looking at the enormous selection of items. They flipped through magazines with pictures of cars, nicely decorated homes, and the latest fashions.

"What do you think of this dress?" Eva held up a picture of a lady in a slender gown that went to the floor and had ruffles around the neck and sleeves.

"That's pretty. Where would you wear it?"

"Maybe one of those fancy balls they hold at the Davenport or the Ridpath."

Eleanor nodded. William had told her about how fancy the Davenport and Ridpath Hotels were. "Have you ever been to a ball?"

"No," Eva sighed. "Balls are for adults. But someday..."

They each got a peppermint stick and sat on the curb. Three girls their age approached wearing store-bought dresses and black polished shoes.

Eva paused. "Oh, no."

The girls stopped. "Hi Eva." The one with long, dark, curly hair looked down at them.

"Hi Helen."

"Look girls, it's Eva." She looked Eleanor up and down. "And who's this ragamuffin?"

Eleanor's face flushed.

"Helen, must you always be so rude?"

"Eva, Eva. I only speak the truth. When will you stop taking in strays?"

"I don't 'take in strays', as you call it. I choose to have different friends than you."

Helen stood in front of Eleanor. "Look at me."

Eleanor lifted her gaze to the girl; her temper rising. She glared back at the girl, whose little nose turned upward.

"Would you look at that red hair?" Helen said. Her two friends giggled.

"Haven't you ever seen red hair?" Eleanor asked.

"Hair like yours belongs on a Raggedy Ann doll."

Eleanor stood and glared into the girl's blue eyes. "Why don't you leave us alone?"

"Oh, she's a feisty Raggedy Ann." The girl reached out to touch Eleanor's hair.

Eleanor grabbed her pale thin wrist and twisted it back. "Don't touch me."

"Oww! Let go. You're hurting me."

"Then don't touch me."

"Alright, alright."

Eleanor let go, and the girl backed away, rubbing her wrist. "You didn't have to do that—Raggedy Ann."

Eleanor took a step toward her. "Stop calling me that."

A mean look flashed across Helen's face. "What are you going to do to stop me, Raggedy Ann?"

Eleanor took another step toward the girl, who stepped back along with her friends. "Next time—" What would she do next time? "Next time, I'll really hurt you."

Helen glanced at the girls standing on either side of her. "Come on Camile, Georgina, let's go get a fountain soda." They marched past Eleanor and Eva; heads held high.

Eleanor hoped there wouldn't be a next time.

Eva grabbed Eleanor's arm. "Wow. No one has ever stood up to her."

Eleanor looked down at the ground. She wasn't sure why she'd responded that way.

Eva touched her arm. "I'm sorry for what she said. I told you she was mean."

Eleanor held out her hand. "Look, I'm shaking." She looked back as Helen and her friends entered Finnegan's. Eleanor really liked Helen's shoes and hair ribbons. She shifted her feet in her too-tight boots, with their scuffed toes. Somehow, she was going to wear new shoes, ribbons, and hopefully a store-bought dress on the first day of school. "Do you know anyone who wants to buy eggs?"

Eva stared at her. "No, but Mother might. You realize you don't have to work so hard; your dad has a job now, remember?"

"I know, but there's also seven people to feed and clothe."

Eva smiled. "Eleanor, you have a mind for business. You're a lot like my mother. She sees opportunities at every turn. I'm sure there are other ways we can make money, too."

"Like what?" Eleanor replied, her mood already changing.

"I'm sure there are things we can make and sell. Mother talked about baking bread and rolls and making potholders, aprons, and embroidering kitchen towels."

Eleanor's mind swam at the thought of all the money they could make. Surely, she could buy several store-bought dresses.

Eva slipped her arm around Eleanor's, and they walked home. "Think of all the people we could help."

Eleanor stopped. "What do you mean, 'people we can help?' I need to save up money to buy winter clothes and fuel."

Eva cocked her head. "Eleanor, don't you wonder if God has given you stuff so you can help others who are cold and hungry?"

Eva's words pressed heavily on Eleanor's chest. She fought the fear and greed that coiled its slithery tentacles around her heart. She looked into Eva's pure blue eyes and resented her generous and caring nature.

The memory of the apple farmer's wife who'd given her the warm green dress, and a nightgown surfaced. She told herself that she'd earned that nice dress.

Eleanor and William walked to their aunt's house to pick up Rose for church. "I hope Suzanne and Albert don't have to come," Eleanor said.

William nodded. "Poor Rose; you could tell she was so embarrassed by their complaining the whole time and not wanting to sit still—"

"Saying they were bored and not wanting to sing," Eleanor added.

"And practically throwing a tantrum when Father wouldn't let them take communion." William shook his head. "Why did Aunt Fiona insist they come?"

"I don't think she likes them."

"Do you blame her? I certainly don't."

"They wouldn't act like that if she'd give them some attention and discipline," Eleanor said.

"Yeah. Rose does more mothering of those two than Aunt Fiona, and it's not her job."

"Hardly much different from me doing everything, especially when we lived in the shanty."

"At least you know Mother loves you."

"I wish she'd say it, or at least show it like when we lived on the farm. Remember how she used to hug us and read to us and bake cookies with us?" Eleanor gazed at a small, but well-kept home as she talked. "Sometimes I'm afraid Lilly is going to end up like Suzanne and Albert. Mother lets her do whatever she wants and hardly ever makes her help."

William nodded, and they walked in silence for a while. "What do you think of Father and this church and God thing?"

"They've helped us a lot. Do you think Father would have his job and we'd have this house if Reverend Hamilton hadn't told him about it?"

"Probably not."

"Father seems..." Eleanor paused, "happier."

"He does," William agreed. "Remember when Mother wanted him to take you all to the children's home?"

"She wanted him to take all of us."

"I told you I wouldn't go. Anyway, he was supposed to go to the children's home that morning and talk to them about taking us."

"I remember."

"But he was really sad and instead of going to the children's home he went the opposite direction, hoping he could find work—not realizing it was Sunday—and ended up in the church instead."

Eleanor stopped and looked at him. "I know. Why are you telling me this?"

"I'm just saying, maybe God is real; that somehow God led Father to the church where he got help; instead of letting him go to the orphanage."

Eleanor hadn't thought of it this way before. She had been so focused on what Reverend Hamilton and the church were doing for them, she'd forgotten about the orphanage. If God were real and helping them, he helped them in more ways than she realized.

They climbed the steps to Aunt Fiona's and knocked.

Rose answered, her hair in a kerchief and flour dusted on the apron she wore over her everyday work dress. "Hi."

Eleanor stared at her sister in surprise. "Rose, why aren't you dressed? Did you forget we were coming to get you?"

Rose shook her head, and Eleanor could see she was trying not to cry.

Aunt Fiona came up behind Rose. "Rosalyn, that meal won't fix itself."

"Yes, ma'am." She leaned into Eleanor and whispered, "Tell Mother I'll be by this week. I have a surprise for her." She hugged Eleanor and hurried past Aunt Fiona.

"Rose has responsibilities and can't be running willy-nilly all over town."

William squinted at her. "Yes, ma'am," his voice was deeper than usual.

Both were silent for a few blocks until Eleanor spoke. "I hate how Aunt Fiona treats Rose."

"Ab-so-lute-ly. It's not fair, but not much in life is fair. Lots of people have things worse—we've seen that firsthand."

Eleanor stopped, and with a hand on her hips, looked at her brother. "Don't you think it's horrible how Aunt Fiona treats her?"

"Yeah."

"But it doesn't bother you?"

"That's not what I said. But while we were cold and starving, Rose at least had warm clothes, a warm and dry home to live in, and plenty to eat."

"Does that mean that Aunt Fiona can treat her like a...like a..."

"Like a slave?" William said.

"Yes, like a slave."

"No. I'm just saying that everyone has some good mixed with problems." William continued walking.

"What's the good we had?" she shouted. As soon as the words were out of her mouth, Eleanor cringed.

William stopped. "Eleanor!"

"I'm sorry. You're right. I guess I'm so used to having all of you around I didn't think what it would be like to be alone."

"When Father and I were out looking for work and not finding any, he always asked me what good I came across that day."

"What did you say?"

"Sometimes I told him about a new neighborhood I found, or that I met someone who was nice, and even though they couldn't hire me, they wished me well and sometimes gave me a glass of water, or a cup of coffee, or maybe a biscuit."

"Like finding the good in what we might get to eat at the church potluck today?"

William nodded, a sad look on his face.

They neared the church, and Mitchell ran to them.

Eleanor mulled over the things William had said. Rose had some things better than they did, but Eleanor wasn't ready to let go of her anger toward Aunt Fiona. "I still hate how Aunt Fiona treats Rose."

Mitchell joined them but said nothing.

"She doesn't care that Rose is her niece; she can't even get her name right. All she cares about is what Rose can do for her."

"How is that different from what you do?" Mitchell asked.

Eleanor stopped, hands on her hips, and scowled at him. "And what does that mean?"

"It means you do the same thing," William added.

She scrunched her eyebrows, confused. "I do not treat Rose that way."

Mitchell shook his head. "No, not Rose."

"Then who?"

Her brothers both pointed up the street at the church. "Reverend and Mrs. Hamilton and the church people—even Eva, who just wants to be your friend," Mitchell said. His blue-gray eyes reflected his sadness.

"I...I...I...that's different!"

William crossed his arms. "How so?"

"We have nothing, and they have lots." She pointed toward the church. "And Aunt Fiona has lots and is taking advantage of Rose, who has nothing."

"Reverend Hamilton and his congregation don't owe us anything," William said. "Everything they do for us; they do out of love and concern. They're good people; yet if you can't get something out of them, you don't seem to want to be at church or want to spend time with them."

"Including Eva," Mitchell said.

A wall of defense rose in Eleanor's chest and mind. "Well...well. I don't have time to pal around and do things that other kids do. I need to make sure the garden produces lots of food and help Mother can as much as possible, so the money you and Father earn can buy clothes and warm blankets and shoes—"

"Eleanor, you still need to have fun," Mitchell countered. "You're changing; you're not as sweet and kind and caring as you once were."

William agreed.

Her eyes and throat burned at their words.

"But...but can't you see I'm trying to help us? To take care of us?"

Her brothers both nodded.

"But that's all you think about," William said. "It's all you do."

"You're...you're so busy with trying to take care of us—" Mitchell was almost in tears. "That you don't seem to love us anymore."

William lifted her chin with his finger. "He's right. It's not that we don't appreciate all that you do; we do. It's just that you only see the stuff that needs to be done and forgot about us."

"But...but those things are important. We needed food to eat and clothes to wear and quilts to keep us warm."

"Yes," William agreed. "We did need those things, but now we're fine."

"God has given us everything we need," Mitchell chirped, his face beaming with joy. He wore an underlying peace she envied.

"For now, but things could change," Eleanor countered. "Who knows what winter will be like? What if Father loses his job, and we have to move back to the shantytown? What if we don't have enough food this winter? Or coal for the stove? Or —"

William held up his hand. "Enough. We can't spend all our days worrying about what might happen."

"Besides," Mitchell said, "God might give us so much food and money that we can help others."

Eleanor looked at Mitchell and then William. Had they been talking to Eva?

"We don't need lots and lots of stuff," Mitchell continued.

Helen White's store bought dress and nice shoes came to mind—how she wanted some of her own.

Mitchell looked up at her. "I've been watching people; some have very little and are happy, and others have lots and are grumpy. Some people, like Reverend Hamilton, have some things, but willingly share and are cheerful and..." he searched for the word.

"Content?" William added.

"Yes."

"Look who's become the little philosopher." William smiled.

Eleanor swallowed hard. Just last night, she'd prayed that if God was real, he would help her make money. Now, what was he trying to tell her?

The church bell rang. Eleanor was sure Raymond had talked Reverend Hamilton into letting him pull the rope. They all moved toward the church.

Eva stood at the top of the stairs and waved. "Eleanor. Eleanor."

Mitchell touched her arm. "At least you have someone who wants to be your friend."

Eleanor looked down at him, squinting back tears. She'd been so busy; she hadn't realized that neither Mitchell nor William had friends. "You're right." She gave his hand a squeeze and called out to Eva before she hurried to the building.

THIRTY-FIVE

THE WOODEN SCREEN DOOR banged behind Raymond as he moseyed down the back steps. "Hurry," Eleanor called. "The sooner we get this weeding done, the sooner you can play."

"Why do we have to weed, anyway? The plants are all growing."

"For now." Eleanor glared at him. She wasn't going to explain to him again the importance of removing weeds that would take water and nutrients from the large vegetable garden Mr. Hugo had planted and left for them. "Finish weeding between the beets and then do the radishes."

"Why do you always get to be in charge?"

"You know why. Now just do it."

"He's just jealous," Mitchell whispered from between the rows of lettuce and spinach. "He's used to being in charge and doing what he wants."

Eleanor nodded. She stood and peered over the already tall green bean patch, which Lilly always claimed for weeding. No Lilly. "Lilly?"

Eleanor headed to the corner of the yard and the strawberry patch with its wood frame and chicken wire to keep the birds out. Lilly stood with her fingers in her mouth and red around her lips. "Lilly, how many times do I have to tell you those are for all of us, not just you?"

"I wasn't eating them."

"Quit lying to me and get back to work."

"I am. I was trying to get a mouse out of there."

"Maybe you should come and work next to me."

"No, I'm weeding the beans."

"Then I'd better see a pile of weeds at the end of the row, and soon."

"When are the apples going to be ready?" Raymond had already wandered from the garden and was looking up at the apple tree planted in the far corner.

"Not 'till this fall, after the first freeze. Now get back—"

Teddy barked.

Eleanor turned to see the dog barking at the gate that led to the alley. "Teddy, stop. Mr. Potter is going to complain to the police if you keep up that barking. Besides, people can walk down the alley." The dog looked at her and barked a few more times, then whined. She turned back to her weeding, tired of keeping an eye on everyone.

"What about the cherries?" Raymond reached up and pulled a pink one from a low-hanging branch.

Eleanor stood and wandered over to the tree, where several chickens pecked. "Probably in a week or two." She fingered the unripe fruit. "I can't wait for cherry pies and cobblers."

"I bet I could eat a gallon," Raymond boasted.

Mitchell now stood beside them, examining the tree. "And get sick."

"Well, we're going to be canning lots, so we have some to eat this winter." She turned. "Come on, let's get back to work—" She stopped and scanned the garden and then the yard. "Lilly?" Nothing. "Lilly?" She ran to the row of beans—it was empty. "Boys, where's Lilly?"

They both shrugged. They looked around the yard, behind the lilac bush and up in the apple tree. Eleanor ran into the house. Moments later she and Mother came out, having called and searched throughout.

"Eleanor," Raymond ran to the back porch. "The gate's open."

"Oh, no." Mother's light-complected face was almost white. "If something happens to her..."

Mitchell squeezed his mother's hand. "We'll find her. God will help us."

Mother looked at him. The despondent look she had in the shantytown had returned to her green eyes.

"Teddy's gone too," Raymond said.

They all ran into the alley, Mitchell and Mother going one way, Raymond and Eleanor the other, all calling after Lilly and Teddy.

Dogs barked behind wood fences. Raymond or Eleanor knocked on the back door of every home that looked like children lived there and ask about Lilly. At the end of the alley, Raymond turned to the block behind them and Eleanor continued to the next alley. Behind them, Mother and Mitchell reached the other cross street. Mother headed for the street that ran in front of the house and Mitchell down the next alley.

Shannon flagged down a passing car and asked the driver if he'd seen a little fair-skinned, brown-haired girl but was told, "no."

They asked neighbors and children, but no one had seen her.

Eleanor chastised herself for not keeping a closer eye on Lilly, but why wouldn't Lilly leave? Before moving to the new house, she'd roamed at will. Surely this wasn't as bad, she tried to convince herself. But how far would Lilly go? The shantytown had definite boundaries; as far as Eleanor could tell, their new neighborhood went on forever. Her stomach tightened.

She crossed another street and entered a third alley. Fear gripped her. Should she pray? No, that was for religious people, she told herself. Besides, she was just a child; why would God listen to her?

Several blocks behind her, Mitchell walked down another alley, call-ing for Lilly and Teddy. Back yards with garages, small barns, and sheds edged the narrow dirt road. Laughter, shouts, and barking emanated from the yard of a two-story house. He ran to a low fence where a group of children were running around chasing a chicken. Among them was Lilly, and running in a circle around the children, barking and trying to herd them together, was Teddy.

Mitchell ran into the yard as the chase headed in his direction. The terrified chicken flapped its wings upon seeing Mitchell, who scooped it up. He held its trembling body close to his.

"Oh, why'd you do that?" A boy about his age asked. "We were having fun."

"Not with my sister's chicken, you're not."

Teddy bounded to him and barked.

"Lilly, you need to come home."

"But I'm having fun."

"Come on."

"You're not my boss."

"You're already in a lot of trouble. Even Mother is looking for you. If you're not coming, I'll get her."

Lilly put her hand on her hip. "She won't do anything."

Mitchell looked at her. "Are you coming, or do I need to bring Mother back?"

"I'm not leaving."

"Fine. Teddy, you stay." The Australian Shepherd looked up at him with his pale blue eyes, seeming to understand his orders. Mitchell carried the hen home and placed it back in the coop.

Eleanor entered the yard moments later. "Did you find her?"

Mitchell nodded. "But she won't come."

"Ugh! That little brat!" She stopped and pointed at the lone chicken in the coop. "What happened?"

"It followed her several blocks down. When I found Lilly, a bunch of children were chasing it."

"Oh, no!"

"I hope she lays again."

"If she even lives." Eleanor was fuming. "I'd better go get her."

"She won't come. Mother needs to go."

In the garden, Eleanor and Raymond could hear Lilly's shouts of disapproval as Mother, with a firm grip on Lilly's arm, pulled her home with Mitchell and Teddy following at a safe distance. "I don't want to work. I want to play. I hate this house. I hate cleaning and weeding. I don't want to go. I want to go back to our other home."

Mother stopped in her tracks, just inside the gate. "You listen here, little missy. This is your home. Don't you ever refer to that shanty as our home. It was only a temporary shelter." Mother looked over the garden. "Now you get in that garden and start weeding the carrots."

"But I weed the beans."

"Not today, you're not."

Lilly slogged to her assigned row.

Mother pulled an old chair left outside by the previous occupants and sat down.

Lilly stopped and glowered at her mother. "What are you doing?"

"I'm going to watch you. And when you're finished, you will go inside, wash up, and spend the rest of the day in your room until your father comes home."

Lilly's eyes were big, and tears pooled in them.

"Do you understand?"

"I don't want to stay in my room."

"You should have thought of that before you snuck off."

"You don't love me!" Lilly wailed.

"Just get to work." Shannon massaged her forehead and turned to the other three, who quickly returned to pulling weeds, trying to look busy.

"Eleanor, do you have any egg money?"

Eleanor looked up at her mother, suppressing the smile that Mother was finally disciplining Lilly. "Yes."

"Why don't you three go and each of you get an ice cream bar?"

"Really?" The twins each jumped up in excitement.

Lilly stood. "That's not—" but stopped when she saw Mother's look.

Eleanor's smile now burst through; she stood and brushed off the dirt. "Come on boys, let's go."

Mrs. Jacobson prattled on about the importance of grass clippings on the garden, but William only half-listened. Every few minutes he'd glance across the street, hoping to see Clara Turner. He was sure she was peering out the window at him, but hid behind the drapes whenever he looked up. Why did she do that? Didn't she like him? Or was she just teasing him?

William took his pay and wandered over to the Turner's. As usual, he'd use the excuse of asking for work, hoping to see Clara. Throughout the spring, they'd spoken often. There were only a few times Clara hadn't come out to see him, usually when she was strapped to the piano practicing, or it was raining. William avoided her house on rainy days, and Clara confined her piano practice to early mornings.

Today, he pulled weeds from Mrs. Turner's flowerbeds and tossed them into the wheelbarrow; his stomach churning as he anticipated Clara's visit. He wiped the sweat off his brow.

"I wasn't sure if it was you or Cary Grant out here loafing around my yard." Clara leaned against a tree, smiling at him.

William blushed. He wished he could be like Raymond with a quick reply, and tell her she looked like a movie star. Instead, he stood and fumbled for words—any words. "You...you startled me. I didn't hear you."

She smiled, obviously pleased with herself. "I was practicing in case I ever need to sneak up on a criminal or away from a kidnapper."

"What have you been reading?"

"Nancy Drew. She's intelligent, skilled, and always solves her cases. Have you ever read her books?"

William shook his head.

She put a fist on her hip and scowled at him. "Shame on you. I'll lend you a couple, and you can tell me what you think."

"Are there fast cars?"

She rolled her eyes. "You boys and cars." She scowled at him. "She drives. Does that count?"

"We'll see." He grinned.

"Would you like some lemonade?"

He wiped his brow again. "Ab-so-lute-ly."

He took a deep breath when she returned with drinks for both of them. "So, I was wondering?" William paused, trying to get the words he'd practiced out.

She flopped down on the grass; her legs stretched out in front of her—distracting him. "Wondering what?"

"Well, I was wondering if you'd like to go to the movies with me Saturday afternoon?"

Clara examined her fingernails. "This Saturday afternoon?"

He swallowed. "Yes."

She sighed and took a sip of lemonade. "I don't know. What movie?"

William shifted his weight. He'd pondered this for several days. "I was thinking, What Price Hollywood?" He looked at her, his stomach in knots.

"What Price Hollywood?" She looked up at the trellis behind William. "Who's in that?"

William was sure she knew. "Constance Bennett and Lowell Sherman." Had he misjudged her? Was she not interested in him?

"Oh, yes. I remember that one. That looks like it will be a swell show."

His hopes climbed. "So, you'll go?"

"I don't know."

William's mouth turned dry, and he took a drink of lemonade. What should he do? He hadn't expected this. He kicked at the pile of weeds. "Well, I'd better—"

"Let me check my diary; make sure I'm not already booked."

William nodded and went back to weeding, not trusting himself to respond.

Clara watched him for a few moments, then left.

"What am I doing?" he chastised himself. "She's way too much a looker to go out with the likes of me. I don't even have a boiler to drive her around in." He'd cleared several feet of her mother's flower bed and decided that she wasn't returning when the screen door banged shut, and he steeled himself for her rejection.

"Ahem," she cleared her throat.

He glanced up. "Clara, never—"

In two strides, she was before him, her finger on his lips, her brown eyes staring into his. "I was going to tease you a bit more, but Mother says it's mean."

He swallowed; not sure he was still breathing.

She looked at him. "Of course, I'll go."

He took a deep breath.

She sat down and pulled him down next to her.

At her touch, he found it hard to breathe again.

She flopped back, gazing up at the blue sky. "My girlfriends thought you'd never ask—just come over here beating your gums. But I told them you would."

He stared at her. "Then why?" He gestured with his hand. "Why the act?" He looked at her, and she batted her lashes at him.

"Don't I make a spectacular actress?"

He wiped the sweat from his forehead. "Swanky."

A coy smile graced her lips. "A woman must keep her sheik guessing."

Sheik? He raised an eyebrow. Was she calling him her boyfriend?

She avoided his gaze.

"So, after the movie, maybe we could go out for a milkshake?"

She let out a giggle. "That sounds nifty."

On his way home, William fingered the coins in his pocket. Now that Father was working, he insisted William keep some of his pay for himself. "I'm finally taking Clara out." He grinned, then chuckled. "And her old man is paying."

THIRTY-SIX

"IT'S NOT FAIR." LILLY tugged at a weed in the next row over from Eleanor. "All the other children on the block get to play. Why do I have to work?"

"Because you're part of the family, you get to eat this food, so you can help grow it."

"I don't like beets or radishes, so I shouldn't have to weed them."

"And I don't like your complaining, so I shouldn't have to listen to it," Eleanor responded.

"That's a good one," Mitchell laughed.

Lilly threw a handful of weeds at him. "Stop teasing me."

"Oh, quit being a baby." Mitchell chucked a handful back at her; some of the dirt splattered over Lilly's dress.

"Oh, yeah?" She grabbed a large pile of weeds from Eleanor's pile and threw them at Mitchell.

Eleanor looked up from the dandelion she was tugging at. "Hey you two, stop it." Thump. A dirt clod with a small weed attached to it hit her in the back of the head. She turned around to see Raymond stand and fling another one at Mitchell.

Before she could stop it, they hit her two more times as weeds and dirt clods hurtled through the air. "That does it. You guys are in so much trouble." Eleanor picked up a pile of weeds and threw them at Raymond, then sent another flying at Mitchell before dumping two handfuls on top of Lilly.

"What are you four doing?"

They all stopped to see Rose standing on the back steps, shaking her head at them.

"Rose!" They all dropped their ammunition and ran to her.

"Whoa, whoa, whoa. No one is coming close to me with all that dirt. Get back there and clean up that mess. Then wash your hands, and I'll bring you out some cookies."

Eleanor waited for the other three to head back to the garden. "How long have you been here?"

"About a half hour. I brought Mother some patterns and material."

"From flower sacks?"

"No, this is some I bought."

"Did Aunt Fiona give you a raise?"

"No. But sometimes I watch the neighbor's three children. They play with the brats, and I'm able to get more of my work done, and she pays me."

"People pay you to watch their children?"

Rose nodded. "It's not a lot, but it adds up."

"Eleanor, you need to help us clean this up," Lilly yelled from the garden.

Eleanor looked back at the garden, wilting weeds hung limply from green bean and tomato plants and threatened to flatten the delicate lettuce and carrot greens. "I'd better get back, or I'll have another revolt on my hands."

"Who started it?"

"Lilly, of course."

"Just don't tell them about the mud pie fights we used to have with William."

Eleanor smiled.

After milk and shortbread cookies, Rose asked if Eleanor could walk with her back home.

They walked most of the first block without speaking, and Eleanor was beginning to wonder why Rose wanted her to come when Rose broke the silence.

"If I tell you something, will you promise not to tell anyone?"

Eleanor's heart swelled. A secret. Rose was trusting her with a secret. "Promise."

"Cross your heart?"

Eleanor drew a cross over her chest. "Cross my heart, hope to die, stick a needle in my eye."

Rose looked around to make sure no one was listening; even though they were the only ones on the sidewalk for several hundred feet. "I'm thinking of leaving Aunt Fiona's employment."

Eleanor stopped. "You are? When?"

"Well, not for a little while."

Eleanor's smile grew big. "Are you going to move home with us?"

Rose shook her head, and Eleanor's shoulders slumped. "Why not?"

"Eleanor, I'm fourteen. I've been living on my own for almost a year. I'm used to having my own room and being in charge of a whole house. It would just seem...hard to go back to being a child under Mother and Father's rules."

Eleanor's excitement drained. "But...I miss you."

Rose put her arm around her sister. "I miss you too. But there's a great big world out there with lots of opportunities."

Eleanor wondered how many opportunities there were when Father and William had such a hard time finding work. "Where will you live?"

"Do you remember my friends Shirley and Marguerite?"

"Are they the ones who came with you to the shanty?"

"Yes. They work cleaning people's homes and share a room at a boarding house. If I move in with them, I can help with their rent and only have to pay my board. I've met some women who know Aunt Fiona, who have asked if I would clean for them, and Shirley knows a few people who need help with cooking."

"Will we get to see you more?"

Rose smiled. "I hope so. But my plans are much larger than that."

Eleanor looked at her. She couldn't imagine what more there could be.

Working for Aunt Fiona and Uncle Harry, I've met many interesting people. They talk about fascinating places. I've decided that I want to travel and see things."

A knot formed in Eleanor's stomach. She didn't know what to say.

Rose caught her by the arm. "Please, don't tell anyone. If Aunt Fiona finds out, she'll be furious; she'll tell me how ungrateful I am and ruin all my prospects."

Eleanor nodded, certain Mother and Father would not like the idea of Rose living on her own. Sadness draped itself over her. She'd always hoped that someday Rose would come home. It was clear now that she never would. Eleanor regretted their first visit to Aunt Fiona; sure their aunt would take them all in. Instead, Aunt Fiona had only taken Rose away from them forever.

Eleanor took her time walking home. "There's a great big world out there with lots of opportunities," Rose had said. What if Rose moved far away? Eleanor wiped away a tear.

Eleanor hemmed the dress Mrs. Hamilton had left. The woman who owned it had promised to pay twenty-five cents to have the hem shortened and the waist taken in. She and mother chatted about a picnic planned with Mrs. Hamilton and Eva at Manito Park.

"Mrs. Hamilton said we'll walk around the Duncan Gardens," Eleanor said. "She says there is a greenhouse and a beautiful granite fountain and lots of flowers." She was about to ask Mother what a greenhouse was when there was a commotion outside.

Mother walked out onto the front porch. "Raymond, boys. What are you doing?"

Eleanor heard a faint, "Nothing." She shook her head. It was never nothing.

"You boys get out of Mrs. Lockland's yard."

"It's alright, she said we could—"

"I said get out. You have backyards and the alley you can play in. You don't need to be in her flowerbed." She returned, shaking her head, a bundle of mail in her hand. "I don't know what I'm going to do about that boy. He seems intent on getting into trouble, and Lilly seems determined to follow him."

Eleanor nodded and threaded her needle as Mother opened the envelopes.

Mother sighed and shoved the mail in a drawer of the built-in cabinet in the dining room. "Where is your father? He's usually home by now."

Eleanor shrugged. "Is it bad news?"

"Yes."

Eleanor sewed in silence. What could be wrong now? She considered the possible bad things, but she took a deep breath and remembered what Mrs. Hamilton had told her. She now made a list of all the good things that had happened to them; then turned her thoughts to the possibility of selling bread. "Mother, if I can get people to buy bread, will you help me bake it?"

Mother looked up from the socks she'd picked up to darn. "Oh. Yes, of course. Hopefully, that will help."

The front door opened, and Father appeared with a package wrapped in butcher paper under one arm. "How was your time with Mrs. Hamilton?"

Shannon smiled. "Fine, I wish I had her energy. She came today with two baskets of mending. Where do you suppose she finds all these people who can't sew?"

"City people differ from country folk. I imagine there are other things they'd rather spend their time doing."

Mother shook her head. "I don't know how city people can afford not to sew."

Father set the package on the table and wrapped his arms around Shannon. "What makes you say that?"

Shannon sighed and retrieved the mail from the china cabinet.

"Mother says it's bad news."

Father looked in each envelope. "Yep, that makes sense. Living in the city and enjoying its luxuries comes at a price."

"I understand the electricity, but we have to pay for water and garbage?"

"Welcome to the city."

Relief poured over Eleanor. "So, no one died, and we don't have to move?" she asked.

Father chuckled. "You don't miss much, do you?"

She suppressed a grin. "Nope."

"We don't need to move. They're just bills."

"Do we have enough money?"

He looked at them again. "I think so."

Mother took the bills. "And to think, just last night we talked about saving up for winter; making sure there was enough for warm coats, sweaters, and boots."

Father lifted her chin with his finger. "And we will. It's just going to take a little longer. God will take care of us, you'll see."

Eleanor could stand it no longer. "What's in the package?"

Charles grinned. "A roast."

Her grin broadened, and even Mother smiled.

"For dinner tomorrow night. Life is looking up, and we're gonna celebrate!"

THIRTY-SEVEN

WILLIAM GLANCED AT HIS reflection in the plate-glass window of Finnegan's Market. He straightened the new shirt Eleanor had sewed him and adjusted his hat. His heart raced, and he wiped his sweaty hands on his nicest trousers as he walked to Clara Turner's house. He tried to think of things they would talk about on their way to the movie and afterward, at the soda shop.

Several times he forced himself to slow down; he didn't want to arrive early and appear too eager. He'd daydreamed about walking beside the slender brunette, and spending the afternoon with the prettiest girl he'd ever seen from the moment she agreed to the date. But it was so much more. He longed to fall into her deep brown eyes and even deeper soul. There was a magnetism about her. A force that frightened him, but drew him to her.

He couldn't wait to hear her laugh and hopefully feel her hands around his forearm as they walked. Should he put his arm around her during the movie? Would she think that too forward? He suspected she'd be disappointed if he didn't.

He turned the corner and approached the white two-story Victorian with its round pillars gracing the wraparound porch. Mr. Turner's Cadillac V-16 Roadster sat in the driveway. William imagined what it would be like to drive such a machine along wide-open country roads with Clara by his side.

William stood at the end of the sidewalk and looked up at the home. The sheer curtain in one of the upstairs windows ruffled, and he hoped Clara was watching for him. He took a deep breath, straightened his shoulders, and walked to the front door. His heart was pounding as loud as the chimes when he rang the bell.

Moments later, the door opened, and he was face-to-face with Mr. Turner.

"Good afternoon, Mr. Turner." William worked the brim of his hat in his hands. "Is Miss Clara here? We have a date at the movies this afternoon."

Mr. Turner stood behind the closed screen door. "No, you don't."

William tilted his head. Had he gotten his days mixed up? No, today was Saturday. "Uh, yes. Yes, sir. I have a date today with Miss Clara. We're going to the movies and then out for a soda."

"No, you're not."

William blinked.

"No Hooverville tenant will date my daughter. You thought you could hide your shame from me? It's a good thing I drove by when you were unloading that truck of junk."

William stared at the man. "What?"

"You heard me, boy. You're a homeless urchin, and no one of your status will date my Clara."

William shook his head in confusion. "I'm not homeless. You saw the home we were moving into."

"I checked in on that. It appears the house you're claiming as yours belongs to the hospital, not your father—a mere maintenance worker."

William's earlier excitement melted—replaced by a growing anger—the anger of being judged unworthy for situations out of his control.

"It surprises me that the hospital would even hire a vagrant to care for their building."

William straightened, his vision hard on Clara's father, who shielded himself behind the screen door. "You listen here," William's voice was strained but grew in strength. "You know nothing. Nothing of me, nothing of my father, and nothing of what we've been through."

"Don't bother making justifications; you homeless wanderers are full of stories and excuses."

William stepped toward the door and pulled it open. Mr. Turner stepped back. "If you were a real man, you'd quit hiding behind that door. Come out on this porch and talk to me."

"You get off my porch," Mr. Turner's voice shook.

William glared at him. "You think we make excuses? You think all of us homeless people are just lazy wanderers? I'd like to see how you'd survive if you lost your job and home. How would you care for your family if you had nothing and no one would give you a steady job?"

"I'm warning you, boy."

"My father and I knocked on door after door and talked to anyone we could find looking for work to feed our family. But most of the time, no one would even give us a chance."

Mr. Turner leaned away—visibly shaken by William's boldness, but unmoved by his words.

William leaned in. "You think my father's lazy? I'll bet he's worked harder every day of his life than you ever have. You think you're pretty special, you with your fancy car and fancy home. Well, we once had a home of our own." William pointed to the Turner's house. "A house bigger than this one. A house and a big huge barn, four-hundred acres, and a whole herd of milk cows. My father ran his own business, and we were never in want of anything..."

Clara stood several feet behind her father, her eyes puffy and red.

William's voice cracked. He swallowed. "Until some greedy crooks came and stole our pay and burned it all down." He looked away from her and glared at her father before slamming the screen door and stomping off.

The door creaked open behind William, and Mr. Turner stepped out onto the porch. "And don't let me ever catch you on my property or around my daughter again."

William kept walking, his heart pounding as he muttered the injustice of it all. He wandered around neighborhoods he was familiar with and ones he'd never entered. Soon he found himself downtown, following a group of fellows his age. William purchased a ticket at the Fox theater and sat a row behind the boys; thinking more than watching a horror movie he was sure Clara wouldn't have enjoyed.

Mitchell walked several steps behind Raymond and Lilly; their chatter about various neighborhood children annoyed him. He followed them into a backyard, where Raymond joined a group of boys playing marbles, and Lilly ran off to jump rope.

Standing alone, he surveyed the scene.

"Cruthers, you want to join us?" asked a boy playing Jacks.

Mitchell shook his head. "I don't have any."

"You can buy some. They sell 'em at Finnegan's."

"I'll sell you some of mine," offered another boy with a look that told Mitchell he'd be paying too much.

"Nah." He wandered over to a group of girls gathered around a box of kittens and squatted down to pet the mother. Five little black and white furballs nuzzled up to nurse.

"There were six," said a little girl with brown braids. "But one died." She pointed to a white kitten with black spots and a splash of black on its face. "I call that one Poco." She turned to Mitchell. "Which of you is the oldest?"

"My brother William."

She cocked her head and scrunched up her nose. "I thought his name was Raymond?"

"Oh." Mitchell's cheeks flushed at his mistake. "I am."

"Then why is he taller?"

Mitchell shrugged.

"You have pretty eyes."

Mitchell blushed more. "Thank you." He looked down at the kittens, unsure what to do or say next.

The girls all giggled, then skipped off.

Mitchell watched his siblings engrossed in their activities, then slipped out the back gate and down the alley.

He wandered for several blocks before exploring a patch of woods surrounded by the city. He inhaled the scents of dry grass and pine needles. The sounds of traffic, dogs, and people slipped away, replaced by the chirps of robins and sparrows. He climbed a basalt outcropping and looked out over the homes and small businesses below.

He didn't like city life. Despite all the people, he was lonely. How was it that Raymond and Lilly could make so many friends, and he couldn't even make one?

School would start in a month and a half. Would he make any friends there? He missed Lenny. Everyone said the boy had polio. It didn't seem fair. But it seemed a lot of things weren't fair.

Mitchell looked up at the blue sky. "God, can you help me find a friend? I don't need a lot, just one would be nice." Then, as an after-thought, "And please help Lenny."

He stood and walked about the top of the rock, surveying the large vacant lot. A short distance away was a small ravine where something shiny reflected the sun. Climbing down, his heart sank at the sight of the natural beauty spoiled with discarded junk.

Mitchell wandered about the abandoned items. There were tires and tin cans, a broken kitchen chair, several crates and a cracked crock, a butter churn, and some broken and mismatched plates and cups.

He picked up the butter churn and examined the broken lid and plunger handle.

He fingered them. Back on the farm, they took turns pumping the plunger up and down until it was too hard to move as the soured cream turned into butter balls. How good that rich fresh butter was! He could almost taste the biscuits Mother baked with the buttermilk.

Mitchell turned the churn over and examined it for cracks or holes, but there was only one. An idea sprang to mind, and he carried the churn home.

It surprised him to find William in the back room of the basement where Father kept what few tools he had. "Look what I found."

William stopped his whittling. "Where'd you get that?"

"In a ravine." Mitchell looked at the shapeless stick in William's hand. "How was the movie?"

William shrugged. "Alright."

"Did Clara like it?"

"I don't know."

Mitchell set the churn down on the workbench. "Did something happen?"

"I don't want to talk about it."

Mitchell returned to the churn, knowing when to be quiet.

"Why aren't you playing with Raymond and Lilly?"

Mitchell fiddled with the plunger. "I don't want to talk about it."

William gave him an understanding nod.

"Do you think we can fix it?"

William looked it over. "Does it leak?"

"I don't know."

"I have an idea." William picked it up and took it to the basement faucet. "Let's fill it up and see." At about half-full, water dribbled out of two small holes. "Quick, go get a piece of chalk."

Mitchell did, and William circled the leaky spots. They cleaned up the churn and filled in the few cracks with small pieces of wood and wax.

"What do you plan to do with this?"

Mitchell shrugged. "I don't know. I miss the milk and cream and butter and..."

"Home."

Mitchell averted his eyes, and they worked in silence for a while. "Do you think Father will let us get a goat?"

William leaned back. "A goat?"

"It could eat the grass, and we could milk it."

"How are you going to keep it out of the garden?"

Mitchell's shoulders slumped. "Oh, yeah. I forgot about that."

For over a week, Eleanor went door-to-door trying to get bread orders, even passing out samples of her mother's bread. Though many people enjoyed the samples; only two customers agreed to purchase a loaf each week.

She'd sat on the curb dejected. She was selling two to three dozen eggs a week, but feared she'd never have enough to get new shoes and a store-bought dress.

A delivery truck parked across the street, and a man in a white uniform shuffled past, milk bottles clinking together. He returned a few moments later with empty bottles in his metal crate. He paused. "What has a young thing like you so down?"

Eleanor looked up and shrugged.

"It must be something. I see lots of children on my route, but very few appear to have the world on their shoulders."

She sighed. "We just moved here and things are tight. My mother and I want to bake bread and sell it, but I'm not very good at selling things."

He pointed to the basket of samples she had. "Do you mind if I try a piece?"

She held it up for him.

He tasted it and licked his lips. "Oh, that's good. You say you and your mother baked this?"

"Yes, sir."

"You know, I think I can help you."

He followed Eleanor into the house and spoke with Mother.

For three weeks, Eleanor and her mother had risen long before sunrise twice a week to bake and package bread. When Mr. Pollack, the milkman, arrived, they gave him a dozen loaves of bread for milk, butter, and a few coins.

Today, Eleanor stumbled into the kitchen late, still groggy, to find Mother already had four loaves of bread rising. "You should have woken me."

Shannon smiled at her and poured two cups of tea. "You were pretty tired. Your plate's on the counter by the stove; let's eat on the front porch."

Eleanor balanced her plate on her lap, eating her toast and egg as Mother gently rocked in the porch swing and drank tea.

Mother pointed to the eastern sky. "There are still a few streaks of pink in the sky. A reward for rising early."

Eleanor smiled.

Soon they were in the kitchen kneading bread. Shannon's soft voice sang an Irish blessing song:

May the road rise to meet you

May the wind be ever at your back

May the sun shine warm upon your face...

Eleanor joined in, loving this time with her mother. But the morning slipped by, and soon they were rushing to wrap the cooled bread in paper.

Eleanor tied a piece of twine around the last loaf as Mr. Pollack climbed the front steps, milk bottles clanking together. Mother opened the door and the milkman entered with their order.

"Can't stay," he said and exchanged full bottles for empties. "It's gonna be a scorcher today—trying to finish early—ice is at a premium these days."

"I'm sure it is." Shannon looked at Eleanor. "Can you carry some of those loaves out to Mr. Pollack's truck?"

"Yes, ma'am."

Mr. Pollack counted out fifteen cents for Shannon and thanked her for the twelve loaves of bread. "I've got folks on my route who rave about your bread, Mrs. Cruthers. One of these days, I need to hide a loaf away for me and the missus to enjoy."

"If we bake more, could you sell it?"

"Oh, you'd better believe it." He leaned in and lowered his voice. "That Mrs. Track's been out again; offering her bread for a penny less. She must have young-uns who watch my deliveries. I've seen her skip homes I deliver only milk to and go directly to those customers who buy your bread."

Eleanor bit her lip.

"Should we lower our price?" Shannon asked.

Mr. Pollack shook his head. "I wouldn't. Your customers like your bread, and I have others asking for it. It's going to take something mighty drastic to make them switch." He turned back to Mother. "You bake more bread, I'll sell it."

Mother looked at Eleanor. "We'll see what we can do."

Mr. Pollack tipped his hat. "Good day, ladies."

Eleanor looked at the three nickels on the kitchen counter. "That's not much for all our work."

Mother sighed. "But it helps offset our milk bill."

"If we let Mitchell get a goat—" She looked at Mother with hope.

"And who's paying for the fence to keep it out of the garden?"

Eleanor nodded, knowing the damage a goat might do could outweigh any advantage it offered.

As they filled the sink with dishes, Mitchell ran up the basement stairs. "Come and see what I found."

Mother and Eleanor followed Mitchell into the basement and to the workroom. There, on the bench, was a sewing machine.

"Mitchell, where did you find that?" Eleanor rushed over to it, and Mother followed. "Does it work?"

"Possibly. I was walking past this really enormous house, and this lady offered to pay me ten cents to haul it to her trash bin. She said her maid couldn't get it to stitch right. I asked her if I could keep it. She said she didn't care as long as she didn't have to look at it."

"Oh, wow! Can you believe it, Mother?"

Shannon shook her head. "I can't imagine just throwing something away like that."

"Do you think you can fix it?" Eleanor asked.

Mitchell nodded. "Something's probably just too tight or too loose. It might need cleaned and oiled. Look." He dug into his pocket and held out his hand. "She even paid me the ten cents to take it."

"Wow!" Eleanor turned to Mother. "Can you imagine not having to sew by hand anymore?"

"Eleanor, that machine is your brother's; he may want to sell it."

Eleanor paused and looked at him.

Mitchell smiled. "I got it for you two..." He paused, something clearly on his mind.

"What is it?" Mother asked.

Mitchell fidgeted with the foot lever. "I was..." he looked up at them then back down. "...just wanted you to see it."

Eleanor watched a shadow of sadness come over him as he turned to work on the machine. She motioned Mother closer and whispered into her ear. "I think he wants us to sew him something."

Shannon smiled and straightened. "Mitchell, we think the first thing we sew should be something for you. Does that sound fair?"

Mitchell raised his head; a huge grin spread across his face. "Can you sew me a shirt?"

"Of course." The look on Mother's face was one of pride. "What color do you want?"

"Blue. Without flowers."

Eleanor laughed.

"Come on Eleanor, let's leave your brother to his tinkering; we've got a kitchen that needs cleaning."

Eleanor turned to her brother. "Do you want to come with me next time Father and I buy feed sacks? You can pick out the pattern you want."

He grinned, "Sure."

William approached Mrs. Jacobson's home with apprehension. He would not give up this job just to stay away from Clara and make Mr. Turner happy. He tried not to look at her house, but he couldn't help it. The sheer curtains in the upstairs windows were closed, and he couldn't tell if she peered through them or not.

Mrs. Jacobson welcomed him and put him to work mowing the lawn before weeding the front flowerbeds. "You're upset," she remarked as he yanked weeds with extra gusto.

"They're holding onto the dirt extra hard today."

She motioned at the weeds. "There's a time to hold on to the dirt, and a time to let go."

He looked up at her, shielding his eyes from the sun behind her. "Excuse me?"

"Let's take a break and have some lemonade on the back lawn."

He dusted the dirt off his hands and glanced up at the window Clara always watched him from. He squinted. Did she just move behind the curtain?

William took a long swig of the cool drink. "Thank you."

Mrs. Jacobson smiled. "It's a hot day, and I don't need you getting heat exhaustion." She refilled his glass. "I don't mean to pry, but I have it on pretty good authority that you had a date with Miss Clara Turner last Saturday."

William choked on his drink. "I was supposed to."

"But Mr. Turner chased you away."

William picked at a weed seed stuck to his shirt. "You could say that."

Mrs. Jacobson waited for William to look up at her. "I imagine I'm partly to blame."

"What? You?" his last word came out angry, which he regretted.

She held up a well-manicured hand. "Oh, not in the way you think. No. Heavens, no. I actually enjoyed watching the friendship between you and Miss Clara develop. It's been such a long time since Mr. Jacobson passed, and even longer since we courted..."

He tried to understand what she was saying.

She sighed. "Anyway, you two are young and are very different people. That's not a bad thing. Mr. Jacobson and I were very different from each other when we first married. The thought of keeping house focused him on working and getting our feet under us. Me, I was young and over-whelmed. I feared making that kind man unhappy. Though it provided its challenges; we also helped each other to grow and be—" she paused, "bigger? No, better, more rounded people."

William swallowed. He had told none of his family about Mr. Turner's refusal to let him date Clara; though he was sure Mitchell had an idea. He really didn't want to talk about it, and he didn't have a clue where she was going with her stories.

"What I mean to say in my roundabout way is that I could see you two were falling for each other and headed for trouble. I don't know Mr. Turner well, but he is a very proud man who sometimes has his priorities jumbled. I'm afraid I could see that he would forbid you dating Miss Clara."

A knot lodged itself in William's throat.

"William?" She placed her clean hand on his dirty one. "Please, never think you're not good enough for her." She waited for him to look at her. "No matter what her father says; what anyone says. Ever since last fall, when you started working for me, I've seen a young man who is kind, hard-working, dependable, and polite—a good man."

William pressed his lips together and nodded at her words. No one had ever spoken so forthrightly to him before. "Thank you, ma'am."

"Someday, you will make a beautiful young woman a wonderful hus-band."

"But not Clara."

She shrugged her shoulders. "Maybe, maybe not. You're young, and you don't know what might happen. You could meet someone else that you like even more. I know that's hard to imagine right now." She let her words sink in, and they drank their lemonade in silence.

William wondered why he even still liked Clara. He was sure she detested him; once her father exposed who he was to her. If only he could explain himself to her; let her know he wasn't bad just because they were now poor, and he had to work to help provide for his family.

Mrs. Jacobson stood and reached into the pocket of her apron and pulled out some money. "Thank you, William, for all your hard work—"

William shook his thoughts away and stood, startled by her sudden announcement.

"I have really appreciated all the work you've done for me, but—"

William struggled to breathe. "Are you firing me?"

Her hand went to her chest. "Oh, heavens no! I have an appointment downtown. Can you come by next week and finish up those flowerbeds? I hope you don't mind."

Relief washed over him. "Oh, no, that's fine, ma'am." He stuffed the coins in his pocket. "Thank you, ma'am."

"William, I have something else for you." She reached into a different pocket and pulled out an envelope. "Miss Clara came by the other day and asked that I give you this."

William's heart swelled, and he reached for the envelope with shaking hands. The paper was smooth beneath his rough fingers, and he caught a whiff of her violet perfume. "Thank you, ma'am."

"I'm not sure what that letter says, but I consented to take any correspondence you may have and deliver it to her. But like those weeds outside, you may choose to hold onto where you're planted, or you may choose to let go."

He thanked her and left with a mixture of anger and hurt, and her kind words about him running around in his head. Did he want to stay planted in a relationship with Clara that might never bloom? Or should he pull up roots and move on?

Thirty-eight

RAYMOND STOOD NEXT TO Eleanor in the back of the truck. "Hey, look at that. It's a house in a tree."

Lilly squeezed in between them. "Not a very big house."

Eleanor squinted. "Where?"

"Right there, in that huge tree next to that house."

"I don't see it."

"Why's it so small?" Lilly asked.

"It's for kids to play in," William answered.

"I still don't see it," Eleanor said.

"It's way back there." Raymond moved to the other side of the truck.

"Wouldn't it be fun to live in a house in a tree?" Mitchell asked.

Raymond and Lilly agreed.

Eleanor was upset she hadn't seen it and tried to ignore her younger siblings as she and William stared silently at the passing scenery. She contemplated the argument between her parents last night. Father wanted to tithe a portion of his income to the church, and Mother was very much opposed. "How can we afford to give away money when we are so poor?"

"Poor? Poor? Shannon, how can you say that? We have a fine home with luxuries we never had back on the farm. We have clothes and never miss a meal. God is providing for us."

"The children are growing out of their clothes; we have very little furniture; winter's coming, and we don't have enough saved up to buy coats and boots for everyone. We don't know how much it's going to cost to buy coal to heat the house. And, if we're going to be driving around as a family, we should sell the truck and purchase something we can all fit in and be out of the elements."

"But God is providing, and he will continue to provide."

"But what if something bad happens again?"

"We'll survive. We survived the loss of our home and a winter in that shanty. It wasn't easy, but we survived. We can't put our trust in money. If the stock market crash should have taught us anything, it's that money is fleeting. One day it's there; the next day it's gone. But God is always there."

"I can see you've already decided, but don't complain when we're all cold and hungry this winter."

Eleanor had peeked around the corner in time to see Father wrap his arm around Mother. "It will be alright," he told Mother.

But Eleanor agreed with Mother. As they drove through the countryside, she thought about the money she was hiding from Lilly, who was always wanting some for candy and ice cream. How much of that would she be able to use for the patent leather saddle shoes and a few store-bought dresses, and how much would the family need for food and coal?

The truck rumbled as Father downshifted and turned off the highway and onto a dirt road. Eleanor took in a deep breath of the clean air with its hint of pine scent. Father pulled off the road and parked near Reverend Hamilton's car. Eva ran and greeted them.

It was a lovely day for a picnic.

"Let's go fishing," Raymond shouted.

"Hold your horses." Mother held up a hand. "I need you children to unload the truck, and take the things over to Mrs. Hamilton. We're going to eat first, then you can play." Her look said no complaining.

After everyone dished up and sat, Reverend Hamilton asked everyone to share something they were thankful for. The boys were thankful for the outing in the woods, as was Eleanor. Mrs. Hamilton was grateful for Shannon's friendship, and Mother agreed.

"Rose, what are you thankful for?" asked the pastor.

She took a deep breath and smiled. "For a chance to get away and spend time with my family."

Mother reached over and squeezed her hand. "And we are thankful you can join us."

"How about you, Charles?"

Father fiddled with his hat. "Of course, I'm thankful for my family, but, well, this is going to sound strange, but...I'm thankful for forgiveness and for you, Jake."

Jake Hamilton smiled. "Expound on the forgiveness part."

"I'm grateful that God has forgiven me for my sins and mistakes. But I'm also glad that you encouraged me to forgive the men who destroyed our home and farm."

His family looked at him in disbelief.

Jake and Olivia smiled and nodded their heads.

"I know I still have a way to go. Several times a day, I think about what they did, and I get angry. Then I ask God to help me forgive them." He chuckled. "I've named them Welby and Maddox and I say, 'Welby, I forgive you; may God change your heart. Maddox, I forgive you; may God change your heart."

Mother stared at her plate and moved the food around with her fork.

Jake smiled. "Brother, that's a wise decision. Forgiveness will set you free from the bondage of hate, anger, and resentment; just to name a few of the chains that can ensnare us."

Eleanor picked at her food. A feeling of betrayal slithered around her. Those men did not deserve forgiveness.

After the meal, the twins and Lilly gathered their homemade fishing poles and can of worms and headed for the river. Father called Rose and Eleanor over to himself. "Girls, please help Mrs. Hamilton and Eva clean up here while I take a walk with your mother."

Charles took Mother's hand and they strolled down to the river, away from the younger children. Behind them, Jake pounded stakes into the ground to play horseshoes.

"Shannon, I can tell you're not happy with me."

"Really Charles, I feel like I don't even know you anymore. Wanting to take money out of our children's mouths and give it away, and now you want to forgiving those horrible men?"

"Have I really changed that much? We've always helped others."

"People we know," she countered.

"And even back in Idaho, I tried to forgive others."

"Those people deserved it. But those...those horrible men. What they did was...well, it was unforgivable, and yet you want to pardon them and let them go about life as if nothing ever happened."

Charles sat on a rock and took her hand. "Shannon, that's not what I said. What they did was wrong, and they deserve to be punished. But I'm trusting that God is good and just, and he will punish them in his own way and in his own time. But my bitterness was chipping away at me, destroying me." He waited until she was looking at him. "Honey, it's doing the same thing to you."

She turned away, not making eye contact.

"This has changed both of us," he continued. "We can allow it to destroy us as people, as a couple, and as a family. Or we can forgive as God has forgiven us and let him heal us."

She stared out at the water as it flowed past, her eyes moist.

Rose followed a trail through the brush in the direction she'd seen William slink off. Father's announcement played over in her mind, but she had a nagging concern that something else bothered William.

She found him sitting on a rock taller than herself, engrossed in reading something. She was going to get him to talk, whether he wanted to or not.

Rose wandered behind the basalt boulder and found the ground higher, with several smaller basalt columns. She climbed her way up the rock, careful not to rip her dress.

"What are you doing?"

She looked up to see William staring down at her; whatever he was reading hidden in one of his pockets. "I wanted to come and see you."

"When was the last time you climbed something?"

"Can you just help me up?"

"And if I don't?"

"I'll throw rocks at you."

He held out a hand and pulled her up. "Would you have thrown those rocks while climbing, on the ground, or as you were falling?" He grinned.

"I'm disinclined to tell you."

"Disinclined? Now that's a fancy word."

"Oh, I've gathered a multitude since working for our gracious aunt and uncle."

He chuckled. "I could have come down."

"It was a delight to climb. I only wish Aunt Fiona could have seen."

"I imagine that would have sent her hairpins flying."

Rose smiled. "It would have been so worth it."

William sat back down, and Rose settled next to him. "Interesting topography."

"Yes, it is; sister with the five-dollar vocabulary."

"So, what do you think of Father's announcement today at lunch?"

"We've talked about it."

"You have? Do you agree with him?"

William caressed the few hairs that graced his chin. "He's...he's at peace. He never was one to show anger or get down. But last winter, when we were struggling—" William shook his head. "He's tried really hard to be upbeat and look at it as an adventure. But it wasn't working. I'd hear him mutter something about those men under his breath."

She listened to him, trying to imagine what it was like.

He picked up a small rock and threw it. "Resentful. He was becoming resentful. But since that first day he went to church and 'went to the altar' as he says, it appears he's let go of his desire for revenge and has accepted that nothing he can do to those men will bring back our farm or make him feel better. There's a peace about him—not always, but more often than not." William shrugged his shoulders. "I don't get it."

"So, you haven't forgiven them?"

He shook his head.

"I wish we were back home." She paused. "I wonder if Johnny would have married me or that other girl?"

William shook his head. "Life is a lot more complicated than I ever imagined."

"It is."

They sat quietly, each contemplating their own thoughts.

"What about you?" she asked after a while. "Do you wish we were back home?"

He gazed at the distant canyon through which the river flowed. "I don't know."

"Are you kidding?"

He shrugged. "I didn't enjoy being hungry and cold and called names just because we were homeless, but I have met some interesting people."

She eyed him. "Would any of those interesting people be a girl?"

He blushed.

A mischievous smile spread across her face; she bit her lower lip, and her eye sparkled. "What's her name?"

"Clara." His shoulders slumped, and he flicked a pebble off the boulder they sat on.

"Don't be so excited," Rose teased. "What's she like?"

"Clara's beautiful, intelligent, fun, and kind with the most beautiful deep brown eyes; she's bold, playful and interesting. She understands things of the world I didn't even know existed—she even wears her hair in a bob," he said with a sad smile and returned to staring into the distance.

Rose cocked her head and peered into William's blue eyes, and in a soft voice she asked, "Does she not like you?"

William sighed. "Oh, she likes me. That's not the problem."

"Then what is?"

"Her father."

Rose waited for him to continue.

"It doesn't matter." He chucked a rock.

"Yes, it does."

"He wouldn't let me date her. Okay?" William growled.

Rose stared at him, confused.

"He said I wasn't good enough for her because we are poor and lived in the shantytown. 'Hooverville', as he called it. We had a date, and he wouldn't even let me see her."

Rose grimaced. That was something she could see Aunt Fiona and Uncle Harry doing. "I'm sorry."

"It's not your fault. I'm sorry for getting angry." He flicked more pebbles. "I don't know what to do. It's not fair. There are so many people and things against us, just because of those men—" He grabbed a handful of loose pebbles and sticks and hurled them. "Just because they destroyed our lives. Why does what they did to us make me a bad person?"

"It doesn't. People like this man and Aunt Fiona and Uncle Harry are small-minded. They refuse to see past their wealth and their isolated and privileged lives. They've only experienced good and don't understand that not everyone has had the benefits and chances they've had."

William nodded. "The thing is, I really like her—" He pulled the letter from his pocket. "And I know she likes me." He fingered the envelope and placed it to his lips, smelling the fading violet perfume, then handed it to his sister.

Rose took it. "You sure?"

He nodded. "I don't know what to do."

She opened it and read:

My Dearest William,

I feel like Romeo and Juliet, separated from each other by the feud between our families. If only my father could see that love is grander than economics and social class. These are troubling times, and we do not know what the future holds. But we are modern young people, not willing to be held back by the conventions of the past. We are bold and willing to tackle the trials that arise before us. For we are destined to a greater future than what they print with crude ink in the daily screamers.

Hold fast with me. We will overcome these tribulations and triumph. My father will see that keeping us apart is an injustice in need of reconciling. Until then, we must act with stealth and cunning. Mrs. Jacobson, being the kind and understanding soul that she is, has agreed to act as a covert intercessor through which we can pass correspondences.

Let us consent to a secret meeting at the elementary school, under the far trees on the west side at eleven am on Wednesday. I have some strategies we can employ in overcoming our obstacle which will allow us to continue our liaison.

Please let me know by Monday if you agree with my proposal. I will wait with heartfelt anticipation.

Truly Yours,

Clara

Rose read it again, surprised by its content.

William looked at her with bewilderment.

"Is she always this...this theatrical?"

"She loves the movies."

Rose shook her head in disbelief. "And you really like her?"

"I do. She's so unique. I've never met anyone like her."

Rose glanced down at the letter. "I'm sure you haven't."

"How should I respond? I want to write her something, but I don't know what to write."

"That is a dilemma." She reread parts of the letter. "Who is this Romeo and Juliet?"

He shrugged.

"What do you want to do?"

"I want to be with her..."

"But you're afraid of her father?"

He clenched his jaw and furrowed his eyebrows. "It's not right."

"I guess your choice is to see her and risk his wrath when he finds out—"

"If he finds out."

She sighed. "Or let her go, and know there are other girls out there."

He pondered her words, then looked at her with a smirk. "Is that what you've done with Johnny?"

She wrapped her arms around her knees. "I've become acquainted with a few nice young men." A shy smile slipped across her face.

"Come, I want to show you something." Eva grabbed Eleanor's hand and the two, followed by Teddy, scurried down an overgrown path. Eva stopped and Eleanor bumped into her.

"Isn't it beautiful?"

"Oh." Eleanor squatted by a narrow stream that spilled into a small pool surrounded by moss and small flowers. "I love it. How did you find it?"

Eva sat down and ran her hand over the soft green moss as a little butterfly flitted about. "Father and I found it while hiking one day."

Eleanor lay back and looked up at the pine needle canopy above. "This place reminds me of our old home with the trees and bushes and birds."

They lay in the moss, enjoying the sound and beauty of the pool. "So," Eva said. "How did Mitchell learn how to fix things? And where does he get all the things I always see him working on?"

Eleanor rolled over on her side and focused on her friend. "I guess Father taught him. When we lived in the shantytown, Father brought home broken items he'd found, and he'd fix them. We would either use them, or he'd sell or barter with them. Mitchell often helped him. Sometimes Mitchell would find damaged things and bring them back."

"But where does he get the stuff he fixes now?"

"He said there's a ravine where people dump things, and sometimes, he goes through people's garbage."

Eva giggled. "He's quite resourceful. Like that knapsack he made?"

"Can you believe that? He met a tanner who gave him some scraps of leather."

"Pretty amazing."

"Have you seen the cap he sewed from our worn-out shoes?"

"Is that what all those different types of leather are?"

Eleanor nodded. She sat up and examined her friend. "Do you like Mitchell?"

Eva cocked her head. "What do you mean?"

"Are you sweet on him?"

"No!" Her pale cheeks warmed. "I just find him interesting and kind." She paused. "He's kind of mature for his age."

Eleanor considered this. "He is. But most people find Raymond interesting and don't even notice Mitchell."

"That's sad, because he has a good heart and is very clever with the way he makes and fixes things."

Eleanor's countenance turned sad.

"What's wrong?"

"I just worry about him, especially when we go back to school. What if he doesn't make any friends? Or kids make fun of him?"

"I agree."

They were quiet for a few minutes, then Eva brightened. "Do you remember my friend Violet, I told you about?"

"Yeah."

"She has a little brother, Paul. I think he might be Mitchell's age."

"But what's he like? Mitchell doesn't care for the neighbor boys that Raymond plays with."

"Paul is small for his age, kind, and very silly. He's always making us laugh at the silly things he says and does. I think he and Mitchell would get along."

Eleanor smiled. "I hope so. He's so lonely."

They stared into the clear pool and watched the water striders skittering across the surface.

Eleanor sat up. "Can I ask you something?"

"Sure."

"Do you think God is always here? Or does he travel around from place to place?"

Eva laughed. "My Father says that God is everywhere. He sees everything and knows everything."

"How?"

"He's a spirit."

"Humm." Eleanor tapped a stick against the dirt. "If he sees and knows everything and can do everything, then why didn't he take care of us?"

Eva picked up a small pile of ponderosa pine needles. "What do you mean?"

"Why did he let us lose our home and live in the shanty and be cold and hungry? Why didn't he take care of us?"

Eva pulled several of the seven-inch-long needles apart and arranged them beside each other. "I don't know why all those things had to happen. Father says that God allows things to happen for lots of reasons." She pulled more needles apart and tried to weave them between the needles set before her. "Father said sometimes God wants to get our attention, or teach us things, or even get us to move, or do things he wants us to do." She tried weaving another pine needle, but it broke.

"Are you saying God wanted us to move here?" Eleanor also picked up some pine needles.

"I don't know. Maybe."

Eleanor pondered this. "But why didn't he take care of us?"

"He did."

"How can you say that?"

"Did any of you get hurt or die in the fire?"

"No."

"Remember those stories you told me about the farmer with the apples and the wool dress? Or how about your sister coming over with fabric and yarn and food? And all the different jobs your father and brother got that provided wood and money?"

Eleanor nodded and tried again to weave the pine needles.

"That was God providing for you. And remember when Raymond got lost?"

Eleanor reached over and gave the dog a scratch behind his ear. "God helped Father and Teddy find him."

Eva smiled.

"But there were times we were starving."

Eva contemplated this. "Father says that sometimes God gives us lots and sometimes just enough, but he's God, and we can't always know why he does what he does."

"I guess that makes sense." She shoved aside the pine needles. "But now Father wants to...tithe? Is that what you call it?"

"Yes," Eva said.

"But how can we give when we don't have enough money for what we need?"

Eva sighed and gave up on weaving her needles as well. "God will always provide. Mother knows an older couple who were really poor. She told Mother that she gave God a tithe of ten percent, even though they didn't have any extra money."

Eleanor leaned in. "What happened?"

"She said that it never worked out on paper, but somehow, there was always enough money to pay the bills and buy the food."

"Huh."

THIRTY-NINE

ELEANOR WIPED THE SWEAT from her brow as steam rose from the canner and the pots of water on the stove. She peeled the peaches from the Hamilton's tree, and Eva sliced them. Next, Mrs. Hamilton placed them in the jars and poured the sugar water over them. Finally, Mother wiped the jar lips clean, placed a lid and ring on each jar, and placed them in the bubbling bath ready to process. Mother then selected more fruit for Eleanor to peel.

Eleanor liked the sense of belonging and community as they worked together, each doing their part. An image of the band that played at the county fair came to mind. Father had explained how each musician's instrument blended to make beautiful music.

The doorbell rang. Teddy barked and scratched at the back door.

"Just a moment," Mother called. She opened the door to a suited man carrying a metal canister with hoses.

He thrust his hand out. "Good morning, ma'am. What a fine home you have, Mrs.—?"

"Cruthers," Shannon's tone indicated she did not share his enthusiasm.

"Hello, Mrs. Cruthers, I'm Mr. Peters, I'm pleased to make your acquaintance. I've stopped by to share with you the wonders of the Eureka number eleven model vacuum cleaner, the best vacuum cleaner on the market. If you'll just let me in, I'll demonstrate what a fine job this modern machine does in cutting your workload in half—"

Shannon eyed the machine with mixed skepticism and curiosity. "Thank you, but now is not a good time."

He stood straight and confident, his right hand on the vacuum's handle. "Mrs. Cruthers, I can see you're pressed for time. But that's where the Eureka number eleven model will help you out. No more carrying rugs outside to beat them. Just run this delightful machine over your carpets and suck the dirt away."

She raised an eyebrow.

"If I can just show—"

She pushed the door closed.

"Mrs. Cruthers, for just $56.50 you'll be the envy of all your neighbors."

"That will be a first," she called and latched the door.

"Mrs.Cruthers. Mrs.Cruthers."

She walked away from his muffled voice.

Mrs. Hamilton filled the sink with hot, soapy water to prepare for the next batch. "Shannon, Eva told me that Mitchell fixed the sewing machine he was given."

"He did. It will cut our sewing time considerably, wouldn't you say, Eleanor?"

"Yes!" She looked at Eva with relief as she measured sugar for the next batch.

"Girls, those jars we canned yesterday have cooled and are in our way. Why don't you put half in the empty crates for Olivia to take home and carry the rest downstairs?"

"Yes, ma'am," they giggled in unison.

Downstairs, Eva held the crate while Eleanor placed the jars on the newspaper lined shelves in the pantry next to jars of green beans, stewed tomatoes, pickles, cherries, and a variety of rhubarb, raspberry, blackberry, and plum jams. "Isn't it beautiful?"

Eva agreed.

Eleanor imagined the other fruit, vegetables, and maybe even pie filling they'd have canned before winter.

"You know, that vacuum salesman gave me an idea."

Eleanor turned from straightening a few jars. "To make money?"

Eva smiled. "What if we used scraps from the flour and feed sacks and sew potholders and kitchen towels? Then we could go door-to-door selling them."

Eleanor grabbed Eva by the shoulders. "That is a great idea. How much should we ask for them?"

Eva scrunched her face. "I don't know. I'll ask Mother. Maybe she'll take us to the five-and-dime, and we can see how much they charge."

Banging on the back door, accompanied by excited shouts and barking, interrupted them.

Eva's eyes widened. "What is that all about?"

"Let's go see."

The girls ran up the stairs.

"What's happening?" Mitchell asked, rushing up from the workshop where he'd been tinkering with a phonograph he'd found.

In the kitchen, Lilly and several neighbor boys spoke in excited voices, while Teddy pranced around yapping, and Mrs. Hamilton and Mother tried to calm everyone down. "Eleanor, grab Teddy and put him outside. The rest of you, get out of the kitchen and into the front room."

"But Mother, Raymond's in trouble." Lilly looked more frightened than Eleanor had seen her in a long time.

"Please, Mrs. Cruthers, you've got to hurry," a boy about Mitchell and Raymond's age pleaded.

Shannon glanced up at the wall clock. "Olivia, can you take those peaches out of the canner while I figure this out?"

"Of course." Mrs. Hamilton eyed the children with concern.

Lilly grabbed Shannon's hand and pulled her to the front door. "Hurry, Mother."

"Alright, alright. What kind of trouble has your brother gotten himself into?"

Lilly and the boys looked at the floor.

"Lilly, what did your brother do?"

"Nothing. But that mean ol' man is going to hurt him."

"He's gonna whip him," added another boy.

"Who's gonna whip him?"

"The man."

"What man? Why?"

Lilly and the boys fell silent.

Shannon held her hands out, palms up in frustration. "Where?"

"Mr. Finnegan's"

"Why?"

No one answered.

Eleanor, Eva and Mitchell listened from the kitchen.

"Oh, my goodness. Olivia?"

Mrs. Hamilton hurried from the kitchen, her apron partially off, and scooped up her purse. "Do you need a ride?"

Mother's expression was strained. "Please?" She turned to the now silent neighbor children. "You boys go home. Lilly, you come with me. Girls?" She looked into the kitchen.

"We'll take care of it," Eleanor said.

As quickly as the uproar began, it was over, and the house was quiet.

Eleanor, Eva, and Mitchell looked at each other.

"I hope he's alright," Eva whispered to Eleanor and Mitchell.

Eleanor nibbled her fingernail.

Neither noticed Mitchell's knowing look.

William cleaned up at Mrs. Brown's spigot after weeding her garden and walked to the school with the small bouquet she'd given him. His stomach churned. He watched the passing cars, hoping not to see Mr. Turner on his way home for lunch.

A group of boys played baseball, and younger children ran about the playground shouting and laughing. He scanned the tree line but didn't see the slender brunette. He sat down with his back against a Maple, grateful for the rest and shade from the hot weather.

He examined the red, pink, and white flowers. Zinnas...Zinias...Zinnias, that's what Mrs. Brown called them. They had little fragrance, but they were bright and cheerful—he smiled—like Clara.

"Look who I should find relaxing in the shade."

William turned around and scrambled to his feet. "Clara..." He smiled and took in her perfect skin, coy smile, the twinkle in her eyes, and her slender waist and limbs accentuated by the snug red dress she wore. "You look—" He thrust out the bouquet. "They're colorful, like you...I mean...um...bright and um...pretty." His cheeks flushed.

She took them, and her fingers brushed against his.

He almost dropped the flowers at her touch.

She smiled. "You are a gentleman."

The air grew hotter, and he discreetly wiped his hand on his pant leg. "Shall we sit?"

He offered his hand as she sat. "I...I've missed you."

"I try to watch you from the window, but Mother's been keeping me busy."

"Why?" He struggled to form the words, to be reminded of his lacking, but he had to hear it from her, that he wasn't good enough for her or—hope beyond hope—that his poverty didn't matter. "Why does your father hate me? He always seemed so...so fine with me."

"He was fine as long as you were doing the work he hated doing. But he has notions I'll marry one of the young men in the firm."

"Firm?"

"Father is a lawyer; he works for the law firm of Connor and Masters. They have a couple of young lawyers he thinks are magnificent prospects and one of his colleagues has a son Father is fond of."

"What do you think?"

"I want something different. Someday, I'll get married and have children, but not yet. I want to travel and see the world, meet interesting people, have experiences."

William swallowed. His thoughts were mostly on finding the next job, earning the next dime or quarter—surviving for another day. He never considered other options. But he wouldn't tell her that. "What will your father do if he...catches us together?"

"He'd send the police to talk to you."

William didn't like the sound of that.

She leaned back. "But that's all they can do. Maybe threaten you, but you're not doing anything wrong."

William absently watched the boys playing ball. His father would be none too pleased if the police had to talk to him, but he kept that to himself as well. In her letter, she said that they were, '...not willing to be held back...bold and willing to tackle the trials that lay ahead.' He was determined that she did not see him as weak. "What were your ideas? The ones on how we can see each other?"

A sly smile spread across her face; she sat up, leaned into him, and in a quiet voice as if someone might hear said, "If you attend school in the fall, we can see each other all the time."

He smiled at her. She was so beautiful and enthusiastic.

"So, what do you think?" Her eyes were bright.

"That's a good idea. A relatively simple solution."

She cocked her head. "It's a brilliant, yet simple idea. What could be wrong with it?"

William twisted some grass between his fingers. "It's just—never mind."

"No, tell me."

"There's just a lot about me you don't know."

"Then tell me."

"It's embarrassing."

"So, you're just going to give up? Ignore our feelings for each other? Walk away from me and never look back?"

He looked up at her, his eyes clouded, eyebrows bunched. "No. I...Your father was right." He looked down at the grass, at the dirt on his thin and faded trousers, trying to gain the courage to tell her. "My family is poor," he blurted. "We used to live in the shantytown—for about a year." He looked up at her, expecting to see disgust, but there was none. "My father and I spent every day looking for work and scraps of whatever we could find to build a shelter. Rose, the oldest of my younger sisters, lives with my aunt and uncle and works for them, but they don't pay her much. My next sister, Eleanor, raised chickens, first to give us eggs to eat and then, when there were extras, to sell. She sewed clothes and quilts out of flour sacks and tried to take care of us."

"What about your mother?"

William sighed. "She's sad a lot. She helped Eleanor, but she also slept a lot. It's better now, but Father and I worry about her."

"Where did you used to live?"

He smiled at the memory, then the pain hit him. "In a big beautiful log home on our dairy farm, in North Idaho. It was so pretty there and quiet. It was a good life, and the stock market crash and all that went with it seemed hundreds if not thousands of miles away."

"Then what happened?"

William told her about the fire, and how they replaced the bare necessities and moved to Spokane. "We planned to find work and a place to live, but so did everyone else."

Her eyes were large and intent upon him. When he finished, she placed her hand on her chest. "William, that is the saddest story I have ever heard. That is just grievous. Have they caught those horrible wretches?"

William shook his head. "A couple months ago, my father got a job with the hospital as head of maintenance. The job came with a house that we live in, but we don't have that much. Me and Father built our dining room table of boards we found; we have a few mismatched chairs and a long bench that we sit on. We really don't have any furniture in our front room; unless we bring a few chairs from the dining room. My parents and little sisters have beds, but I share a mattress with my twin brothers on the floor."

"Oh my, I had no idea you'd endured such a saga."

He swallowed, unsure exactly what a saga was.

"But what does this have to do with school?"

"Father's job is good, but we have a lot of catching up to do. I need to work to help buy winter clothes and food that my mother and sister can't grow."

She stared at him, her hand on her chest. "William Cruthers, I declare, you astound me!"

He didn't know how to respond. "Meeting you, seeing you, was...well, it was a bright spot in my week. I was afraid if you knew the truth, you wouldn't want to be around me."

Clara's face became stern. "William Cruthers!"

He looked at her, startled.

"How dare you think that of me! If anything, I have greater respect for you. Father thinks everyone in the Hooverville is lazy; that they just aren't trying hard enough."

William shook his head. "It's the exact opposite. Some men abandon their families, and I feel bad for the wives and children left behind. But many are like Father and me, every day looking for work. Sometimes you might get a job for a few hours or even a few days, but usually when we asked for work, we were told, 'No.' Businesses now hang signs that read, 'No Work Here.' "

"So, you don't think you can come to school?"

William sighed. "I'd like to, if only to see you. But by now, I'm so far behind, I'd be a grade behind you."

She looked up into the branches above them. He expected her to be discouraged, but she wasn't. Her gaze returned to him. "I suppose I'll have to come up with another plan."

"I'm sorry. I don't even have any ideas."

"Well, until then, we'll have to keep having these clandestine meetings and communicate through letters."

William sensed she might want to leave and sought to keep her for a few more minutes. "I was really disappointed we couldn't go to the movies."

"Me too. I refused to speak to my father for three days. He finally threatened to ground me to my room unless I started speaking to him again."

He smiled at her tenacity. "I'm sure your father thinks he's just doing what is best for you."

A shadow blocked the light, and they both looked up into the silhouette of a male figure.

William's breathing stopped.

"Clara, what are you doing here?"

She shaded her eyes. "Marvin Thayer?"

A youth in ironed trousers and a white button-up shirt sauntered close to Clara. "Is this hood trying to boondoggle you?"

William scrambled to his feet, noticing that he stood several inches shorter than the boy. "Clara is quite safe and smart enough to make her own decisions about who she spends time with."

The boy looked down at William, then over at Clara. "Is he bothering you?"

"Ab-so-lute-ly not! Why don't you mind your own beeswax?"

"Where you're concerned, I am."

"Well, it's time you get over this archaic idea that I am your baby."

Marvin bent down and brushed her cheek. "You know we're destined to be together; our fathers talk about it all the time."

"Well, my father doesn't choose who I spend my time with. I do."

"That's not the story I got." He focused his attention on William. "Is this the Hooverville scamp your father turned away a few weeks ago?"

William stiffened. "What we're doing here doesn't involve you. So, leave!"

In a flash, Marvin grabbed William by his shirt collar and pulled him to within inches of his face. "But it is my business; because I am her future and you're not. So, listen here, Hoover scum, you'd better get it through your head, you're out of your league here. Leave her alone." He let go of William's shirt and shoved him backward.

William stumbled and caught himself.

Marvin held out his arm. "Come on Clara, I'll walk you home."

"No." she protested and stepped back.

No sooner had she moved away from Marvin when William plowed into the boy, head aimed at his side, and knocked him down. The two wrestled about on the ground, William pinning Marvin for a few seconds before Marvin flipped him off and was on top.

"Fight!" shouted several boys playing ball, and both teams rushed to the scene.

William wrestled free and jumped to his feet, as did Marvin, and they moved about in a circle, each with his fists ready.

"Come on, you hobo, let me teach you a lesson."

William resisted the bait. Over the past year, he'd seen his share of fights. He'd seen fellas drawn in by their emotions, blindly swinging, only to get beat up. He'd already given in to that rage once with Marvin. That wouldn't happen again.

"You Hoovervillers have taken over our city. It's time I run some of you out."

"I ain't going nowhere."

"We'll see about that."

"Why don't you go back to where you came from? Can't you see she doesn't want you?" William taunted as they continued to move about in a circle.

"Punch him Marvin," a kid yelled.

"Yeah, hit him," said another.

"Fight. Fight. Fight. Fight," chanted the boys.

Marvin grinned at their calls, and William swung, hitting him on the jaw.

"Get him Marvin."

"Don't take that from him."

Marvin squinted at him. "You think you're pretty smart, don't you, hobo?"

William faked a punch to Marvin's face, and the boy raised his fists to block it. William punched him in the gut twice, then the chin when the boy lowered his fists.

"Ooh," several boys hollered.

"That's four to zero," one boy commented.

"Shut your mouth, you little monkeys, or I'll beat you up next."

"Sure thing there, Thayer."

"Thayer, the slayer, isn't as dangerous as he thinks he is," said another boy.

Marvin glared at William and pounced, arms flying, fists pelting. William lowered his head and drilled the boy several times in the gut before William was able to land an uppercut. When they backed up, William's ears rang from the punches, and he shook his head, trying to clear the sound.

Marvin charged, and William stepped aside and hit him in the side. Marvin turned and struck William in the cheek.

"Yeah," shouted a boy. "Now that's what I call fighting."

William struck back, giving his opponent a bloody nose.

Marvin stumbled backward, and his hands went to his face. "You worthless hobo, now you've broken my nose."

William stood ready in case Marvin charged again.

When Marvin stood, he looked around at the boys watching. "Get out of here. No one invited you."

Several boys shrugged and wandered back to the baseball field while others poked fun at the smartly dressed boy.

"Good job, fella," one of them called.

William half smiled.

"Yeah, good job," added several others.

William watched Marvin slink away, then turned to Clara. The stand of trees where they had met was empty. He looked around the field and playground, but there was no sign of her.

He scooped his hat off the ground and washed up in the water fountain. How long until the police came to talk to him? He didn't know which was worse, talking to the police or the conversation afterward with Father.

FORTY

AT FINNEGAN'S MARKET, SHANNON jumped out of Olivia's car and ran into the shop. "Lilly, where were they?"

Lilly pointed to the rear of the store. "He took him to the back."

"Can I help you ma'am," a teenage boy asked as Shannon looked about the store.

"I'm looking for my son; I was told he was being hurt." Her words came in short bursts, as if she was trying to catch her breath. "He's about yay high." She held her hand to about four feet. "Brown wavy hair, his name is Raymond Cruthers, my daughter—" She pulled Lilly to her and ran her hand over Lilly's head.

Lilly squirmed under the man's scrutiny.

"Oh, that boy." He motioned with his thumb to the wall behind him. "He's in the alley with Mr. Finnegan getting a whipping for stealing."

"Stealing?" Shannon's eyes widened, and she turned to Lilly. "You never mentioned that he was stealing."

"I didn't know."

"She knew, ma'am," the teen countered.

"You go sit in the car with Mrs. Hamilton; I'll deal with you later."

"But, Mother—"

"Now, missy."

Lilly stuck her tongue out at the teen and stomped out of the store.

Shannon composed herself and left the store. Once out front, she walked around the building to the back corner.

Wussh. Slap.

She stopped and took a deep breath.

"Ouch! Stop. You're hurting me."

"You don't seem to care that your stealing is hurting me."

"We're not hurting you. You've got lots of stuff."

"You street urchins need to be taught a lesson. I've worked hard to build up this business and keep it running during these hard times. I don't need a bunch of hooligans walking off with all my merchandise."

Snap.

"Oww! Why are you picking on me?"

Wussh. Snap.

"I'm not the only one. I only took a comic book."

"This time."

Wussh. Slap.

"Oww! I never stole anything from you before."

Snap.

"Don't lie to me, boy. I've been watching you and your little gang—"

Shannon stepped around the corner. "And what have they been doing, Mr. Finnegan?"

Raymond let go of his ankles and stood. "Mother, he's hurting me." He took a step toward Shannon, but Mr. Finnegan stopped him. "You hold up there, lad."

"Mother—"

Shannon held up her hand. "Raymond, you just be quiet. I want to hear what Mr. Finnegan has to say."

"But—"

Shannon gave Raymond a stern look that stopped his protest.

"Ma'am, this is your son?"

"He is."

"Well, ma'am." Mr. Finnegan leaned against the half-inch board he'd used as a paddle and pointed to Raymond. "He and a group of boys come around several times a week. First, they would snatch apples from the front of the store and run off. Then several would create a diversion while a few others stole something of greater value, usually candy bars, comic books, gum or soda, one time even a watermelon."

Shannon took a step toward Raymond. "Is this true?"

"No Mother, he's lying."

Shannon raised a shaking hand—about ready to strike. "Raymond Allen Cruthers, don't you lie to me. I wasn't born yesterday."

"But—"

"You be quiet. I've seen those boys you run around with and heard snippets of stories. Your father is going to hear all about this, and you can be sure he won't be any too happy. Now you owe Mr. Finnegan an apology."

"But—" He stopped and with a set jaw and squinted eyes mumbled, "I'm sorry."

"I didn't hear you and I don't think Mr. Finnegan did either."

"I'm sorry." He turned to Shannon. "Can I go now?"

"No."

"Mr. Finnegan, what all has my son stolen?"

"He's stolen apples, at least one comic book, gum, and candy. I also suspect he stole more before we caught on to what he and his gang of hooligans were doing."

"How much does he owe you?"

"I suspect two-and-a-half, maybe three-and-a-half dollars."

"What?" Raymond exclaimed.

Shannon looked at Raymond. "You will pay him back!"

"But I don't have any money."

"Then you'll work it off." Her green eyes flashed like fire and bored into him.

"But, Mother—" He stopped when he saw her look.

"I am very disappointed in you, and I know your father will be too."

Raymond hung his head. "Yes, ma'am."

Shannon stretched out her hand to Mr. Finnegan. "I am so sorry for the trouble Raymond has caused you. My husband and Raymond will be back tomorrow morning to discuss how Raymond can work off his debt to you."

Mr. Finnegan shook her hand. "Thank you, ma'am."

"And you, young man." She had a hold of Raymond by the ear. "You are going home and sweeping both porches and the basement. Then I'll find something else for you to do."

When he opened his mouth to object, she raised an eyebrow, and he stopped.

Eleanor and Mitchell exchanged looks as everyone ate in silence that evening. William, with his black eye, didn't look up from his plate. Mother picked at her food; her sadness from the shantytown returning.

Father set his silverware across his half empty plate. "Boys, on Saturday we're going to go wood chopping."

"I have some yard work to do," William announced.

"Well, get it done before Saturday."

"Yes, sir."

"Why do we all have to go?" Raymond asked. "Can't you and William do it?"

Charles looked directly at his youngest son. "Raymond, you are one reason we're doing this."

Raymond opened his mouth to argue, then shut it.

"I am very disappointed in you, Raymond. You know better than stealing."

"Yes, sir."

"And you, William, what were you thinking?"

"I don't know, sir. I was wrong."

"I want to go to the woods. Do I get to go?" Mitchell asked.

Father smiled. "Yes, you get to go too."

"What are we going to do with the wood?" Mitchell asked.

"We're going to make firewood, and I think the first load should go to Mr. Finnegan."

Raymond put down his fork. "The first load?"

"Oh yes, this is going to be your new chore. I'll get some trees cut down on Saturday and then you boys can go back during the week to saw, chop, and load them into the truck."

William's shoulders slumped. "What about my other jobs?"

"If you can find time to fight, you can condense your jobs and make a few days a week to go get wood."

William sighed. "Yes, Father."

Eleanor glanced at Lilly, who pushed her peas around on her plate with a smug grin.

"Lilly," Mother's voice was firm.

The six-year-old bolted upright, her brown braids bounced forward.

"Quit playing with your food. And don't think that you won't have consequences."

"But I—"

"Lilly." Charles' voice was stern. "You will not speak to your mother that way. Do you understand?"

She glared at the table. "Yes, sir."

"Lilly," Shannon continued, "it's time you help out around the house."

Lilly's little head jerked up. "Me? What about Eleanor?"

Mother looked intently at her youngest. "Eleanor is none of your concern; she has proven herself trustworthy."

Eleanor's heart warmed at Mother's words. "She has proven herself trustworthy." It was as if Mother had hugged her and said, "I love you."

"You, on the other hand, have a few things to learn."

Lilly opened her mouth to protest, but Father cleared his throat, and she stopped herself. "Can I be excused?"

"After you finish the meal and clear the table."

Lilly pursed her lips and picked at her remaining bites.

"Don't think you can get out of it by lollygagging," Mother continued. "That will only get you helping with the dishes."

At this, Lilly shoveled the remaining bites into her mouth and was about to guzzle her water when Mother reprimanded her for not eating lady-like.

She chewed and glared at Eleanor, who inwardly cheered that Mother was holding Lilly accountable.

Mitchell saw it, and when Lilly took her plate and cup to the kitchen, he leaned over. "What was that for?"

"I don't know."

Lilly cleared everyone's dinnerware except Eleanor's and was about to go outside when Mother called her back. "Lilly, aren't you forgetting something?"

She stomped back and took Eleanor's plate and cup. "This is your job, and I'll get you for this," she whispered.

"I highly doubt that."

"Oh, you just wait. I'm going to get you big."

Eleanor shook her head, but still decided to keep an eye on her.

"I don't want any." The lady shut the door, knocking the potholder Eva was holding to the porch.

She dusted it off. "This is harder than I expected. How are we ever going to earn enough money to help the people in the shantytown?"

Or buy a store-bought dress and patent leather shoes, Eleanor wondered.

They plodded along, offering the kitchen towels and potholders along with samples of bread. After several hours, they had sold two sets of towels and had seven bread orders.

"I'm done!" Eleanor plopped down on the curb.

Eva looked up the street. "Hey, is that your truck?"

Eleanor looked to where she pointed. "Yes, it is." They ran down the street to find William stacking wood near the tailgate. Mitchell stood near a driveway and handed the wood to Raymond, who carried and stacked it against a white house. "Hey guys, what are you doing?"

"Helping Raymond," William grumbled.

"Is this Mr. Finnegan's house?"

"Yeah." Raymond took a deep breath. "You would think if he's rich enough to own his own store, he'd have a much bigger house."

"Get to work," William ordered. "I'm tired of wasting my time because of your stupidity."

Eleanor examined the half-unloaded truck. "Will you be done cutting wood after this?"

"No. Father has plans for us to get more wood and thinks this is good for us; keeps someone out of trouble."

"You're in trouble too," Raymond hissed.

Mitchell grabbed another piece of firewood. "Come on, guys, can we just get this done?"

"I agree." William returned to his task, but stopped and jumped down from the truck. "Mitchell, I think I've got enough within reach. Can you move some more forward if Raymond catches up?"

"Yeah, but—"

William was already running up the street toward a girl.

"Where's he going?" Eleanor asked.

Mitchell eyed the girl.

"Mitchell," Eleanor leaned in. "Where's he going?"

"To talk to that girl."

"What girl?"

"The one up there." Mitchell pointed.

Eleanor squinted. "Who is she?"

"I...I...I'm not...sure."

Eleanor grabbed her brother and turned him around. "Who do you think she is?"

Eva leaned in.

"Wait," Mitchell whispered, then filled Raymond's arms with more wood. After his twin was out of earshot, Mitchell leaned in. "It might be Clara."

"Who's Clara?"

"His girlfriend."

"Girlfriend?" both girls shrieked.

"Shush. No one's supposed to know."

"Why?"

"Her dad doesn't want them seeing each other."

"Why?"

They paused, and Mitchell reloaded Raymond's arms and sent him off. "He doesn't like William because we were homeless."

"That's stupid," Eva said.

"Yeah," Eleanor agreed. How long would their being poor and homeless stalk them?

Mitchell looked anxiously up the street at William and Clara and then at a passing car. "Please, don't tell him I told you, and don't tell anyone—not even Mother and Father. William could be in real trouble if her father sees them."

William had a girlfriend! A thrill shot up Eleanor's spine and arms. "Promise," she told Mitchell. She took one last look in William's direction, then they headed home. She calculated the money she and Eva hoped to make. Sure, the people in the shantytown needed it. But she so wanted nice clothes. She dreaded Helen White calling her a Raggedy Ann or ragamuffin.

FORTY-ONE

"CLARA."

The slender girl in a deep blue dress turned around. "William! You never answered my letter?"

"I never got your letter."

Her face scrunched. "Why? Are you not working for Mrs. Jacobson?"

"Yes, just at different times." He told her about Raymond getting into trouble, and how he had to rearrange his jobs to take his brothers wood cutting.

Clara's eyes were wide. "You chop down trees?"

"No, my father does that on Saturdays, and I help him. Then my brothers and I saw them into pieces." He held his hands apart about sixteen inches. "And chop them into firewood. That takes us about three days a week."

She looked at his arms and chest. "You sure have lots of muscles."

He blushed. "So, why'd you leave?"

She looked down at the sidewalk. "I'm sorry. I was afraid."

"Of what?"

"That my father would catch me."

"Clara, it was your idea."

"I know." She fiddled with her necklace. "But I hadn't considered that someone like Marvin Thayer would see us. I only expected little kids would be at the school ground. I knew Marvin would tell my father, or at least his father, who would tell my father."

William shifted his weight. "So how did running away keep him from telling your old man?"

"It didn't, but I was home, baking cookies when Father got home for lunch, so when Marvin claimed I was with you, I could say, 'No, I wasn't at the school ground; I was at home baking cookies, remember Father?'"

William looked at her. "Did it work?"

A coy smile spread across her lips. "Of course, it did." They laughed for a moment. "So, who won?"

William grinned. "Who do you think?"

She smiled and ran her hand over his bare arm. "I figured you would."

He blushed again.

"William," Raymond yelled. "Come on, we need your help."

"I'd better get going." He took a few backward steps.

"Have you talked to your folks about school?"

"Not yet. I'm waiting for the right moment." He hoped chopping wood would give them the extra money they needed so he could go to school. He had never imagined that he'd want to go to school.

"Ninety-seven, ninety-eight, ninety-nine. Six dollars and ninety-nine cents." Eva and Eleanor stared at the pile of coins. Eleanor straightened a stack of coins. "Wow, that's a lot of money." Eleanor struggled to suppress her desire to use her half of the money for new dresses and shoes.

"I know. Think how much food we can buy to give to the Lee family."

Guilt nagged at Eleanor. The Lees had been so thin and frail the last time she'd seen them. Memories of never-ending hunger squeezed her stomach. Though Mother rarely allowed them to gorge themselves, the pain of hunger and weakness was gone. "Father says that the Lees are a proud people. They may not accept the food we want to give them."

"Hmm." Eva had that look of determination she got when posed with an obstacle to something she really wanted to do. "Maybe we could put it on the front door, knock, and hide."

Eleanor pondered this.

"Or we could give it to them, and if they insist they work for it, we could have them do some work around the church."

"That's a good idea."

A few days later, William drove the girls down to the shantytown. It seemed like the shantytown had grown; Eleanor recognized some people, but there were new people living in other shacks. Her heart sank at the memory of it all.

"Look, our shanty's gone." Eleanor exclaimed as she examined a small building where theirs once stood.

"I imagine people tore it down, taking what they could for their homes."

"Why couldn't another family move into it?"

William stared at the newer building. "I suppose there would be a fight over who got it. This way, lots of people benefited."

"I suppose."

They stood in front of the Lees' shanty, and William knocked on the door. A tired and gaunt woman with a faded dress answered the door. "What do you want?"

They stared at her.

"What's wrong? Did you come to gawk at me in my troubles?"

"Oh, no ma'am," Eva responded. "We were expecting someone else."

"Ain't no one else here but me and my kin. Who is it you lookin' for?"

William spoke up. "There was a family here this spring, the Lees. They were a Chinese family."

"Well, they ain't here anymore."

"Do you know where they are?"

"How would I know? They just up an' left one day and we'se moved in."

"Oh."

The woman now eyed the crate of food.

Eva nudged Eleanor. "Can we?" She motioned at the woman.

Eleanor shrugged. This had not turned out like she had hoped.

Eva's smile grew. "May I ask what your name is?"

The woman squinted at her. "Why?"

"Well—" Eva paused. "We've worked hard to earn some money to help the Lees, but if they're no longer here, we'd like to give this food to you."

The woman's scowl softened. "Is you pullin' my leg?"

"No ma'am," William spoke up. "We used to live in a shanty that was over there." He motioned with his thumb at the shanty now sitting where theirs had been. "We can't help everyone, but we would like to help someone."

The woman's eyes softened. "My husband and two sons look for work every day, but they don't find any. They left two weeks ago to find work in Seattle, but I ain't heard from them."

Eva's hand went to her chest.

William held the crate out to the woman. "Please, take it."

Eleanor pointed to some items in the box. "There's produce from our garden and a loaf of bread we baked and some strawberry preserves we made. And you can use the flour and salt bags for sewing clothes and quilts. That's what we did."

The woman took it and just stared. "This...this is one of the nicest things anyone's ever done for me." Her voice cracked.

"Ma'am," William bent to look into her eyes, "How are you fixed for firewood?"

She shook her head.

"I'm headed up into the woods tomorrow. I'll get you some and split it, too."

She turned her face to her sleeve and wiped her eyes. "Would you?"

He smiled. "I'd be glad to."

They left the shantytown in silence. Hooverville residents watched them leave; their eyes devoid of hope. Driving through town, a blue dress in a store window drew Eleanor's attention. Empathy fought with desire and a rising anxiety.

Eleanor was still thinking about the department store dress when she and William walked into the house.

"Where's father?" William asked.

"In the living room," Mother called while Lilly stood on a stool beside her, snapping beans and scowling.

Father sat in a kitchen chair, reading the newspaper, his eyebrows bunched up. Eleanor sat near him on the floor.

William leaned against the wall next to him. "Father, I was wondering..."

Charles looked up. "Oh, you two were supposed to go to the shanty-town this afternoon; how was your visit?"

"The Lees are gone and so is our house—shanty," Eleanor corrected herself.

"I imagine."

They told him about the woman they had met and given the food the girls had bought.

Charles shook his head. "People are starving, farmers aren't bringing in their crops..." He stabbed at the paper. "And sometimes, the government pays farmers to destroy them."

Eleanor stared at him in disbelief.

"Why?" William asked.

"The newspaper says there's an oversupply of food which is driving the prices down. The cost to harvest the crops is more than the farmers would earn."

Eleanor cocked her head. "How is that?"

"The money they'd spend for fuel, labor, and storage would be more than they'd make at market."

"Oh."

William shifted. "So, the government is going to pay them to destroy the crops?"

Father nodded. "It will keep the farmers in business and hopefully drive up the prices so they can support themselves."

"That doesn't seem right. What about the people who can't afford food right now?" William's voice vibrated with agitation.

Father sighed. "I don't know. If you let the farmers go out of business, then no one has any food."

"But if they raise the prices; more people starve." Frustration crowded William's countenance.

Charles nodded.

Eleanor's thoughts played tug-of-war between the pretty blue dress and the starving woman.

"You know that thicket Raymond got lost in?" William changed the subject.

Charles looked up at him.

"It's gone. There are only a few scraggly bushes, and I'm sure they'll be gone before long. People are even building shacks there."

Father shook his head. "This has got to stop."

"Well, I was thinking." William shifted to face his father. "Why don't we take this next load of wood down there for those people?"

A smile spread across Father's face. He looked up at William, then Eleanor. "Was this your idea?"

Eleanor pointed to her brother.

"That lady we gave the food to doesn't have any fuel," William said.

"That's a great idea. I'll talk to Reverend Hamilton. He wanted to help the people out." Father looked down at the newspaper and tapped the article he was reading. "I'm also going to talk to him about this crop situation and the story of Ruth I was reading."

"Ruth?" William looked at him quizzically.

"Ruth was a Moabite widow living in Israel with her widowed mother-in-law. They were very poor, so her mother-in-law suggested she glean grain in the field of a relative named Boaz. In those days, it was customary for farmers to leave grain along the edges of the fields and not to go back over the already harvested fields. Poor people could go behind the harvesters and glean any grain left behind. This was God's way of providing for the poor who were willing to work."

"Huh."

"It's something to consider in our current economic situation," Father said; he watched his daughter. "Eleanor, you look as if something is bothering you."

She shrugged.

"What is it, Kitten?"

"Well...what if someone worked really hard to save up for something they really wanted and kind of needed, but then learned of someone with a greater need? Would they be wrong to use the money they'd worked really hard for to buy what they wanted? Or should they share what they had with the person who didn't have much?"

Father leaned back in his chair and rubbed his chin. "Wow, that's a pretty tough dilemma. What do you think, William?"

William started from his own thoughts; surprised Father had asked him. "Um, well..."

"Is this something you're struggling with, too?"

He nodded.

Father looked at both of them. "What do you suppose is the main issue here?"

"Our needs versus others' needs?" William asked.

"Maybe. What do you think, Eleanor?"

"Greed or selfishness versus giving and kindness?"

"Maybe. You've both brought up some excellent points. We have needs, as do others, and God wants us to help others who are in need."

Mitchell slipped in and sat on the floor, his back to the wall.

"But what if we're in need, too?"

"Good question, Eleanor. We know what it's like to be in need, don't we?"

"Uh huh," they all agreed.

"Do any of you remember being hungry when we lived on the farm?" They were quiet.

"I remember plenty of times each of you said you were hungry...starving in fact. But were you?"

They shrugged, not sure how to answer.

"Of course, you were. But, compared to the hunger we experienced after the fire, you each struggled to say you were hungry back then."

"But...what does this have to do with my question?" Eleanor asked.

"I'm trying to help you see that there are different levels of need. Two people can both be hungry, but their hunger isn't always the same."

William played with a loose string on his shirt. Eleanor's eyes widened in understanding.

"It's easy to look around us and see people with more than us or nicer things than we have and feel like we have great needs. But we can also look around us and see people with less than us and see our abundance. Jesus pointed out to his disciples a poor widow who only gave two small coins to the Lord—"

Mitchell's face brightened, and he leaned in.

"Do you know this story?" Father asked him.

"I do." His eyes lit up.

"What happened next?"

"Jesus said the poor lady who only gave two small coins gave more than the rich people who put in lots of money."

Father smiled. "Yes. He said that she gave all that she had."

Eleanor's usual smile was downward. "Should I give all the money I earned and was saving to the woman in the shantytown?"

"God loves it when we give—with a joyful heart." He paused. "But he also knows our needs and rewards us when we work by providing for our needs and even some of our wants."

William and Eleanor pondered this.

"I won't tell you what to do. You have both worked hard to help us as a family and to earn some money for yourselves. God understands, and he cares about you, too. He knows your needs and wants. He desires to give you good gifts, but he also wants you to have hearts that care about what he cares about—which is people."

Tears streamed down Eleanor's face. "So, how do we know what to do?"

Father motioned her to him and lifted her chin. "You need to pray and examine your motives."

"William," Mother called from the kitchen.

"Coming."

Shannon looked up from the pot of water she was pouring fresh peas into. "Did I hear you and your father talking about getting wood tomorrow?"

"Yes, ma'am."

"Why don't you get your brothers and clear out those weeds along the side of the house to stack it?"

William shifted his weight and plucked a pea out of a pod.

"What is it?" she asked.

"I can get the boys and we can do it...it's just that—"

She put a hand on her hip and glared. "What?"

"We were going to take this load to some people in the shantytown—" He watched her eyes widen and her pale skin redden. "Mother, they don't have any wood. The thicket is gone."

"What about us?"

He looked about the house, bewildered. "We have the furnace, and you have the electric range—" He pointed to the stove behind her.

"And this winter—what if we can't afford to buy coal? How will we heat this house?"

William took a step back. "We'll get wood...it's just that...they have nothing."

"And if we don't stock up, we won't have anything either."

Charles entered and placed a hand on William's back. "What's the problem?"

Eleanor watched Mother's eyes grow wild.

"William here tells me you're planning to take the wood you chop tomorrow to the shantytown instead of stocking up for our own needs," Mother spat, visibly shaken.

Father took a few steps toward her; his hand low and flat to motion for her to calm down. "Shannon, it's alright. We'll get wood for ourselves; don't worry. But right now, we have, and they don't."

"And Pastor Hamilton? He didn't have any coal? You had to give him some wood?"

Eleanor bit her nail, and Mitchell mumbled quietly next to her.

"Shannon, you know how much they've helped us. I just wanted to show our appreciation."

"And those two elderly ladies you gave wood to?"

"Shannon, they have little money, and yet they hired me and William plenty of times before I got this job."

"I still work for one of them," William interjected.

"Charles, it's not enough that you insist on giving some of your pay to the church, but now you're giving away the work of your hands that could keep us warm this winter?" Tears filled her eyes.

From the doorway, Raymond motioned to Lilly, who slipped away from the kitchen unnoticed and into Raymond's bedroom.

"Honey, we will be fine. It's still summer; me and the boys have time to get us several loads of wood. But God has been generous, and we can give to those who are in greater need than us."

"He's been generous to us? Charles, do you hear yourself? Your god let those monsters destroy our home and farm. He let us almost freeze and starve to death." Her body convulsed with sobs, and her skin was blotchy red. "And now we're here in the city. Our oldest daughter isn't living with us, and our youngest son is getting into trouble. You call that generous?"

Eleanor's stomach churned. She wiped away the tears that now flowed.

"Shannon," his voice was firm. "That's enough. It's time you let go of the fire and all that we've lost. How long will you carry that millstone of resentment and bitterness around your neck? We can't change the past, so we might as well embrace where we are and move forward."

"You say we're moving forward? Come here." She marched past him and William into the living room, followed by the others. "Look at this?" She spread her arm around the almost empty room. "You have to take a chair from the dining room just to have someplace to sit."

"Yes, look around this room and this entire house." Father's eyes were intent on her. "Last year at this time we were sleeping in the back of the truck, and the boys were on the ground. You were cooking over a fire, and now you have a big beautiful kitchen with features you never had on the farm. We have indoor plumbing, electricity, and hot water. Shannon, count your blessings, not the few things you don't have."

"We're never going back, are we?"

Father shook his head. "I don't see how we can. Farmers all over this country are leaving their farms; food prices are so low, most can't break even."

Mother clutched her apron to her face, turned, and rushed out of the room.

Father hung his head, then looked at Eleanor. "You can't see today's beauty when you're always looking at yesterday's storm."

He was right; Eleanor knew that. It was time to set aside her hopes of returning to the farm.

She could see some of the beauty here—especially now that they were out of the shantytown. This house wasn't as nice as their log home, but she had to admit, she liked—no, loved—indoor plumbing. She loved hot water, electric lights, and her friendship with Eva.

Their earlier conversation reminded her of her dilemma—give her hard earned money to those in need or buy new clothes? If only she could do both.

An idea sprouted. Maybe she could.

FORTY-TWO

CHARLES AND WILLIAM, FOLLOWED by Reverend Hamilton, found over twenty men waiting when they arrived at the shantytown. "Father, how are we going to transport them all?"

Charles whistled. "Getting them there will not be the problem, it's getting them home."

"Good morning, men." Jake's tall, slender frame cast an even longer shadow in the early morning light. "I appreciate you all showing up; we hope today will help you provide for your families. In the Bible, God helped care for the poor in Israel by requiring farmers to leave the grain the harvesters missed for those in need to glean."

The men listened with obvious eagerness.

William contemplated the concept. It certainly had merits.

"My good friend here, Charles Cruthers," continued Jake. "Spent most of last year in this very community. He's worked out a similar plan with some local farmers. The cost of wheat and other crops is so low that many farmers can't afford to bring in their harvest. We have spoken to a few who have given us permission to bring a group of you out to their fields with the express purpose of helping them harvest some of their crops. You'll receive wheat as payment, and we hope this helps the farmers break even and not lose their farms."

"Are you saying we're not getting paid?" a man asked.

"Not in cash," Jake replied. "Instead, you'll each receive five or six bundles of wheat."

There was a murmur among the men.

"What are we supposed to do with that?" another man asked.

William tensed. Would the whole idea fall apart?

Charles stepped up. "I will show you how to thresh the wheat from the stalks. Then, you can grind it with a coffee grinder or pestle to make flour. You can also boil it and eat it like a porridge or rice, or add it to other foods like beans or spam. It can replace meat. People fry it."

Many of the men looked skeptical, as did a few of the women who stood by out of interest.

"You can also use the stalks for mattress ticking or wind them up and burn them," William added.

Father smiled at him.

"If this works," Jake continued, "we're hoping to talk with farmers who raise corn, barley, and apples."

"Sounds like a lot of work for nothing," said a man, who turned and left. A few others followed.

"Does anyone else want to leave?" Charles asked.

"My son and I will try it," said a man in the front.

"Me too," said another.

Others nodded in agreement.

"Great." Jake picked out five of the frailer men and sent them to his car. "The rest of you climb in Mr. Cruthers' truck."

William worked alongside the men in the heat and dust. They worked hard and enjoyed a good noon meal. That afternoon, the men loaded bundles of wheat onto the truck and then climbed on top for the trip back to town. In the shantytown, Charles laid a burlap sack on the ground and showed the men and their families how to thresh the wheat.

"How long do you think that will last them?" William asked on the drive home.

Charles shrugged. "Not as long as I had hoped. Maybe a few weeks."

William nodded. "Are you disappointed?"

"I guess I was being unrealistic. In Bible times, the people would have gone out to the fields every day except the Sabbath, but I can't leave work to take these men out there."

"What if I drove?"

Father considered this. "That's an immense responsibility."

"I can do it."

Father smiled at him. "I know you can, and I'm proud of how hard you've worked and all you do. I'll talk with Jake and the farmer. But school will start soon, and I promised your mother we'd get at least one more load of wood in before your brothers head back."

William grew quiet, and Father looked over at him. "You're holding your cards pretty close to your chest. What are you thinking?"

"It's nothing."

"Does it have to do with school?"

William worked a blister on his hand. "I...Never mind."

"Are you wanting to head back to school?"

"Clara wanted me to."

"But do you want to?"

"I want to see Clara."

"That's not what I asked."

William shrugged. "Yes, and no."

"An education is like an ace in your hand. It increases your potential for success..."

"But?"

"But I'm not sure we can afford the loss of your income."

William stared out the window. "I'd probably be pretty far behind, anyway."

"That's no reason not to return."

"I really just wanted to see Clara."

"Don't you see her when you work for her father?"

William stared out the window at the Saturday shoppers.

"William."

"No!" he answered, a little more emphatically than he meant to. "I'm sorry."

"Why not?"

William refused to look at his father. "He won't let me see her."

"Why not?"

"He thinks I'm not good enough; because we were homeless, and we don't own our own home anymore." William hit the truck door with the outside of his fist.

Now Charles was silent.

"But if I was at school..."

"You'd be courting trouble."

"It's not fair!"

"No. It's not. But it shows what kind of man he is. If he would judge you based on external situations, you have little or no control over..." Father shook his head.

"He thinks all homeless people are lazy."

"Yet he sees how hard you work for him?"

William pondered this. His father was right. "Maybe if I graduated from high school, he'd think I was good enough for Clara."

Charles sighed. "I'm afraid this has less to do with you and more to do with some unspoken expectations he has that most fellas won't measure up to."

William stared out the window but saw nothing. Maybe he should give up on her. Who was he fooling? She'd get bored with him someday, and her old man would never consent to him seeing her.

The more he dwelt on this, the more the idea left him adrift in loneliness.

FALL 1932

"Isn't this exciting?" Rose pulled a dress off one rack and a sweater off another at the downtown department store and showed them to her little sister. "The first time you've gone clothes shopping." Her eyes sparkled.

Eleanor's hands shook with excitement. She turned a corner and paused at a table of hats, shoes, and purses. "Where do these all come from?"

"Factories, silly." Rose pulled her to a case. "Look at these."

Eleanor stared at a display of gloves, stockings, hair combs, and jewelry. How would she ever decide? She strode back to the table. "Let's start with shoes."

Rose shook her head. "Aunt Fiona always says you begin with the dress and accessorize with the shoes, purse, gloves, and jewelry."

Eleanor put a hand on her hip. "Rose!"

Her sister grinned. "I know, but it's useful information for when we get older and can."

Eleanor examined a pair of red Mary Janes. "Do you think we'll ever have enough money to buy more than the bare necessities?" She set the pair down and picked up another. "Rose?"

"Huh?"

Eleanor followed her sister's gaze to see a young man with dark hair and strong bone structure smile at Rose, then occupy himself with a rack of shirts. "Rose, did you hear me?"

"I'm sorry, what?"

"Do you think we'll ever have enough money—"

Rose smiled and batted her eyelashes at the young man.

"Never mind." Eleanor moved to a rack and pulled out a dress.

Rose followed her. "If a girl wants money, she needs a daddy."

"A daddy?"

Rose glanced at the boy, then looked away. "Yeah, a boyfriend with dough," she whispered, and a coy smile spread across her lips. "He might work."

Eleanor made a face. Boys were odd, and she'd rather keep them at a distance. "Weren't you going to move out of Aunt Fiona's—"

"Shush." Rose pulled Eleanor away from a sales clerk. "They all know both Auntie and me. I don't want her knowing."

"May I help you girls? Oh, Rose, is that you?"

Rose straightened and smiled. "Yes, hello Mrs. Osborn, this is my sister, Eleanor. She's looking for a new dress and shoes for school."

The woman looked Eleanor up and down. "Size eight, I'd say. Blue, green, red, lavender, or brown would look best on you. Which would you prefer?"

"I have a green dress and was thinking of orange."

"Oh no, dear, not with your coloring. Let's look at some blues and lavenders. Follow me." She plucked several dresses from a rack, held

them up to Eleanor, hemmed and hawed over a couple and settled on
four, which she hung in a dressing room.

Eleanor's stomach churned, and she nibbled a nail.

The clerk grimaced at Eleanor's worn boots. "Now, let's find a few
pairs of shoes. Phillip," she called to a clerk in the shoe department.
"Please measure this young lady's feet and get me a pair of Mary Jane's
in black and another in blue."

Eleanor tugged on Rose's arm after the man named Phillip measured
her feet. "Rose, I don't have enough money for all this," she whispered.

Rose chuckled. "You don't have to buy it all. You try it on and decide
which ones you want."

"Oh." Eleanor blushed at her own naivety.

The bells on the store's front door tinkled, followed by girlish laughter. "So, Helen, which dress are you going to get?"

"Oh, I don't know. I really can't decide. Probably both."

Eleanor turned to see Helen White and her two shadows approaching. She ducked behind a rack of sweaters. "Where are they? Are they
coming over here?"

"Eleanor, what are you doing?"

"Shush. Don't let them see me. Are they coming our way?"

"They stopped to talk with the sales clerk. What is going on?"

Eleanor popped her head above the rack; the girls had their backs
to her. She scurried into the changing room, her back bent like an old
woman, and pulled the curtain closed.

Outside, the clerk gave Rose the shoes and hurried away to help
another customer.

Eleanor cowered in the dressing room, chewing her thumbnail until
Rose entered.

"Do you want to explain to me what that was all about?"

"Shush, keep your voice down. I don't want them to know I'm here."

"Who are they?"

"Helen White and her two disciples."

Rose held out her hands, palms up. "So?"

"She's really mean."

"Will she be going to your school?"

Eleanor nodded.

"Are there dressing rooms at school for you to hide in?"

"Of course not."

"Then why are you hiding here?"

"Because I don't want to get into a fight here."

"You know you'll get into a fight?"

She nodded again.

"Why?"

"Because she's mean, and she calls me names."

Rose stared at her. "So?"

"So?" Eleanor's hands went to her hips. "I don't like the names she calls me. I told her if she did it again, she'd be sorry."

"You're digging yourself into a pit. Leave her be. If she's as mean as you say she is, she's not worth wasting your time on. Now, are you going to try on these dresses or not?"

"Yes."

Eleanor stared at herself in the mirror. Of all the dresses she'd tried on, the lavender one was by far her favorite, and the brand-new Mary Jane's finished the outfit nicely.

"White stockings would look really nice with that," Rose said. "Should I get a pair for you to try on?"

Eleanor looked at the price tag. Two-twenty-nine for the dress and another three dollars and eighty-five cents for the shoes. "How much are they?"

"Fifty cents for one pair, one dollar for three."

Eleanor did the math in her head. "No. They'll have to wait. I only have $6.45."

"And there's tax."

Eleanor sighed. "How much is that?"

"Probably an additional six or seven cents."

"How are you girls doing in there?"

"We're almost finished," Rose called.

At the cash register, Eleanor looked about, hoping Helen and company wouldn't see her.

"That will be six dollars and twenty-one cents," said the woman, who now wrapped the items.

Eleanor tried to count out her money without dumping it all out. She flushed. Why hadn't she asked Father to exchange it for bills? "Five-twelve, five-twenty, five-thirty-five, five-forty, five-forty-seven—" She struggled to breathe. Sweat grew on her forehead and hands.

Rose looked at her. "What's wrong?"

"I only have five-forty-seven." She shook her head. "I don't understand. Last night, when I counted it, there was six-forty-five."

"Take a deep breath. Let me count. Maybe you made a mistake."

Eleanor's throat constricted, and her heart pounded. "I don't understand." She shook her homemade change purse, but nothing came out. She checked her pockets—empty.

"Eleanor, there's only five-forty-seven here. Are you sure you had more?"

She nodded; tears welled in her eyes.

"Do you think you dropped them along the way?"

"I don't know." Eleanor looked up to see the sales clerk watching with a scowl.

Just then, Helen, Georgina, and Camile approached the counter with their purchases. "Oh, look girls, if it isn't Raggedy Ann!"

The other two snickered.

Eleanor's lip quivered as disappointment, anger, hurt, and embarrassment pulsed through her veins. Her eyes pleaded with Rose, who only shook her head.

"What will it be, Miss?"

Eleanor's shoulders slumped, the image of herself in the new dress and shoes vivid in her mind. She just had to have them, especially now that Helen had seen her.

"Oh, does Raggedy Ann not have enough money?" Helen taunted.

Eleanor scooped up her change and shoved it in her coin purse. "I've changed my mind," she told the clerk, avoiding Helen.

"Oh, poor Raggedy Ann has to go home empty-handed and keep wearing her country-bumpkin dresses."

Eleanor turned to Helen. She hated the girl. Why did such people have to exist? "I told you not to call me Raggedy Ann."

Rose placed a hand on her shoulder. "Leave her be," she whispered.

"I don't remember that. But then again, I don't take orders from ragamuffins."

"Well, you're going to start." Eleanor kicked the girl in the shin.

"Oww!" screeched the girl.

"Maybe that will help you remember." Eleanor turned and marched out of the store; tears burned her eyes and blurred her vision.

"Eleanor, wait up." Rose scurried to catch up.

Eleanor crossed the street and was halfway up the next block before she ducked into the doorway of a vacant building. "It's not fair," she cried. "It's just not fair. I don't know what happened to my money. Why did Helen have to be there? Why?"

Rose wrapped her arms around her as she sobbed. When Eleanor had calmed down, Rose brushed a strand of red hair from her sister's face. "I don't understand; Mother told me you've been working really hard, baking bread, selling eggs, even selling towels. I thought you would have more money."

Eleanor wiped the tears from her face. "I did. I used some of it to buy food for the Lee family, who lived across from us in the shantytown, but they moved and there was a lady living in their shack who didn't have any food, so we gave it to her."

"Oh."

"That was probably pretty stupid of me, wasn't it?"

Rose shrugged. "I don't know. It's hard to argue that a pair of shoes or a dress are more important than someone starving."

Eleanor sighed. Rose was right, but it still hurt. Was this how God was blessing her for the good she did?

"Can I see your coin purse?" Rose examined it. "Wow, you did a good job on this. I don't see how any money could have fallen out."

Eleanor took in a jagged breath. "I just don't understand."

"Well, if you earn some more money and want to go shopping, I'll come with you. But it's getting late, and I need to get back and fix supper."

They walked without speaking for a couple of blocks until Eleanor broke the silence. "Why haven't you moved out of Aunt Fiona's?"

"I don't have any money, and I don't have a job."

"Weren't you earning money watching people's children?"

"I was," Rose's voice dropped an octave. "But I think Aunt Fiona realized they were paying me more than she was and was afraid I'd start demanding she pay me more. She hasn't let me watch anyone else's children and keeps me busy so I can't look for other work."

"I'm sorry. Maybe you could move back in with us?" Eleanor's countenance brightened.

"I can't do that. You all are just getting on your feet. You don't need another mouth to feed and body to clothe."

"But you could help Mother bake bread when I'm at school."

"I don't know; it would be odd coming back home and being treated like a child again."

Eleanor wished she could tell Rose it wouldn't be like that, but she knew different.

"Well, here's where we part. I hope you enjoy school."

"I'm sure I'd enjoy it a lot more if I had my new clothes and Helen White wasn't there."

"You could still buy the dress."

Eleanor shrugged.

"Look on the bright side, at least you get to go to school."

Memories of spending last winter huddled under quilts in the cold shanty, unable to attend school, came to mind. Yes, at least she got to attend school. She balanced the good against the day's disappointment.

FORTY-THREE

MRS. NEWBERG PLACED THE math test upside-down on Eleanor's desk. Eleanor swallowed; her teacher hadn't placed everyone's test upside down.

Helen turned around from her chair and looked back at Eleanor's paper. "What'd you get? I got an A." She grabbed Eleanor's upside-down paper off the desk. "Oh, Raggedy Ann, you got a D!" Nearby students looked at Eleanor. "The poor ragamuffin. Not only does she have to rotate her three flour-bag dresses, but she's also stupid. Look." She waved the paper about. "This D proves it. I guess it's hard to do math when you don't need to count higher than three."

Eleanor lunged at Helen. "Give me that."

Helen held it just out of Eleanor's reach. "Look at her. She's wild, just like an animal from the woods of Idaho."

"Give me that."

"Miss Cruthers!"

The room grew quiet and Eleanor looked up to see Mrs. Newberg looking right at her. "What is the problem?"

"Helen won't give me my test."

"Mrs. Newberg." Helen looked directly at the teacher. "In a fit of rage, Eleanor threw her test onto the floor. I was just picking it up to give it back to her."

Eleanor stared at the girl in shock, unable to respond.

The teacher eyed Helen. "Miss Cruthers, Miss White, look at me."

Eleanor squinted at Helen, then turned to her teacher.

"We don't take our disappointment out on others. Do you understand?"

"But—"

"Miss Cruthers, I want you to stay in during recess."

Eleanor's eyes stung. She nodded. "Yes, Mrs. Newberg."

"Miss White."

Helen gave the teacher a smug look.

"In the future, I'd appreciate it if you didn't touch Miss Cruthers' things."

"But she threw—"

"You can stay in during recess as well."

Helen scowled at Eleanor, who shifted under her glare.

Across the room, Eva and Violet wore sad expressions.

"You've got to ignore her," Violet whispered.

"She's just trying to get you upset," added Eva.

Pauline, a girl in the other class, nodded her agreement. "She likes to upset people. When I stopped showing her she bothered me, she stopped picking on me. It's no longer fun for her if she can't make you angry or cry."

The girls were walking home from school, and Eleanor listened as she watched her brothers and sister walk ahead of them. Mitchell and Paul, Violet's little brother, stopped to examine an ants' nest.

"But she's so mean—it hurts. I want to hit her to keep from crying. How do you make it not hurt?" Eleanor asked.

"Oh, it hurts," Pauline said. "You just don't let her see that it hurts."

"And you pray for her?" Eva asked.

"Pray for her? Why would I want to do that?"

"Mother says Helen must be pretty miserable inside to be so mean. Mother thinks she's taking out her hurt on others to feel better about herself."

Eleanor mulled this over. She thought about her cousins; were Suzanne and Albert little brats because her aunt and uncle ignored them?

Pauline and Eva said their goodbyes and turned toward their homes. "It's really sad that she is so miserable," Violet said. "Can you imagine feeling so bad that you want to make other people hurt?"

Eleanor shook her head as she watched Raymond and Lilly pass a paper between them before Raymond shoved it into a bush.

"I'm glad Paul and your brother get along so well. Paul really struggles to make friends. He's not tough and athletic as the other boys."

Eleanor smiled. "I am too. Mitchell has only had one friend since we moved here, and he ended up getting polio."

"Oh, that's so sad."

Eleanor pulled the paper from the bush and slipped it in her pocket. "Do you understand the math we're doing?"

"Yes."

"I really struggle to understand Mrs. Newberg's explanations on the board. Maybe at recess tomorrow you could help me?"

A big smile spread across Violet's lips. "Sure. You really want my help?"

"Yes. I just don't understand it. I must be stupid."

"You're not stupid; it's basically multiplication in reverse." Violet stopped. "Here's our street. I'll see you tomorrow. Come on, Paul."

Eleanor hurried to catch up with Mitchell.

"Hey, there's William." Mitchell pointed to their father's truck parked on the next block about thirty yards away. "Who's the girl with him?"

Eleanor squinted. "What girl? I don't even see William."

"There." Mitchell pointed. "See him there; in front of that boarded-up market by the truck."

"No."

Ahead of them, Raymond and Lilly turned around. "Honestly Eleanor," Raymond teased, "are you blind? He's behind the sign that says, 'Firewood for sale.' "

Eleanor stopped. "Quit it."

"Quit what?"

"Teasing me."

Mitchell put his hand on her arm. "Do you really not see him?"

Eleanor's eyes welled with tears. "I..." She swallowed hard. "I just see...blurry..."

"Can you see me?" Raymond asked.

"Of course, I can."

"How about me?" Lilly asked and waved her hands about.

"Stop it, you guys," Mitchell ordered.

"I want to go see William," Lilly begged.

"You can go if Raymond will take you," Mitchell said, not giving Eleanor a chance to speak.

Raymond and Lilly waited for a passing car before running across the street.

"Can you read the sign on the gas station?" Mitchell asked in a quiet voice.

"Mobilgas, I see the red horse with wings."

"But can you read the words?"

She squinted again. "Mo...b...l...is that a g?" She turned to him; her eyebrows knit together.

"What about the gas price?" He pointed to smaller signs by each pump.

She shook her head. "Am I going blind?"

He held up his book. "Can you read this?"

"The Work-Play Books, Pleasant Lands, Gates and Ayer."

"Now look over there." He pointed to William and the truck.

"Just fuzzy, colored shapes."

"Let's keep walking. Tell me when you see him."

"I think you should tell them." Mitchell picked up a hammer from the basement workbench.

"No." Eleanor tightened her grip on the wood she was holding for him.

"But it could be serious," Mitchell insisted.

"I'm fine. I can see just fine to read and cook and clean—"

"And not walk out in front of a car?"

Eleanor hesitated. "Y—e—s."

"And read the blackboard at school."

"Y—e—s."

"You can't read the blackboard; can you?"

"Yes, I can—unless she writes really small," Eleanor conceded.

"You probably just need glasses."

Eleanor turned pale. "No. I don't. I can't. Helen already makes fun of me. If I get glasses...she'll call me four-eyes and all kinds of other names."

"But you'll see."

"So what?" She grabbed Mitchell by the shoulders. "Don't tell them. Promise?" Eleanor glared into her little brother's eyes until he squirmed. "Besides, we don't have money for glasses."

"Maybe you can buy a pair from the five-and-dime."

"No. I'm not wearing glasses, and you won't tell them."

A tin can clanged against the concrete floor of the basement.

"What was that?" Eleanor whispered, and they both looked about.

Mitchell pointed at several crates stacked under the stairs, and they tiptoed to the spot. Mitchell pulled a crate off the stack. "Boo!"

"Ahh," Lilly's eyes were wide.

"What are you doing?" he asked.

"Just pretending."

"How much did you hear?" Eleanor asked.

A smug smile spread across Lilly's thin lips. "Everything."

Eleanor leaned down until her face was inches from her little sister's. "You don't tell anyone. Do you understand?"

"How much are you going to pay me?"

"Pay you?" Eleanor straightened. "I'm not paying you anything."

"Maybe I'll tell your secret—" she folded her arms. "And maybe I won't."

"Fine, I'll give you three cents."

"Twenty-five," Lilly countered.

"No. I worked hard for that. I'll give you five."

"Twenty."

"Five," Eleanor insisted. "I have to get up early to help Mother mix that bread and collect eggs. You do nothing."

"I have to help Mother wash the dishes and set the table."

"Big deal."

"Fifteen," Lilly bargained.

"Seven, and that's my last offer."

Lilly's shoulders slumped. "I hate big people."

"Well, someday, you'll be one."

"Lilly?" Mother called down the stairs from the kitchen. "Lilly Ann Cruthers, you get up here right this minute."

Lilly rolled her small blue eyes. "See, I hate big people." She marched up the stairs, and Eleanor and Mitchell followed.

"Lilly Ann Cruthers," Mother repeated. "What is this?" She held out the crumpled paper Eleanor had pulled from the bush.

Lilly's eyes enlarged, and she reached for it, but Mother pulled it back.

"It appears to be a note from your teacher saying that you aren't paying attention in class, talking, picking on other children, and not doing your assignments," Mother said.

"Where did you get it?"

"It was on my pillow. Are you telling me you didn't put it there?"

"No. Why would I do that? Raymond shoved it in a..." Lilly stopped. Mother's face was stern.

"Oops."

"Is that why it's all wrinkled?"

"It was an accident. I dropped it..." Lilly turned and looked at Mitchell and Eleanor. "You guys. You found it and gave it to her, didn't you?"

"Found it where?" Mother asked.

"You?" Lilly turned on Eleanor. "You tell me to keep your secrets, but tell mine."

Eleanor stiffened. "I left it for Mother before I—"

"Eleanor?" Mother now scrutinized Eleanor.

"It's nothing." Eleanor's face flushed and her breath caught.

"Eleanor's going blind," Lilly spat.

"Shut up."

"Eleanor, what on earth?" Mother glared at her. "You don't talk to your sister that way. What is going on?"

"Nothing," Eleanor said and glared at Lilly, who straightened her three-foot frame.

"Eleanor is going blind; she couldn't see William and his girlfriend or even the truck today."

"I could too."

Mitchell put a hand on Eleanor's arm to calm her.

Lilly squinted at her. "Liar."

"You're just trying to get Mother to forget about your teacher's note," Eleanor retorted.

"Eleanor's blind. She can't see anything."

"Yes, I can."

"Eleanor is blind. Eleanor is blind."

"Stop." Eleanor's eyes welled with tears.

Mother grabbed Lilly by the shoulder. "That's enough, young lady. You go to your room while I talk to your sister; then I'll deal with you."

Lilly stuck her tongue out at Eleanor and stomped off.

"Mitchell, can you leave us alone?"

"Yes, ma'am."

"Eleanor, what is this all about?"

Eleanor slumped. "I didn't want to worry you."

Shannon studied her face, then poured two glasses of milk and put several oatmeal cookies on a plate. "Come, let's sit on the front porch."

They swung back and forth, taking in the late afternoon. Despite the subject, a tinge of joy coursed through Eleanor. Mother was attempting to make this special.

"So, what happened today?"

Eleanor took a deep breath to suppress the fear growing inside her. What would she do if she went blind? She told her about William and the truck. Mother only nodded.

"I'll speak with your father about finding an optometrist."

"A what?"

Shannon smiled. "A doctor who treats eyes."

"Will I have to wear glasses?"

"Let's hope we can fix it with glasses."

"Oh." What if glasses couldn't fix it?

"I'll talk to your father when he gets home." Mother sighed. "I guess I'd better have a talk with Lilly. Can you send her out?"

"Yes, ma'am."

"Oh, and you'd better take the plate and cups in, or I'll never hear the end of it."

Eleanor fretted over the idea of wearing glasses. "Lilly, Mother wants you to—" She stopped. "What are you doing?"

Lilly straightened; her hands behind her back.

Eleanor marched into their sparse room and reached for the baking soda can Lilly hid behind her back.

"Leave me alone. Don't touch me." Lilly twisted away from her sister.

"What are you doing? That's mine."

"You owe me."

"I do not."

Eleanor wrestled her money can away from Lilly and thirty-five cents fell from her sister's hand. Anger rose in her. "You've been taking my money."

"It's not fair that you get money and I don't."

"I work really hard for my money."

"So. It's still not fair."

"You've taken money from my can before—haven't you?"

"No."

Eleanor scrutinized her little sister. "Tell me the truth."

"What does it matter?"

"You have. You've been taking my money."

"So." Lilly folded her arms and lifted her chin in a show of defiance.

Eleanor leaned into Lilly. "It's because of you I couldn't buy the dress I'd worked and saved up for," she screamed.

"What is going on here?"

They both looked up to see Mother in the doorway.

FORTY-FOUR

SHANNON HANDED OLIVIA A child's coat and two men's shirts, then turned to the next woman, who gave her a bundle of used clothing wrapped in twine. "Thank you. We so appreciate your generosity."

"I hope this will help them," said a woman.

"I can promise you it will."

"Someone needs to help those poor souls," said another.

Shannon placed a fruit box of clothing on a table and turned around to find herself face-to-face with Fiona.

"Oh, Shannon." Fiona's voice of superiority rang out. "Surprise me seeing you here. The poor collecting for the poor." Her eyes widened, and she lowered her voice. "Don't tell me this is a scheme to collect items for your family?"

Shannon froze, her pale skin tone reddening.

Olivia stepped in. "Mrs. Morgan, we appreciate your donation, but I assure you, Mrs. Cruthers here is a member of this congregation in very good standing, and it is out of a kind and caring heart that she is donating her time, energy, and resources to help those affected by this horrible economic plight."

Shannon's sister lifted her chin. "Well, I was just saying—"

Olivia looked her straight in the eye. "Excuse me, Mrs. Morgan, but we have others who need to drop off their donations."

"Yes, well, I hope you know those people there are lazy and just looking for handouts."

Shannon's embarrassment turned to indignation. "Have a good day." She held her hand open in the door's direction. "Who's next?"

Fiona gave her sister a look of surprise and strutted out; her head held high.

"I think what you're doing is wonderful," said a woman of modest dress who came with a laundry bag of items. "These were the clothes that were in the best of condition. I have a small pile at home with holes that I'm going to make a quilt or two out of. Would you be able to give those to a family?"

Shannon smiled. "They would very much appreciate the quilts you make."

After several hours, they closed the doors and started sorting through the items. "How do you know Mrs. Morgan?" Olivia asked.

Shannon chuckled, "She's my sister."

Olivia's brown eyes widened, and a deep-throated laugh spilled from her lips. "I would have never guessed. You two are so different! I'm sorry if she hurt you."

Shannon looked down at the shirt she was folding and bit her lip. "Thank you. I don't understand her. As hard as I try to tell myself that what she thinks of me doesn't matter, it still hurts."

"Of course, it does. You love her, and she means a lot to you. She should be supportive, but for some reason, she feels threatened by you."

Shannon paused. "She feels what?"

"Threatened."

"Why? How? I have nothing and she has her big beautiful home and all her needs met..."

"So, it would appear. But something is missing—something you have that she can't seem to attain or grasp—as hard as she tries."

Shannon pondered this new idea. "You really think so?"

Olivia nodded. "I've known Fiona for quite some time and have seen that something is missing in her life. There is something she is striving for, a love or acceptance that she feels she's lacking."

Shannon picked at a piece of lint on a jacket before folding it, Olivia's words sifting through her mind. In high school, Fiona won competitions for memorizing poetry and making political speeches. Everything Shannon had done, Fiona tried to do better. Maybe Olivia was right.

"Eleanor." Mitchell ran up to her in the hall before school began. "Eleanor, you've got to help." He was panting and pulling on her arm.

"Whoa, whoa, what's wrong?"

"It's Raymond. Some boy's gonna beat him up."

"What'd he do?"

"He conned a fourth grader out of a slingshot."

Eleanor walked against the flow of students entering the building and out to the schoolyard. "How'd he do that?"

"Tiddlywinks."

"This betting of his is getting out of hand," Eleanor murmured.

A cluster of boys surrounded Raymond and the larger boy.

"Give me my slingshot, or I'll punch you."

"If you didn't want to lose it; you shouldn't have bet it," Raymond said, the item in question gripped in his hand.

"You cheated."

"You can't prove that."

"Andy saw you."

Raymond looked around at the group of boys, most of them his friends. "Did anyone else see me cheat?"

They all shook their heads.

"So, it's all of us against you and your one measly friend." Raymond glared at the older boy.

The older boy grabbed Raymond by the collar and pulled him to himself. "I want my slingshot back."

Raymond swung at the boy.

"Stop it!" Eleanor shoved her way into the group. "Just stop it, both of you." She pulled Raymond from the other boy's grip. "Give him back the slingshot."

"It's mine; I won it."

"You cheated," interjected the other boy.

"If you want it, you can win it back," Raymond dared.

"Enough. All of you," Eleanor commanded.

The bell rang.

"Raymond, give him the slingshot—now!" She looked about. "The rest of you get to class."

Scowling, Raymond handed over the slingshot.

"You need to stop this betting," Eleanor reprimanded.

"It's how I get stuff."

"Well, maybe you should try working. Now get to class."

Eleanor hurried inside, her skin sticky from running, and her heart racing from the adrenalin. She rushed through the classroom door and ran right into Helen White.

"Watch where you're going." Helen brushed imaginary dirt from her blouse, then looked at Eleanor. "Oh, look who's got glasses." She turned her head to the classroom behind her. "Look, Raggedy Ann now has four eyes and she still can't see."

Eleanor's chest shook as she tried to control her emotions. Her entire class focused on her and several laughed.

Why couldn't she have just walked into the classroom unannounced—let the others make up their own minds?

Everyone waited to see how she'd respond.

Frustration, hurt, and anger rose in her. She wanted to shove Helen, to punch her. She heard Violet's words, "Ignore Helen." Tears welled in her eyes, and she hoped Helen couldn't see them. Eleanor took a deep breath and stood straight. "I need you to move."

"And if I don't?"

"Then Mrs. Newberg will see you disturbing the class."

"I can just tell her you won't move out of my way."

Eleanor's anger flashed back. "Turn the other cheek," Reverend Hamilton had said yesterday.

"How many fingers am I holding up?" Helen taunted.

The room was quiet as everyone watched the interchange.

Eleanor struggled to keep her cool. She stepped aside. "There, you need to go—go."

Helen didn't move. "I asked you a question. How many fingers am I holding up?"

"If you don't know, I'm not telling you." Eleanor slipped around Helen and suppressed a grin at Helen's shocked expression.

"Good job," Eva whispered as Eleanor walked past her to her own desk.

"I like your glasses," said the girl behind her.

Eleanor smiled.

"This isn't fair," Lilly complained from the dining room table where she wrote out her lessons.

Shannon rolled her eyes at Eleanor, who sat with her back against the living room wall knitting. Eleanor's suppressed grin told Shannon that Eleanor was worn out with Lilly, too. Across the room, Mitchell fiddled with the dials on the radio while William prepared a game of dominoes.

"I shouldn't have to pay half my allowance to Eleanor," Lilly called.

"That's enough," Father scolded, "you stole. Now you must repay—with interest."

Another sharp pang of disappointment stabbed at Shannon's heart. Eleanor had worked so hard to save up for a new dress and shoes. It was bad enough to have strangers take everything from them. But her own sister? She hoped Eleanor and Lilly's relationship wouldn't end up like her and Fiona's.

Mitchell's radio sprang to life and Jack Benny's slightly nasal voice filtered into the room as The Jack Benny Canada Dry Program began. Shannon shook her head at his back-handed compliments. Their laughter had just subsided when a knock on the door sent Teddy barking.

"I'll get it." Shannon opened the door to a cheerful, "Hello," from Rose.

Her eldest daughter turned to the dog. "Teddy, have you forgotten me?" Rose ruffled the dog's fur.

"Goodness," Mother threw her arms around Rose. "It's almost dark. What on earth are you doing out at this hour? Is everything alright?"

"It must be." Father stood in the doorway leading to the living room. "Look at that smile, Shannon." He turned to Rose. "We're just listening to the radio. Come on in."

Rose took off her sweater. "Brr, it's getting chilly out there." She examined the wooden box as a radio personality announced the next program. "I can't believe you guys fixed that old thing."

"Most of the damage was to the case," William said. "We just built a new one."

"I thought it didn't work."

"It didn't," Mitchell said, a big smile on his face. "There was a broken radio tube and a few loose wires that just needed to be twisted around the conductors to get it working."

"That's great." Rose looked at the table it sat on. "Where did this come from?"

Father beamed. "You like that?"

"Yes, that's nice."

"William built that."

Rose ran her fingers over the smooth wood, then turned to her brother. "You made this?"

He nodded, color flushing his cheeks.

"That is nice."

"So, what are you doing out and about at this hour?" Charles asked.

Shannon wondered the same thing and sensed more change coming.

Rose sat on a chair mother had brought from the dining room. "Well..." Her eyes were wide and bright, and her face glowed. "I've given Aunt Fiona my notice. Starting Monday, I'll be working a new job."

"That's great!" William said.

"Good for you," Father congratulated.

"Where at?" Eleanor and Mother asked.

"Well, actually, I have a few other jobs. I have several cleaning jobs, and jobs cooking for the renters in several boarding houses so the women who run them can have a day off."

Shannon's face brightened. "Look at you, so industrious. When will you be moving back?"

Rose looked at the floor. "I won't be."

A knot grew in Shannon's throat, and she struggled to breathe. "What do you mean? Surely you won't stay with Aunt Fiona and Uncle Harry?"

"Oh, no. Certainly not."

"Then where will you live?"

"I'm going to be sharing a room with Marguerite and Shirley. In fact, it's Mrs. Wagner, the boardinghouse mistress, who suggested I offer my cooking skills. She's one of the boardinghouse mistresses I'll be cooking for one day a week. That's part of my room and board." Rose's excitement was now tempered with apprehension. She watched her parents' response.

"A young girl of fourteen living on her own—when she has family right here?" Mother wrung her hands. "Rose, I don't think that's a good idea." Shannon looked at her husband. "Charles, what do you think?"

"What kind of people are living in this boarding house?"

"Good people, Father."

"Rose, you know that it's not appropriate for young girls or even young ladies to live with men they're not married to."

"Yes, Mother."

"Are there single men?"

"Of course not. Mrs. Wagner only rents out rooms to women, except for Mrs. Johnson and her son."

"How old is her son?" Mother asked.

"I'm not sure, seven or eight. Lenny is such a sweet boy; the poor thing got polio last winter, which crippled him."

Mitchell was now at his sister's side, tugging at her arm. "Rose, who is the boy?"

"Lenny." She looked at her brother, who was suddenly very interested.

"Lenny? Lenny Johnson?"

"Yes, do you know him?"

Mitchell nodded; his bright blue-gray eyes sparkled.

"Not him?" Raymond grumbled. "He's Mitchell's stupid friend from the school we used to go to."

"He's not stupid."

"Yes, he is," Raymond sneered.

Mitchell charged Raymond and knocked his unsuspecting brother to the ground. "He's not stupid. Your friends are stupid."

Shannon stared at the scuffle in surprise.

"Whoa, whoa. What is this all about?" Father said, pulling his two sons apart with William's help. "We don't call anyone stupid. Do you understand?"

"Yes, Father."

"Yes, sir."

"Now apologize to each other."

The boys each mumbled a half-hearted apology.

"We are going to talk about this later," Father promised.

"But I want to go see him," Mitchell insisted.

"We'll see if we can arrange that, but right now, I want you two boys to go get ready for bed. You too Lilly."

Mother watched them leave. "I don't know," she said to Rose. "I still don't like the idea of you staying in a boarding house. Why can't you come back home?"

Father put a hand on Shannon's shoulder.

"Mother, I haven't lived at home for over a year. I've taken on the responsibility of caring for children and preparing meals. I practically run Aunt Fiona's house. I'm used to making my own decisions and being treated like an adult."

Shannon's countenance dropped, and she tried not to cry. The sadness was filling her up like milk in a mason jar.

"Besides, I need to be there in the morning to help fix breakfast and watch Lenny as his mother has to be at her job by seven."

Charles drew Shannon close to him. "Rose, your mother and I are very proud of you and the wonderful young woman you've become. It's just happened sooner than we expected."

Shannon stared at her feet.

Rose kneeled before her mother's chair. "I don't mean to hurt you. I love you. It would just be hard to move back home and be a child again. But I'll have more time and freedom to come and visit."

Shannon nodded, then looked out the dark window. "You'd probably better get headed back—to Fiona's. William, will you walk with her?"

"Yes, Mother."

The click of the door as it shut stabbed her in the heart.

FORTY-FIVE

ELEANOR FUMED OVER THE "D" she had received on her history test. How was she supposed to know that information? She'd never even heard most of it? Mrs. Newberg said it was a review from last year. Eleanor regretted all the months last year that she and her siblings had stayed in the cold shanty instead of attending school.

All last winter she had missed school; now she hated it. "Face it," she told herself. "You're dumb." Even though she could now see what Mrs. Newberg wrote on the board, she still struggled to understand some of it. At least she'd learned to snatch up her papers when the teacher returned them; before Helen could see.

Now Mrs. Newberg wanted to talk with Mother, and Eleanor needed to get Mother and Father's signatures on the test. She was trying to figure out how to tell them when Teddy started barking on the front porch, and a woman called out from the street.

"Shannon. Shannon. I need to speak to you. Come get this vicious creature."

"What on earth?" Mother came to the kitchen door, wiping her hands on her apron. "Eleanor, can you go see who's there?"

"Yes, Mother." Eleanor ran to the front door and calmed the dog. "Oh, hi Aunt Fiona." She looked down at the dog. "Teddy, calm down. It's just Aunt Fiona." She turned to her aunt, who stood shielded by the partially open car door. "Come on in."

"Not until you do something with that ferocious beast. He should be in a cage."

Eleanor led the dog off the porch toward the back gate. "Oh, he won't hurt you unless you try to hurt one of us."

"I wouldn't be so sure of that. Is your mother home?"

"Yes, she's in the house. We're getting ready to bake bread for tomorrow's deliveries."

Aunt Fiona raised a penciled eyebrow. "You help her bake?"

"Yes, ma'am."

Eleanor entered the back door into the kitchen just as Aunt Fiona was questioning Mother.

"Shannon, please tell me you warned Rosalyn against leaving us?"

"Honestly Fiona, I only learned of it last night."

"And you didn't think to tell me?"

"I thought Rose had already told you."

"No, she didn't." Fiona looked about the sparsely furnished home, then finally settled on an old kitchen chair. "Rose told me this afternoon, shortly before the children came home from school. She simply couldn't have chosen a worse time." Aunt Fiona looked up at Eleanor. "Child, what are you looking at?"

Eleanor stammered, not sure what to say.

"Eleanor, darling. Can you make some coffee for your aunt and me and make up a plate of those cookies we baked yesterday?"

"Yes, Mother."

"I thought Rose had already told you." Shannon called through the kitchen door. "Eleanor, isn't that what Rose said?"

"Yes, Mother."

Fiona waved her hand. "She mentioned something to me last night, when I was exhausted from the day's events, and I assumed she was just prattling."

Shannon shrugged. "One woman's prattling is another woman's proclamation."

Fiona waved her words away. "Regardless, I don't know how she could do this to me."

"Well Fiona, it's possible you asked too much and gave too little."

"You're just full of pithy little statements, aren't you?"

In the kitchen, Eleanor smiled at Mother's remarks. She sounded more like her old self.

"I'm just pointing out the obvious."

"The obvious, my dear sister, is that Rosalyn belongs with us, not cavorting with commoners. You simply must make her change her mind. We offered her that position when you needed help. It's your turn now to help me. I have a full schedule and no time for these menial tasks."

Eleanor peeked into the dining room to see how Mother was responding. She watched her mother take a deep breath and straighten, her back stiff.

"Fiona, you can't be serious."

"Of course, I am. You're her mother; she should do what you say."

"If you haven't noticed, she's growing up into a young lady who has a mind of her own—as she reminded me last evening."

Eleanor brought in the cookies and coffee.

"But she has an obligation to me." Aunt Fiona was emphatic.

Shannon shrugged. "Rose is spreading her wings and trying new things."

"I'd hardly say cooking and cleaning is anything new."

"Maybe not, but she'll meet new people and have new experiences."

"She had lots of opportunities working for me. She met many very sophisticated people, and it surprises me you'd prefer she rub elbows with riff-raff rather than high society."

Mother took a sip of her coffee. "The decision is final. I won't try to stop Rose from leaving your employment."

Eleanor picked up her school work to take into her bedroom. Aunt Fiona looked more ruffled than when she arrived, and Eleanor decided it was best to leave.

"Well, what am I supposed to do? I have a tea next Monday and my Bridge group over for luncheon on Wednesday. I simply must have Rose there to prepare. And who's going to watch little Suzanne and Albert every day after school?"

"You're their mother," Shannon said. "Why don't you watch them?"

Eleanor wanted to cheer.

Fiona gave her a look of shock. "You don't understand. I have very important work I do for the community."

"Caring for your family is caring for the community," Shannon said.

Aunt Fiona set her cookie down. "So, this is how you treat me after all I've done for you?"

"All you've done for me?"

"Why yes," Fiona looked surprised. "We sacrificed to bring Rosalyn in and board her as well as pay her wages."

"Her name is Rose, and it looks to me like you received a wagon of gold more than Rose or any of us did."

Fiona paused, her cup mid-way to her lips. "What on earth do you mean?"

"Never mind. The answer is 'No.'"

"Really Shannon, you are being so stubborn!"

Eleanor returned to the room to retrieve her pencil, even though she could hear the entire conversation.

Aunt Fiona glanced up at her, and a thin smile spread across her painted lips.

Eleanor felt like a mouse just seen by a fat cat.

"Eleanor darling."

Aunt Fiona's words snaked around her like a snare.

"How would you like to come and work for me? You could make your own money and have your own bedroom." A forced smile implied kindness and generosity.

Apprehension wiggled at Eleanor's mind. Did she really want to work for Aunt Fiona? Watch the "Little Demons" as Rose called her cousins?

Eleanor pushed her glasses up on her nose and the memory of Helen White making fun of her and the "D" on her history test came into sharper view. She was stupid. She didn't need school, anyway.

Excitement and apprehension dueled inside her. Her income would be all hers. Yet she already earned more than Rose—money Lilly stole. She could have her own room and no Lilly. But also, no Mitchell and William, no Mother and Father, and she would miss Raymond and Lilly. Would she be replacing the latter two for Suzanne and Albert? She shivered at the memory of Aunt Fiona's spacious home. For all its beauty, it was cold.

"I'd make it worth your while," Aunt Fiona said. "You could take the children to the movies and live in a grand house."

Eleanor opened her mouth—

"No."

Mother's word snapped Eleanor from her fantasy.

"Absolutely not."

Fiona fanned herself. "You allow Rose to make her own decisions, but not Eleanor?" Fiona directed her words at Mother, but she looked at Eleanor when she spoke them.

"Mother, I'd—"

"Eleanor has school and friends."

She'd considered school with its "D's", teacher's notes, and Helen White. But would she ever see Eva, Violet, and Pauline? A sadness pressed into her.

Aunt Fiona gave Eleanor a look of disappointment, then turned to her sister. "Really, Shannon, what good is an education going to do her? She's a girl—a girl destined for service."

Her aunt's words stabbed her, and she dropped the hopes she'd gathered.

"That is enough," Shannon demanded. "Rose worked seven days a week, twelve to fourteen hours a day for a mere pittance, not even earning enough to buy herself a dress, let alone help us while we almost froze and starved to death. I will not have Eleanor doing the same."

"Oh, Shannon, you're exaggerating, as usual."

"I do not exaggerate." Shannon shoved her coffee away and glared at her sister. "And while she was cooking, cleaning, running errands, and watching your children, you were off flitting about town as if you hadn't a care or responsibility in the world."

Fiona stood. "You know nothing."

Shannon bolted up from her chair. "No Fiona, you're the one who knows nothing. You know nothing of people's struggles, and you know nothing of what they need."

Eleanor's heart swelled at this unexpected turn of events.

"I can see that once again, you're going to be difficult." Fiona scooped up her purse and stormed out of the house, slamming the door behind her.

In the quiet, Eleanor took in all that had happened. Any hopes of working for her aunt were gone, but that was fine—no, that was good.

Mother held out her hand. "Eleanor, look I'm shaking." Then, to Eleanor's surprise, Mother chuckled and put an arm around her. "I've never stood up to my sister." She wept and laughed. "I can't believe it. I really stood up to her." She took a deep breath. "I only wish I would have stood up and not let her take advantage of Rose."

She dabbed at her eyes, though rather than revealing sadness, they were alive and confident. "I failed to protect Rose from her. I just couldn't stand by and let her do that to you." She pulled Eleanor to her and kissed her cheek. "I love you so much."

Eleanor threw her arms around Mother. She was sure her chest would explode, but she didn't care. "I love you too."

FORTY-SIX

ELEANOR FINGERED THE COLORED construction paper Father had given them.

"Why do the boys get to go sledding and we have to stay home and make dumb decorations?" Lilly asked.

Eleanor looked at the paper. It was pretty, but she would have enjoyed sledding more.

Mother wrapped her arms around her disappointed daughters. "I'm sure your father will take you sledding. He just wanted to spend some time with the boys alone." She looked at the paper. "And I suppose he thought we'd enjoy making decorations together."

"I won't." Lilly pouted.

Eleanor tried to cheer them all up. "At least we get to have decorations this year. What are we going to make?"

"Let's make a paper chain and some stars—" Mother paused. "I know." She hurried to the kitchen and returned with some cookie cutters. "Olivia lent me these. We could trace the shapes onto some cardboard and use it as a pattern."

They worked for several hours, taking a break to eat lunch and bake some sugar cookies before returning to the decorations.

Lilly drew faces on the little paper gingerbread men. Every half hour, she would go to the window. "Why aren't they home?"

After several hours, Mother looked out the window at the falling snow. "I really didn't think they'd be gone this long."

Eleanor joined them; she worried there'd been an accident. "I hope the truck didn't break down."

"Me too."

"Aren't you glad we're not in the shanty?" Eleanor asked.

"Yes, very much so." Shannon pulled her sweater tighter around her. "Just the memory of those days makes me shiver."

Lilly looked over the table full of paper shapes, including angels, snowflakes, candles, and reindeer. "Won't they be surprised to see all the pretty things we made?"

Mother smiled at the day's work. "Surprised and hungry, I imagine. Let's put the decorations in the living room and start the stew."

"Aren't we going to hang them up?" Lilly asked, disappointment in her voice.

"Of course, we will. We'll do it after dinner when the boys are here to help."

In the kitchen, Mother watched the clock and sighed every fifteen minutes or so. Eleanor worried too, but chatted about Christmas memories to keep Mother from worrying.

Mother pulled the rolls from the oven. "It's already dark. Where on earth could they be?"

Eleanor looked at the clock. They'd been gone for eight hours. Something must have happened. "Maybe I should go see if Reverend Hamilton knows where they went. If he does, maybe he can go look for them."

Lilly wrapped her arms around Mother's waist. "I'm scared."

Mother motioned Eleanor over and pulled both girls close to her. "We'll give them another fifteen minutes, then you can go, Eleanor."

"Can I go too?"

Mother brushed a stray hair out of Lilly's eyes. "Yes."

Outside, there was the slam of a door and voices.

"They're here!" Lilly ran to the door and flung it open. She paused and stared. "Oh, Mother!"

Father and the boys arrived with loud voices and much stomping of boots on the front porch.

"Merry Christmas!" Father called with an echo from the boys.

Lilly squealed.

"What?" Mother and Eleanor backed up out of their way.

Eleanor stared in awe.

"Oh, Charles! Boys!" Shannon's cheeks flushed with excitement. "Oh, you shouldn't have. But I'm glad you did." She threw her arms around Father, then stepped back to get a better look at the tree the boys held up. "It's beautiful."

Eleanor couldn't stop smiling. "That's why you had us make Christmas decorations."

"That's right Kitten."

"Where do you want us to put it?" William asked.

Father held his hand out to Mother. "Shannon, the choice is yours."

"Oh, my goodness!" She looked about the dining room, then went into the living room. "Over there, in front of the window. Oh, Charles, thank you." She wiped a tear from her eye.

"Mother! Why are you crying?" Raymond asked.

She put her arm around him. "They're tears of joy. Last winter, I never imagined I'd see a day like this. But here we are."

Eleanor and William exchanged glances.

"Yes," Father agreed. "I've never regretted stopping in Jake's church that morning. So many good things have come as we've learned to rely on God. He has been faithful and cared for us."

Mitchell wore a wide grin, and his eyes twinkled. "And Mother, guess what?"

Shannon touched his rosy cheek. "What?"

"We cut a small tree and took it to Lenny Johnson and his mother. They were really happy."

Mother smiled and hugged him. "I'm glad."

Eleanor helped string the colorful garland, amazed at how much their life had changed again, this time for the better. Hopefully, the bad was all behind them. She couldn't imagine what else could go wrong.

Shannon's palms sweat with nervous excitement. What if they didn't have enough? She wasn't even sure she wanted to go. It had been seven months since they moved from the shantytown, which everyone said had grown. Now she was returning, not as a resident, but to help. She hoped so much that it would go well.

Before they had met Reverend Hamilton, he had come regularly to the shantytown with food and clothes but had always given everything away before reaching all the shanties.

She didn't want that to happen today, not on Christmas Eve. She arrived at the church to a bustle of activity; the energy filled her insides and staved off the fears lurking there.

Outside, Charles and William helped cut and split firewood while the twins helped load it onto several trucks. Inside, Eleanor and Eva helped the children wrap all the socks the church had purchased.

Shannon and Rose placed the rolls and pumpkin pies they'd baked on a table with others and joined the women in the kitchen. She prepared the gravy next to a chatty woman who sliced a ham. For a moment, it was as if she was back in Idaho at the Glendales' during harvest. She smiled.

At four o'clock, Reverend Hamilton gathered everyone together. "Jesus, as you multiplied the loaves and fishes, we pray you will multiply this humble offering, and fill every belly and heart tonight."

Shannon hoped God would answer his prayer. She didn't think she could bear to tell someone they had no more food.

They loaded food, tables, and gifts into waiting cars and trucks and headed to the shantytown. With windows rolled down, they joined another congregation and entered, singing Christmas carols.

Charles smiled at her as she sang.

People peered out windows, and children ran into shacks, announcing their arrival. Others stood in lines, plates, bowls, and cups in hand. Eleanor and Eva handed out the small brown paper packages of socks, which residents accepted and stuffed into their pockets.

Shannon dished out mashed potatoes and prayed they wouldn't run out.

"Thank you, this is the first actual meal we've had in two weeks," one mother said.

"We'd all but given up on Christmas," several others said.

"You don't know how much this means to us," said a slender mother wearing one of the coats they'd passed out several months earlier.

Shannon's eyes filled with tears; she placed an icy hand on the mother's hand. "I know; we spent last winter in a shanty just over there." She pointed. "I had given up on life itself," she paused. "But God rescued us, and he will rescue you."

The woman forced a smile. "Thank you; you give me hope."

"What is your name?" Shannon asked.

"Fern."

"Fern, I'll pray for you."

"Thank you."

"And we'll be back."

"Thank you."

Shannon looked down at the third and last large pot of potatoes. It was half empty and there were still many people in line.

The woman next to her whispered something about running low on gravy. Shannon's hand shook. She couldn't do this.

"God, I know I don't talk to you much, but please multiply this food," she whispered. "These people have been through enough; they don't need another disappointment."

She watched Charles and other men passing out bundles of firewood to each shanty and hoped they didn't run out either. Even now, a year later, she felt the cold of last winter deep in her bones.

As a group of women and children sang carols, the potatoes in her pot dwindled. She tried to put on a good face, but she only had a few more spoonfuls. What would she tell them? She understood these people's hunger and constant disappointment. She didn't want to be part of that.

Shannon scraped the edges of the pot. She was down to only two more scoops of potatoes. "God, please, now," she whispered under her breath. She placed the second to last scoop of potatoes on a child's plate.

Behind them, a large car pulled up and two women she'd never seen jumped out. "Olivia, I am so sorry," said the driver.

Shannon dropped the last spoonful of potatoes on a young boy's plate, his mother standing behind him with disappointment and fear in her eyes.

"If you'll just wait a moment," Shannon told her. "I'll be right back."

She turned to Olivia and the women who'd just arrived. "Olivia, I'm all out of potatoes." She hoped her whisper hadn't carried to those waiting.

The lady who had just arrived moved to the trunk and unlocked it. "We've brought more food; how are you holding up?"

Shannon stared, her anxiety quieting.

Olivia let out a sigh, and a big smile spread across her lips. "I've often said that God likes to wait until the last-minute. He wants to keep us trusting. Hillary, this is my friend Shannon. Can you give her some potatoes?"

Shannon walked to the table as if in a trance. She looked up at the mother and smiled, blinking away the tears in her eyes. "These are still warm." She put a large serving on the woman's plate and called her son back to add to his portion.

"I was worried," said the mother, her voice weak.

Shannon took a deep breath. "I was too. But—" She swallowed at the realization. "God has provided."

Eleanor awakened to the smell of cinnamon rolls and Father calling "Ho, ho, ho, Merry Christmas. Is anyone awake?"

She was late; her plans to make a special breakfast ruined. Eleanor hurried out of bed and joined the others. Everyone but William wore the robes she and Mother had sewn. She thought of the gift for Mother and hoped she hadn't ruined the surprise. She'd tried so hard to work on it without Mother seeing it. But then, last week, Eleanor was sure Mother saw the beautiful fabric. She hated disappointing the others who had also worked hard to make and hide Mother's gift.

Charles stood by the living room entry and shooed anyone away who tried to enter. "Your mother cooked a fine breakfast; let's enjoy that first."

Guilt draped itself over her as she pulled out her chair and looked over the table with cinnamon rolls, scrambled eggs from her chickens, and a glass of milk at each child's place. "Mother, you should have woken me up; I could have helped you."

Shannon stopped her bustling and smiled. "Eleanor, this is part of my Christmas gift to you. Last year, you worked so hard to give us a nice Christmas breakfast when we had so little. So many mornings you've gotten up early to help bake bread or sew before school. I wanted you to sleep in."

It touched Eleanor to know her mother had cared so much for her gift last year. A tear slipped from her eye, though she didn't know why.

"Who's the extra place setting for?" Lilly asked.

"For me, silly." Rose peaked out from the kitchen with a pot of coffee.

Eleanor joined in the chorus of cheers. For the first time in a year and a half, it actually seemed like old times.

After breakfast, Father and William blindfolded Mother and led her into the living room.

"Charles Cruthers! What is this all about?"

"You'll see."

Eleanor's excitement grew as everyone followed and they watched as Father removed the bandanna.

Mother's eyes grew wide, and her mouth opened in surprise. "Charles! It's...it's beautiful. How on earth did you afford it?"

Eleanor's smile broadened.

"This wasn't all me, Shannon. Your children had a lot to do with it. In fact, William here procured it."

Mother turned to her eldest. "You?" Her eyes moistened, and she put a hand to his cheek.

"I traded half a cord of wood for it, but the others helped fix it up."

Mother moved to the yellow American Empire sofa and ran her hand over the rolled arms and admired the decorative mahogany feet and the dipped back. She sat on the newly re-upholstered cushions. "This is so beautiful."

Eleanor beamed with delight as the younger children wiggled with excitement.

"William helped the boys sand and stain the wood," Father explained. "While Rose and Eleanor sewed the cushion covers."

"And I helped pin the fabric and put the cushions back in," Lilly announced.

Mother stood up and walked around it. "It's just beautiful." She hugged them all, then looked again at the couch. "But this fabric must have cost a lot of money."

Father and the boys exchanged looks. "We have a confession, Shannon."

Her face went pale. "What is it?"

He smiled. "Nothing bad. The day we cut this Christmas tree, we also cut some others and sold them. That's part of why we were gone so long."

She threw her arms around him.

Eleanor blinked back tears. Over the past few months, Mother had changed. She was leaving the winter of her depression and now bloomed like her yellow roses back on the farm. The same yellow as the new sofa.

They took their time opening the gifts they'd worked together to either buy or make. Father opened his box to find a nice Fedora. "Oh, you shouldn't have."

"Father," Rose spoke up, "you have an important job in the hospital. You need to dress the part."

"Oh, I don't know about that."

Mitchell squirmed with excitement as each family member opened the small handmade wooden boxes he and William had built.

After everyone had opened their gifts, Charles peered under the tree. "I say, what is that there between the branches, in the back?"

The children all jumped up to investigate.

"Eleanor, see if you can retrieve it."

"Yes, Father." She squeezed between the tree and the window and wiggled a lightweight box out between two branches.

"Who's it for?" asked her siblings.

She fumbled with the tag and read, "To Eleanor." She looked up in surprise. "Me?"

Father and Mother nodded.

"What is it?" Lilly asked, her eyes wide.

Eleanor removed the tape, careful not to tear the paper. She lifted the lid on the box and gasped. "The dress! The lavender dress." She held it up to herself, not daring to believe it was real. "How did you know?"

"Rose told us," Mother said.

"I'm going to try it on." She rushed from the room and returned moments later to "oohs" and "aahs."

William stood. "Is it alright if I go now?" he asked Father.

Charles nodded, a slight grin on his face.

Eleanor paused, confused.

"Where's he going?" Raymond asked.

"None of your business," Father said.

"Mother, where are those rolls?"

"In that floral bag, there are some cookies for her."

"Thank you, Mother."

"Don't be too late. We're having the turkey the hospital gave your father and your sister has brought some cranberries for sauce."

William smiled. "Don't worry, I won't miss that." He put on the work gloves Rose and Eleanor had given him and his worn cap, patted the pocket of his coat, and headed out the door, bag in hand.

Eleanor worked to push the rising sadness aside. She wanted it to be like old times. All of them together.

Rose leaned in. "Be happy for him," she whispered.

Her sister was right, and she found herself saying a quick prayer for him.

William walked with purpose to Mrs. Jacobson's and slipped through the alley to her back porch. He hadn't finished knocking when Clara opened the door.

He stared speechless at her. Her light-milky complexion contrasted with the slender mid-calf deep blue dress that showed off her tiny waist and delicate ankles.

"Breathe," she teased.

He kneaded the hat in his hands. "Just when I thought you couldn't get any more beautiful—" he swallowed. "I'm sorry. I didn't mean to be so forward."

A coy smile spread across her lips. "Ain't that how a sheik ought to talk to his sheba?"

William blushed.

She grabbed his hand and pulled him inside. "Come on, I don't have long. Father has company coming over soon."

William shook off his coat and hat and gave Mrs. Jacobson the bag of rolls and cookies.

"William, you didn't need to bring these."

He shrugged. "It's the least I can do for all your kindness."

"Pshaw!" The older lady waved a hand. "It's my pleasure." She handed them each a small glass plate with homemade Russian tea cakes, jam thumbprints, and date pinwheels. A glass cup of eggnog sat in a ring on the edge of each plate. "Now you two go in and spend a few minutes together before Clara has to leave."

They sat awkwardly on the couch and nibbled on their treats.

"Did you have a nice Christmas?" she asked.

William nodded and shared about the sofa they'd given his mother.

"I can't imagine all the excitement and noise with all your siblings. It must be so much fun!"

"It certainly isn't dull."

"That's what my holidays are like. Actually, stuffy. Father invites clients Mother and I don't know, and we have to entertain them. Then, this year, he's also invited Mr. And Mrs. Thayer and their sap of a son, Marvin Jr."

William tried to calm the frustration rising inside him.

Clara watched him with her deep brown eyes and placed a hand on his. "Don't worry. I don't like Marvin. I never will."

William nodded. "I wish you could spend the day with my family."

She smiled and giggled. "I have something for you." She opened her small handbag and pulled out a slender, wrapped box.

"Me first," he said, and retrieved the package from his coat pocket. "I hope you like it."

Clara looked at the small package wrapped in red paper and shook it. "It's kind of heavy."

He grinned.

She untied the ribbon and peeled back the tape to reveal a handmade wooden box. "Oh, my goodness. William, did you make this?"

He nodded. She ran her finger over the flower carved into its lid. "No one has ever made me a gift before."

"Open it up."

She gently shook it, then looked at him with mischief. She lifted the lid and pulled out a silver filigree necklace with a small teardrop shaped crystal. "Oh, William, it's beautiful!"

"You really like it?"

"Yes. Now come over here and put it on me."

His hands shook as he fumbled with the clasp and fastened it behind her neck.

She ran to a wall mirror and examined it. "I love it."

He beamed.

"Now you have to open mine." She gave him the slender box.

He opened it to find a pocketknife with his name engraved on it. "Do you like it?"

"Wow! That is the nicest pocketknife I've ever seen. Yes. Thank you."

Mrs. Jacobson's wall clock chimed, and Clara turned to look at it. "Oh no, I have to get home." She touched William's cheek. "Seeing you has made this the best Christmas."

William nodded. "I only wish you didn't have to go."

Clara nodded. "But first, I need to show you something." She pulled him into the dining room.

He looked about the room at Mrs. Jacobson's decorations. "What did you want to show me?"

Her eyes twinkled, and she pointed above them.

"Mistletoe," she whispered.

FORTY-SEVEN

JANUARY 1933

RAYMOND RAN INTO THE house, panting. "Mother, Father, where are you?"

Mother hurried into the entry from the living room, needlepoint still in hand; her heart pounding.

Father scrambled up the basement stairs two at a time.

"Mother—" Raymond panted to catch his breath. "Father—" More panting.

Shannon grabbed his mittened hands. "Where's Mitchell? Where's Lilly?"

Charles put a hand on his youngest son's shoulder. "Calm down, what is it?"

"What's wrong?" Mother asked. "Are they hurt?"

Raymond shook his head. He took one last gasp of air. "Can I go sledding with some friends from school?"

Shannon stepped back and took a deep breath. "Sledding? All this was about sledding?" She looked at Charles with mixed bewilderment and relief.

"Where do you plan to go sledding?" Father asked.

"At Manito Park."

Father nodded. "And who are these boys?"

"Just some friends from school. They live near Aunt Fiona."

The front door opened, and Mitchell slipped in.

"Where's your sister?" Mother asked.

"Outside playing with her friends."

Shannon looked at Mitchell's downcast expression and bit her lip. Why did he struggle so much to make friends?

Father scratched at his stubble. "I don't see why you two can't go."

Raymond glanced at his brother, then gazed up at Father. "But they invited me, not Mitchell."

"Either you go together, or you don't go at all."

Raymond's shoulders slumped. "Alright." He turned to Mitchell. "Come on, let's go find some garbage can lids."

Mitchell's eyes brightened. "We could, or we could use the toboggan in the shed rafters."

Raymond's eyes widened, and Shannon smiled at Mitchell's 'ace in the hole,' as her husband would say. But how long could he stay in the game?

Mitchell pulled the long toboggan, suppressing his excitement in case things didn't go well. He would have to ask Paul to come with him next time—if there ever was a next time.

"Hurry up," Raymond urged.

"You could help."

"If you get hurt, you'd better not cry." Raymond warned and yanked the rope from his hand.

"I won't."

"Try not to do or say anything stupid and embarrass me."

Mitchell's hopeful enthusiasm softened like spring snow. "Okay."

"Help me pull this," Raymond ordered as they neared the park.

"Raymond, Raymond, over here," shouted several boys, all waving their arms. They glanced at Mitchell as the twins joined the group, but no one said anything. "We're climbing to the top of that hill and aiming for that jump," one of them said and pointed to a two-foot slick mound partway down the hill.

"Billy wrecked really bad," said a dark-haired boy, and pointing to another boy with snow caked into his sweater and wool pants.

"Anybody make it?" Raymond asked.

"We did," a couple of athletic boys bragged.

Raymond yanked the toboggan's rope from Mitchell's hand. "Come on, let's go."

Mitchell trudged behind the boys, who shoved and pushed each other as they called one another names and talked up their sledding skills.

Raymond placed the sled on the cusp of the hill, aiming at the jump. "I'm riding up front," he announced and climbed on. "You push us and then jump on."

Mitchell gave the toboggan a shove and scrambled on as it tilted downward. Cold air stung his face as they sped downward.

"We're gonna miss it," Raymond yelled.

Mitchell leaned to the left, and the sled corrected somewhat. They hit the mound at an angle, went airborne momentarily, landed hard, and traveled at a crooked angle across the hill, toward a large Ponderosa Pine.

"Pull on the right rope," Mitchell yelled as he leaned to the left. They missed the tree but toppled over as they hit unpacked snow. "That was fun!" Mitchell stood and dusted the snow off himself.

Raymond jumped up and yelled to the boys at the top of the hill, "Bet you can't go as fast as us!"

Several others hooted and hollered as they sped by on red Flexible Fliers.

Raymond knocked the snow off the toboggan. "Come on, let's catch up."

They rode down several more times before other boys wanted to try the toboggan. Occasionally Mitchell rode another boy's sled down the hill, but usually he waited, watching Raymond ride their toboggan with other boys. When one of the boys began throwing snowballs at other children, the rest joined in and Mitchell wandered off.

He explored the old zoo area and the formal gardens. He watched Rose walking with a boy in the distance. The sun was setting when he returned to the sledding hill. "There you are," grumbled Raymond. "Come on, you need to help me drag this home."

Raymond's face was red from the cold.

"What happened?"

"Where were you? If you were here, I wouldn't have gotten into trouble. But now Jonathan Howard's old man won't let me play with him."

Mitchell stared at his brother. "Why is that my fault?"

"I don't want to talk about it." Raymond stomped off, leaving Mitchell to pull the sled.

Mitchell watched his brother disappear into the growing shadows. "My fault. How is it my fault?" Raymond and the other boys were the ones throwing snowballs at younger children.

Why were they so mean? If Raymond and his friends got in trouble, it was their fault, not his. Yes. No more feeling guilty for Raymond's actions. Yeah, it wasn't his fault. Raymond did this kind of stuff all the time. Raymond should have seen this coming.

He glared at his brother, half a block away.

Indignation surged through him. "Don't blame me for your dumb choices," Mitchell yelled. "You got what you deserved."

Raymond turned and hurled a snowball at him.

Mitchell didn't care.

Forty-eight

SHANNON FORCED HERSELF TO press forward with her spring cleaning. It had been almost two years since they lost the farm, and she thought about it often when the children were at school. There was so little of that life left.

She swept cobwebs off the living room ceiling, all the while missing the large log beams that had run along the living and dining room ceilings of their old home. Even though the brick fireplace was easier to clean than the old stone fireplace with the muzzleloader hanging over the mantle, she still missed it.

She conjured the memories of kerosene lamps set around the rooms and fixed into the walls. The beautiful wool-braided rug in the living room, pictures of her and Charles' parents, the family picture when Lilly was just a baby. Could they could afford to have another picture taken? Before William and Rose grew up. This move had matured both of them.

She wiped away a tear. The longings for the farm returned that morning with the smell of fresh earth and the chirp of birds. At first it had brought a smile, but then she remembered the row of muck boots and galoshes along the front porch, and her heart sank.

She wondered who had purchased the property. Charles had written the county assessor; he learned the county had foreclosed on it for back taxes, and the delinquent debt for the tractor that the bank was unwilling to write off, even though it was in their possession.

Shannon carried the mop bucket and rags into Eleanor and Lilly's room. She wiped down the window frames, baseboards, and the closet door. Shannon stood on the stool William had built and reached to the back corner of the closet shelf, hoping not to find a spider or mouse.

Her hand bumped against a lumpy object, and she yanked it back. What if it was a dead rodent? She shuddered and lit a candle.

The object turned out to be an old, ten-pound sugar bag. As she pulled it out, a spider crawled onto her hand, and she dropped it onto the hardwood floor with a crash.

"Oh, no." Shannon gingerly lifted the bag, and its contents ground together with the sound of metal and porcelain. She untied the string around it and peered in; a blade from a pair of ice skates loomed large among a mangled spoon, a metal button, a cup handle, and the now broken pieces of one of her good dinner plates. She pulled an edge piece out and fingered the hand painted pink roses and gold trim as tears poured forth.

"What have I done?" Shannon massaged her forehead. "What have I done?"

The doorbell rang, and Teddy barked. Shannon wiped her eyes with her apron and set the bag of items on the dining room table as she went to the door.

"Shannon, what on earth is wrong? You look as white as a ghost." Olivia stepped in and placed a caring hand on Shannon's arm.

"Look what I found in the girls' closet." Shannon pulled the items out one by one, placing each broken plate piece gently on the table. "I'm afraid I broke the plate," her voice was low and melancholy.

"It appears to have been broken already." Olivia picked up a piece and pointed to the charred stains on a broken edge. "But what a lovely pattern."

Shannon nodded. "It was my mother's; I had an entire set. It was all I had left of her."

The pastor's wife squeezed back her own tears. "A very special memento."

"But what am I going to do? Eleanor must have hidden this for a reason."

Teddy barked and startled both women. "Teddy, what on—" The doorbell rang and Shannon gave Olivia a look that said, 'Who could that be?'

The door opened. "Mother?"

"Rose!"

The fourteen-year-old gave her mother a hug. "I have a little time between jobs and thought I'd stop by. Oh, hello, Mrs. Hamilton."

"Hello Rose. Look at you, you're becoming a beautiful young woman." Rose blushed.

"Come in." Shannon pulled her eldest daughter in. "Come see what I found."

Rose picked up a piece of the broken plate. "I'd forgotten Eleanor had this. How'd it get broken?"

Shannon hung her head. "I dropped it when I was cleaning the girls' room. To think, all this time, one of my mother's plates survived the fire."

"Not a whole one," Rose said, picking up another piece. "It was broke."

"But why? Why did she hide it? Why didn't she show it to me?"

Rose turned to her mother. "She did."

"No, she didn't."

"Yes, when she found it."

"I don't remember."

"You weren't yourself. You told her you didn't want it and to get rid of it."

Shannon lowered herself into a chair. "Oh, my. Poor Eleanor." She rearranged the pieces, trying to put them back together. "I'm so glad she didn't listen to me. But now what do we do? I just can't bring myself to toss it out."

Olivia arranged several pieces on the table. "There must be something we can do."

Rose walked around the table, looking at the pieces. "You know, a friend of Aunt Fiona's shared about some art she'd seen in Greece. She said they made it of small pieces of ceramic or stone. What did she call that?"

"Oh." Olivia's eyes lit up. "I know what you're talking about. I've seen those in museums and art galleries in Chicago. Mo...mo...mosaic."

"Yes, that's it," Rose said.

"That's what we can do," excitement filled Olivia's voice. "We can make a mosaic with these pieces—if it's alright with Eleanor."

The others nodded

Olivia turned pieces over to see the pattern, intermingling the plain white pieces with the floral ones.

Shannon and Rose joined her.

"Maybe we can have William carve a wooden trivet with a place in the center that we can arrange these pieces into a new design," Olivia said. "Then you can have it on the table to set hot dishes on or hang it on the wall."

A sense of anticipation washed away Shannon's disappointment. "What a beautiful way to keep this special heirloom. I think my mother would have liked this." She added a few pieces to the group Olivia had. "It should be oval."

"I agree. Something new from something old from your old home for your new home."

"Yes." Shannon sniffled. "Yes." They sat in silence, turning over pieces and arranging them into a decorative design. "How will we get them to stay in the wood trivet?"

"Jake knows a man who does tiling. I'm sure he has some kind of glue or mortar."

"Which reminds me." Shannon stood to put water on for tea and looked at her daughter. "I need to ask you about something."

"What?"

"About this boy one of your siblings spotted you with."

Rose blushed. "Oh, which one?"

"Which one?" Shannon's voice rose an octave. "What do you mean, which one?" She looked at Olivia in apprehension.

Eleanor beamed with excitement as the family gathered around the dining table. In the center was a wood tray William and Mitchell had built, with an oval indent about three-eighths of an inch deep that Father had carved-out. Rose entered with a bowl of plaster she'd mixed.

Mother shared again how Eleanor had found the dish in the log home's ashes and saved it. How she had accidentally broken it, but that they were going to make something new for their new home and life from the broken pieces of their old home and life. Mother insisted they make it as a family.

They each had several pieces of the broken plate in front of them. Mother spread the plaster into the carved out center of the wooden tray as if she were icing a cake. She then placed her pieces into the plaster and passed it to Lilly, who stood next to her.

As each family member arranged their pieces on the tray, they shared stories of meals together. Rose recalled the time an injured squirrel squirmed out of Mitchell's pocket and scampered across the table. Raymond reminded them of the cookies Rose had baked with a few wrong ingredients.

There were memories of holiday meals with Grandma and Grandpa Cruthers before they moved to the Midwest, and the jokes Father's brother, Uncle Levi used to share.

When they had finished, Rose smoothed the remaining plaster into the spaces between the fragments and wiped the excess off of the ceramic pieces. They all leaned in to admire it. Eleanor had to admit, it was pretty in its own unique way—kind of like their new life.

FORTY-NINE

SUMMER 1933

THE GREAT DEPRESSION HAD reached its lowest point with fifteen million people out of work. On Saturdays, Father and William went to the woods and felled trees. During the week, all three boys chopped the trees into firewood, loaded it on the truck, and knocked on doors selling their hard work for small profits.

Several times a month, Father insisted they take a load to the shantytown and share with those in need. In this way, Father sought to keep them busy and out of trouble. He also hoped the experience would teach them good work ethics, charity, and the value and sense of accomplishment as they helped provide for the family's needs.

On a hot day in July, William and the twins cut and stacked the rest of the trees Father and William had felled. They were hot, tired, irritable, and ready to be finished.

"We're done!" Raymond exclaimed and jumped up on the tailgate to sit down.

William looked at the extra space; there was still room for two more rows. "We need to fill it."

"But there are no more cut trees," Raymond argued.

"Then I'll cut a few."

Raymond and Mitchell looked at each other. Raymond shrugged, but Mitchell pressed his lips together. "Are you sure?"

William sharpened the axe. "I've helped Father do it plenty of times."

Mitchell took a deep breath.

"Get me the wedge." William swung the axe over his shoulder and headed to the tree line that marked the area they'd already cleared for a friend of Father's. "Come on, I'll show you how it's done." He selected a Douglas Fir about ten inches in diameter and chopped a "V" about a third of the way into the trunk on the side facing the clearing. His body was lean, and his muscles solid.

He moved to the back side and did the same thing. Soon, only a few inches remained holding up the tree. "Watch out, stand behind me."

Raymond and Mitchell scurried behind but peeked around, not wanting to miss a thing.

The tree wavered, the wood creaked, and the branches above them shook and brushed against those of other trees.

William chopped the tree a few more times then called, "Timber!"

"Timber!" echoed the twins.

The tree leaned into the opening and fell with a crash.

"Whoa! That was neat," Raymond shouted.

Mitchell stared at the long tree before him. "Yeah. Wow."

"Did you feel the ground shake?" Raymond asked.

Mitchell nodded his head, his eyes wide. The boys headed toward the closest branches with their small hatchets.

"Wait, you two, I'm not finished."

"You're going to chop down another one?" Raymond's face was bright with excitement.

William nodded.

The boys jumped up and down.

"Watch it with those hatchets. You're likely to hurt yourselves."

William selected another tree of similar size and swung his axe at the tree's base. Raymond bent down to peer into the branches of the fallen tree.

Mitchell stood between his brothers. "Raymond, come on, we need to stand by Will."

"Just a minute. There's something moving in there."

Mitchell looked between his twin and William who had just about finished with the cut on the front side. Mitchell's heart pounded. "Raymond, now."

William stepped to the back of the tree. "Come on, you two. Get over here, now."

Mitchell hurried toward William. "Come on, Raymond."

The sound of the axe against wood rang out.

Raymond stood and took one last look into the branches. "I think there's an animal in there, a squirrel or something." He went behind William, then took a few steps to William's right and squatted down to watch the axe assault the wood. "Can I try?"

"Not today," William panted between swings.

"How come?"

William took another swing and chips of wood flew out. "I want to get this done so we can go home."

"Please?"

William stopped and wiped his brow. "Raymond, this is hard work. You'll get to do it soon enough."

"It doesn't look that hard."

A breeze kicked up and Mitchell watched the tree's upper branches sway. "William?"

"Not now, Mitchell." William waved Mitchell off and glared at Raymond. "I said, not today."

"You're just like Mother and Father," Raymond complained. "You think I'm too young to do anything. I bet I could chop a tree down all by—"

"William?"

William turned to Mitchell at the tone in his voice.

Mitchell's eyes were wide, and he pointed to the tree. Near the top, the branches swayed in the wind and the trunk leaned farther than the surrounding trees.

Raymond stood, then leaned in to look at the cut William had chopped on the side by the clearing.

A moan emanated from the tree.

"Raymond, get over here," William ordered.

"Huh?" He looked up.

A gust of wind blew through the forest.

Creak.

The branches shuddered, and slowly the top tilted. The tree twisted. Then, with increasing speed and power, the tree sliced through the upper branches of nearby trees.

William shoved Mitchell back with his hand. "Raymond, look out." And reached for him.

Mitchell stared, unable to move or call out.

Another gust of wind blew, and the tree swayed.

Crack. The trunk splintered.

"Run to the trees," William yelled.

Needles, pine cones, bark, and twigs rained down upon them. Air forced away by the falling tree rushed past them, carrying dirt and debris.

The sound behind them was deafening as the tree crashed past other trees in its rush to meet the ground.

Branches and twigs scraped Mitchell's arms, face, and legs as he ran. Behind him, the sound of panting and pounding feet approached.

Thud.

The ground shook, and the branches swooshed. Dust flew up.

Mitchell covered his eyes until the rain of needles and sticks subsided, his heart hammered.

William panted next to him.

Quiet settled about them.

Mitchell opened his eyes. Something was wrong. He sensed it.

They looked about.

"Raymond!" Mitchell struggled to breathe. "Where's Raymond?"

"Raymond." William called; his voice was more manly than Mitchell had ever heard it. "Raymond."

They scanned the surrounding woods. Nothing.

An ache strangled Mitchell's chest, and he shivered. "Raymond."

As if on cue, they ran to the tree. "Raymond."

William and Mitchell peered into the tangle of branches, pine needles, and cones. "Raymond. Where are you?"

"There he is." Mitchell pulled at a branch, yanking off only a handful of needles and getting pitch on his gloves.

William tried to pull the branches apart. "Raymond, can you hear me?"

"Help," Raymond's word was a whisper. "I...I can't...I can't...breathe."

"Mitchell, hand me your hatchet."

Mitchell ran back and retrieved it.

"Raymond, don't worry. We're gonna get you out."

Raymond groaned.

Mitchell swallowed—his mouth was dry and dusty.

Sweat poured off William's forehead and soaked his clothes as he chopped at the branches that Mitchell pulled away. "Stay with us Raymond. Stay with us. We're gonna get you out."

Mitchell looked on as William chopped. He struggled to keep his tears at bay; his lips moved with silent prayers.

"I need the small saw."

Mitchell ran to the truck.

"And the tarp," William hollered.

Mitchell returned in time to pull another branch away. There was now a three-foot path to the tree trunk that hovered over Raymond. Several branches poked into the ground around Raymond. They minimized the trunk's weight on Raymond but entrapped him like a cage. Mitchell could see his twin, pale and bleeding. A stick, about the size of his forefinger, stuck out of Raymond's chest. Mitchell stared, unmoving.

"Find Raymond's hatchet. I need you to help me. We need to clear a space big enough to get him out, but don't cut those branches that are holding up the tree. Not yet."

Mitchell searched for the hatchet and found it near his brother. He crawled on his belly under branches to retrieve it, then chopped with all his might.

"I think that's big enough. Get the tarp and lay it out beside him."

Mitchell shook as he followed William's instructions. His brother lay on his back, motionless except for his quivering lips that drew in shallow breaths. Tears slipped down Raymond's cheeks from his closed eyes.

"What about the..." Mitchell pointed to the stick in Raymond's chest, his voice barely audible.

"Stay with us Raymond. We've almost got you out." William turned to Mitchell and whispered, "We'll cut this branch, that one, and this one."

He pointed to the ones that stood in their way. "I don't know how much they're holding up or if it will shift the weight."

Mitchell nodded.

"Where's the saw?"

Mitchell handed it to him.

"Once we get these two cut, I'm going to shimmy in there and cut that one—" He motioned to the one sticking in Raymond's chest. "And make sure there's nothing else causing problems; then we'll cut the bigger branch and pull him out."

"Are you going to pull it out of him?"

William shook his head.

They worked without a word as the shadows grew longer, and insects buzzed about them.

Mitchell watched as William lay on his side, one hand on the small branch sticking in Raymond's chest, the other sawing it off.

Raymond whimpered and gasped for air.

"You're doing good, Raymond. I've got to cut this so we can get you out."

"Hurts," Raymond whispered.

"I'm trying not to move it."

Mitchell watched, praying, praying, praying. "Hold on Raymond. It won't be long now."

William cut through the stick, and the tree shifted. He grabbed the nearest branch to stop the tree's downward movement. "Mitchell, grab that branch." He motioned with his head. "Help hold it up."

Mitchell did as he was told. His tired arms shook under the strain.

William scurried out from under the tree, scanned the debris, then pulled two limbs over and worked them under several branches near the trunk to brace the tree.

Mitchell watched in awe.

"Help—" Raymond shivered.

"We're almost done." William grabbed the canvas tarp, crawled back next to Raymond, and motioned for Mitchell to join him.

"Be careful not to kick any of those braces."

Mitchell nodded.

"Okay, you grab his feet—be gentle. On the count of three, lift him onto the tarp."

Mitchell sat in the back of the truck with Raymond, trying to keep splinters and small chunks of wood and bark off his brother and out of his own eyes and mouth as William drove to the hospital. "Please God, please," Mitchell begged. "Don't let him die."

The road was bumpy, and with each jolt, Raymond grimaced and moaned. It seemed to Mitchell that the drive took longer than normal.

William pulled up to the hospital's front doors; set the brake, and jumped out the door, yelling for help, and opening the tailgate.

A couple of orderlies and a nurse ran to the truck. "What do you have—" The orderly stopped at the sight of Raymond, pale and barely breathing, dark blood around the stick in his chest. "Get a stretcher. Someone notify Dr. Gray."

"A tree fell on him," William spoke to no one in particular.

There was a flurry of activity, and within minutes they carried Raymond away. Mitchell tried to follow.

A large nurse stepped in front of him. "Whoa there, lad, where do you think you're going?"

"My brother—" Mitchell tried to get around her.

She stood like a wall in front of him, her arms crossed. "No children allowed. You go back to the waiting room."

"But—" He peeked around her to see several men carry Raymond's stretcher into a room.

"Mitchell."

He turned. "Go down to the maintenance department and tell Father. I'm going to go get Mother."

Mitchell nodded, his legs already moving.

"Young man, this is a hospital," bellowed the nurse who'd stopped him in the hall. "Don't run."

But she was far behind him.

FIFTY

"WHY CHARLES? WHY?"

Father comforted Mother, whose body shook as she wept. Rose sat next to her; holding Mother's hand.

Eleanor watched this exchange and squirmed in one of the waiting room's hard wooden chairs. She hated not having something to do.

"Where's Raymond?" Lilly asked after her umpteenth lap around the room. "I want to play with Raymond."

Father motioned with a nod of his head to Eleanor.

"Come on Lilly, let's go for another walk."

"To the water fountain?"

"Sure." She wished she'd brought the handkerchief she was embroidering.

They passed William, who sat back against a wall, brooding. Next to him, Mitchell tried to console him. "Raymond shouldn't have argued with you. He should have stayed where you told him to stand."

"I shouldn't have tried chopping down those trees is what I should have done. There's a reason Father leaves you two at home when he and I go out." His voice was harsh.

Mitchell's veil of strength tore. He turned his face away from his brother and rose to leave.

William pulled his little brother back. "I'm sorry. I wish he'd give me a whipping; instead, he says nothing. At least yell at me."

Eleanor squeezed back a tear as she passed them. Her mind turned to the bread orders. She and Mother were to make sixteen loaves of bread tomorrow. They would need the money more than ever to pay for the hospital.

"Can we look at the statue?" Lilly asked.

"Sure." Eleanor allowed Lilly to guide her to the statue of Jesus outside the front door. From there, they walked back and forth in front of the large brick building as pinks and oranges filled the western sky.

"Hi," said a pretty teenage girl.

"Hi," Eleanor's voice was almost inaudible.

"Who is she?" Lilly asked.

"I don't—" Eleanor turned and watched the slender girl with bobbed hair and a red dress climb the steps. "Oh."

"William!" Clara's heels clicked as she ran down the tiled hall.

William pulled his legs tighter to his chest, but left his head buried in his arms. He simultaneously wanted her here and wished she'd never come. He sensed her next to him, inhaled her violet perfume. Her presence stung like salt in a cut.

"William?" her voice was soft.

He raised his gaze to hers.

When he didn't stand, she squatted as best as she could in her tight-fitting dress. "William, I'm so sorry. I just heard."

He glared up at her. "Does the whole town know?"

She jerked back. "What? No. Mrs. Jacobson was visiting a sick friend when she saw you pull up."

He returned to his earlier posture; face hidden. A short distance away, he could hear his mother's sobs and Father's attempts to comfort her.

Clara reached out her hand and touched his dirty arm. "What happened?"

William's tongue rolled the words around his mouth for a few moments before thrusting them out. "I've probably killed by brother." His voice was rough and raspy.

She looked at him in confusion.

"I felled a tree on him."

Clara's deep brown eyes grew wide, and her hand went to her mouth. Several orderlies walked by.

"But you didn't mean to."

"Of course not. But I still did it. I should have never tried to fell those trees with them there. I—" He stopped, and examined the blood on his hands. "If he..." The words refused sound. "...I wish it was me and not him."

She reached out and took his shaking hand, but said nothing.

William was grateful for the silence, but feared what she was thinking. Her father had told her he was worthless—this proved it. It wouldn't be long before she left, and he never saw her again.

Eleanor and Lilly walked by. "Look, there's that girl."

"Shush," Eleanor pulled her little sister toward the waiting room. "Leave them be."

"I'm tired of sitting here. I want to see Raymond. Where is he?"

William's chest tightened. He watched Eleanor sit down across from Rose and their parents. Mitchell sat next to her, flipping through a Bible he'd found somewhere.

Lilly wandered around the room, listless.

"Look at them. Look at the pain I've caused them."

Clara squeezed his hand. "I'm so sorry."

He watched Rose motion Lilly to her, then pull his little sister onto her lap.

William shook his head. He was worthless. He couldn't do anything right.

Clara touched his chin and pulled his face toward hers. "Are you alright?"

"Yeah."

"Charles."

William looked up to see Pastor Hamilton enter, followed by Olivia and Eva.

"I am so sorry. Have you heard anything?"

Father shook his head. "They're operating on him right now."

Rose stood so Olivia could sit next to Mother.

"Why?" Mother asked. "Why is this happening? My little boy. I...I..."

At his mother's words, William's chest shook, and he laid his head back down. Olivia asked what had happened, and he wept at his father's reply.

Clara shifted her weight and gently touched his back.

William wanted to pull her close to him and bury his face in her neck. "You should leave," he said, not looking up.

He sensed her hurt. When she didn't respond, he dared a glance at her.

She stared at him with those determined brown eyes. "I'm not leaving you."

"Until your father finds you."

"I told him I don't want to marry Marvin Thayer or any other boy he chooses." She smiled at him.

How desperately he wanted to believe her. Believe they could be together. "You don't want me. I'm no good."

Her smile turned to resolve. "William Douglas Cruthers! You can be so stubborn." Her look was stern. "You just stop this nonsense right now. You don't give yourself credit for all the good you do, and the man of character you are. And I will not listen to you speak such lies—"

"I don't mean to interrupt." Rose stood before them.

William shifted, wishing everyone would leave him alone.

"Father wants you to join us."

William sighed and struggled to his feet before offering a hand to Clara. They joined the others as Reverend Hamilton turned to Mitchell. "How are you doing?"

Mitchell's blue-gray eyes were watery. "I prayed the whole way here. I told Raymond I was sorry for when I'd been mean to him." Mitchell wiped at his eyes. "I told him I wished we liked more of the same things. He nodded that he did, too. I told him how I asked Jesus to forgive me for my sins, and how good I felt afterward. I told him that Jesus would forgive his sins too; he just had to ask."

Jake nodded and let Mitchell gather his words.

Worthlessness washed over William as he listened to his little brother.

Mitchell took a deep breath. "Raymond couldn't talk, so I asked him if he wanted Jesus to forgive him, and he nodded yes. So, I prayed for him. I told him that Jesus could heal him, but that maybe Jesus wanted Raymond to come live with him in heaven." At this, Mitchell's voice wavered, and tears streamed down his cheeks.

Pastor Hamilton put an arm around Mitchell. "I'm sure you brought Raymond a lot of comfort."

William bowed his head; he wanted to be anywhere but here.

"It always amazes me how fast our lives can change," Jake said.

William looked up. The reverend watched him with eyes full of compassion. William averted his gaze; he didn't want to talk.

"These things are never easy," Jake said. "But it sounds like you kept your wits about you and saved your brother."

William shrugged. "I shouldn't have had to save him. He's hurt because of me."

"William, I know this is hard on you. You feel responsible."

"I am responsible."

Jake didn't argue with him. "This is the kind of thing that defines a man."

William stared at the floor.

"Sometimes we make choices with no idea of the potential outcome."

William nodded—still avoiding eye contact. He was acutely aware of Clara's hand in his; her other hand caressing his arm.

"But that isn't the only decision that matters. How you respond to the results will mold your character and your life. Even what seem like small, inconsequential decisions are big."

Reverend Hamilton's words were a jumble in William's mind. He just wanted this day to be over—to be miles away from all of this.

"The decision I'm talking about is to forgive yourself."

William's head jerked up. Was this man crazy? The pastor looked at him with understanding and compassion that angered him.

"It's hard, but necessary. If you don't, you won't move forward, and this will cripple you. Think about that."

William shrugged, but wanted to blurt that he'd never forgive himself. "Do you mind if I pray for you all?"

Father worked the rim of his hat in his hands. "We'd appreciate that, Jake."

William stole a glance at each family member as Jake prayed. Mother looked as hopeless and lost as she had when the house burned down, and Father held her hand; he looked older than just that morning. Lilly fidgeted, and Rose was pale and sad. Eleanor nibbled on her finger and exchanged sad looks with Eva. Mitchell kept rubbing his chest, as if it hurt too. William looked at Clara, who squeezed his hand and smiled at him with sad eyes.

Reverend Hamilton had just finished praying when the doctor approached.

"Mr. Cruthers?"

"That's me." Father turned to meet the man. Mother and the rest of the family encircled him. The Hamiltons and Clara stepped back.

William took a deep breath and braced himself for the doctor's words.

"I'm Dr. Richards."

"How is he?" Mother asked. "Will he be alright?"

Dr. Richard's expression was grim. "He's in critical condition." He focused on William. "Are you the one who brought him in?"

William nodded. "Yes, sir."

"You were wise not to remove that branch from his chest."

Some of the tension in William's frame left. He breathed.

Dr. Richards turned back to Mother and Father. "Your son's lung has collapsed—"

"Oh, my." Shannon wilted and Father held her.

"Keeping that branch in prevented more air from filling the chest cavity and pushing on the lung. We could remove much of the air from the cavity as we sewed shut the puncture."

"That's good, isn't it?" Father asked.

"It is. But he's not out of the woods yet." Dr. Richards looked up. "I'm sorry." He cleared his throat and collected his thoughts. "When the chest cavity fills with air, it not only affects breathing but also puts pressure on the heart. We will monitor his heart and also watch for infection."

"Can we see him?" Mother asked.

Dr. Richards looked about at the huge clan. "He's still under some anesthesia." He focused on Father and Mother. "I think for now it's best for just you two and only for a few minutes."

A collective quiet groan rose as shoulders, and heads dropped. William stepped back from the group.

Father nodded, and Jake stepped up. "We'll take the children home with us."

"And get them something to eat," Olivia added.

"You two take all the time you need," Jake continued. "Come over when you're ready." He grasped Father's hand and pulled him into a hug. "We'll be praying for you."

"Thank you." Charles turned to his family. "We'll let Raymond know how much you all love him. In the meantime, you all go with the Hamiltons."

Rose leaned in. "I really need to get back to work."

Mother and Father nodded.

William stayed back as the rest gathered around the Hamiltons. "Father?"

Charles paused as he and Mother turned to follow Dr. Richards. "Yes."

"I'm not up to being around many people right now."

Father looked over at Clara, who stood outside the circle, watching. "I understand."

"Please," William paused, steadied his voice. "Please tell Raymond I'm sorry. I never meant for him to get hurt."

Charles pulled his eldest son into an embrace. "I know, and I'm sure he does, too. We all make mistakes. You did well in getting him out from under the tree and here to get help. Show yourself some grace."

William pulled away; his eyes averted to the ground.

Fifty-one

"Why are you crying? You don't even like him."

Eleanor cringed at the memory of Lilly's words. Maybe Lilly was right. She had been hard on Raymond; she tried to remember the last time she'd said anything nice to him. He was always disobeying, sneaking around, taking things that weren't his, and telling lies. He made it hard to be nice to him.

Her eyes burned from crying. Next to her, Lilly inhaled a jagged breath and whimpered in her sleep. Eleanor had tried to hug Lilly, but her little sister refused Eleanor's comfort.

Mitchell had told the family how Raymond wouldn't listen to William and stand behind the tree. It was so typical of him. Anger rose within her. Why did Raymond have to be so difficult? Why couldn't he just do what he was told?

Life was just getting back to normal. Mother wasn't sad, and they had food and clothes and a nice place to live. Now what would happen? She worried about Mother, who looked again like she had when they lived in the shanty.

She thought about the hospital bill. How would they pay for it? Tomorrow was bread day; it was more important than ever to get their orders out, but Father had already said they'd return to the hospital first thing in the morning.

A rustle outside her door startled her.

"Where have you been?"

"Does it matter?"

"You know it matters."

"What's going on here?"

Eleanor slipped from under her sheet and pressed her ear to the door, straining to hear.

"William, are you drunk?" Mother's voice was shrill.

"Shannon, not so loud," Father whispered.

Mother glared at him. "Where on earth did—"

"I know people," he spat.

"Enough, you two." Father's voice was stern. "Your brother lies in a hospital bed, and you decide to go get drunk?"

"Yeah."

"William," Father's voice was calm. Eleanor opened the door a sliver to hear better. "I know you feel guilty. But no amount of alcohol will wash away that guilt."

"I'm a failure. Admit it. You know I am." William's voice rose.

"Not so loud. Your siblings are sleeping," Father reminded.

"You don't deny it."

"That's not what I said. You know you're not a failure."

"I can't get a job, Clara's father won't let me see her, and because of me Raymond is—"

"You have lots of jobs," Mother protested.

"Nothing steady. Nothing I can count on. Rose can support herself, and Eleanor brings in money with her eggs and bread..."

"And you bring in money with your yard work and wood cutting and help me with the boys by teaching them to work."

"More like putting them in danger."

"William," Father's voice was firm yet compassionate. "Mitchell told us what happened—how Raymond was arguing and not doing what you told him. We don't blame you."

"You should. I'm a no-good, worthless son."

"You know that's not true," Father said. "It's been a hard day, and you're tired, and now drunk. Go to bed. We'll discuss this later."

Eleanor slid her door shut and slipped back into bed. William's words echoed in her mind.

How could he think he was worthless? She considered Mitchell's brief description of what happened, and how William had worked to get Raymond out. What would she have done? She probably wouldn't have known what to do.

She and Raymond had argued just that morning. She couldn't make him well, but she could help her family.

Eleanor arose earlier than usual, mixed and kneaded the ingredients for the bread orders, and was placed the first batch in the oiled bowls to rise when Mother entered.

"Eleanor, what are you doing? We need to go to the hospital."

"But we have orders; people are expecting us to deliver their bread."

"They'll understand."

"Will they? That Mrs. Track is always trying to steal our business away. She'll use this," Eleanor countered, a worried look crossed her face. "And we'll have hospital bills."

Mother stared at her. "But your brother."

Father entered and looked about at the dough rising in the smooth wooden troughs he had helped William and Mitchell build.

"If I go, all I do is sit. They won't let us see him."

"I really think you should be there," Father said. "Raymond may be doing better."

Eleanor looked about at all her hard work. "And waste all this?" She turned to him. "How are we going to pay for the hospital?"

"That's my responsibility."

They all turned to see a disheveled William still wearing his clothes from the previous day. "I'm the one who hurt him. I'm the one who will pay his hospital bill."

"That responsibility belongs to neither of you," Father asserted. "I'm still the head of this house—"

"He wouldn't be there if it wasn't for me."

"Shannon, make some coffee and get some breakfast ready. William, go take a shower and get some clean clothes." Father turned to Eleanor. "And you, Kitten, finish up this batch and come to the hospital."

"But Father, this will only—"

He lifted a finger. "Family first."

Eleanor sighed. "Yes, Father."

Behind her, a bowl fell and shattered on the floor. Mother let out a sob and crumpled beside it. Eleanor stared, motionless, while Father rushed to her side. "I'm scared," she cried.

He lifted her to her feet and helped her into the living room.

Mitchell and Lilly came into the kitchen, wide eyed. "Is Ray—?" Mitchell's eyes were wide and his complexion pale.

Eleanor shook her head. "Put some bread in the oven to toast while I get the coffee and eggs. You'll be leaving for the hospital soon."

Mitchell stopped. "Aren't you coming?"

"I have customers who are expecting bread today."

Mitchell didn't move. "But...Raymond."

"What can I do there? We can't go in and see him. All I can do is sit there. I might as well do something productive."

"But..."

"The toast, Mitchell. The toast."

No one ate much for breakfast, and before long they left for the hospital with instructions for Eleanor to come as soon as the bread was out of the oven and not to bake any more.

Eleanor watched them leave and tried to push the rising guilt away. She loved Raymond, really, she did; even though he could be so difficult.

She felt so helpless at the hospital; at least here she could help. She didn't know how much Raymond's operation and hospital stay would be, but she was sure it was more than they had.

She punched down the rising dough a little harder than normal, shaped the loaves, and put them in the pans to rise. Tears came as the water poured into the sink to wash the dishes. "Why God? Why?" She wiped her tears with her sleeve. "Haven't we had enough troubles?" She placed the clean dishes on the counter. "God, Pastor Hamilton and Father say you can do anything. That you can heal." She inhaled a sharp breath; tears now mingled with the dishwater. "They also say that sometimes you choose not to—" She let the mixing bowl slide back into the soapy water and ran to her room, yanking off the apron on the way.

She threw herself down on her bed and cried; her sobs, the only sound in the empty house. She wished she'd gone with her family. Why did she have to be so practical? Why did she have to worry so much about money? She wished someone was here to hug her. What if Raymond—? She would not think about it. She went into the bathroom, washed her face, and re-braided her hair. Soon the bread would be ready to bake.

Passing the table, Eleanor paused at the trivet they had created out of the broken dish she'd kept. She could still feel Mother's hug when she came home from school the day Mother had found and broken the plate. Mother had apologized for telling her to get rid of it, not realizing Eleanor's kind gesture, and thanked her for saving it. Mother's hug and kind words were like a flower growing in her heart. Eleanor had dwelt on them for days. How she could use a hug from Mother now.

She looked at the mosaic trivet and remembered the broken bowl this morning. Mother was fragile and needed a hug, too. She put the bread in the oven and checked the clock. It would cost at least a half hour, maybe more, before the loaves were done. She sighed, wishing she was finished. A knock at the door startled her.

Fifty-Two

SHE OPENED THE DOOR to find a winded, wide-eyed Eva. "Come," she panted and grabbed her arm. "You need to come. Now."

"What happened?"

"Raymond." More panting. "He...he's not doing well." Eva blinked back tears. "They sent me to get you."

"What's wrong?"

"I don't know; I was just sent to come and get you. They said to hurry."

Eleanor looked back at the oven. "I just put bread in."

Eva peered around her friend. "I'll watch it. You go."

Eleanor nodded, took off her apron, and handed it to Eva. "Look in on it at twenty-five after."

"I will." Eva hugged her.

Eleanor ran to the hospital. "Oh God, help me get there in time. Oh." Various scenarios zipped through her mind. Maybe he needed another operation; maybe the doctor needed to talk to them.

She took the front steps two at a time and flung the door open. The lady behind the counter glared at her.

"Eleanor." Rose hurried to her from the waiting room. "Finally." She grabbed Eleanor's hand and pulled her further down the hall.

"What's going on?"

"Raymond's not doing well."

Eleanor slid to a stop, pulling Rose with her. "He's not going to—" Her chest tightened; she struggled to breathe. "Die...is he?" For the first time Eleanor noticed her sister's red eyes.

"Come on," Rose urged. They passed Reverend and Mrs. Hamilton standing in the hall, their heads bowed together, clasping each other's hands, praying.

Rose led Eleanor into a long room with four beds on either wall, and several nurses helping patients. Several beds were empty, but one bed held a boy younger than Raymond, who whimpered for his mother. Two other boys were in beds. One had a bandage wrapped around both hands, his arms, and his face, which left only a small space for his mouth and eyes. The other boy had a leg in a cast that was lifted in the air at an angle with a pole and cables at the foot of his bed.

"Hi there, cutie," said the latter boy to Rose.

"Russell, shush," commanded a middle-aged nurse with thick, powdery makeup.

Rose ignored the boy and motioned Eleanor to the bed in the corner where their family was gathered around.

William looked up as they approached, his blue eyes bloodshot, and his usual wide grin flat. It was only a moment before he bowed his head again.

Father turned and held out an arm to Eleanor, who slowed her pace, suddenly unsure if she wanted to see him.

"Come," Father said.

Eleanor slipped in next to Father, who wrapped his muscular arm around her. She first looked across the bed at Mother, whose slender frame looked thinner than just the day before. Mother was pale, her eyes moist and rimmed in red.

Eleanor looked down at Raymond, pale and still. She couldn't remember a time he'd been so still. His eyes were closed, and his breathing shallow. Sometimes he'd take a breath and then—nothing. They would all stare at him; fear rose in Eleanor's heart when this happened. Then he'd take another breath, and she'd realize she was holding her own breath.

"Take his hand." Father lifted Raymond's hand for her to hold.

She stared at its smallness. There was pitch on several fingers, a sliver in his thumb, and dirt under the nails.

"Talk to him," Father said.

Eleanor's mouth went dry. What should she say?

"Let him know you're here."

"Can he hear me?"

Father nodded.

"Raymond?" Her voice shook. "Raymond, it's me, El...Eleanor. I...I...I wish you weren't hurt." Tears streamed down her face.

Father squeezed her arm. "You're doing good. Tell him you love him."

"Raymond, I...I know I don't say it...but...I love you." She wiped the tears with her hand. "I do. I love you." She sniffled. "I'm sorry I didn't tell you more often. I'm sorry I wasn't nicer to you." Tears dropped on the blanket.

Raymond's hand moved just barely inside hers. She squeezed back and looked into his pale face, his jaw slack, no breath.

Her chest tightened. "Raymond!"

His body quivered, and he took another breath.

Her shoulders dropped; her muscles relaxed, and she exhaled. "Oh, Raymond." She ran her other hand over the back of his and looked across the bed at William. He looked horrible—his jaw set, and his eyes—his eyes looked angry yet empty at the same time. He had a look about him, of someone who was utterly lost. Grief welled in her chest as much for him as for Raymond.

One by one she took in each family member, all gathered around the hospital bed. She never wanted to forget this scene. Rose stood next to William; her makeup smeared, head cocked, watching Raymond breathe. Eleanor wondered what Rose was thinking. Before the fire, they had been close, and she could read her sister's expression—that time was gone.

Next to her, Mother stroked Raymond's cheek, her lips moved, but Eleanor couldn't make out the words, if they were words at all.

To her right, Father stood, speaking softly to Raymond, "I love you; God loves you; God has prepared a very special place for you." Then, Father would quote Bible verses he'd shared at supper; that God would never leave him, or about believing and receiving salvation. His words brought her comfort.

To her left, Lilly pressed in tight and wrapped her arms around Eleanor. Lilly hadn't been affectionate toward Eleanor in a long time. Eleanor warmed at this surprise. Lilly tugged at her arm, and Eleanor bent down to listen.

"When is Raymond coming home?"

Eleanor grimaced and looked around for help. William turned his head and left the room. Eleanor took a deep breath. "Well…" This wasn't fair. Why did she have to tell her sister?

Mitchell, who'd been praying at the foot of the bed, looked up. "Raymond is going to a new home."

Lilly's eyebrows bunched. "Are we moving?"

Mitchell shook his head.

"What your brother is trying to say," Father explained. "Is that Raymond is going home with Jesus."

"But then I can't see him." Big tears welled in Lilly's eyes.

Eleanor reached down and lifted her sister, who was getting so big. Father took her from Eleanor's arms, and the child sobbed.

"Mr. Cruthers," the grouchy nurse approached with a scowl on her face. "I'm going to have to ask you all to leave. There shouldn't be this many people in here."

Father nodded. "Please, may my wife stay?"

The nurse looked at Shannon's grief-stricken expression, then down at the dying boy and agreed.

They each took one last look at Raymond; a few touched his hand or sheets and whispered their love to him. In silence, they followed Father, who carried the crying Lilly out of the room.

In the hall, Reverend Hamilton, Olivia, and Eva met them. Olivia's large brown eyes looked at Charles. He shook his head and tears streamed down Olivia's already blotched cheeks. They went to a waiting room. William sat in the corner. Father handed Lilly to Rose and sat with him. Jake Hamilton motioned for the others to leave them alone.

Lilly soon fell asleep with her head on Rose's shoulder, leaving Eleanor to ponder all that had happened. She chastised herself for baking bread instead of being with her family. She'd only had a few minutes with Raymond, and now she might never see him again.

Father and William sat without words. Several people entered while nurses and orderlies passed by in the hall.

"I know you blame yourself. I would too," Father finally said.

"You wouldn't have done it," William spat. He hated himself more and more with each passing minute.

Father shook his head. "You don't know that."

"You think before you act."

"Not always. It's a skill I've learned over the years. But I've done my share of things that could or should have turned out bad." Father examined his hands. "One time, when I was working in the mill with your grandfather, I was supposed to be guiding a board through the saw; I got distracted by some other fellows, and the board got pinched between the blade and the guide. It swung out and knocked over the man I was working with. He had a gash in the arm and a goose egg on his head. It was a miracle he wasn't hurt worse or even killed. Your grandfather gave me a whoopin' I never forgot."

"I wish you'd give me one."

"You know me. I've never been one for whipping you kids." He sighed. "Maybe if I had, Raymond wouldn't have been such a handful."

"I feel like I've taken Raymond away from all of us."

"You haven't taken him away from us. We are all given a certain amount of time—some long, some short. We need to cherish the time that we have."

William tried to contemplate this, but all he could see was his guilt.

The hand on the wall clock had moved less than forty minutes when Mother entered; her lips quivering.

William's heart sank.

FIFTY-THREE

ELEANOR TRUDGED INTO THE house; every step heavy, as though she was dragging a bag of sand. She struggled to accept the events of the past twenty-four hours.

Teddy greeted the family. His tail was down and the usual excitement was gone. He worked his nose under each hand as they filed silently into the house. A bouquet of red, yellow, and orange dahlias sat on the table with a handwritten note. Mother stopped, stared at them, then shuffled to her and Charles' bedroom, and shut the door—the note unread.

Teddy followed her partway, then stopped; he turned, and his pale blue eyes searched each family member.

Eleanor and Mitchell exchanged looks. Worry bunched Mitchell's brows. Eleanor bit her lip. Would Mother slip into the sadness she wore in the shantytown? "Please God, no," her voice was barely audible. She picked up the note and read the kind words from one of their bread customers.

She looked around the kitchen; the bread was gone. Eva must have waited for Mr. Pollack, who would have told their customers what had happened. She was exhausted, more tired than she'd felt in a long time.

Teddy nudged his nose under her hand.

She looked down at his pleading eyes and dropped to her knees; she wrapped her arms around his neck and sobbed.

Lilly and Mitchell joined her. All three huddled around the dog, who licked their tears and nuzzled them.

At some point William mumble something to Father, and Eleanor looked up at the clock. It read noon. She should fix lunch, but the thought of food repulsed her. She took a deep breath, wiped her face, and stood. "Father?" her voice was shaky as she sucked in jagged breaths.

He fingered a slingshot the nurse had given him from Raymond's pocket and looked up at her.

"Should I fix lunch?"

He looked at the clock for a long moment. "I suppose. Not much; I'm not hungry."

William turned from the living room window he'd been staring out. "None for me." He picked up his hat and walked out the kitchen door.

Mitchell shook his head, no, his attention on his brother.

Outside, Eleanor heard the axe striking wood as William chopped unneeded firewood.

Lilly, quieter than usual, pressed against Eleanor's side.

"And you?" Eleanor looked down and ran her hand over her little sister's messy brown hair.

"Toast...please...in a bowl of milk?"

Eleanor traced Lilly's cheek with her finger. Mother rarely allowed Lilly that indulgence in the middle of the day, but what could it hurt? "Let's go see what we can find?"

Eleanor, Rose, and Lilly rode in the back seat of Gerald and Margaret Boyer's car. Margaret sniffled and dabbed at her eyes. Behind them, William and Mitchell rode with Mrs. Jacobson and Clara. Ahead of them, Mother and Father rode with Reverend and Mrs. Hamilton and Eva. Other cars followed, and at the very front was a shiny black painted wagon pulled by two black draft horses.

Eleanor sighed as the car stopped at the cemetery. Rose squeezed her hand, and together, with Lilly, they followed Mother and Father to a row of chairs set several feet from a deep hole. Eleanor failed to swallow a cry at the image she had of her little brother buried in that pit—all alone. She focused on Father's words, that it was only Raymond's body; his soul was already in heaven with God and his angels. She glanced up at heaven; could Raymond see them?

Aunt Fiona, Uncle Harry, Suzanne and Albert sat in the row across from them, on the other side of the hole. Eleanor wondered about several boards laid across the hole.

Reverend Hamilton stood at the head of the hole with Mrs. Hamilton next to him. She sang "Amazing Grace" as four men carried the plain wood coffin from the wagon and laid it on the boards.

At the sight of it, Mother cried out and buried her face in Father's chest. He patted her back, his gaze fixed on the wooden box before him.

Across from them, Aunt Fiona gasped. "It's—so small." She pressed an embroidered hankie to her lips; her body trembling.

Eleanor tried to listen to Reverend Hamilton, but she couldn't stop thinking that she would never see her brother again. She replayed past interactions with him in her mind. Thinking of all the times she'd gotten mad at him. Why did he have to be so...so...so stubborn? Always having to do things his way?

"Some people claim you have to be good to get to heaven."

Reverend Hamilton's words brought Eleanor back to the funeral. Good was not a word she would have used to describe Raymond.

"But good is not enough," continued the preacher.

A knot grew in Eleanor's throat. She had tried so hard to help her family—didn't that count for anything with God? Wouldn't that get her into heaven?

"None of us are good enough." Reverend Hamilton paused and looked around at those gathered. "No. On our own, none of us are good enough to stand in the presence of God and live in his heavenly kingdom."

"Uh!" Aunt Fiona was pale; her eyes were wide.

"Our sin is an enormous debt against God that we can never repay. But he loves us, so he, himself, provided a way to pay off that debt. A way to make us better than good. A way to cleanse us from all our sins."

Eleanor leaned in. She had worked so hard to help provide for her family, but no matter how hard she worked, she always felt lacking. And that drive to 'do more' had kept her from the hospital. It had kept her from time with her brother.

Tears now streamed down her cheeks.

Reverend Hamilton looked at her with empathy; his voice was kind, and hopeful. "Through Christ's death on the cross and resurrection, we can each have forgiveness from our sins. We can each have our burdens lifted and someday experience eternity in heaven with our loving Father."

Forgiveness—her burden lifted. A swelling of hope and joy arose in Eleanor's chest at the idea. For so long, she'd chased after security and never found it. But now, with Reverend Hamilton's words, she realized that she'd been looking in the wrong place. Security was only temporary here, because...she looked around at the cemetery with its stone and wood markers, long dying grasses, and flowers left to wilt by headstones. This world was temporal. Nothing lasted. Not their home in Idaho, not the shanty, and not their bodies.

She looked at the wooden box that now housed Raymond's "earthly home" as Mrs. Hamilton had explained to her and Lilly. He wasn't here. He was in heaven with God and a new body—forever. That was security. That was what she wanted. She turned to Reverend Hamilton.

"Before Raymond died," the pastor continued, "he asked God to forgive him for his sins and believed in God's son, Jesus Christ. We too can have the hope that God has promised to save us, and that he has prepared a place for us."

The weight that she'd never see Raymond again pressed in on her.

"But not everyone has the opportunity right before they die to believe and ask for forgiveness, as Raymond did. So, each of us should do that now. None of us knows how long we will live. I'm sure Raymond thought he had many decades ahead of him." Reverend Hamilton looked around at the mourners.

"When I spoke to Raymond in the hospital, I asked him if he believed Jesus was Lord, and that God had raised him from the dead. He nodded he did. I reminded him that because of his belief, there was nothing to fear. That heaven was a beautiful place, and Jesus was waiting for him there."

Eleanor sat on the edge of her seat.

Reverend Hamilton smiled at all in attendance. "A peace swept over Raymond's face, his muscles relaxed, and he smiled as best he could."

Eleanor wiped the tears from her face as a smile spread across her lips. She glanced up to see Aunt Fiona crying uncontrollably.

"Each one of us can carry that peace with us every day," Reverend Hamilton said. "We don't need to wait until our death bed. In fact, I implore you not to wait. For some, death is sudden, and there is no other chance."

Eleanor bowed her head. "Father, forgive me," she whispered. "I have fought against you and your ways. I have tried to do things my way. Please, make me clean like Reverend Hamilton said you can."

FIFTY-FOUR

THE NEXT WEEK WAS quiet and somber. Father returned to work and Eleanor wished she had somewhere to go. She worked in the garden; her tears mingling with the dirt. Mother spent most of her days in bed; the curtains drawn. William refused to return to the woods and combed the surrounding neighborhoods, looking for yard work. Mitchell helped in the garden in the morning, then disappeared after lunch with Teddy to roam the rocky wooded areas around Manito Park. Sometimes he wandering as far as High Drive and climbed down the steep bluff to Hangman's creek. "I know me and Raymond weren't getting along," Mitchell told Eleanor one day. "But I feel like..." he searched for the words to explain his emotions. "I feel like part of me died with Raymond. Part of who I am."

Eleanor hugged him until he shrugged her off.

"I don't know what I'd feel if I knew I'd never see him again...you know, in heaven."

She nodded.

Most mornings, Lilly climbed into bed with Mother after Father left, then remained close to Eleanor and Mitchell until the afternoon when she'd look at Eleanor with sad eyes and ask if she could play with the neighbor's children. "Of course, you may," Eleanor would hug her and send her on her way. Sometimes it seemed Raymond's death hadn't affected Lilly much. Though when she was tired, the tears would come, and Father or Eleanor would spend an hour or more holding and calming her.

Often one or another of them would ask: "Why did Raymond have to die?" Of which, there was no answer.

Rose came every day to help Eleanor while neighbors, bread customers, and church members often brought food, so there was little cooking to do.

In the ensuing weeks, Mother began to venture from her room in late morning for coffee and toast, look about the kitchen, and the bread Eleanor was baking, or the vegetables from the garden she was preparing to can. Occasionally she would help with the canning, but often she'd return to her room with barely a word.

Father always arrived home from work looking haggard, and Eleanor could tell he was losing weight. "Aren't you eating the lunch I pack?" She finally asked him one evening.

He forced a smile. "I try to Kitten, I'm just not real hungry." He squeezed her shoulder and looked at the meal Eleanor was trying to finish. "Has your mother been out of her room today?"

"Briefly."

He nodded and went to wash up for dinner.

Some evenings, he took the children for walks around the neighborhood or around the gardens and trees at Manito. Other evenings, he sat on the front porch and read his Bible or went walking with Jake Hamilton. Often, he would leave for work early and go to a small wooded area near the hospital, where he would sit and weep.

William would come home in time for dinner, eat, then retreat downstairs to the small workshop, where he would sometimes allow Mitchell to help him with a piece of furniture he was rebuilding. Other times, when he was in a bad mood, he'd shoo Mitchell away, saying he wanted to be alone. Then he'd slip out the basement door. When Father asked where he was, Mitchell would give partial directions, often having followed William until he left the neighborhood.

Mitchell spent more and more time alone. He occasionally played with Paul, but only when Violet brought him during one of her and Eva's visits with Eleanor.

Eleanor loved these visits with her two best friends. It gave her a break from thoughts of Raymond and feelings of guilt that she should have been nicer or could have done things differently with him. She wondered if she could ever laugh and talk like she used to without the ache and sadness that seemed to walk alongside her.

She wasn't alone in this. Even though Father didn't lie in bed crying like Mother, she'd seen his eyes mist up and he often sighed for no apparent reason.

And so, the days went. The produce in the garden and on the trees needed more work than Mitchell and Lilly could provide.

"I'm worried about Mother," Rose said one day as she sat on the back steps and helped Eleanor shell peas.

Eleanor dropped the handful of peas she'd just picked up. "I don't want to do this again."

"Again?" Rose emptied her bowl of peas into the larger strainer. "What do you mean, again?"

"You weren't there."

"Where?"

"In the shanty. Mother shriveled up, like—" she looked at the pea pod she'd just picked up. "Like a dried-up green bean. She was sad all the time and stayed in bed most days. I did most of the cooking and cleaning and trying to get Lilly and the twins—" she paused at the last word and swallowed hard. "To help and study."

Rose's eyes widened. "Oh, Eleanor, I didn't know."

Tears welled in Eleanor's eyes. "It's bad enough with Raymond...but to have Mother hiding away in her room...it's...it's like...like she's died, too."

Rose nodded.

"I feel like everything is falling apart."

Rose looked down at the bowl in her lap and pushed more peas out of a pod.

Eleanor stiffened. "What? What is it?"

"You remember my friend Marguerite?"

Eleanor nodded.

"Well, she's friends with Clara."

"William's girlfriend?"

"Yeah, well, she's not his girlfriend anymore."

"How come?"

"Apparently, William broke up with her. Said he wasn't good enough for her. That he'd never be able to provide for her, and that Raymond's death proved he'd be a horrible father."

"That's awful. Didn't he hear Reverend Hamilton at the funeral?"

Rose shrugged. "If God loves us, why did he let Raymond die?"

Rose's words stabbed at Eleanor's infant faith. "I...I...I don't know."

"Anyway," Rose continued, "William doesn't think he deserves forgiveness, not from God or anyone else."

"Oh, William!" Eleanor recalled her own heavy burden, lifted when she trusted Jesus. Despite Raymond's death, she had hope and, oddly, joy. She only thought of Raymond in heaven—where she would see him again, rather than gone—never to be seen in this life.

"If Jesus can forgive the criminal on the cross next to him and the people who crucified him, surely God will forgive William for an accident. Why can't he see that?"

Rose emptied another pea pod. "I don't know. I'm still not sure I believe any of it."

"Rose!" Eleanor's hands were on the step as she leaned forward, surprised at her sister. "Why not? It's knowing that God is with me, being able to talk to him about all of this, and knowing that I'll someday see both him and Raymond that helps me do all this, day after day."

"I'm happy for you. I'm not ready to believe all that, and apparently William isn't either."

Eleanor sank back and her heart with her.

"According to Clara, William is hanging around with some guys who drink a lot, get in fights, and chase after not-so-nice girls."

Eleanor had a vague idea of what not-so-nice girls meant, but she didn't want to ask Rose, who, since moving out of Aunt Fiona's, seemed to know much more about the world than even Mother and Father would have liked. "Why?" she asked, recalling several arguments between William and Father.

"He told Clara when he drinks, he forgets."

"Forgets? Forgets what? Forgets Raymond ever lived? Forgets that he has a family that loves him? Forgets..." Eleanor stood and stomped off with the pan of pea pods and threw them at the compost pile. "That solves nothing," she yelled. "Raymond's death is always going to be there. He can't stay drunk and forget it forever."

"Some people do."

"That's stupid."

"Calm down and quit yelling."

"No. I won't."

It had been over a month since Raymond's death and everyone but Mother sat around the table eating. "Children," Father waited until he had everyone's attention. "I've asked Reverend and Mrs. Hamilton to take you on an outing after supper tonight."

Lilly perked up. "Where to?"

"That's up to them, but I believe there will be ice cream involved."

"Yay!" Lilly clapped.

"Yay," William grumbled. "I've got plans tonight."

"Well," Father said, "You'll have to cancel them."

"Father! I'm not a little child."

"No, you're not. But I'm asking you to do this for me. Mr. Hamilton has some things he wants to show you."

"Great, another sermon."

"William, come downstairs to the workshop with me."

"Fine."

Downstairs, Father shut the door to the shop and ran his hand over the smoke chair William was repairing. "You do good work."

William only nodded.

"I've told you before, I don't like the path you're headed down, and I know someday you won't either."

"Yeah, well, you don't have to live with the regret of killing your brother."

Father looked down at the sandpaper on the workbench. "No, I have to live with the regret that my decision to move from our land and livelihood in Idaho left my family starving, cold, and homeless."

"But we survived that only to have me kill—"

"Son, you didn't kill him. You never saw a tree turn like that one and fall the wrong way. You had no way of knowing that could or would happen."

"But it did. I disobeyed you...if I'd obeyed, Ray—he'd still be here. Why can't I do anything right? I can't get a steady job and support myself like my little sister can. Clara's dad thinks I'm not good enough for her, and now I can't even keep my little brothers safe."

Charles pulled William into an embrace. William sobbed. "It's alright son, get it out."

Twenty minutes later, Reverend Hamilton tapped on the workshop door.

"Come in Jake."

The lean-faced, slender Scandinavian entered. "Charles." He nodded at Father. "William."

"Hi, Pastor." William dried his face on his shirtsleeve.

"I just wanted you to know that we're here and ready to leave when you are."

William took a deep breath. "I'm ready."

Charles raised his eyebrows at Jake and motioned at William.

Jake gave him a knowing nod.

Father watched the Hamiltons drive off with the four children and shut the door. The clock's ticking echoed in the quiet house. Teddy nudged his nose under Charles' hand and he ruffled the dog's fur. "One down and one to go, old boy."

He walked down the hall to the room he and Shannon shared. He opened the door; his eyes adjusting to the dark before partially opening the curtain.

"Charles, don't."

"No, Shannon. It's time."

"Time for what?"

He sat on the edge of the bed, caressing her face and hair. "Time to get up."

"I can't. I'm tired."

He steeled himself. "We all are. But it's time you get up and join us. It's time to reenter life."

She rolled over and glared at him. "You don't care, do you? Our son's dead—dead Charles, dead!" her voice increased in volume and intensity. "Raymond's dead, but you carry on, going to work and church as if nothing happened."

Charles said nothing, allowing her to vent. When she'd spent her anger in words, the sobs came, and he pulled her to himself, and together, they wept.

After a while she looked up at him, her light complexion blotchy. "Why don't you cry?"

He brushed a strand of hair from her face. "Oh, Shannon. I do. I cry when you're asleep, and I cry as I walk to work and on my way home. I grieve Raymond's death deeply. I always will."

"But still you go."

"Yes, I go on. I need to provide for our family, and parent our remaining children."

"First, we lose our home and farm and now our son." Her tears came again. "How am I supposed to go back to life the way it was?"

"I don't know. But you can't keep living this way either. I know you're hurting, so am I, but so, also, are the children. Shannon, they are hurting too. They need our love and comfort. They don't deserve to be neglected."

Her sobbing slowed, and she wiped her face with her hand. "I know. I...I want to. But then the sadness comes. I miss him. I miss him, Charles." Her sobs muffled in his chest.

He held her close again. "I miss him too, Shannon. Every day," his voice cracked. "The children miss him, too."

She drew in a jagged breath.

He smoothed her uncombed hair. "They miss you too. Lilly asks me daily why you don't spend time with us anymore. She asks why you don't love us. Love them."

Shannon looked at her husband. "Oh Charles. I don't know how to do this. I love them, but I miss him. This hurt consumes me. It's all I can see."

He nodded. "I know. But we can't let it swallow us. We are still in the land of the living, and we need to live. Our children need us to live."

"But how?"

"One day at a time."

Shannon nodded.

"I've asked Olivia to come over tomorrow. I think you need another woman to talk with."

"No, Charles. I'm not ready."

"But we are."

Shannon read over the note Eleanor gave her from Olivia. "I don't know. I feel guilty enjoying myself with Raymond gone."

Eleanor nodded. "I do to. But..."

"But?" Shannon's voice came out terser than she would have liked. She watched as Eleanor straightened her posture as if steeling herself.

"But I don't want to spend the rest of my life feeling sad." Eleanor paused, then continued. "Father said we needed to learn how to smile and laugh again. I'm trying to do that."

Shannon sighed. "There's no getting out of this, is there?"

Eleanor shook her head.

"Then I guess I'd better go bathe."

Shannon washed and wound her long braid into a bun. She looked at her hair. Maybe she should cut it. That was the style nowadays. She even applied a little lipstick. But when Olivia rang the doorbell, she panicked and turned to go to her room. Eleanor stopped her while Mitchell opened the door. Shannon turned around in defeat.

"Shannon, it's so good to see you." Olivia hugged her and kissed her cheek. "It's a beautiful day out there, and I hear the petunias and gladiolas are gorgeous."

Shannon tried to smile. "I'm not sure this is a good idea."

"Just a short outing. The sunshine, flowers, and friendship will do you good."

Shannon consented. Maybe a quick trip wouldn't be bad.

Olivia put a hand on Shannon's arm as they walked out of the house. "I want you to tell me some of your funniest memories of Raymond."

A slow smile spread across her face. "You don't mind listening to me talk about him?"

"Of course not. Why would I?"

"Oh, most people want to talk about everything but him."

Olivia squeezed Mother's hand. "You are welcome to talk about him whenever you want—as much and as long as you like. He was your son, and you loved him."

Mother's eyes moistened. "Thank you, Olivia. You are a loyal friend."

FIFTY-FIVE

"Do we have to go?"

Eleanor watched from the kitchen as Father, William, and Mitchell prepared to leave.

"I'm really not up to celebrating Thanksgiving, let alone..."

Father stopped and turned to William. "I understand. This is hard on all of us."

"Then why do we have to make it worse?" William massaged his temples.

Beside him, Mitchell was somber and looked on with sad eyes.

Eleanor wondered the same thing.

"There are others in need, and it's time you two returned to the woods and faced what happened. If you'd fallen off a horse, I'd have you get back on. This is the same thing."

William picked at a hole in his sleeve, then looked up. "But why today? Why Thanksgiving?"

Father examined his gloves. "The folks in the shanty camp need wood, and we have an extra day off, so we have the time to help them."

William groaned, and they left.

Eleanor stared past them, not really seeing anything. While Father and the boys chopped wood with other men from the church, Eleanor needed to distract Mother from her grief in order to fix the Thanksgiving meal. Eleanor had a plan and shared it with Eva after she and Mrs. Hamilton arrived.

Peeling potatoes and yams, Eleanor and Eva talked Mother and Mrs. Hamilton into sharing stories of their childhoods in Chicago. At first, Mother balked at the idea, but after Mrs. Hamilton shared a few memories, Mother joined in.

Eleanor had never gotten Mother to say much about her childhood, so she hung on every word. She cringed at Mother's description of the narrow Chicago alleys, fenced in by tall brick buildings, with clothes lines displaying personal dainties above the trash and raw sewage on the street. No wonder mother loved the privacy of the farm and hated the shantytown. But even that didn't dampen Eleanor's desire to visit the big city.

Before supper, Eleanor joined Father and the boys in passing out food and firewood to the families in the shantytown. When they arrived home, Rose, Marguerite, and Liam were there, helping Mother dish up the food. Father carved the turkey, and the girls put relishes and jams on the table that Lilly had set. With everyone seated, Father asked Reverend Hamilton to bless the meal.

Eleanor glanced at Mother, who was now pale; her light green eyes with their dark orbs teared up. There was a tremor in Mother's hand. Soon Mother would escape to her room, not to return.

They'd put so much work into the meal, and everyone, including Rose and her friends and the Hamiltons, were here. She needed to stop Mother from leaving. Before sitting, she gave Mother a hug.

"Thank you," Mother whispered.

Eleanor watched as Mother's attention was drawn to the hall. She leaned into Reverend Hamilton. "I'm afraid Mother's having a hard time. She may leave."

He nodded and tapped a spoon against a glass. "Can I have everyone's attention? I have an idea. Before I pray, let's take a few minutes and everyone who wants can share something about Raymond that they're thankful for."

Everyone nodded except Eleanor; she watched Mother slowly crumple into herself.

Jake started, "I'm thankful for Raymond's exuberance for life—every Sunday he would run up to me and ask if he could ring the bell."

They all smiled at the memory.

"I'm thankful that Raymond was my twin," Mitchell said. "When we were younger, I always had someone to play with, and because of Raymond I got extra cookies and sweets."

Mother looked at him. "How is that?"

Mitchell blushed and looked down at his plate. "Well...he would have me ask you a question, or have you come and help me with something, then he would slip into the kitchen and sneak off with some cookies."

Mother shook her head. "That little rascal! And I used to wonder why my recipes sometimes made less than at other times."

As Mother relaxed and smiled at everyone's memories of Raymond, a fresh fear arose in Eleanor—what would she share? She looked across the table at William, who sat quietly as everyone shared, and shook his head when it was his turn.

"That's alright," consoled Reverend Hamilton.

One by one, they shared things they were thankful for until only Eleanor and Mother were left. Eleanor shifted in her chair. What should she share? She sensed everyone's eyes on her.

"Is there a story you want to tell?"

Eleanor nodded at the pastor. She recounted the weed fight they'd had over a year ago. The image of dirt clods flying through the air and bursting against their clothes, and wilted weeds clinging to their hair and hanging from the tomato and bean plants even had William chuckling. Eleanor smiled at the recollection and decided she would write that memory in her new journal, so she was sure not to lose it.

It was now Mother's turn, and everyone turned to watch her. Eleanor hoped she wouldn't find this too hard and escape to her room. She picked at the tablecloth. "Raymond could drive a body crazy," she announced. Everyone nodded. "But I am thankful for how he always added something interesting to what was often a regular day." She smiled to herself. "Charles, do you remember when you insisted that we have that photographer in town take a family portrait?"

Father smiled at the recollection.

Mother turned to Olivia. "The twins were only four or five years old, and Lilly was just a toddler. The day before the photographer arrived, Raymond escaped from the house, and I found him just inside the woods in a patch of poison ivy we'd never seen before."

"Oh, no!" Olivia exclaimed.

Eleanor's eyes widened, and she itched at the memory of her own experience with poison ivy.

"Me and Charles and that photographer had to work extra hard to keep Raymond still for the picture. He was wiggling around and scratching and pulling at his clothes. Oh, my, I was about to call the whole thing off."

"I'm glad you didn't," Father said. "That photographer did a good job."

Mother sighed. "Yes, he did. It's too bad the fire destroyed the photo."

Charles rubbed his chin and looked at the ceiling as if he could see something up there. "I can't remember, Shannon. What was that fellow's name who took that portrait?"

"Oh my, John, James, Jack—James...James Johnson, that was it."

"Yes, that's right."

As Reverend Hamilton thanked God for the food, Eleanor tried to remember the picture; she'd seen it every day for most of her life until the last year-and-a-half. Where was she standing? What was she wearing? Why had she forgotten it? The older she grew, the stranger life seemed.

After supper, Reverend Hamilton announced he had a surprise.

Eleanor and Eva exchanged glances.

"Oh, Jake," Olivia said. "Please don't tell me it's ice cream. I don't think I can eat another bite."

"Me either," Mother agreed.

"You don't want any ice cream?" Pastor Hamilton teased.

Olivia looked sternly at her husband. "Don't tell me you hid the ice cream maker in the trunk?" She turned to Shannon. "That man would eat ice cream three meals a day if I let him and still not gain any weight. It's just not fair."

Mother shook her head—a grin on her lips.

Reverend Hamilton stood. "You children give your mothers a break and clean up while Charles and I go get our little surprise."

"What do you think it is?" they asked each other as they collected dirty dishes.

"I don't know," Eva said. "But Father got a package from one of his brothers in Chicago last week, and he wouldn't show us what it was."

They all whispered what it might be; even Liam offered a few ideas.

Soon they were seated around the table, with Reverend Hamilton standing at the head holding a package wrapped in brown paper. "I have here, in my hands, straight from Chicago, one of the most popular games people are playing." With a flourish, he pulled out a box and held it up for everyone to see. "I present, 'The Landlord's Game.'"

They all stared at him, unsure what to make of it.

"Each player has a game piece and with the roll of the die, moves their piece around the board. On some spots you can buy property, others you pay rent, taxes or fees. The winner is the player with the most money."

William groaned.

Eleanor examined the game board and soon noticed some squares were better places to land on than others.

"But I don't have any money." Lilly's countenance darkened.

Father smiled. "That's alright, my little Mountain Flower; the game has its own play money."

"Can I use the money to buy candy?"

Father grinned. "Sorry Lilly, it only works in the game."

"Oh."

Soon, they were moaning or hooting as their pieces moved around the board. "Jail?" Eleanor hollered.

"I'll be keeping an eye on you," Reverend Hamilton teased.

"Public Utility Ting-A-Ling Telephone Company, fifty-dollars!" Rose said. "I'd rather work there."

Liam looked at the few dollars he had left in his hand. "This game is too much like real life."

"I agree," Olivia said.

"Hey," Rose turned to Liam. "Tell everyone what your boss gave you."

SMITH

IDA SMITH

They all looked at the ruddy Liam with his sandy blond hair. His blue eyes twinkled and dimples deepened as he grinned. "My boss gave me a raise. Soon I'll be able to move into a boarding house. Hopefully, before winter."

"Good for you." "Congratulations."

Eleanor eyed Liam. She liked him and suspected he had feelings for Rose, though Rose seemed to treat him like a brother.

Liam leaned into William. "You should think about moving in with me. We could split the rent."

Eleanor watched her brother. He seemed both enticed and discouraged by the idea. "I'll think about it."

Next to her, Mitchell fidgeted. He and William had grown closer, and he wasn't ready to lose his remaining brother. She wasn't either, but sensed William's restlessness and desire for independence.

"William, how much scratch you got?" Rose tried to peek at her brother's stash.

He covered it with his hands. "None of your beeswax, you little gold-digger."

"Ooh," Liam chuckled.

Rose slugged Liam and shook a fist at her brother. "Look who's become a Scrooge?" she teased.

"Beat it." A smirk tugged at the ends of William's lips.

"Do I need to pass the offering plate?" Reverend Hamilton teased.

Eleanor smiled at the joking. She was pleased that no one noticed her purchase of Fifth Avenue. Now she could collect one-hundred dollars rent from every player who landed on it. She waited with guilty glee for her first victim.

This morning she'd been sad and missed Raymond. Now, concerns about William leaving hovered overhead, but she would not let that ruin what had turned into a good day. She was thankful, despite her grief. If Raymond was here, he would be "wheeling and dealing" as Father called it, and having a good time—like he did when he was alive. In some strange way, this game seemed to honor him.

FIFTY-SIX

"ARE YOU SURE?" MOTHER asked.

"Yes, I've been keeping a record." Eleanor pulled a piece of paper from her apron pocket. "See. Every day or two, there are fewer jars."

Shannon looked it over. "That's interesting."

"What?" Eleanor leaned in.

"It's never vegetables or soup or anything that has to be cooked."

"You're right. It's always the fruit or pie filling, jam, or pickled preserves, except for the relish and beets."

Mother turned back to the spam she was cutting for sandwiches. "If this keeps up, we could run low on food this winter."

"That's what I was thinking. Should we set a trap?"

"Oh, Eleanor. You've been reading too many books."

"Maybe someone is sneaking into the basement at night. If we put a bell on the door, we could hear it."

"I'm sure if someone was sneaking in, Teddy would warn us."

"Maybe we should sprinkle some flour on the floor, then we would see their tracks."

"Along with a bunch of ant tracks."

"Mother, I'm trying to stop this."

Shannon tapped the tip of Eleanor's nose. "Every man is sociable until a cow invades his garden."

"Well, I'm meaning to catch this cow. Do we have any extra string?"

Mother placed slices of spam on the bread Eleanor had buttered. "Eleanor, just help me make lunches."

Mitchell wandered into the kitchen. "Can I take some bread and hard-boiled eggs to school?"

Mother and Eleanor looked up from their task.

"For lunch?" Mother asked.

Mitchell fidgeted. "Sort of."

Lilly skirted around them and slipped down the basement stairs.

"Sort of?" Mother gave him a skeptical look and raised an eyebrow at Eleanor. "Mitchell, what is going on?"

He let out a deep breath. "Mom, there are children at school who are hungry."

Shannon squeezed her eyes shut and pressed her lips into a tight line. "So, you're proposing we feed these children?"

Mitchell nodded.

Memories of the persistent hunger they endured while living in the shanty gnawed at Eleanor. Even now, it wasn't like they always left the table with full bellies, but at least they weren't starving.

Mother looked up as Father and William entered the dining room. "Charles, what do you think? Mitchell wants to take some eggs and bread to some of his classmates."

Father put a hand on Mitchell's shoulder. "You've got some lads without food?"

"Yes, sir."

"I don't see why he can't take them some food. God has provided for our daily needs and filled our storehouse."

"I need to talk to you about that," Mother said, her eyebrows bunched.

"Shannon, he has provided."

"Oh, I agree, but someone has been helping themselves to that provision." She looked at Mitchell. "Have you been taking food from the pantry?"

Mitchell's expression turned to one of hurt. "No. I share my lunch, but I haven't taken extra food. That's why I asked."

"Well, somebody has."

"I think we should set a trap," Eleanor offered.

"Enough, Eleanor."

"Maybe you're just imagining it," Charles said and put the sandwich Mother handed him into his tin lunch pail.

"No," Shannon countered. "Eleanor's been keeping track."

"If I move out, you'll have one less mouth to feed."

They all stopped and looked at William. "What?"

William shrugged. "I'm eighteen. Rose has been living on her own for several years. Why can't I?"

"Do you know how much it costs to live on your own? Buy your own food and clothes?" Mother asked.

William scowled.

Eleanor cringed at the idea of William leaving. Beside her, Mitchell's shoulders slumped and his countenance shifted.

"Besides," Shannon continued. "I'm not happy with some choices your sister is making. Bobbing her hair, dating all those different boys, and now getting a job with the telephone company."

"I wish I had the opportunities Rose has." William shoved his lunch into the old sugar sack he used.

"This depression hasn't been easy on any of us," Father said. "But especially not on men who want to support a family." He gave his eldest son a look that William ignored.

Eleanor watched Lilly sneak up the stairs and creep past everyone, her sweater pockets bulging. "Lilly?"

Lilly stopped, her blue eyes wide and avoiding Eleanor's gaze.

"What have you got there?"

"Nothing. I need to go."

"Mother—" Eleanor started.

"Mother, Eleanor's picking on me. I need to go or I'll be late."

Shannon glanced up at the clock. "You don't need to leave for another ten or fifteen minutes."

"Mother," Eleanor tried again. "She's got—"

"I told Emily I'd play hopscotch with her before school," Lilly interrupted.

"Mother," Eleanor's voice was now frantic. "She's got food."

"I do not, I have to go."

Father reached out and pulled her back. "Hold up there, my Little Mountain Flower." He examined her lumpy pockets. "Empty them."

She pulled an apple from each pocket and glared at Eleanor. "There. Are you happy?"

Father gave her a look. "Don't take that tone with me or your sister."

"I just want a snack at school."

"We pack you a lunch," Mother said.

"But I want more."

"Check her school bag," Eleanor said.

"There's nothing in it."

William strolled over to it. "Let's see what kind of boondoggle you got going here."

Lilly yanked it away, and glass jars clanked together.

"Lilly, give that to your brother," Father ordered.

"Why?"

Father gave her a look, and she thrust the bag at her brother. William pulled out a quart jar of peaches and a jar of dill pickles.

"Lilly Ann Cruthers," Mother gasped. "Why on earth..."

William dug around a bit more and pulled out a few hard-boiled eggs.

"Lilly Ann!" Mother continued. "That food is for all of us."

"There's plenty down there."

Father gave her another look.

She scowled. "There is."

"That will be enough," Father said. "That food needs to last us until the garden produces again."

"What'd she do with the jars?" Eleanor asked.

Everyone looked at Lilly.

"Quit staring at me."

"Well," Mother asked. "Where are they?"

"I threw them away."

Eleanor's hands flew up in the air. "Oh, my goodness." She stared at her parents in exasperation.

"I need to go. I'm going to be late for school," Lilly announced.

"You need to go to your room for a few minutes," Father said.

"But—"

Father's look silenced her protest.

"What are we going to do with her?" Eleanor asked.

"You won't to do anything," Father told her. "Your mother and I will discuss this. In the meantime, get Mitchell the bread and eggs he asked for."

"Yes, Father."

Charles turned to William. "If you want to move out, I can't stop you, but I'd suggest you ask around and see what it will cost you, and look at your income. I'd feel better about it if you had at least fifty dollars saved up for unexpected expenses."

"I can take Liam up on his offer," William said.

"I don't need to remind you," Father continued. "That you can make good money cutting wood."

A darkness fell over William's countenance. "Or I could run a gin mill. They make lots of dough."

"William!" Mother's hand went to her mouth.

Father's straight shoulders stiffened. "That's a fine path to jail."

Mother grabbed William's hand. "Please! I don't want you becoming like your grandfather—all alone—not caring about those who loved him."

Eleanor and her brothers both stared at Mother's confession about the father she rarely spoke of.

FIFTY-SEVEN

WILLIAM WAITED UNTIL THE rest of the family was busy before pulling the old block of wood from the top shelf in the basement workshop. He made sure no one had followed him downstairs before pressing the hidden lock and sliding the top off the block to reveal the hidden compartment he'd carved. Inside was the money he'd saved up over the past month. He'd been careful not to spend much after Father had told him to keep all his earnings.

He counted the few dollar bills and the coins he kept in an old sock to minimize noise in case someone, mostly Lilly, went scavenging through his stuff. He looked at the small pile of money, barely half what Rose told him he would need, and that didn't include the "emergency fund" Father wanted him to have.

How did Rose do it? Too bad he couldn't ask someone for free room and board for yard work and handyman jobs. He looked at the wooden bank he was carving in the shape of a house like the metal one he'd seen in a store window and the rake handle he'd carved for one of his customers. A birdhouse, small stool, several wooden kitchen spoons, and toolbox he'd built and attempted to sell sat on the workbench with several tools.

He slammed his fist on the worktable. How would he ever have enough to move out? William looked at the items, and with one sweep of the hand, flung them onto the floor. He marched out of the workshop, up the outside stairs, and out the back gate. No matter how hard he tried, he was a failure. He walked down the alley and past several teenage girls waiting for the trolley.

"Hi," they called in a chorus.

He tried to suppress a smile. "Hi."

"You going to the movies?" one of them asked.

William glanced back. "Naw."

"You should come with us," another called.

He fingered the dime and piece of lint in his otherwise empty pocket and kept walking. Moments later, the trolley clanged by, and the girls shouted the name of a movie out the windows to him. He watched the trolley glide down the hill and grumbled to himself, "I can't make enough money to support myself, let alone go to the movies with cute girls." He kicked a rock and kept walking.

Clara's father drove by in his Cadillac Roadster, and William kicked the next rock even harder. He missed her, and when he was really lonely, he would walk past her house at night, glance up at her window, then remind himself that he wasn't good enough for her.

He wandered past downtown clothing stores, gas stations, banks, hotels, and offices. Businesses occupied some buildings, others vacant—almost all had "Not Hiring" signs in their windows.

He stopped in front of one store and stared at the display of furniture, the same store he'd gotten the idea for the stool he'd built.

"Isn't that just the bee's knees?"

William turned to see a girl about his age window shopping.

"That hutch." She pointed to a corner hutch painted white with scalloped edges. "I love coming down here and looking at the furniture. That piece is my favorite."

William studied the cabinet. "It's swell. I wonder how they cut those... scallops?" he asked, uncertainty in his voice.

"I don't know, but I really like it." She turned and examined him. "What are you looking at?"

William blushed. "Nothing in particular." He pointed at the stool. "I made a stool sort of like that one."

"Nifty."

"Guess I was just looking for ideas."

"You should make a hutch like that one." Her blue eyes brightened. "I imagine your girlfriend would really like it."

William blushed even more. "Yeah, I don't know."

"Oh, any girl who received a gift like that would be mad not to like it." He smiled.

"Have you seen the furniture at Harvey's Home and Office?"

He shook his head.

"It is pos-i-tive-ly swell. If you like making furniture, you need to see the goods they carry." She grabbed his shirtsleeve and pulled him. He walked beside her, listening to her chatter. They stood outside the window of a high-end furniture store as she pointed out the pieces of furniture she liked. There were end-tables, armchairs, and a settee similar to the one they had refinished for Mother. "If you want to make furniture, this is where you want to work."

William fingered the dime in his pocket. He should save it in case he ever had enough to move out. He looked at the blue-eyed girl with blond hair pulled up in ribbons. She had more curves than Clara and dressed more like his sisters. Still, he liked her. "What's your name?" he blurted and immediately regretted it.

She stopped her chatter and smiled. "Delphine."

"Delphine, I'm William. Would you like a cola?"

She looked back in the direction they'd come, appeared to be thinking, then agreed.

They found a booth at the crowded soda shop and ordered two colas. Delphine continued to talk while William listened to her. She talked about her family and shared stories about people he didn't know.

"I don't think I've seen you at school. What grade are you in?"

William shifted in his seat and twirled the straw between his fingers. "I don't go to school."

She seemed only slightly surprised. "Oh. What do you do?"

"Work."

"Making furniture?"

"No, that's just a hobby. Mostly yard work, fix things for people."

"Oh." She paused only momentarily before continuing. "We have a garden, and Mother has a terrible time keeping up with it. Maybe you could—"

"Delphine." A blond boy slightly older than William approached. "Delphine, we were supposed to meet in front of Broemelings?" He glared at William. "Who's this hood?"

William tensed.

The cheerful girl stopped—eyes wide. "I waited, but you didn't—"

"So, you hooked up with this—" He looked William up and down. "This bum."

William clenched his fist and glared at the guy with his store-bought shirt.

"Johnny, he's not. We met at the furniture store and I wanted to show—"

"Delphine, I don't care about furniture."

"But you said to wait there—"

"To get you off my back."

Delphine's enthusiasm melted like ice in July.

William took a swig of his drink and looked at Delphine. "Thanks for showing me that furniture; it's real nice. But I've got to get going." He tried to stand, but the guy blocked his way.

"I'd say. I don't take too kindly to some sap homing in on my girl."

"Didn't know she was yours. We were just talking."

"Yeah, right? I know you homeless types; take her for a walk in the park, steal her money, and do shameful things—"

William stood, grabbed the boy's shirt collar, and pulled him even closer. "You take that back."

People around them stopped their conversations.

Johnny glared at him with a big grin. "Which part? That you're a tramp or a thief and a rapist?"

"All of it." William shoved him back.

Johnny stumbled, caught himself, and charged.

William stepped to the side at the last minute, but stuck his foot out. Johnny stumbled forward into the booth.

Delphine screamed, and the other patrons moved out of the way. Some left, while others watched.

Johnny righted himself, faced William, and stepped toward him. "Not any good with your fists; I see."

"Wrong again." William threw a punch, which was blocked, and received a fist in the gut. He absorbed the blow and threw an uppercut to the guy's chin.

"Hey, what's going on?" A man with a white apron hurried over. "You two knock this off."

Johnny reached back and flung a blow at William, who ducked and threw a gut punch of his own.

"Break it up." The man tried to worm his way in between them.

William backed off while the other boy continued to press against the aproned man and spew degrading comments about William.

"Johnny, stop." Delphine pleaded.

"I didn't ask your opinion, dumb Dora," Johnny spat.

"And I didn't ask you to fight in my soda shop," said the man. "Now beat it, both of you." He pushed Johnny out the door as a soda jerk escorted William out.

"Johnny, please I was just—"

"Stop beating your gums."

William took a step closer to Johnny, who was brushing Delphine's arm away. He grabbed the guy's arm and spun him around. "You don't need to talk to her that way."

The guy grabbed William by the neck of his shirt and pulled him to within inches of his face. "I'll talk to her however I want to, and you won't interfere."

The soda shop customers watched from the windows and door.

"Johnny, leave him alone."

"My father taught me to treat women with respect." William poked his finger into the guy's chest. "Looks like your old man failed to teach you anything."

"Boy, you're gonna wish you never laid eyes on me." Johnny swung and hit William in the jaw.

William stumbled back, shook his head, and rushed at him. He knocked Johnny off balance, and the boy fell backwards. In a flash, William jumped on the boy and pummeled him.

"William, stop it," Delphine screamed.

Pedestrians hurried past the two, giving them a breadth of space.

"Help. Someone, stop them."

Two men from Harvey's Home and Office pulled the two boys apart as a woman waved down a police car. "That tan boy with the wavy brown hair almost killed that other one," said the woman. "He's a dangerous one, probably one of those roving hooligans from that Hooverville by the river."

"Yes, ma'am," said an officer and approached the two battered youths. William had a black eye, several cuts, and a bruise appearing on his cheek. The other boy's right eye was swelling shut; he had multiple cuts, a split lip, and wiped at a bloody nose. "What's this all about?" asked the officer.

"This bum was messing with my girl; planning to take her to some lonely place and rape her."

"I was not." William's blue eyes flashed, and he straightened his muscular frame and leaned toward Johnny, restrained by the man who held him. "If anyone is going to hurt her, it's him."

"Why don't you go back to your shack in Hooverville and leave us alone?"

"Enough, both of you." The older officer looked first at Johnny, then at William. "Is that where you live?"

William glared at the officer. "No. I live up on the hill."

"With your folks?" His stance was skeptical.

"Yes."

The officer looked at Johnny. "Go home and clean up. Next time, try to settle your disputes without violence."

"What about him?" Johnny pointed at William.

"Don't you worry about him. We're going to go have a talk with his father."

William's anger shifted to self-loathing. What if Father sent him back into the woods? Maybe he would be a hobo, ride the rails—working wasn't getting him anywhere.

William remained in the back of the police car, as he was told. From the open window, he listened to the police talk with Father. He picked at the blood on his hands. Ever since moving to Spokane, life had been one disappointment after another. He was tired of it. He needed a change.

An officer opened the door. "We're leaving you in your father's custody. Stay out of trouble, or next time you'll find yourself in the cooler."

William glanced at the house before getting out. Mother and his three younger siblings stood watching. The look of grief on Mitchell's face stabbed him. He got out but said nothing. Father motioned him to the truck, and he sauntered over, gaze on the road.

"I've heard the police story; now what's your side?"

William shrugged. "Accept it, I'm a flat tire."

"If by 'flat tire' you mean you're worthless; you're wrong."

"Why am I here? I don't make enough to support myself. I can't make friends. Everyone thinks I'm a homeless tramp. I'm a disappointment to everyone. I'm—"

Father held up his hand for William to stop. "You are not the only man in this situation, and you know it."

"But I'm the only one in this family who can't support myself and make friends." He was done with this place. The first chance he got; he was leaving.

"Go get yourself cleaned up; we're going to go see Jake."

"So he can preach at me?" Anger tightened in his chest.

"He wants to talk to us about your future."

William grimaced. What future? Life on the rails had to be better than this. He slumped at Mother's gaze. After Mother's Day, he would leave.

FIFTY-EIGHT

SHANNON TOOK A DEEP breath and suppressed her thoughts about Raymond. He was so young! Why did he have to die? This was the worst Mother's Day ever. She wiped away the tears and ran her hands over the yellow dress with pink and white flowers Eleanor had sewn for her. It was a sweet gesture. Eleanor had become quite the seamstress, and it fit Shannon handsomely.

In the hall, Eleanor and Lilly's voices rang out. "Stand still. I can't get the ribbons in your hair with you moving."

"I don't know why I have to wear a ribbon, anyway. I hate ribbons."

"But Mother likes them, and this is her special day."

Shannon smiled and slipped from her room to see Lilly stop with a huff before Charles who gave their youngest a look that said, "behave." Lilly folded her arms, her back to Shannon who imagined Lilly scowling as Eleanor tied ribbons in Lilly's long braided pigtails. "When I grow up, I'm going to bob my hair like Rose."

Shannon shook her head. Though in reality, she'd even considered cutting her own hair, but not as short as a bob.

Charles glanced at the clock. "Hurry, we need to get going."

William, Mitchell, and Rose appeared from outside, and William handed Charles the keys to Reverend Hamilton's car. She couldn't help notice the mischief in their eyes.

Eleanor smiled at her. "Mother, do you like the dress?"

"I do, It's very nice. I love the color."

"When I saw the feed sacks, I knew you would."

"I helped pick out the buttons," Lilly added.

"And they are very nice, too." Shannon turned to Charles. "But I'm not sure why we're all dressed up today; Mother's Day isn't until tomorrow." In reality, she just wanted to go back to bed and sleep forever, not celebrate the fact that, as a mother, she had lost one of her children.

"We have our reasons." He looked around. "Is everyone ready?"

Teddy barked.

"Not you fellow."

Eleanor reached down and wrapped an arm around the dog. "Oh, Father, please."

Mitchell joined her. "Teddy has to come; he's part of the family."

Teddy cocked his head and pawed at the air.

"I must be nuts," Charles said. "Is that why you children were bathing him?"

Mitchell and Lilly nodded.

Charles shook his head. "He needs to stay in the back seat and off your mother's new dress."

"He will."

Shannon smiled at Charles' soft heart. She shoved aside her desire to escape into grief and steadied herself. "What are you up to?"

"You'll see." Charles grinned, as did the children.

Minutes later, they pulled in front of a downtown shop. "Charles," Shannon looked at the display window, trying to make sense of it. "What are we doing here?"

Charles opened the passenger door for her and Rose. "Shannon, you said something at Thanksgiving that got me thinking." He pointed to the sign in the window.

Mother gasped, joy and grief both tugged at her heart. "Charles. Really?"

He nodded and led her to the door, followed by the others.

A wiry man with a big smile welcomed them, then raised an eyebrow at Teddy.

"I hope you don't mind; he's part of the family," Father offered.

Shannon struggled to suppress the grief and guilt that Raymond wasn't with them.

The man put his finger on his chin and walked around the multi-colored Australian Shepherd. Teddy appeared to smile. "He is beautiful." He turned and looked over the rest of the family, then began issuing directions. "Mrs. Cruthers, I'll have you sit there in that chair and you, little Missy." He pointed to Lilly. "I'll have you stand next to her."

When they were all arranged, he stepped behind a tripod and ducked under a black cape. "You all look so lovely. Smiles everyone. On the count of three—one, two, three." A bright light flashed and Teddy barked. "Beautiful. Don't move, we'll take one more."

After Shannon selected a frame, the family headed back to the car.

Lilly put her hand in Shannon's. "Mother, why are you crying? Don't you like the gift?"

Shannon swallowed the rising emotions and ran her hand over Lilly's hair. "Oh, Lilly, yes, of course I do." She paused and dabbed at her eyes with her handkerchief. "I just wish—" She composed herself. "I just wish Raymond was here."

They all nodded.

"Thank you, Charles." She looked around at her family. "Thank you all. This means so much."

"But there's more," Lilly announced.

"More?"

Charles held open the door for her and Rose. "Your children have packed a delicious lunch, so we're headed to the river for a picnic and a few other surprises."

"More surprises?" Overwhelmed, she felt undeserving of her family's love.

Rose and Eleanor laid out the cold fried chicken, deviled eggs, biscuits, honey, and coleslaw on the blankets the boys had carried to the riverbank.

Shannon looked at it all and then at each of her children. "You have all become such wonderful people. I'm so proud of all of you." She looked directly at William, who stared at the blanket beneath him. She'd seen a change in William lately. His restlessness had mellowed, but she was still concerned. "William."

He looked up at her.

"You too. You have given up school and friends and worked hard at whatever opportunity came your way; all to help us. I know things haven't turned out like you've wanted, and it's been very hard."

He nodded.

"Life is like a cup of tea; it's all in how you make it!" She paused, and a tear slipped out. "There are times I have forgotten that, but I'm working to remember it. Life goes in cycles of good and bad; life won't stay this way. I believe that better days are coming. You will find your place, and you will succeed." She smiled at him and squeezed his hand.

He hugged her, then stood. "Mitchell and I have something for you." He turned to his brother. "Come on." The boys scrambled up the hill to the car and returned with a wooden box.

Shannon's mouth opened in surprise, and she covered it with her hand. "Oh, my." She looked up at the boys. "Did you two make this?"

They both nodded with wide grins.

"It's lovely." She ran her hands across the carved flowers and lifted the lid. "Is that cedar I smell?"

William nodded.

She pulled out one drawer, then another. "Oh my, look at this."

"I remember back at the farm you used to do embroidery," William said. "You could put your projects in the top and your thread and needles in one drawer and the patterns in the other."

She smiled and gave them each a hug. "Yes, I need to get back to my embroidering. It's beautiful, thank you."

"Now ours, now ours." Lilly squirmed and poked at her sisters.

"Oh my, you mean there's more? This meal was plenty."

Rose handed her mother a small bundle wrapped in white muslin and tied with twine.

"You all are making me feel like a queen."

Father smiled. "That is the point."

She opened the bundle to find more white and off-white muslin, a pair of small scissors, embroidery needles, and a handful of colored embroidery floss. "Oh, now I don't have any excuse, do I?"

Eleanor beamed at her mother's pleasure. "Nope."

"And you can put it in the box Willy and Mitchell built you," Lilly said.

She laughed. "Yes, I can. Come here, and let me hug you all."

After lunch, Eleanor and Rose served chocolate cake, and they laughed at the silly faces and stories Lilly shared.

"Thank you all for making this day so special." Mother took a deep breath. "I was dreading this day without Raymond, but you all have made it very memorable."

"Well, Shannon, I've got one more gift for you."

She turned to her husband. "Oh Charles, really, you've already done so much."

Charles sat down next to her with a package wrapped in brown paper. "I expected this day would be hard for you, and I wanted to give you something to remember Raymond by."

A heaviness rose in her chest.

He handed her the gift.

She looked at him with confusion on her face. "What is it?"

"Open it."

She pulled the string and peeled back the paper. The children gathered around.

"What is it, Father?" Lilly asked.

Father put his finger to his lips. "Be patient."

Mother pulled back the paper and lifted out a framed family portrait. Her eyes widened. "Oh, oh Charles. The... the family portrait from when the children were little." She touched the small face of a five-year-old Raymond. She turned to Charles, smiling through her tears. "How?"

He smiled. "Remember at Thanksgiving when you mentioned the photograph?"

She nodded.

"I asked you the photographer's name and then wrote him. He had to search for a little while, but he found the negative and..."

She smiled and kissed him, grateful for this day they had together. She would hold on to this day forever, knowing she could endure the coming changes.

FIFTY-NINE

WILLIAM HELD HIS BREATH as the truck approached the address. Excitement mixed with nerves mingled inside his chest. "This is a golden opportunity," Reverend Hamilton and Father had both said. He had to agree, but why did it have to take him back into the woods?

Mitchell stuck close beside him, barely leaving his side. His heart ached for his little brother, but both Father and Mr. Hamilton assured him this was the right thing to do; Mitchell would manage.

The truck turned the corner, and he gasped, as did Mitchell. Before them was a long row of trucks smaller than theirs, some with bench-like seats with backs, others with wood rails.

"Wow, thirteen, fourteen, fifteen." Mitchell's eyes were wide.

Hundreds of people milled around while young men dressed in identical green pants, white t-shirts, and green long-sleeved shirts formed a line for their final check in.

His sisters took in the scene, and Rose leaned in to Eleanor. "Have you ever seen so many cute guys?"

"I've never even seen so many guys," Eleanor said.

William watched as young men hugged mothers and shook the hands of fathers, grabbed duffel bags, suitcases, or knapsacks, and joined others in line.

Mitchell's excitement at the scene before them dwindled, and William feared he would cry. "I wish you didn't have to go."

William nodded. "I wish I didn't either. But for the first time in three years, I have a genuine job."

Mitchell bit his lip.

"It won't be forever. I'll be back."

"But not to stay. You'll move out, just like Rose."

William gave his little brother a playful slug. Mitchell might only be ten, but he was wise to the world around him.

They exited the truck, and everyone gathered around him. William shifted his weight and kept looking over his shoulder. Guys were loading onto the waiting trucks, and he didn't want to be left behind. "Well, I guess this is it."

Father squeezed his shoulder. "This is a great opportunity our President has created."

William nodded.

"I know you're nervous about going back into the woods and being away from home," Father added. "But this will give you steady income, opportunities, and friends."

"I know." He reminded himself of this whenever the panic crept in.

"Please don't go." Mitchell wrapped his slender arms around William's waist.

William ruffled Mitchell's hair, then kneeled down and wiped a tear off his little brother's cheek. Why did Mitchell have to make this so hard? He looked his little brother in the eye. "Be strong. I need you to look after your sisters while I'm gone."

Mitchell sucked in a quivering breath and put on a brave face.

"You can use all my tools while I'm gone. I know you'll take good care of them, and I look forward to seeing what you make."

Mitchell dug into his pocket and thrust out a piece of cloth. "Here, I made this for you."

William took it and unwrapped a small carving of an Australian Shepherd. William smiled. "Is this Teddy?"

Mitchell nodded, squeezing back tears.

"I'll look at it every day."

A man's voice boomed something through a bullhorn.

William straightened. "I guess this is it." His heart pounded in his chest.

Mitchell threw his arms around him again and squeezed, then each family member took their turn hugging him.

Finally, William came to Father. "Probably not the best Father's Day present."

Father smiled. "Knowing you have this opportunity is the best present I could have. Besides, I have a very nice night table you built me."

"You like it?"

Father's smile broadened. "Very much. I'll think of you every time I see it, and I'll pray for you too."

"Thanks. I'm sure I'll need it."

"Son, your mother and I have packed a small Bible in your bag. Use it to guide you."

William nodded, tapped Mitchell on the chin with his fist and joined the two-hundred-some other young men, now part of the Civilian Conservation Corps. By tomorrow, he'd be wielding an axe and shovel, building roads, trails, and shelters on top of Mount Spokane.

The idea scared the bejeebers out of him. What if he killed someone else? He pushed the thought aside. "Sometimes we have to do things we don't like and overcome our fears," Father had said. He hoped that's what he would do.

"Hi." A red-haired youth nodded to William. "Looks like it's going to be a wild adventure."

William took in the large group and the men in charge, yelling orders. "Yes, a wild adventure it will be."

"Mitchell! Lilly!" Eleanor stood on the back steps, listening for any response. She called again; still nothing. She went back through the house and called from the front porch. No answer. Hadn't she seen them go outside? Had they slipped into the basement? A quick search revealed neither of her siblings. She let out a long sigh.

She had a lot to do, and no one to help her; she didn't have time to look for them. Eleanor returned to the backyard and retrieved a few more onions, peppers, and cloves of garlic. Some things never changed.

Eleanor chopped the vegetables and tomatoes, mixing them into the already heating pot. Several more cups of peeled tomatoes sat in a bowl. "Might as well use those, too." She looked out the window again. Where were they? Had they slipped back into the house?

Eleanor checked in Mitchell's bedroom—empty, as was her and Lilly's room. Lilly loved being outside. Eleanor opened the door and glanced about. Empty too... she paused. The curtain hung limp outside the open window. Where was the screen?

Back in her bedroom, Eleanor leaned out the window. The screen was cut and dangling. "Oh, no!" She turned around and scanned the room. Several items of clothing spilled from under the bed, and Lilly's pillow was gone. The closet door was open, and Lilly's school bag was also missing, as was her doll.

She ran back into Mitchell's room, but nothing appeared out of place.

"Mother, Mother." She banged on the locked door where Mother lay under the covers, trying to hide from her depression.

"Mother."

There was only a mumble from inside.

"I think Lilly's run away."

Nothing.

"Did you hear me?"

"Yes."

"Well?"

"Then go find her."

"I'm cooking stewed tomatoes."

There was a pause. "I'm sure she's fine. She's probably just at the neighbors."

Eleanor clenched her fist.

From the kitchen, she could hear the lid on the pot rattle as the tomatoes and vinegar boiled. She ran in and with a pot holder removed the lid to stir. Hot juice splattered up and onto her arm. "Ouch!" She ran to the sink as more red bubbles popped, splattering their juice everywhere. "Mother."

Eleanor glared toward Mother's bedroom, but no help came.

She turned the burner down and stirred. When the contents calmed down, she returned to the garden and picked a few more peppers. Why was she always the one doing all the work? She pulled on an onion and the top broke off, toppling her backwards into the dirt. She flung the onion tops, then grabbed a dirt clod and threw it against the fence. "It's not fair!" She hurled another. "Everyone else eats the food. Why can't they help?"

Eleanor stomped back into the house, banging and slamming things around and chopping vegetables while wiping away onion induced tears mixed with hurt and frustration.

She filled the canner with water and carried it to the stove, her arms shaking with its weight. On the back porch, she yelled again for Lilly and Mitchell, then struggled to carry a crate of empty jars from the basement. But as she put them in the sink to wash, one slipped from her hand and shattered against the counter.

"Ugh. That's it! I'm tired of this!" She grabbed another jar and hurled it across the room, where it slammed into the back door and broke.

"It's not fair!" she sobbed. "It's just not fair."

"What is going on here?"

Eleanor looked up to see Mother staring wide-eyed; strands of her red hair poking in all directions from her disheveled bun. "Why does everything get dumped on my plate? I can't do this all by myself. I'm tired of doing most of the work around here. You told William, 'Life is like a cup of tea, it's all in how you make it!' and yet you stay in bed mourning Rose, Raymond and now William, while I'm here trying to help. Do I have to die to mean anything to you?" Eleanor's hands shook.

Mother stared at her in shock. "Eleanor, I think you're exaggerating."

"No, I'm not. I'm thirteen, and I've spent the last three years being a cook, housewife, and mother." She let the final word sting.

Mother's face contorted in pain. "You do not know what it's like to lose a child...in some respects, I've lost three."

"I could make it four."

Mother opened her mouth. "What—?"

"I'm as old as Rose was when she went to work for Aunt Fiona. I could get a job and move out." She watched fear grow in her mother's eyes.

"And let's not forget Lilly, who packed her things, sliced the screen on our window and appears to have run away."

Shannon grew paler and steadied herself against the counter.

"While you're mourning your losses, our lives keep going on, moving farther and farther from you."

Shannon gasped for air, sweat beading on her forehead. She fled from the room.

Moments later Eleanor heard retching, but she didn't care. The canner was boiling, and she needed to get the stewed tomatoes processing—after she cleaned up the glass. One thing was certain, this was the last time she'd be doing this by herself.

SIXTY

TEDDY YAPPED AND MITCHELL peered around the corner of the house to see Lilly's legs dangling from her and Eleanor's bedroom window. On the grass below her sat her school bag, doll, and pillow with Teddy standing guard. He watched as she lowered her body, let go, and dropped to the ground. He ducked back when she glanced his way.

Lilly coaxed Teddy out the back gate, looked back to make sure no one had seen her, and closed the gate.

Mitchell grabbed the rhubarb stick he'd cut to munch on and slipped out the back gate.

Lilly was already half a block away, headed west, rather than her usual east. He followed at a distance, staying at the alley's edge in case he needed to hide. Several times she looked back, then continued on. Occasionally, Teddy stopped and looked at him, but Mitchell waved the dog on and he obeyed.

She turned north on Lincoln and headed down the hill toward downtown. Sometimes she dropped an item and shifted her grasp on them. A few people looked at her, but no one did anything. Mitchell was closing the distance, hiding behind power poles and parked cars, when she stopped and looked about.

A man in a 1930's Chevrolet Sedan slowed to watch her.

Mitchell's chest tightened, and he glanced about for a rock.

The man drove off, only to return a few minutes later. At first Lilly didn't appear to notice him, but on his third pass she watched him, hugging her bundle closer to her chest. Teddy's fur raised and he barked.

She turned off Lincoln onto a side street, Teddy by her side, and Mitchell half a block behind. She wandered up and down streets for nearly an hour. The sedan was sometimes parallel on another street or parked behind another car on a cross street.

Mitchell's stomach churned, and he prayed the man would leave. He could stop Lilly, but something told him just to follow, so he did.

Finally, she plopped down on a sidewalk across from a vacant lot.

While Mitchell debated what to do, the man in the car approached, this time stopping in front of her. Mitchell moved closer.

Teddy stood by Lilly, his muscles stiff and hair raised.

The man leaned across the front seat and talked to her through the open passenger side window. "That's a pretty dog you have."

Lilly glanced up at him, then back to the ground.

"I'm looking for a lost dog. Maybe you could help me."

Mitchell palmed the rock in his hand and moved closer.

"You seem sad. I bet an ice cream cone would cheer you up."

Lilly eyed the man.

"What's your name?"

"Lilly."

"Oh, that's a pretty name. Well Lilly, why don't you climb on in, and I'll take you to an ice cream shop I know of."

Lilly cocked her head, as if considering the idea.

Mitchell's heart pounded in his chest as he scurried alongside a couple of parked cars, his back bent so the man wouldn't see him.

"They have vanilla, chocolate, and strawberry. Do you like strawberry?"

Lilly stood. "I like strawberry."

The man smiled. "Then come on in. You can even ride in the front seat."

She took a step.

Teddy growled, not moving from her side.

Mitchell ran to her, grabbed her arm with his left hand and raised his right hand to throw the rock. "Leave her alone."

Teddy barked, the hair bristling on his back.

The man wavered, but only for a moment. "Oh, you want some ice cream too?"

"No, now go away and leave my sister alone."

The man grinned. "Looks like she doesn't want to live with you and your family. Looks like she's running away. Maybe she'd like to live with me."

Beside him, Lilly recoiled. "No. No. I...I..." Tears welled in her eyes.

"Leave before I throw this rock at you."

The man chortled. "I doubt you could even hit me." He unlatched the door and pushed it open. "Come on Lilly. Let's go get some ice cream."

She shook her head.

"Lilly, let's get some ice cream."

Mitchell held her back. "Go away, now!" He looked about, hoping someone was around, but the street was empty.

The man stepped out of his car.

Mitchell struggled to swallow at the sight of the tall, broad-shouldered man.

He walked around the car's front. "That's right, there's no one here to see you two."

"Stop or I'll throw this rock."

The man laughed.

Mitchell hurled the rock, and it whizzed past the man's ear.

"Boy, you're messing with the wrong fella."

"Run Lilly, run."

She turned to run, but in two long strides, the man was there, his hand around her wrist. "Help. Let me go." Lilly writhed, hitting and kicking him.

Mitchell grabbed the man's other arm. "Leave my sister alone."

Teddy barked and jumped, nipping at the man's trousers.

The man tried to shake Mitchell off, but he held on tight. "Fine, you both want to go." He lifted both of the children, kicking and struggling, and strode to the car, with Teddy barking in circles around the three.

At the car door, he set Mitchell down. Mitchell stomped on the man's foot then kicked his kneecap hard. There was a crack, and the man let go. "Run."

"My doll."

"Just run."

Mitchell grabbed her bag from her, and the two ran.

"Where's Teddy?"

Mitchell turned to see the dog facing off with the man, teeth bared. "Stopping him."

They ran several blocks before hiding in the doorway of an abandoned storefront, both panting, trying to catch their breath.

Lilly was pale. "Where is Teddy?"

Mitchell peeked out from their hiding place, afraid of what he might see. But the road and sidewalk were empty, except for someone a block and a half away, coming toward them. "Do you think you can run some more?"

Lilly looked like she would cry.

Mitchell peeked out again. "Oh, look."

He pointed at the figure coming their way.

"Teddy," Lilly shrieked.

The dog recognized them and ran toward them.

"Look, he has my doll!" Lilly wrapped her arms around the toy and cried.

Mitchell guided her to a spot on the curb between two parked cars, and they sat. Mitchell's hands shook, and he buried his face in Teddy's fur, hiding his own tears of fear and relief, hoping the man wouldn't came back.

After a bit, her crying stopped.

"Are you ready to go home now?"

Lilly shook her head. "I want to see Raymond. I want to go to the park where Raymond is."

"The cemetery?"

She nodded.

"Is that where you were going?"

"Uh, huh. Are you going to tell on me?"

Mitchell was silent for a bit, then shook his head. "Only if you promise not to do it again."

"But I want to see Raymond."

Mitchell wrapped his arm around her. "I'll ask Father if he can take us. But he's not there."

"But I want to see him. I miss him." Dirty tears streamed down her face.

"Me too." The now familiar pain that part of him was missing squeezed his heart.

Lilly looked up at him. "Why did God take him? Why can't he bring him back?"

Mitchell shook his head, the familiar sadness and questions reasserting themselves. "I don't know why he took him."

"But why can't he bring Raymond back? Like he did Lazarus?"

"I don't think God does that very often."

"I don't like God."

"If Raymond would have obeyed William, that tree wouldn't have fallen on him."

"But God could have stopped the tree."

Mitchell agreed and contemplated her questions, which mirrored his. "I think sometimes when we disobey, God lets us experience what would naturally happen, to teach us that he knows more than us—so we will trust him."

Lilly pondered this. "Even when it means you could die?"

Mitchell nodded.

Lilly stared across the street at a filling station. "Do you think Raymond learned God knows more than us?"

A brightness filled Mitchell's eyes. "Yes."

"Why?"

"He believed in Jesus and asked God to forgive his sins."

Lilly fidgeted. "Is that why you say he's in heaven?"

He nodded. "It's the only way."

Lilly scribbled shapes in the dust with a stick. "I want to go to heaven and see Raymond, but I don't like to obey."

Mitchell twisted a dry leaf between his fingers. "Which do you want more?"

Lilly continued her scribbling in the dirt while Mitchell waited. "Raymond didn't like to obey either," she said. "We had fun."

"But disobeying hurt him."

She considered his words.

"Lilly, when you love someone, do you want to make them happy?"

She nodded.

"Me too. When I read about Jesus in the Bible, it's like I know him. He's smart and brave and kind and caring and can do so many amazing things. I think of how he let others lie about him, beat him, and kill him, so I can know him and go to heaven. That makes me love him and want to make him happy. So, I obey."

She looked at her doll. "What would that man have done to me?"

Mitchell shivered, despite the warm summer day. "I think he would have hurt you."

"I thought you'd say that."

They sat in silence for a while.

"Mitchell, can you help me do that?"

"Do what?"

"Obey Jesus."

Mitchell smiled and put his arm back around her. "Sure."

SIXTY-ONE

THIS MORNING ELEANOR PLANNED to let Mother do all the baking. She wanted Mother to feel what it was like to do all the work alone. Eleanor steeled herself before walking into the kitchen.

It was nine-thirty in the morning. Would Mother be mad at her? They usually had eight to ten loaves baked by now. She took a deep breath, hoping to calm the bubbling in her stomach before entering the kitchen.

"Good morning." Mother slid a knife over the top of the measuring cup of flour. "Are you hungry?"

Eleanor shook her head. "I had some berries from the garden." What was her mother doing? There were six loaves cooling, two more in the oven and two rising. She was falling behind. They wouldn't have enough. Was this a trick?

"What are you staring at?" Mother emptied the last cup of flour into the sifter.

"Why aren't you in bed?" Eleanor asked, almost accusing.

Mother hit the side of the flour sifter against the inside of her palm, releasing the last of the flour. "Because I'm done with that."

Eleanor had heard that before. Still, Mother had more bread done than she expected. She reviewed their fight and considered her plans to not bake, to make Mother do it alone. But today, Mother was here, working. They could work together.

"Eleanor," Mitchell wandered into the kitchen. "When is the movie?"

"Eleven."

He hurried out.

Guilt weighed heavily on her. Maybe she should stay and help. Maybe they could go to the one o'clock movie. She reached for her apron.

Mother turned the dough onto a floured board and stopped. "What are you doing?"

"I'm going to help."

"No, you're not."

"Why not?"

"You're a child. It's time you act like one."

Eleanor stopped, her apron half on. Pressure rose in her chest. What was this? After all she'd done, now Mother had the nerve to tell her to act like a child?

Tears welled in her eyes. She looked about the kitchen, at the counters with the mixing bowls, measuring cups, eggs, yeast, and flour. This had been her domain for the past three years.

Her lip quivered. Was Mother really going to take over her job?

The timer rang and Mother moved to remove two more golden loaves of bread—loaves that looked smoother and larger than hers.

"See, I can take care of this. You enjoy yourself at the movies."

There it was. Just like that. She was no longer needed. Like a worn rag, she was being tossed aside.

"But..." For the past few years, Eleanor had measured her self-worth with all she did. And now, in one morning, Mother had taken that all away.

She recalled their fight last week. Did she really want to spend her time with friends? Did she really want to be a child?

"Eleanor?" Mother crossed the floor and cupped her flour covered hand against Eleanor's wet freckled cheek. "What's wrong?"

Eleanor jerked back. "You...I..." She squeezed back the tears. This wasn't what she wanted, was it? Eleanor didn't want to have to do it all—but—she looked at her mother and the bread. She looked at the clock and remembered the movie and the fun she'd planned to have with Eva, Mitchell, Violet, and Paul. She had thought of little else for several days. But... Her chest heaved, and she gasped for air. "You don't need me?"

Mother tilted her head. "I would never say I don't need you."

"But you don't want me in here anymore—do you?"

A tear slipped down Mother's cheek. "Oh, Eleanor." She rubbed her finger over Eleanor's eyebrow and cheek. "That is not it at all. This family owes you our lives. You have done so much to help provide and care for us all." Mother paused. "Your words the other day cut deep."

Mother was getting even with her. Still, guilt and shame stabbed her conscience. "I'm sorry. I—"

Mother put a finger over Eleanor's lips. "No, you were right. I was so consumed with what I'd lost, I was ignoring all the blessings before me. I know I haven't told you how much I've appreciated all you've done around here the past few years. I'm sorry."

Eleanor nodded, but the ideas she'd formed of her worthlessness argued with Mother's words.

"I wasn't the mother you needed me to be. I'm sorry. But I want you to know that I'm so proud of you for stepping up and taking care of everyone when I couldn't."

Eleanor's heart softened. Mother appreciated her!

"But now it's time you return to childhood."

Mother's last words stabbed her. The feeling of joy now mingled with hurt. Did she have to let go of one thing to have the other?

"Look at you." Mother touched Eleanor's face. "You now have streaks of flour paste down your cheeks." Mother smiled. "You should go wash up before you join your friends."

Eleanor nodded, still unsure if she wanted to leave.

"You need to get going, or you'll miss your movie."

Eleanor turned and took a few steps then ran back and wrapped her arms around Mother. She looked up into Mother's eyes. "Can..." She sniffled. "Can I still help you sometimes?"

Mother's smile spread wide. "Of course, you can. I expect you to. I just don't want this burden to be on your shoulders anymore. It never should have. It's time you enjoy your childhood. Before you have to do this all the time."

All of Eleanor's misconceptions tumbled down. She blinked away the tears, nodding in understanding. "Thank you. Thank you, Mother."

"No, thank you. Now hurry along, lassie, or you'll miss your show."

SIXTY-TWO

ELEANOR, MITCHELL, AND LILLY stood clinging to the truck's wood rails as they bounced and swayed on the bumpy road.

Eleanor took a deep breath. "Smell that."

The other two followed.

"I love it," Mitchell declared.

"I don't smell anything," Lilly said.

Mitchell and Eleanor exchanged glances.

"Hawk." Eleanor pointed out the raptor. "I miss the woods."

"Me, too." He paused. "Most of the time."

She nodded, knowing the woods would always remind him of Raymond.

"All these trees are boring," Lilly complained.

Eleanor ignored her, discounting her opinion as the result of growing up in town. She was excited to see William. She missed him but was sure that Mitchell missed him even more. Deep down, she hoped he'd come home with them.

She fingered Clara's letter in her pocket and debated if she should give it to William. She'd spent the past two days arguing with herself about reading it. She'd almost steamed the envelope open, but was afraid she'd get caught. Now she wished she had.

Father slowed at the sign which read: "Camp Francis H. Cook — Civilian Conservation Corps Company 611."

Tents stood in rows, and young men milled around, some smoking, others playing cards, talking, or playing horseshoes. A group shouted around a makeshift boxing ring. As the truck crept past, Mitchell pointed. "Look, there's William."

Eleanor stared in surprise as the boy in the ring with him swung a punch and William stumbled backward. Eleanor's hand flew to her mouth, and she stared in horror. She glanced at Mitchell, who only raised his eyebrows.

But when she looked back at William, he'd caught himself and blocked another jab before delivering one to his opponent's chin. Why did boys like to fight? That was something she'd never understood.

Lilly jumped up and down. "Go Willy, go Willy!"

Eleanor held her breath and hoped Mother hadn't seen the fight. But the look of horror on Mother's reflection in the truck's mirror said she had.

Father parked, and everyone climbed out.

"What is he doing fighting?" Mother asked, eyebrows and lips bunched in consternation.

Eleanor bit her nail and opted to gather one of the picnic baskets while Rose and Lilly scooped up the blankets.

"There's nothing to worry about," Father assured Mother. "Fighting in that ring with gloves on and someone refereeing is safer than down some alley with bare fists." He handed the other basket to Mitchell and lifted the old milk can half-full of cold water.

Mother shook her head. "I still don't like it."

Young men watched them as they walked. "I feel like I'm on parade," Rose whispered to Eleanor.

"You are," Mitchell said, a smirk on his face.

Eleanor giggled, and Rose nudged her. "It's not funny."

Eleanor snickered as her sister's suppressed smiled, then look away from a few of the young men.

William met them before they reached the boxing ring, sweat glistening on his tan, muscled skin. "I've been waiting all week for you."

Everyone gathered around talking at once.

To Eleanor, William appeared calmer and content.

"If you don't mind hiking a little way, there's a spot with a beautiful view."

Father patted William on the back. "Lead the way."

William carried the milk can and pointed out the tent he shared with several others, the mess tent, and other camp features. He shared about the work they were doing clearing trails, building roads, and shelters in the park, and the fellows he'd befriended. "Just the other day, we scared a small bear out of the bushes."

Eleanor looked about her to make sure there weren't any others.

Mother shook her head. "That's one thing I don't miss."

They reached a level spot and spread out a few quilts.

"It's good to have a steady job and not always out looking for work." William reached into his pocket and pulled out a small wad of bills. "Father, can you put this with the rest of my pay they sent you?"

"Sure, but don't you want some spending money?"

"I have enough. I have some plans and want to save as much as I can."

"Sure son."

"Do you like it here?" Eleanor asked, hoping he'd say "no."

He smiled at her. "I do, and what have you been up to?"

She tried to hide her disappointment and pulled the sketch pad from her satchel. "Mrs. Hamilton's teaching me how to draw." She showed him some of her sketches.

"Those are pretty good. You used to draw when we lived on the farm."

She nodded. "But those were terrible compared to these."

He examined one of Teddy sitting alert by the back fence. "You were a lot younger then." He pointed to the sketch. "Can I have this one?"

"Sure." She tore it from the pad and gave it to him.

"You know, though, it's missing something."

She leaned in. "What?"

"Your signature."

She slugged him, then signed it, pride swelling inside her.

He examined it before folding it and putting it in his pocket. He pulled out an envelope and tapped it against his hand. "Remember Mrs. Jacobson, the lady I introduced you to?"

She nodded as a knot grew in her stomach.

He paused, then handed her the letter. "Give this to Mrs. Jacobson. Ask her to give it to Clara."

Eleanor took it and put it in her pocket.

He gave her a look of expectation, and she squirmed under his gaze. He sighed, and a look of disappointment passed over his face then disappeared, and he motioned everyone to him. "Hey," he raised his voice. "I've had some ideas since I've been up here."

Eleanor sat on a stump and turned to a clean sheet of paper. She sketched her brother. His expression was full of hope and energy. Eleanor would keep this one for herself and maybe make another for Clara. She squelched the reminder of Clara's letter. She liked Clara, she really did, but she didn't want to see William get hurt.

They all listened as William shared about getting the attention of one of his supervisors after making a few stools and tables. "He thinks I should make furniture and maybe open a shop."

"But no one has any money," Rose said.

"Not now," William continued, "but our foreman and all the supervisors think President Roosevelt will get things turned around."

Father nodded. "I hear talk along those lines, too."

"How about you?" William tossed a small pinecone into Mitchell's lap. "Have you been putting my tools to good use?"

Mitchell grinned. "I've been fixing things I find and then Father and I take them down to the shantytown. I figure they need chairs and tables and stuff."

William ruffled his brother's hair. "Good for you. Maybe when I open my furniture store, we can work together. We can call it Cruthers and Cruthers."

Eleanor smiled as Mitchell beamed like a lighthouse. She sketched Mitchell's expression of joy. Her brother may not be coming home soon, but he hadn't forgotten them.

William stood. "Father, I want to show you something."

Eleanor fingered the envelope from Clara and tried to ignore the guilt pressing against her. She hadn't seen William so encouraged since they left the farm. What if Clara's letter said something that would discourage him again?

Father and William walked down the path alone.

Eleanor battled her conflicting emotions. William had asked her to carry letters between him and Clara before he left.

They were nearing a bend.

She slipped Clara's letter from her pocket and examined it. Clara had written William's name in fancy letters. If this letter brought him pain, she'd have a hard time forgiving Clara. But what if it brought him joy?

"Eleanor?"

She looked up.

"What are you doing?" Mother asked.

"Um...I just remembered something." She raced after her brother.

"Eleanor, they want to be alone."

"I'll just be a minute."

"William." She caught up with them, panting from the steep climb.

They paused and waited for her.

"William, I almost forgot." She handed him the envelope.

William took the letter, but gave her a knowing look.

She bent her head, afraid of how Clara's letter might hurt him. She looked up at William. He wasn't just her big brother anymore; he was a man.

He ran his finger across the lettering, then inhaled the violet scent, a look of serenity on his face. "Thank you."

William and Father paused on their climb up Mount Spokane. "This hasn't been easy, and I was pretty mad at you for the first few weeks," William said.

They took in the beautiful views, a whole mountain range, valleys, and lakes.

"Isn't it beautiful?" William beamed with pride.

"It sure is."

"Thanks for encouraging me to join the CCC."

Father nodded.

"I had mixed feelings. I wanted the work, but really didn't want to be in the woods."

"I know."

"They had us felling trees when we first arrived."

Charles sat in silence.

"I had nightmares almost every night. But you knew I needed this." William took in the view. "I was losing hope. I thought I'd never work, that I couldn't do anything right—" he paused. "I was lonely."

Father listened.

"You always encouraged me with my woodwork, but I guess I needed to hear it from others. And I have friends." He turned to Father. "I've been praying. Being in nature has helped me. It's reminded me that God is real and was watching over us. Sure, we lost our home, but no one was hurt or killed."

Charles took a deep breath. "He was watching over us."

"And God also gave Raymond a chance to turn to him."

Father wiped a tear. "Yes, he did."

"You know, Father," William paused. "Raymond was getting into lots of trouble?"

Charles nodded. "I had my suspicions."

"He was never happy. He always wanted something more."

Father looked up to the bright blue heavens above. "Well, now he has the best."

"Yes, he does."

SIXTY-THREE

Red, orange, and yellow leaves floated from the trees at Manito Park as Eleanor walked behind her parents and younger siblings, tugging on the leash Teddy so hated. "I wish Rose could have joined us."

Mother looked back at her. "I do too, but her job at the telephone company is keeping her pretty busy."

"And that boy," Mitchell added.

"Oh, Mitchell, Liam's a fine young man." Mother wrapped her arm around Father's. "I'm just glad she finally noticed him."

Eleanor reached down and scratched the dog's head. "I was afraid she'd never date him."

"I guess she first needed to see who else was out there." Father cast a glance at Shannon, who blushed.

"I sure like him a lot better than Johnny," Eleanor added. "Besides, Johnny's in Bonners Ferry and Liam is here, that means she'll be closer to us."

Mother smiled.

Across the green, her aunt, uncle, and cousins strolled down a path, Suzanne with a doll stroller, and Albert with a kite. Wouldn't Rose be surprised to see this?

"Can I go play on the swings?" Lilly was already straying in that direction.

Mother nodded, and Lilly wasted no time running off while Mitchell joined a couple of boys playing catch.

Eleanor strolled to the pond and let Teddy off his leash. She threw sticks, which he retrieved until dropping them in favor of herding ducks. She pulled out her notebook and sketched Teddy standing by the pond, head cocked, staring at the birds now swimming out of reach.

Across the pond, her parents walked hand-in-hand. She smiled at how far Mother had come. The trauma of the past three years was healing, and she was a better version of who she'd been on the farm. They all were.

In her mind, Eleanor reviewed the finishing touches she needed to make on her entries into the school art show. She had painted each family member in different scenes from the past three years. Still, she wanted something special for the last piece.

As Eleanor neared the park bench where Father and Mother sat, Teddy broke off, rounding up Lilly and Mitchell, and herding them to the bench.

She grabbed her notebook and sketched the scene before her. Here was her final piece—the image of Teddy—guarding what remained.

DID YOU ENJOY GUARDING WHAT REMAINS?

YOUR FEEDBACK HELPS ME provide the best quality stories and allows other readers, like you, to discover great books.

It would mean the world to me if you took 2 minutes to share your thoughts about this book as a review at your favorite retailer.

Thank you!

Ida Smith

https://idasmithbooks.com/Review-Guarding-What-Remains

1920's & 30's Slang

Ab-so-lute-ly - affirmative
Bearcat - a fiery woman
Beating your gums - idle talk
Bees Knees - great, fabulous, outstanding...
Beeswax - business, i.e. "none of your beeswax"
Big six - a strong man
Bob - hair style
Boiler - a car
Boondoggle - a con game
Breezer - a topless auto
Cooler - Jail
Daddy - a young woman's wealthy boyfriend or lover
Darb - a great person or thing
Dough - money
Dumb Dora - a dumb bell,
Dry Up - get lost
Fella - fellow. Used like "man" or "guy" is today.
Flat tire - worthless (verify)
Hood - hoodlum
Hooligans - a young troublemaker, often violent
Hooverville - a shantytown named after President Herbert Hoover
Looker - an attractive woman
Nifty - great
Rag-a-Muffin - a dirty or disheveled individual
Sap - a fool, an idiot
Scratch - money
Shantytown - a collection of crude built makeshift dwellings
Sheba - one's girlfriend; a woman with sex appeal
Sheik - one's boyfriend; a man with sex appeal
Soda jerk - someone who operates a soda machine
Swell - terrific, wonderful, great...

Book Club Discussion Questions

1. Which main character became your favorite? Your least favorite? How did your opinions of the major characters change throughout the story?

2. Guarding What Remains starts with ten-year-old Eleanor, convinced there's trouble, but helpless to stop it. How does that affect her response to the events that occur? Is her response believable? What does it say about the guilt we carry? The guilt children harbor?

3. The initial tragedy Eleanor and her family experienced results from other people's actions. Why are some people cruel? What do the different responses of the characters say about their personalities?

4. With the theft of their pay and the destruction of their home and barn, Charles leaves the farm and moves his family to Spokane, Washington. Why do you think he chose this? Do you agree or disagree with this decision? Why or why not?

5. Each family member responded differently to the trauma of living in a shantytown after losing their home, lifestyle, and moving to Spokane. For Shannon, something deep inside triggers depression. Why do you think she responded this way? What does it tell us about the power of circumstances over our mental health? The power of our own thoughts, attitudes, and will to live? Do you think some people are more disposed to depression than others?

6. That first winter, the family is starving and cold. Shannon begs Charles to take the children to an orphanage. What do you think of Shannon's request? Was she asking this out of cruelty or love? What do you think of Charles' response to his wife's request? How would you respond in a similar situation?

7. On his way to a children's home, Charles finds himself in a church. He confesses his stubbornness and asks God for help. Why did it take him so long to ask for help? Reverend Hamilton encourages Charles to forgive the men who caused their pain. What was Reverend Hamilton's reasoning? What do you think of this idea?

8. Throughout the story, we see people who were helpful, and some who were cruel, regardless of their social and economic status. Did

it surprise you who helped and who didn't? What determines how a person treats those in need? Charles tells Reverend Hamilton, "What we really need is work. Without work, we're never going to stay fed. It's just a patch on the hole in our bellies." Do you agree with this? How can we relate this to our present-day homeless situation?

9. Raymond's accident and death affects each character differently. What do you think of Eleanor's decision to stay at the house and bake bread? William's decision to get drunk? Shannon's slip back into depression?

10. Where do you envision the characters a year after the story ends? Five years later?

ABOUT THE AUTHOR

IDA SMITH writes stories of people traveling jagged journeys. She's fascinated with the complexities of how life experiences, personality, culture, thought processes, and other people meld to create the choices which form our lives.

She credits her love of story and history to a childhood filled with travel and tales of her parents' adventures in the 1940's and beyond. Ida lives in the Pacific Northwest with her family where she's traveled her own jagged path with unexpected twists, mountains, and sinkholes.

Learn more about Ida and her books. Sign up for her short story e-Zine, *Jagged Journeys* at IdaSmithBooks.com.

Follow her on social media.

https://www.facebook.com/AuthorIdaSmith

https://www.bookbub.com/authors/ida-smith
Photo by Julie McGill

Also By Ida Smith

NEIL GATLIN THRILLERS

Neil Gatlin wants nothing more than to return home to Indiana and girlfriend, Sunshine. But with truck problems and little money, Neil enters a pool game, misreads the cues, and finds himself falsely accused of murder. Read the fast-paced thriller, *The Invisible Cipher,* and follow Neil Gatlin as he deciphers secret codes to untangle himself from prison and the dangerous criminals closing in on him. https://books2read.com/NeilG1

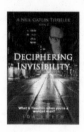

Life outside prison isn't as easy as Neil hoped. With no money, Neil finds himself back in Cleavemont, Illinois where most residents still think he's a killer. Labeled a villain in a town where no one wants him, Neil finds himself a hunted man with few options in Book Two of the *Neil Gatlin Thriller Series, Deciphering Invisibility.* https://books2read.com/NeilG2

HISTORICAL FICTION

All his life, Uzziel has heard the prophesies of a great king who will rescue his people from oppression. Believing he has discovered the promised one, his hope is destroyed in a morning of extraordinary violence, and his hatred of Rome cemented. Decades later, two leaders emerge—each with very different ideas and methods. Could one of these men be the Anticipated one? If so, which one? https://books2read.com/Uzziel

AVAILABLE IN E-BOOK AND PAPERBACK.
AUDIOBOOKS FORTHCOMING.

Made in United States
North Haven, CT
11 December 2024

62205610R00236